To my Tokyo Family:
Makiko, Pei Chen, Mai, Sana,
Lisa, Yuko, Hiroko, and Renna.
~ Marjorie

If you lost the way, go back to your
stem and innocence. What you have
already available is enough.
~ Sana

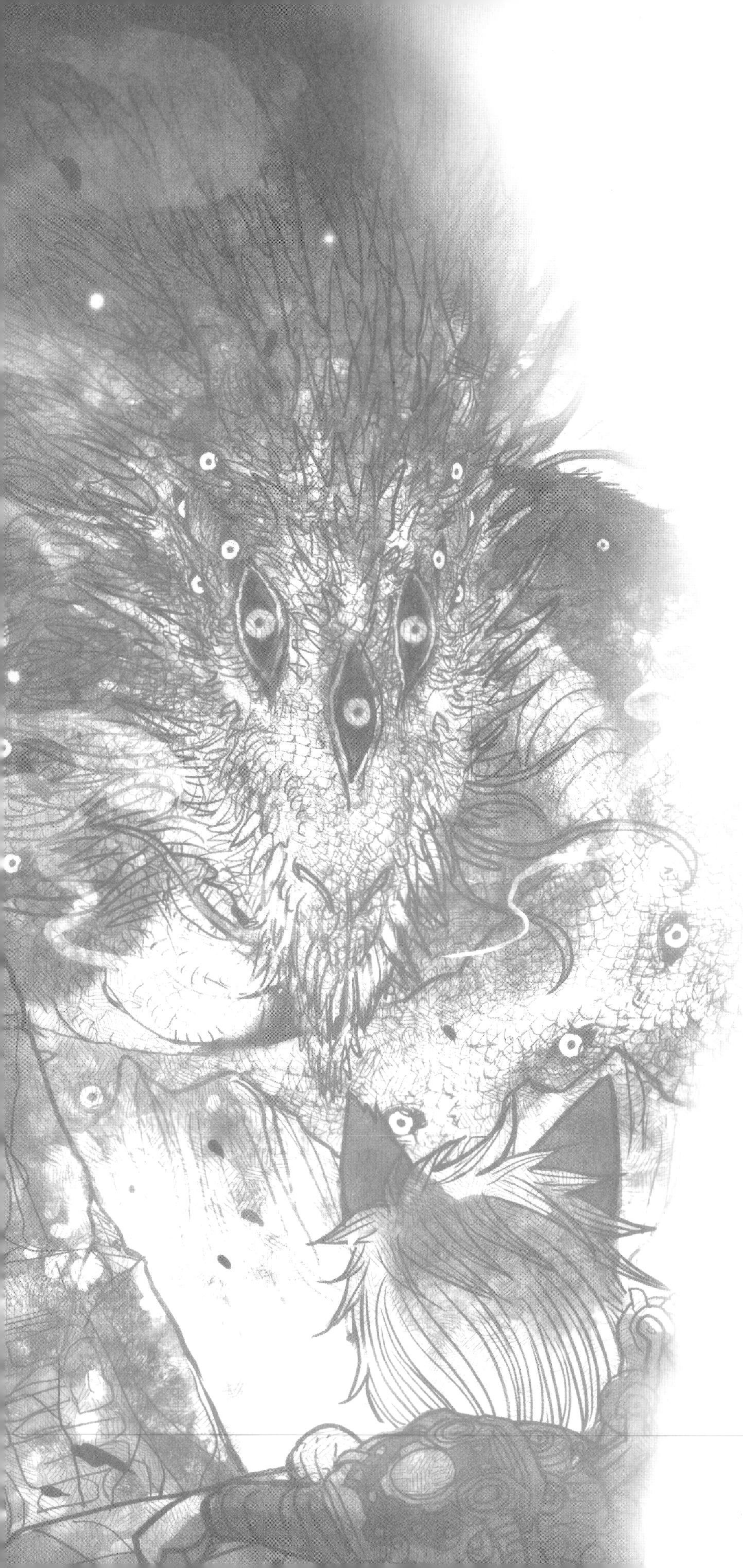

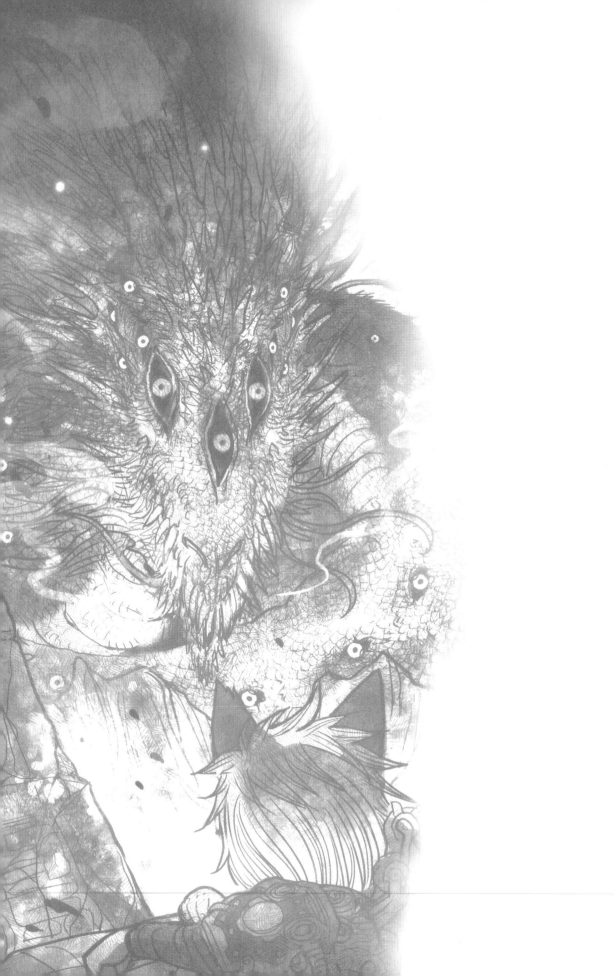

MONSTRESS

VOLUME FOUR
THE CHOSEN

Collecting
MONSTRESS
Issues 19-24

MARJORIE LIU
WRITER

SANA TAKEDA
ARTIST

RUS WOOTON
LETTERING & DESIGN

JENNIFER M. SMITH
EDITOR

SHANNA MATUSZAK
PRODUCTION ARTIST

CERI RILEY
EDITORIAL ASSISTANT ·

MONSTRESS
created by
MARJORIE LIU &
SANA TAKEDA

CHAPTER NINETEEN

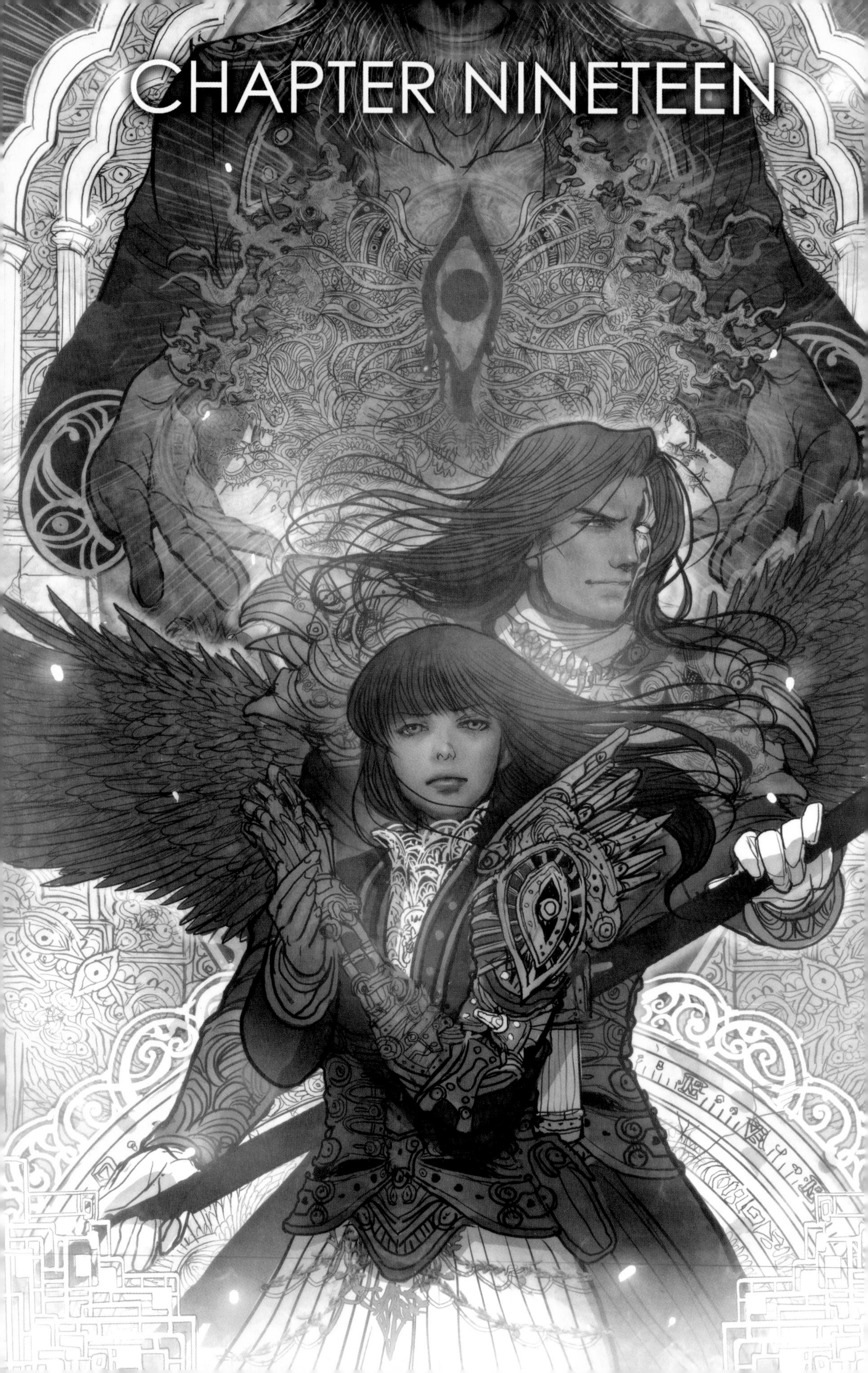

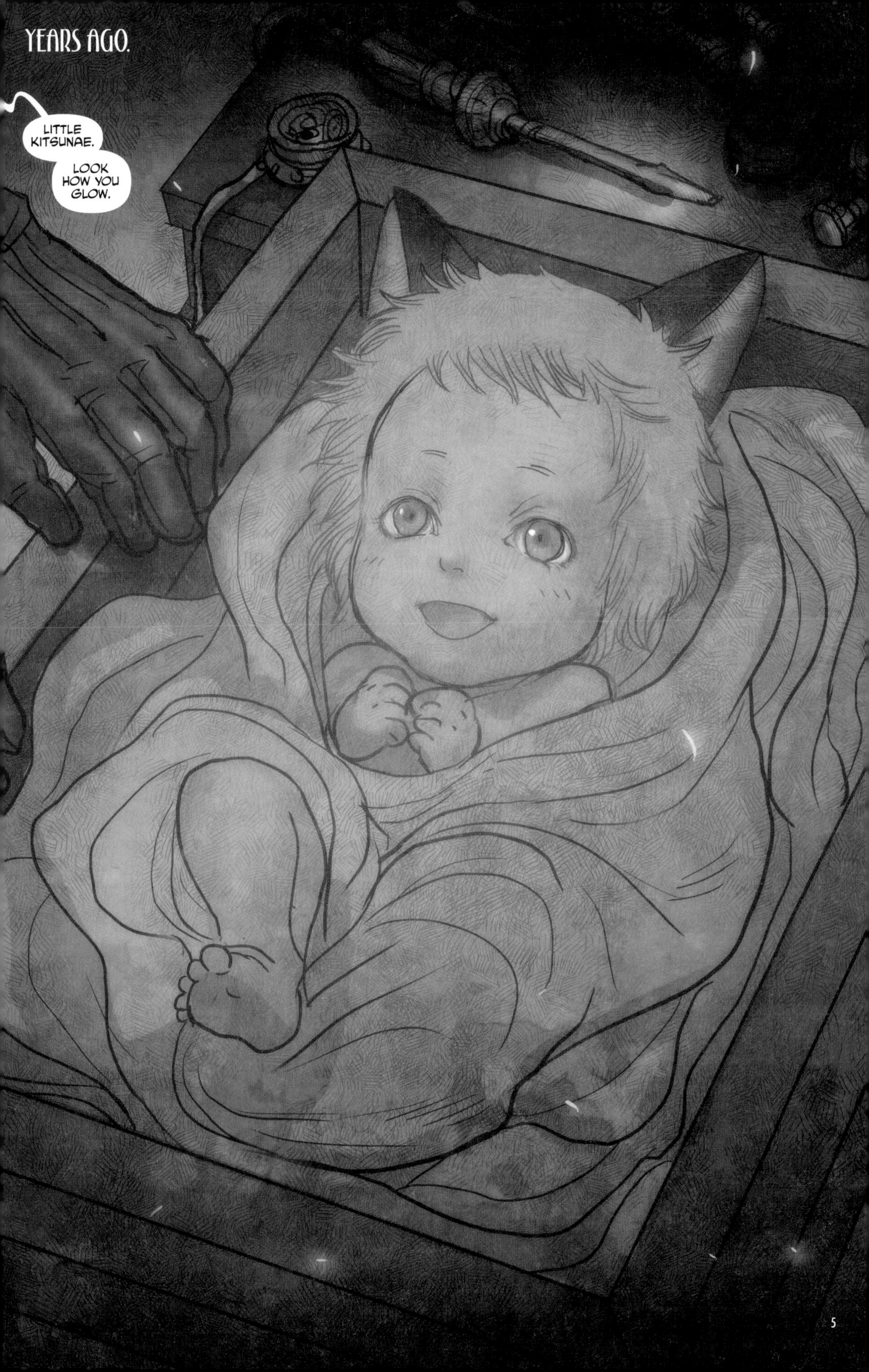
YEARS AGO.
LITTLE KITSUNAE.
LOOK HOW YOU GLOW.

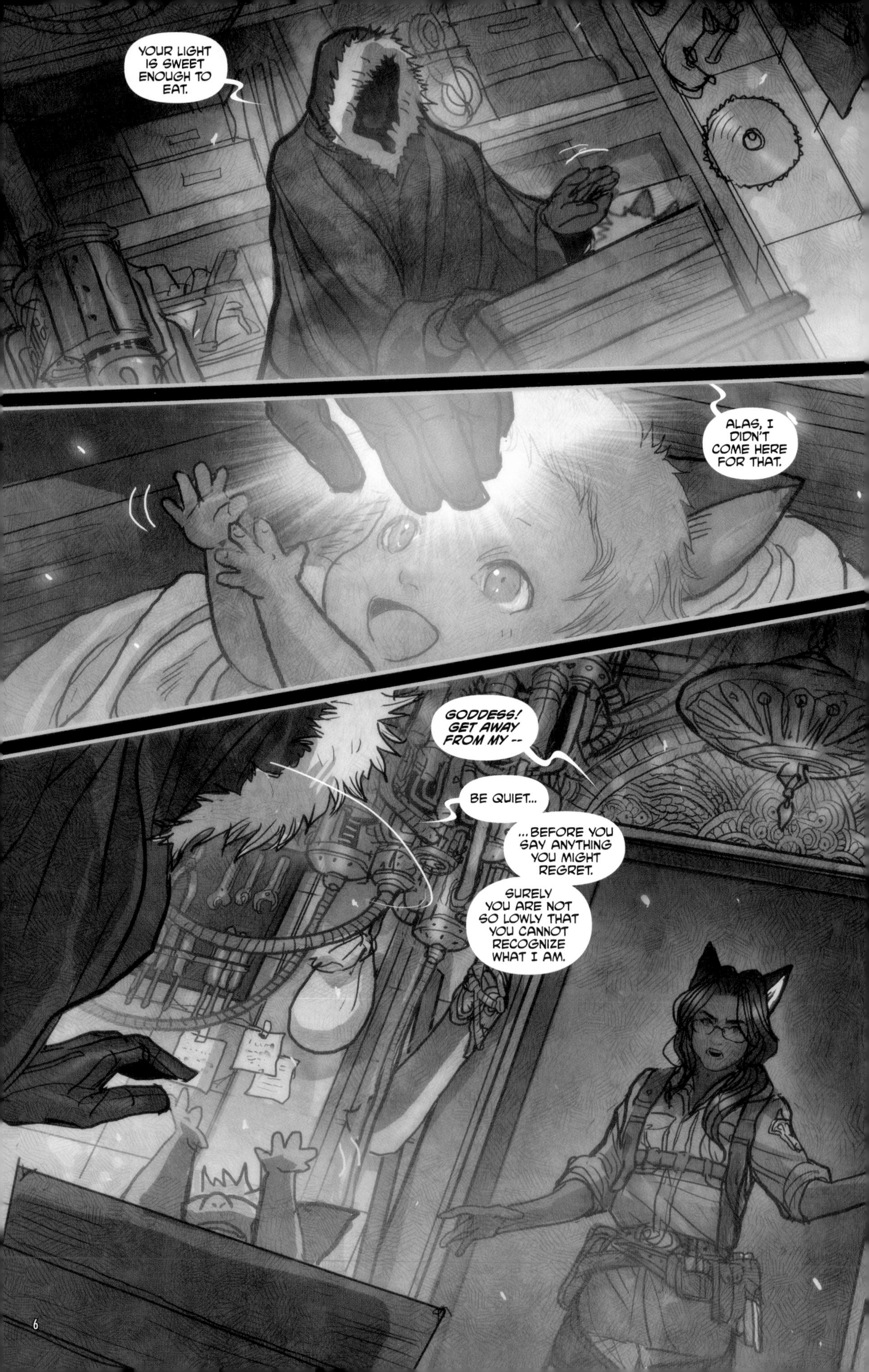
YOUR LIGHT IS SWEET ENOUGH TO EAT.
ALAS, I DIDN'T COME HERE FOR THAT.
GODDESS! GET AWAY FROM MY --
BE QUIET...
...BEFORE YOU SAY ANYTHING YOU MIGHT REGRET.
SURELY YOU ARE NOT SO LOWLY THAT YOU CANNOT RECOGNIZE WHAT I AM.

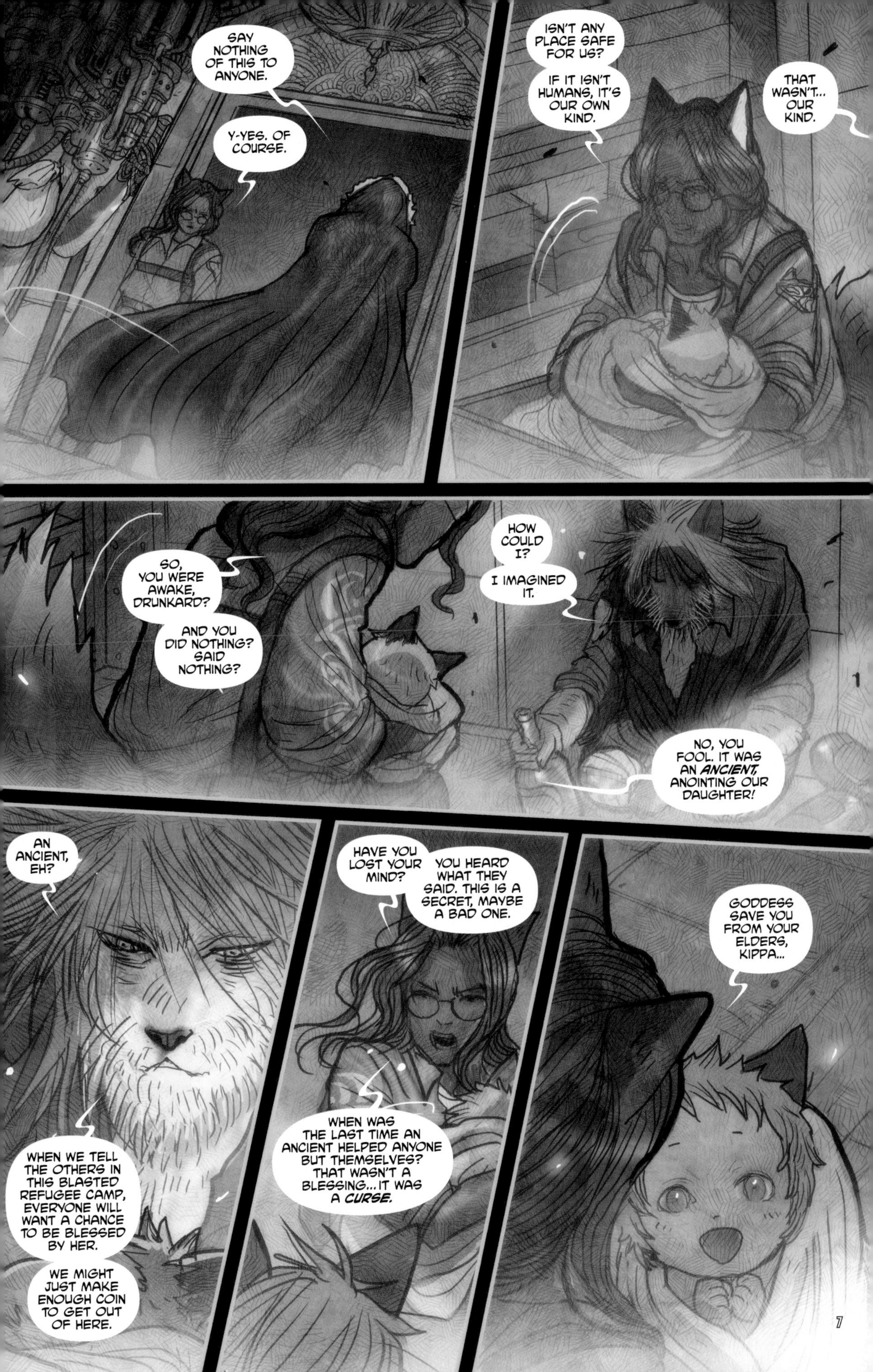
SAY NOTHING OF THIS TO ANYONE.
Y-YES. OF COURSE.
ISN'T ANY PLACE SAFE FOR US?
IF IT ISN'T HUMANS, IT'S OUR OWN KIND.
THAT WASN'T... OUR KIND.
SO, YOU WERE AWAKE, DRUNKARD?
AND YOU DID NOTHING? SAID NOTHING?
HOW COULD I?
I IMAGINED IT.
NO, YOU FOOL. IT WAS AN ANCIENT, ANOINTING OUR DAUGHTER!
AN ANCIENT, EH?
WHEN WE TELL THE OTHERS IN THIS BLASTED REFUGEE CAMP, EVERYONE WILL WANT A CHANCE TO BE BLESSED BY HER.
WE MIGHT JUST MAKE ENOUGH COIN TO GET OUT OF HERE.
HAVE YOU LOST YOUR MIND?
YOU HEARD WHAT THEY SAID. THIS IS A SECRET, MAYBE A BAD ONE.
WHEN WAS THE LAST TIME AN ANCIENT HELPED ANYONE BUT THEMSELVES? THAT WASN'T A BLESSING...IT WAS A CURSE.
GODDESS SAVE YOU FROM YOUR ELDERS, KIPPA...

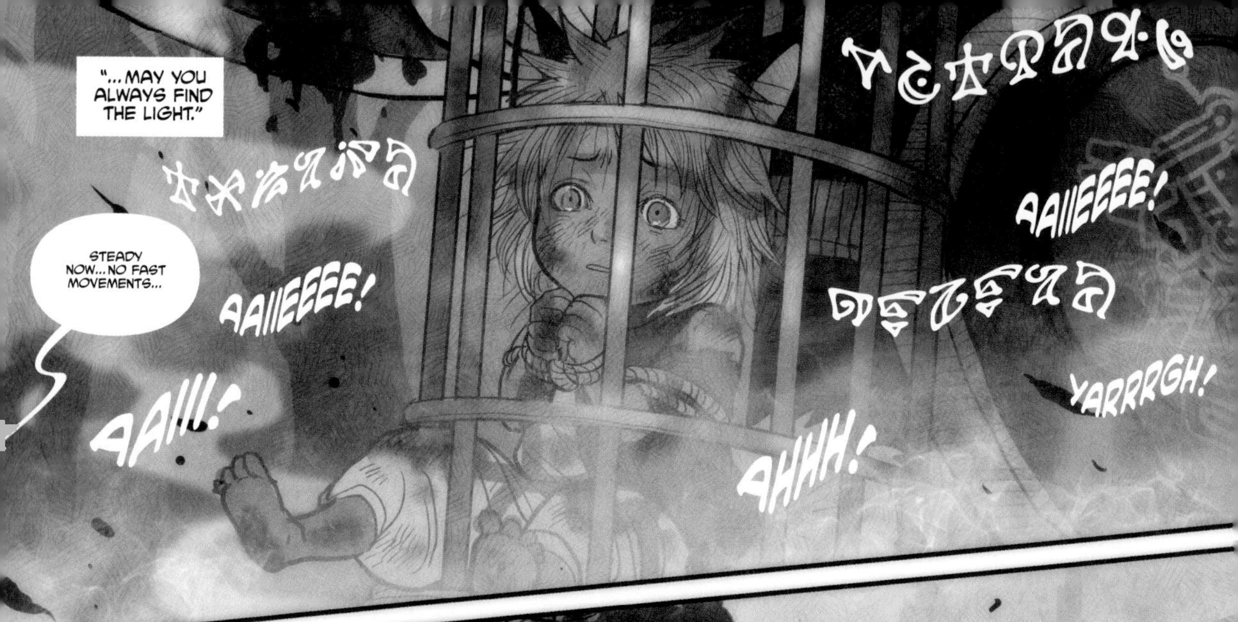
"...MAY YOU ALWAYS FIND THE LIGHT."
STEADY NOW...NO FAST MOVEMENTS...
AAIIEEEE!
AAIIEEEE!
AAIII!
AHHH!
YARRRGH!

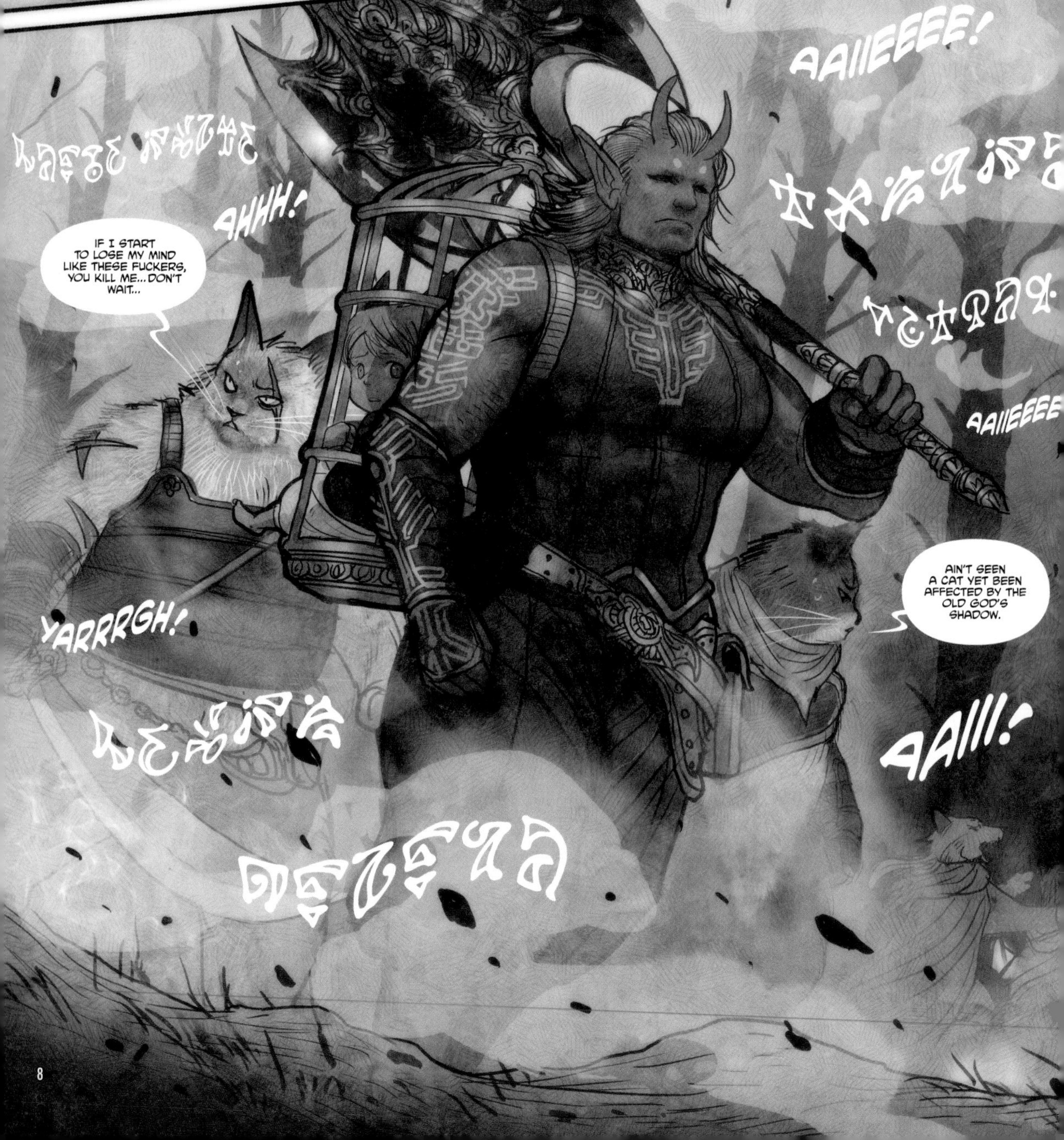
AAIIEEEE!
AHHH!
IF I START TO LOSE MY MIND LIKE THESE FUCKERS, YOU KILL ME...DON'T WAIT...
AAIIEEEE
AIN'T SEEN A CAT YET BEEN AFFECTED BY THE OLD GOD'S SHADOW.
YARRRGH!
AAIII!

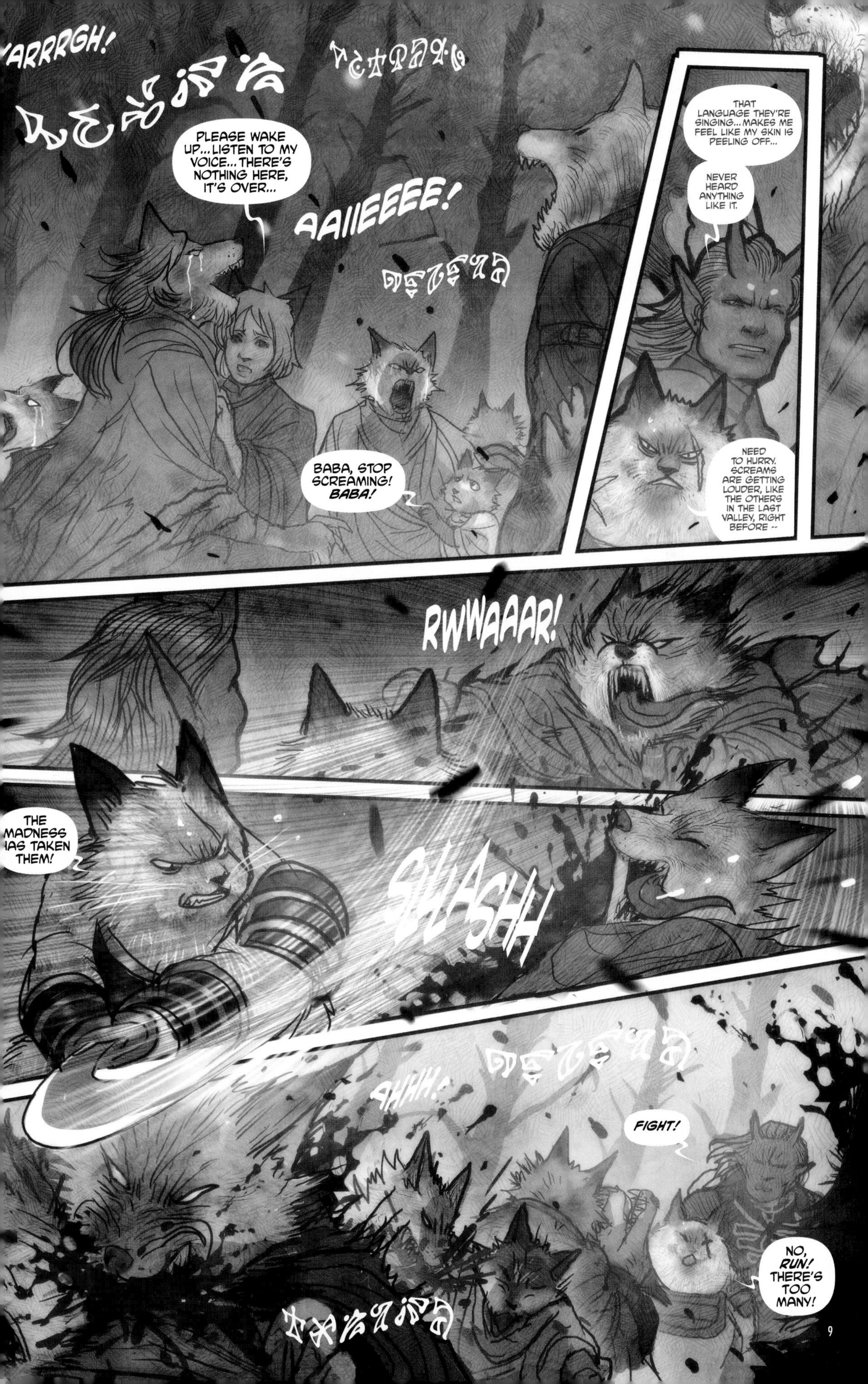

ARRRGH!
PLEASE WAKE UP... LISTEN TO MY VOICE... THERE'S NOTHING HERE, IT'S OVER...
AAIIEEEE!
BABA, STOP SCREAMING! BABA!
THAT LANGUAGE THEY'RE SINGING... MAKES ME FEEL LIKE MY SKIN IS PEELING OFF...
NEVER HEARD ANYTHING LIKE IT.
NEED TO HURRY. SCREAMS ARE GETTING LOUDER, LIKE THE OTHERS IN THE LAST VALLEY, RIGHT BEFORE --
RWWAAAR!
THE MADNESS HAS TAKEN THEM!
SHLASHH
AHHH!
FIGHT!
NO, RUN! THERE'S TOO MANY!

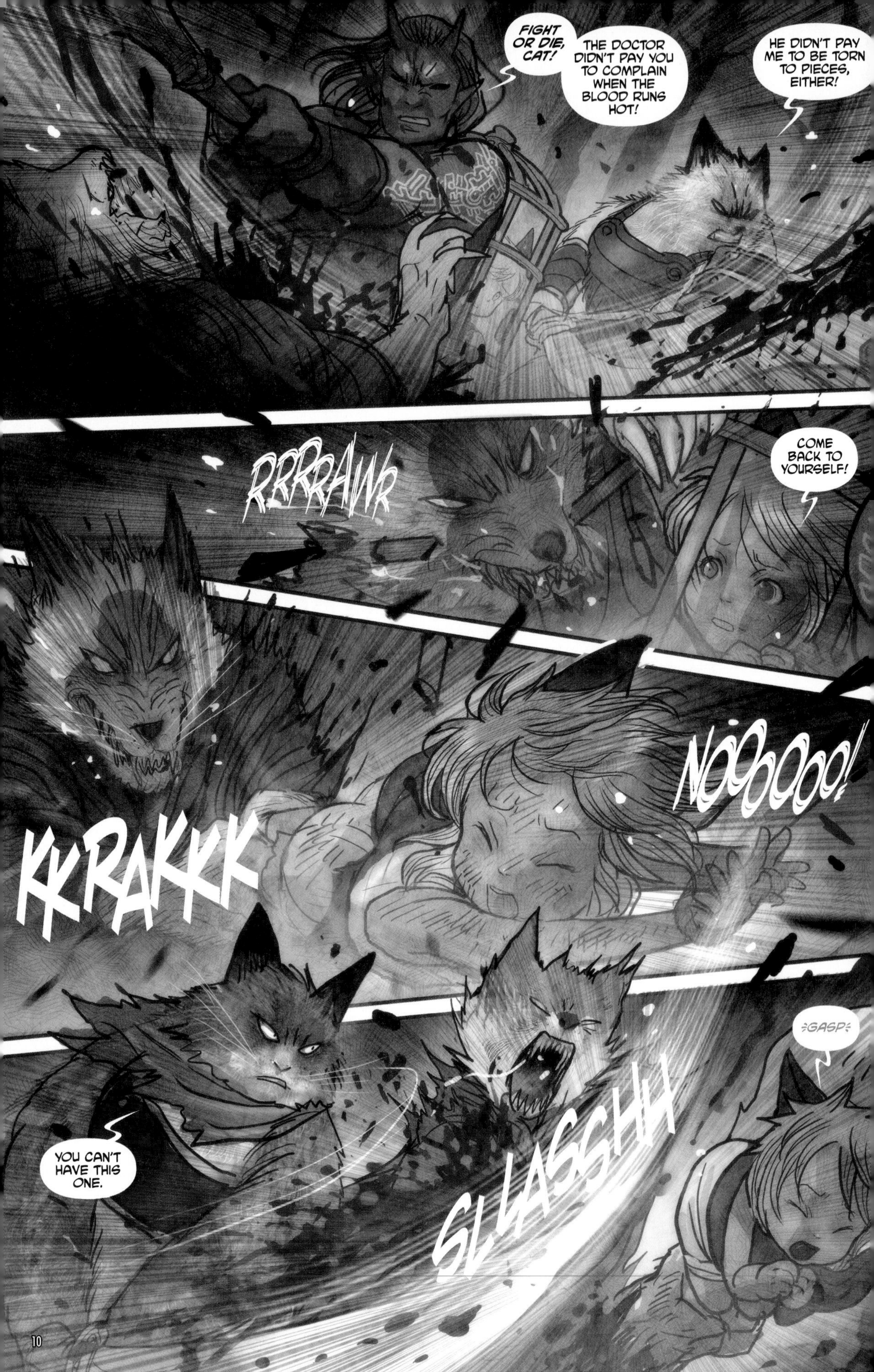

FIGHT OR DIE, CAT!
THE DOCTOR DIDN'T PAY YOU TO COMPLAIN WHEN THE BLOOD RUNS HOT!
HE DIDN'T PAY ME TO BE TORN TO PIECES, EITHER!
RRRRAWR
COME BACK TO YOURSELF!
NOOOOOO!
KKRAKKK
GASP
YOU CAN'T HAVE THIS ONE.
SLLASSHH

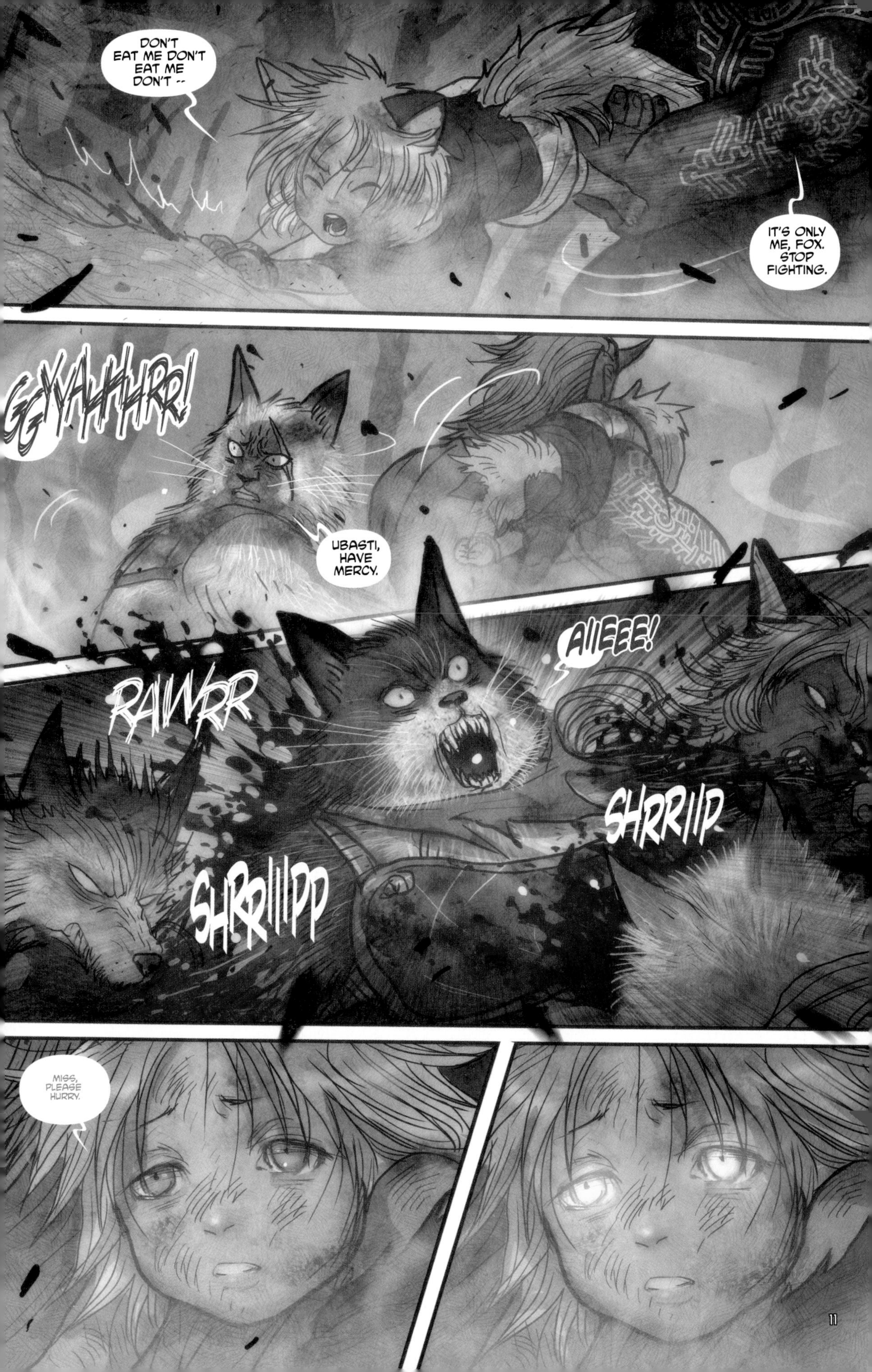
DON'T EAT ME DON'T EAT ME DON'T --
IT'S ONLY ME, FOX. STOP FIGHTING.
GGYYAHHRR!
UBASTI, HAVE MERCY.
AIIEEE!
RAWRR
SHRRIIP
SHRRIIIPP
MISS, PLEASE HURRY.

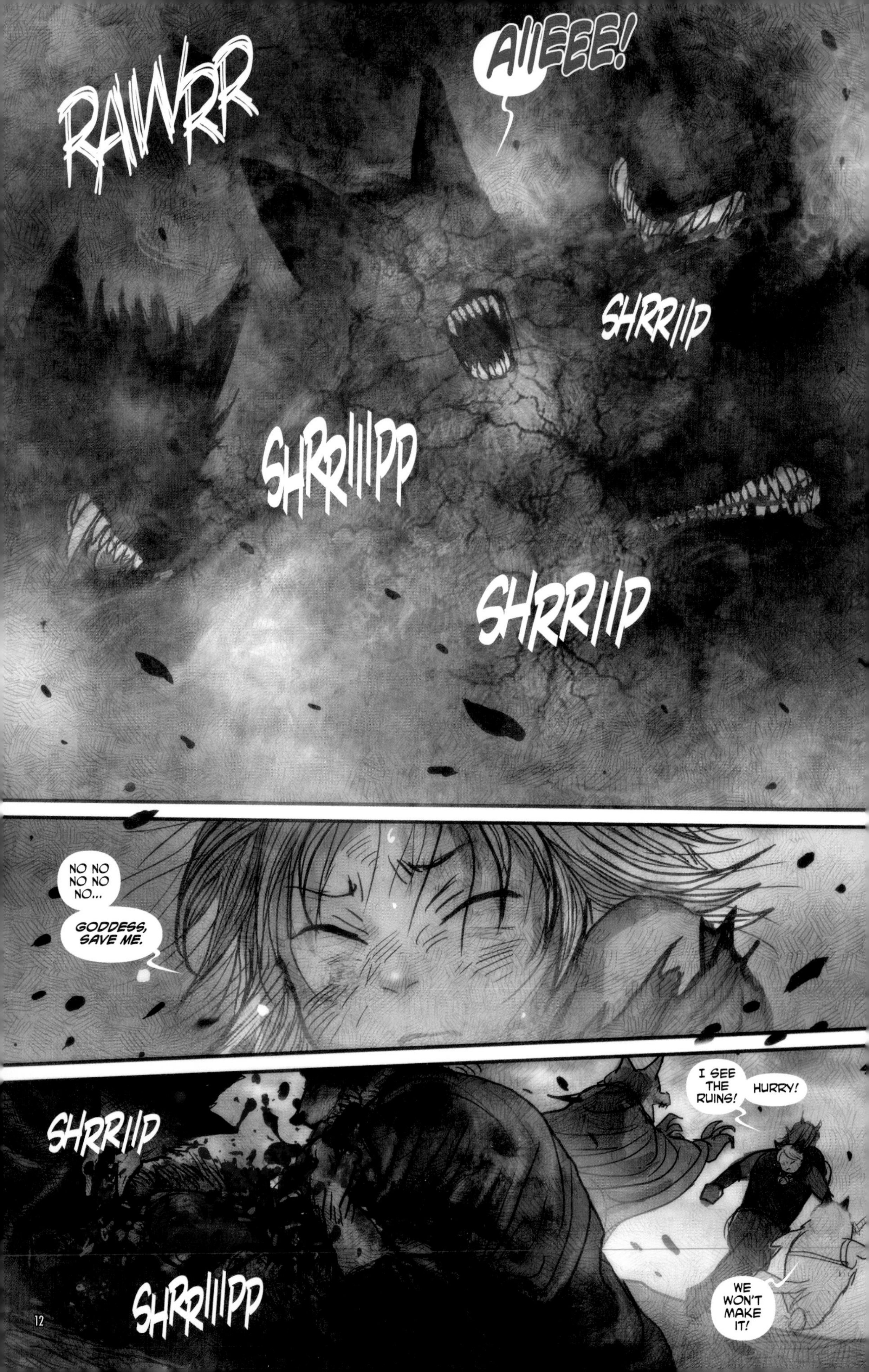
RAWRR
AIIEEE!
SHRRIIP
SHRRIIIIPP
SHRRIIP
NO NO
NO NO
NO...
GODDESS,
SAVE ME.
SHRRIIP
I SEE
THE
RUINS!
HURRY!
SHRRIIIIPP
WE
WON'T
MAKE
IT!

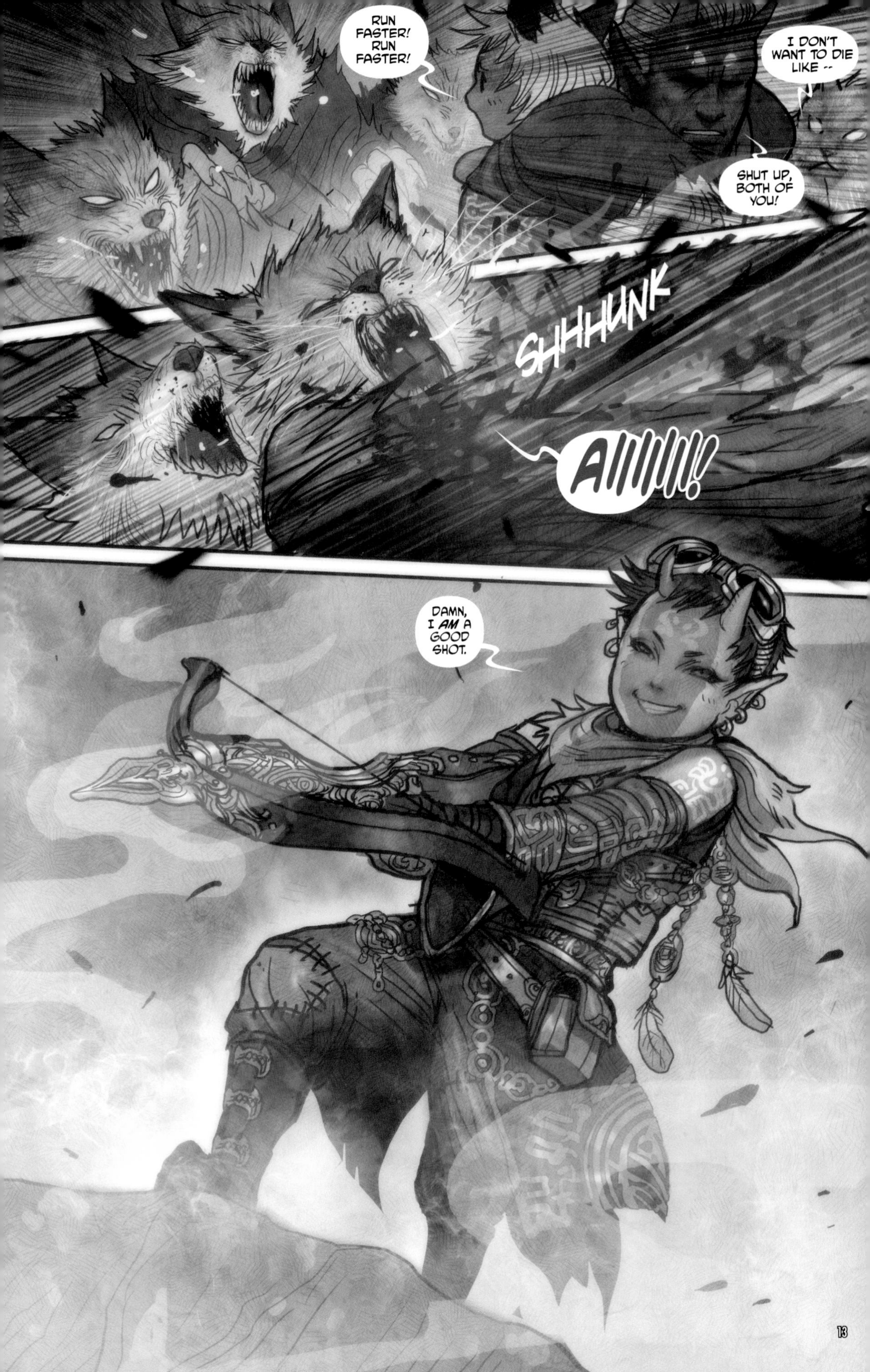
RUN FASTER! RUN FASTER!
I DON'T WANT TO DIE LIKE --
SHUT UP, BOTH OF YOU!
SHHHUNK
AIIIIIIII!
DAMN, I *AM* A GOOD SHOT.

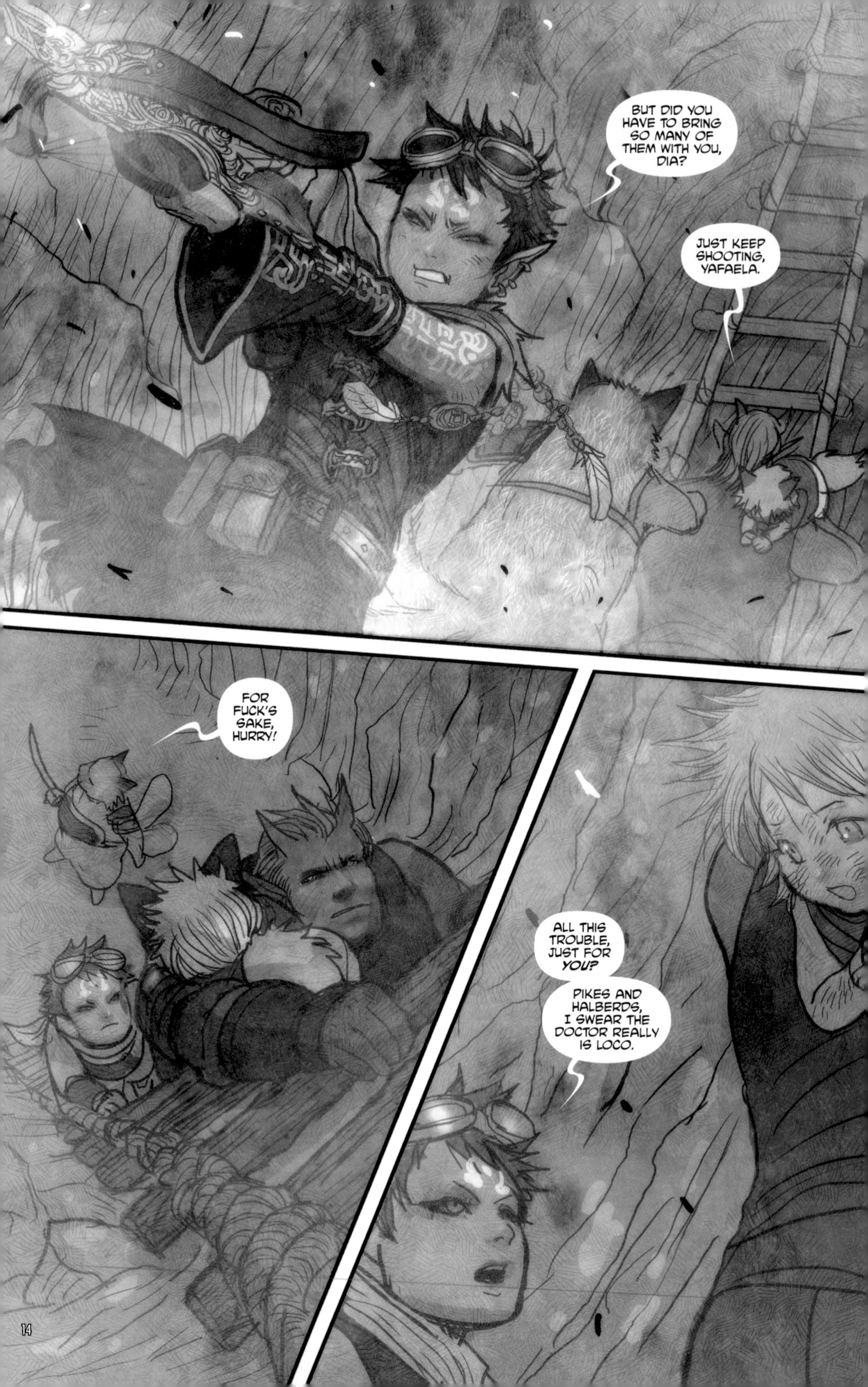
BUT DID YOU HAVE TO BRING SO MANY OF THEM WITH YOU, DIA?
JUST KEEP SHOOTING, YAFAELA.
FOR FUCK'S SAKE, HURRY!
ALL THIS TROUBLE, JUST FOR *YOU?*
PIKES AND HALBERDS, I SWEAR THE DOCTOR REALLY IS LOCO.

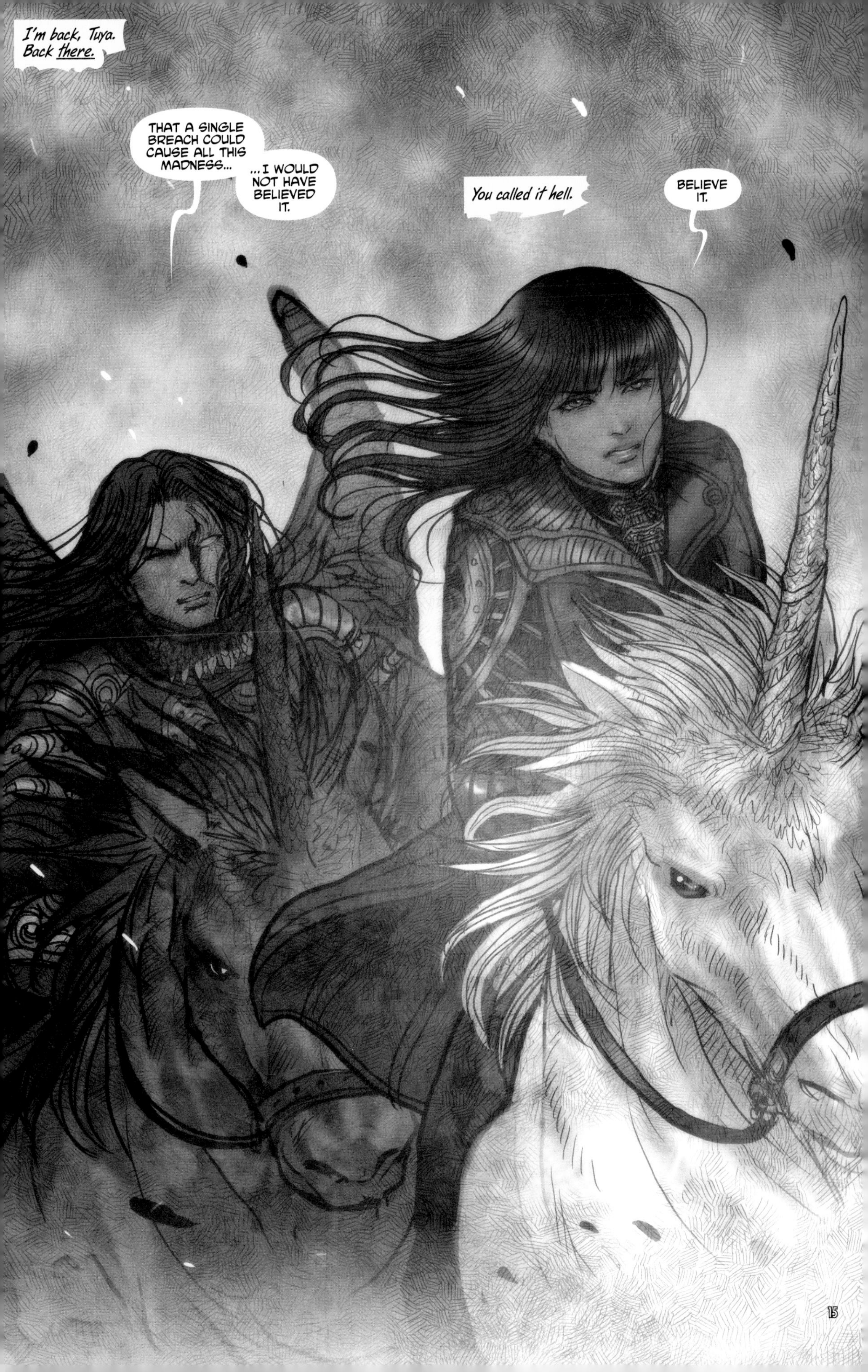
I'm back, Tuya. Back there.
THAT A SINGLE BREACH COULD CAUSE ALL THIS MADNESS...
...I WOULD NOT HAVE BELIEVED IT.
You called it hell.
BELIEVE IT.

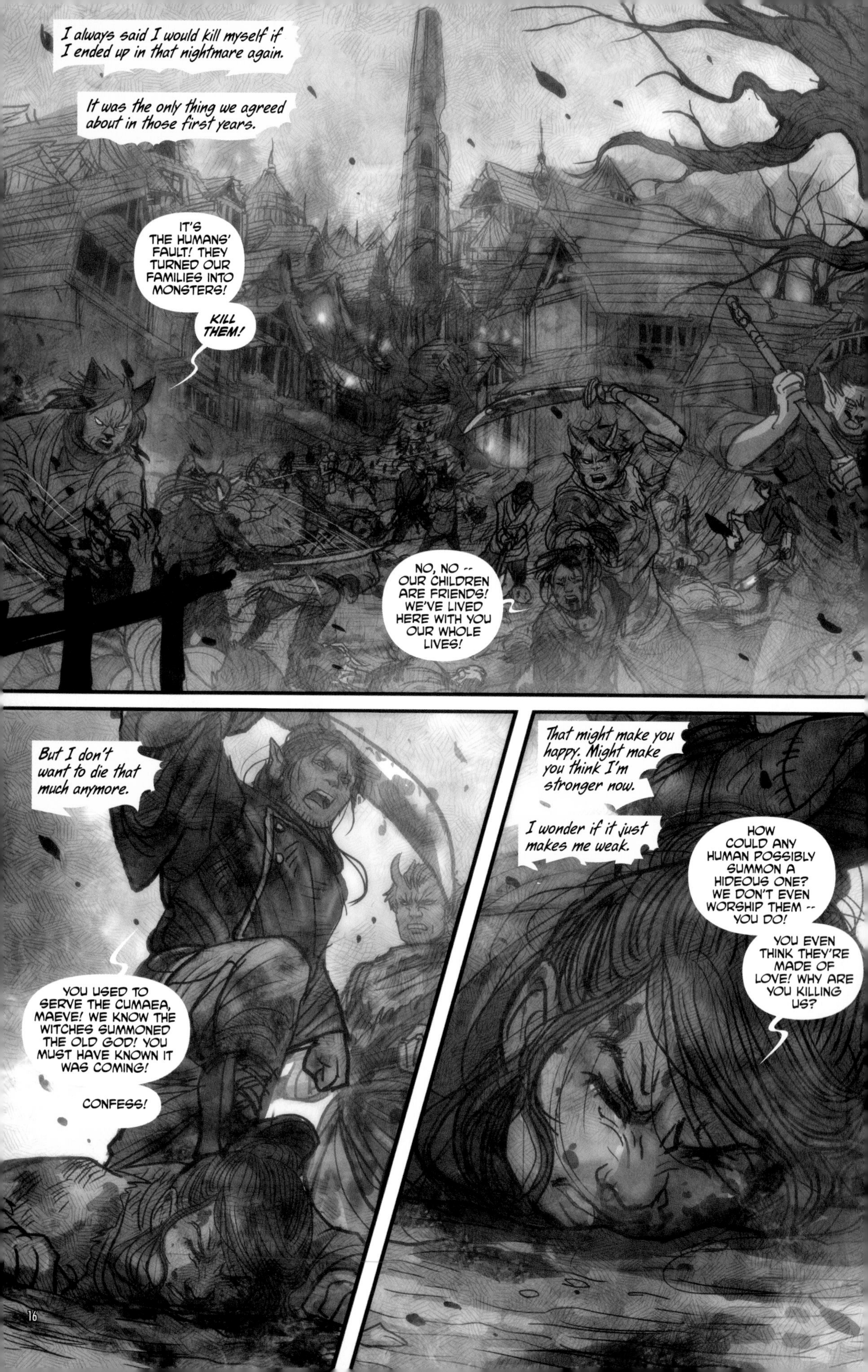
I always said I would kill myself if I ended up in that nightmare again.
It was the only thing we agreed about in those first years.
IT'S THE HUMANS' FAULT! THEY TURNED OUR FAMILIES INTO MONSTERS!
KILL THEM!
NO, NO -- OUR CHILDREN ARE FRIENDS! WE'VE LIVED HERE WITH YOU OUR WHOLE LIVES!
But I don't want to die that much anymore.
YOU USED TO SERVE THE CUMAEA, MAEVE! WE KNOW THE WITCHES SUMMONED THE OLD GOD! YOU MUST HAVE KNOWN IT WAS COMING!
CONFESS!
That might make you happy. Might make you think I'm stronger now.
I wonder if it just makes me weak.
HOW COULD ANY HUMAN POSSIBLY SUMMON A HIDEOUS ONE? WE DON'T EVEN WORSHIP THEM -- YOU DO!
YOU EVEN THINK THEY'RE MADE OF LOVE! WHY ARE YOU KILLING US?

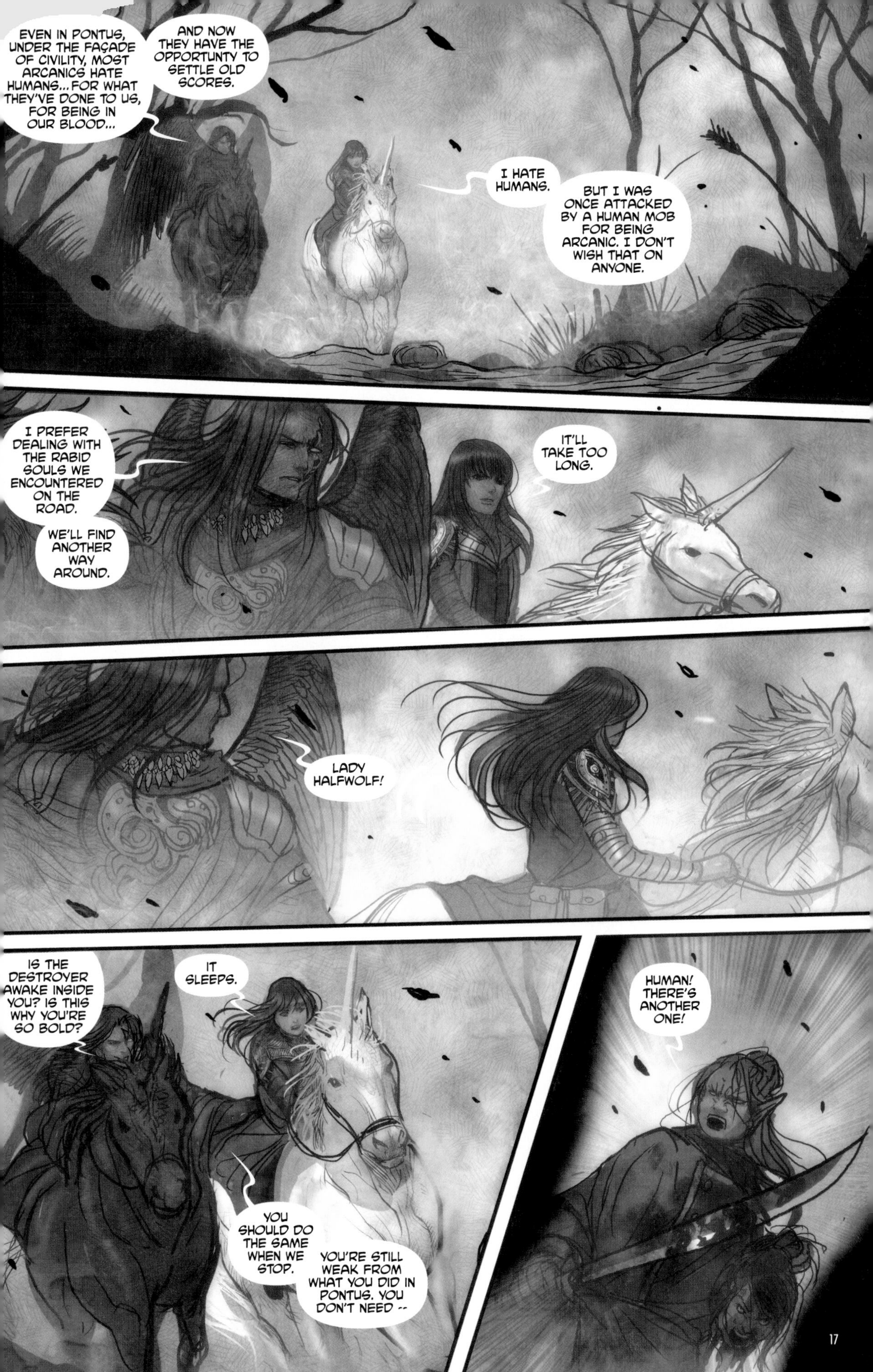
EVEN IN PONTUS, UNDER THE FAÇADE OF CIVILITY, MOST ARCANICS HATE HUMANS... FOR WHAT THEY'VE DONE TO US, FOR BEING IN OUR BLOOD...
AND NOW THEY HAVE THE OPPORTUNTY TO SETTLE OLD SCORES.
I HATE HUMANS.
BUT I WAS ONCE ATTACKED BY A HUMAN MOB FOR BEING ARCANIC. I DON'T WISH THAT ON ANYONE.
I PREFER DEALING WITH THE RABID SOULS WE ENCOUNTERED ON THE ROAD.
WE'LL FIND ANOTHER WAY AROUND.
IT'LL TAKE TOO LONG.
LADY HALFWOLF!
IS THE DESTROYER AWAKE INSIDE YOU? IS THIS WHY YOU'RE SO BOLD?
IT SLEEPS.
YOU SHOULD DO THE SAME WHEN WE STOP.
YOU'RE STILL WEAK FROM WHAT YOU DID IN PONTUS. YOU DON'T NEED --
HUMAN! THERE'S ANOTHER ONE!

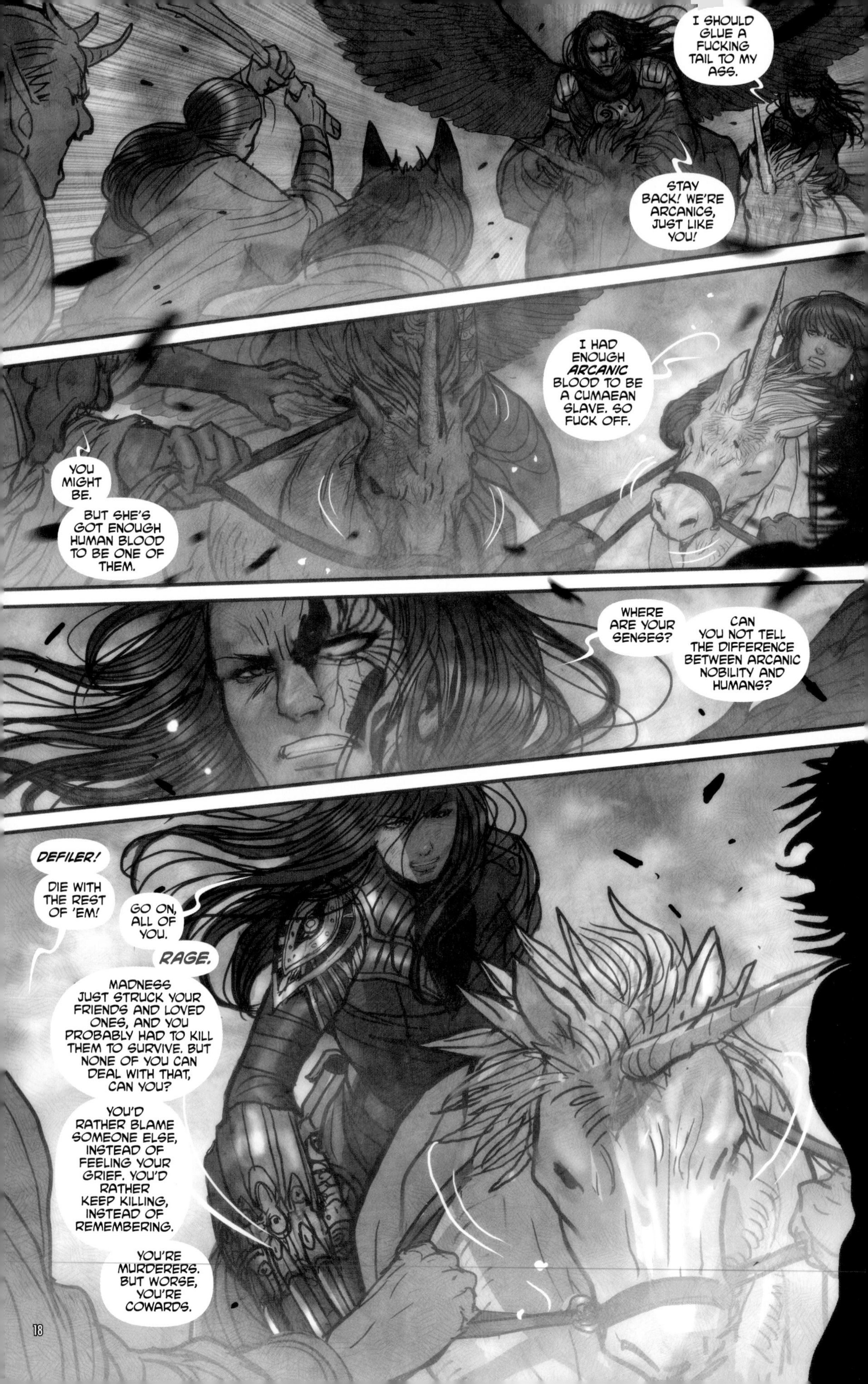
I SHOULD GLUE A FUCKING TAIL TO MY ASS.
STAY BACK! WE'RE ARCANICS, JUST LIKE YOU!
I HAD ENOUGH *ARCANIC* BLOOD TO BE A CUMAEAN SLAVE. SO FUCK OFF.
YOU MIGHT BE.
BUT SHE'S GOT ENOUGH HUMAN BLOOD TO BE ONE OF THEM.
WHERE ARE YOUR SENSES?
CAN YOU NOT TELL THE DIFFERENCE BETWEEN ARCANIC NOBILITY AND HUMANS?
DEFILER!
DIE WITH THE REST OF 'EM!
GO ON, ALL OF YOU.
RAGE.
MADNESS JUST STRUCK YOUR FRIENDS AND LOVED ONES, AND YOU PROBABLY HAD TO KILL THEM TO SURVIVE. BUT NONE OF YOU CAN DEAL WITH THAT, CAN YOU?
YOU'D RATHER BLAME SOMEONE ELSE, INSTEAD OF FEELING YOUR GRIEF. YOU'D RATHER KEEP KILLING, INSTEAD OF REMEMBERING.
YOU'RE MURDERERS. BUT WORSE, YOU'RE COWARDS.

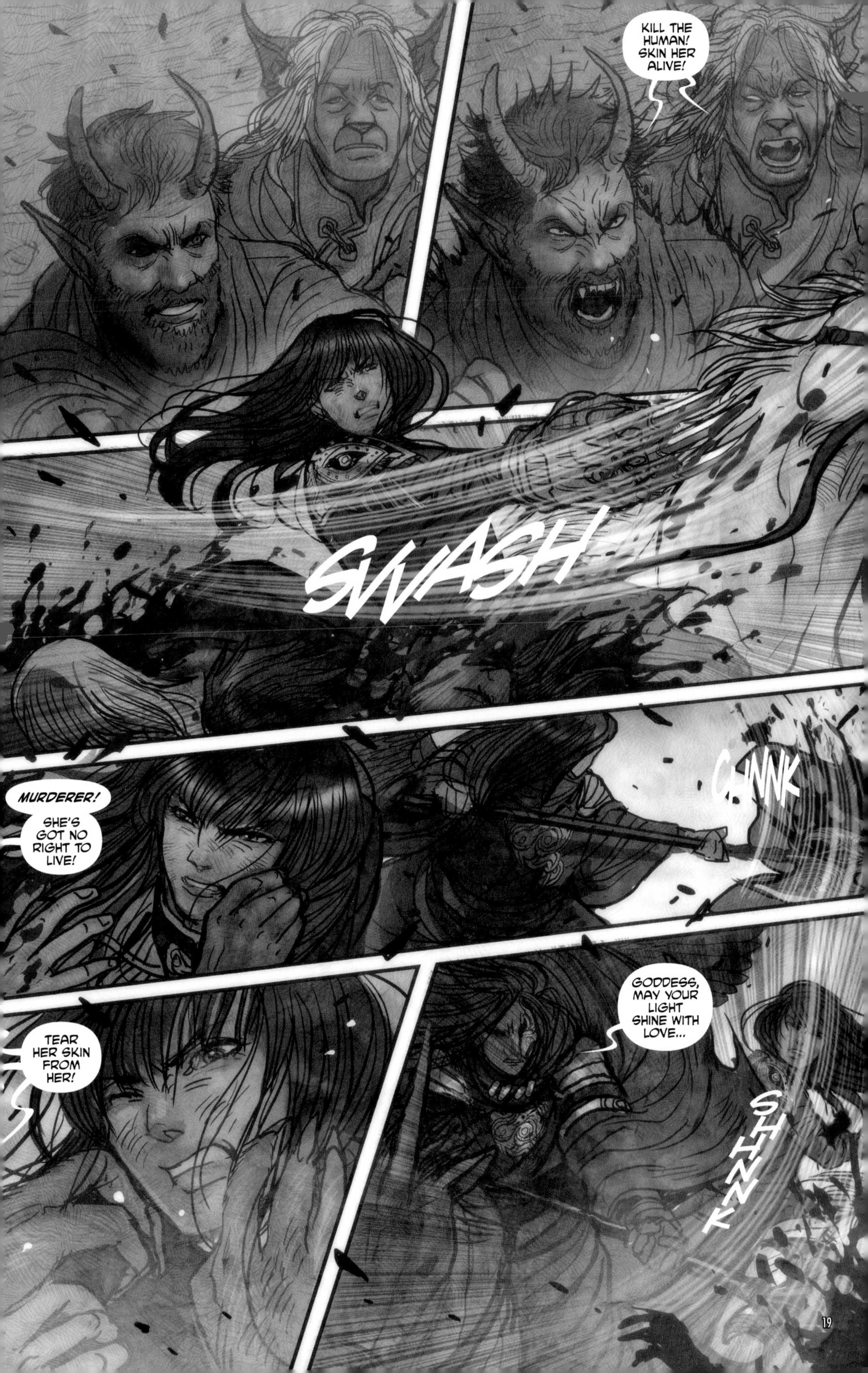
KILL THE HUMAN! SKIN HER ALIVE!
SWASH
MURDERER!
SHE'S GOT NO RIGHT TO LIVE!
CHNNK
TEAR HER SKIN FROM HER!
GODDESS, MAY YOUR LIGHT SHINE WITH LOVE...
SHHNNK

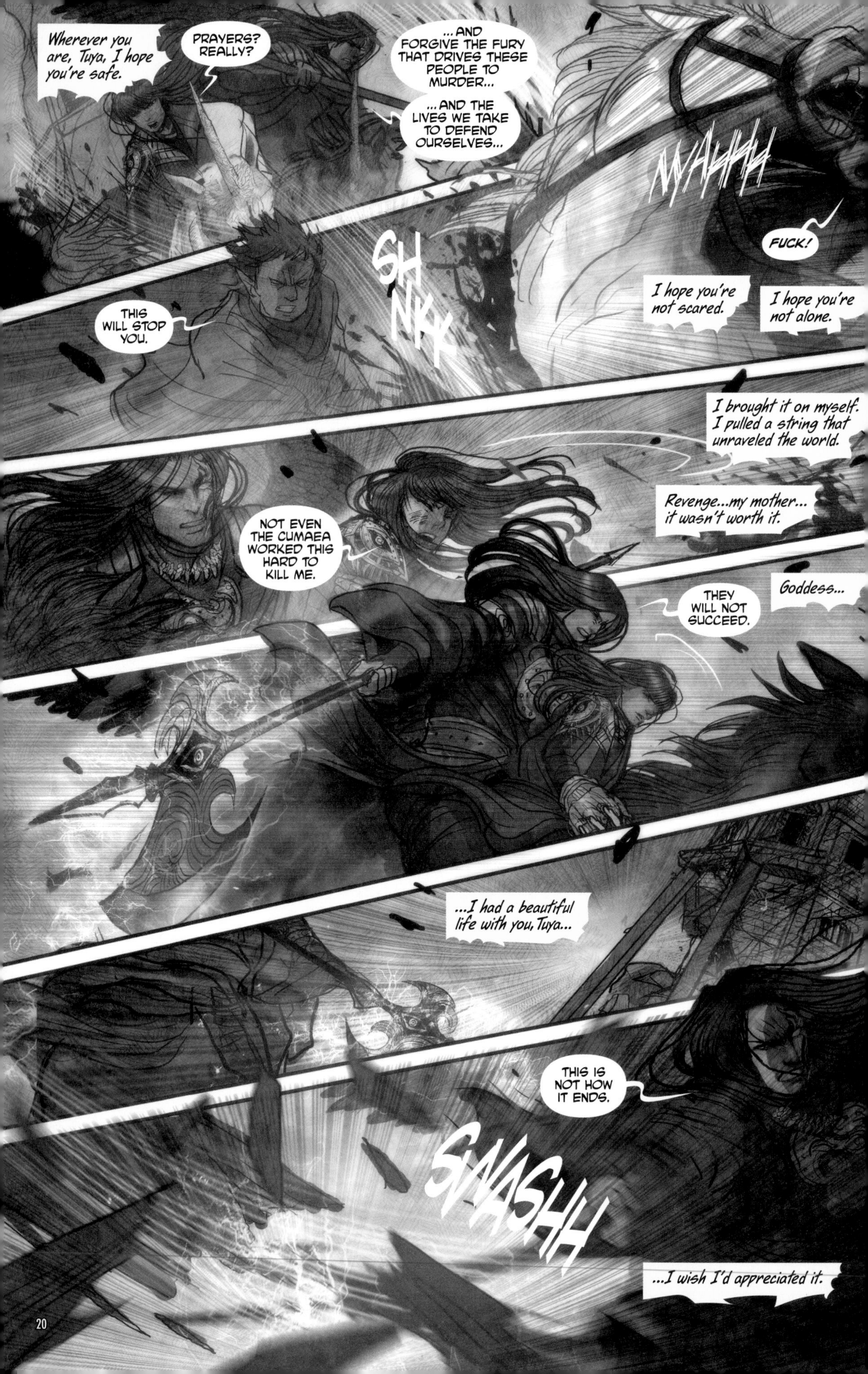
Wherever you are, Tuya, I hope you're safe.
PRAYERS? REALLY?
...AND FORGIVE THE FURY THAT DRIVES THESE PEOPLE TO MURDER...
...AND THE LIVES WE TAKE TO DEFEND OURSELVES...
NYAHHH
FUCK!
SHNKK
THIS WILL STOP YOU.
I hope you're not scared.
I hope you're not alone.
I brought it on myself. I pulled a string that unraveled the world.
Revenge...my mother... it wasn't worth it.
NOT EVEN THE CUMAEA WORKED THIS HARD TO KILL ME.
THEY WILL NOT SUCCEED.
Goddess...
...I had a beautiful life with you, Tuya...
THIS IS NOT HOW IT ENDS.
SWASHH
...I wish I'd appreciated it.

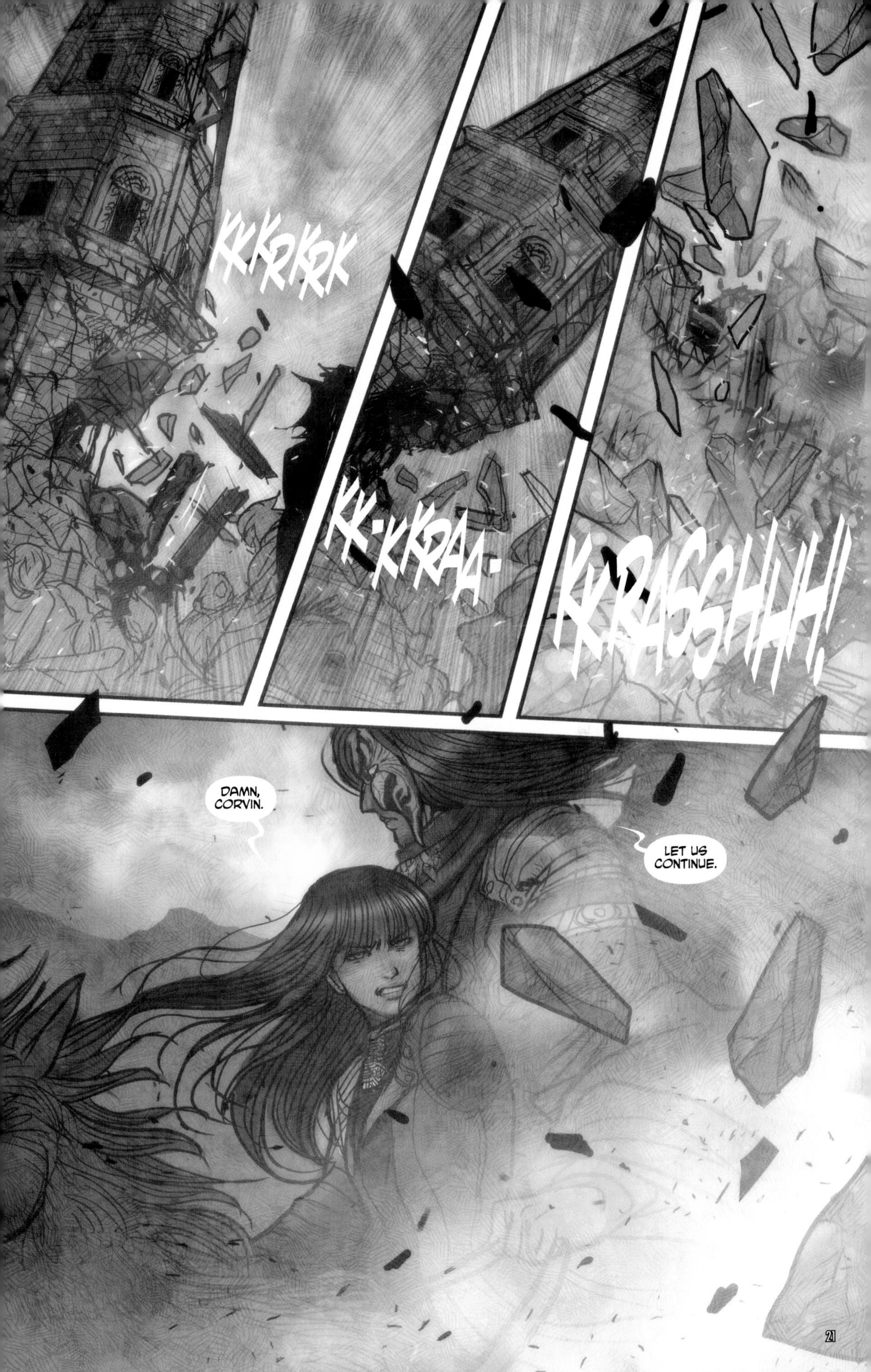
KKKRKRK
KK-KKRAA-
KKRASSHHH!
DAMN, CORVIN.
LET US CONTINUE.

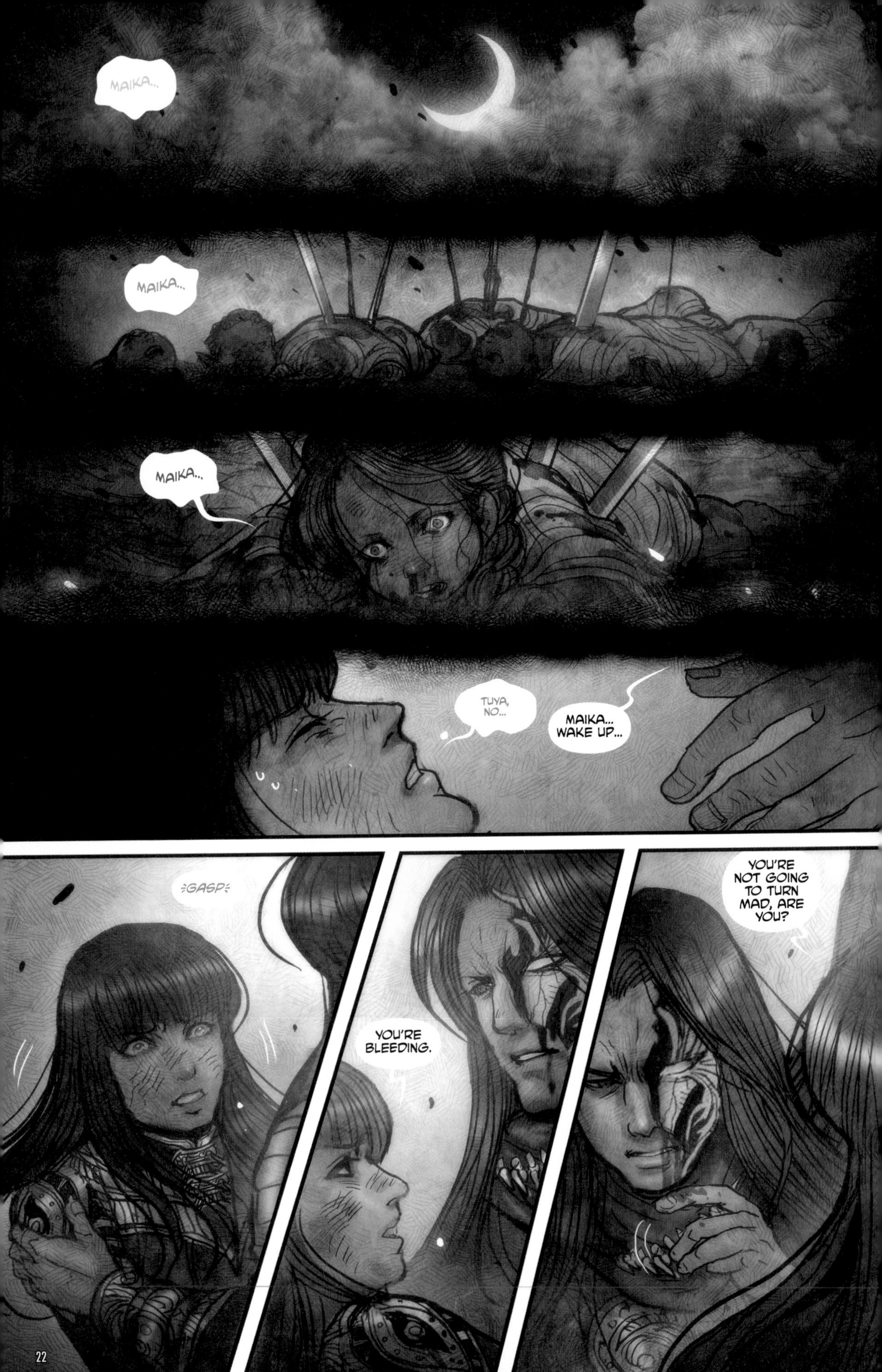
MAIKA...
MAIKA...
MAIKA...
TUYA, NO...
MAIKA... WAKE UP...
GASP
YOU'RE BLEEDING.
YOU'RE NOT GOING TO TURN MAD, ARE YOU?

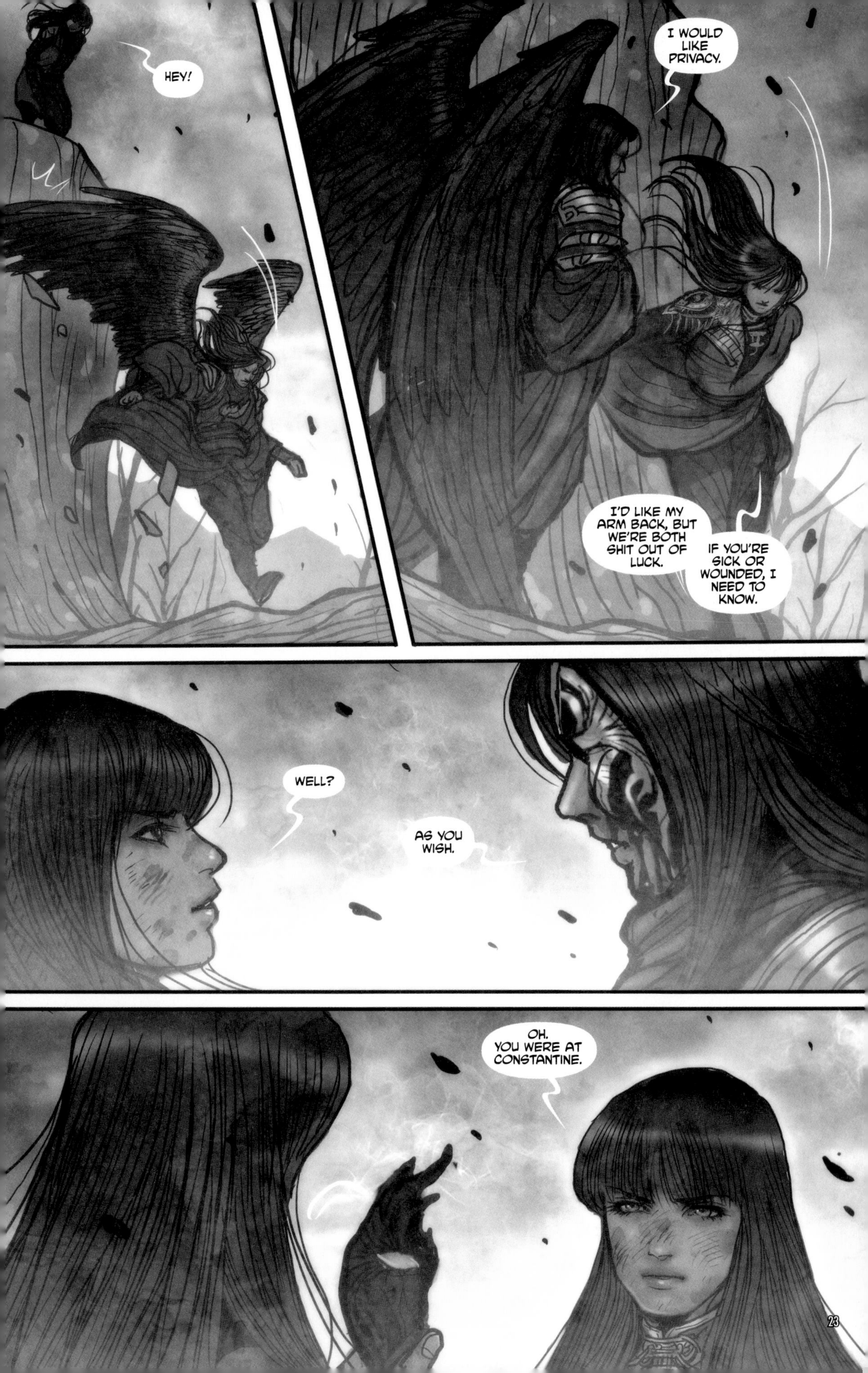
HEY!
I WOULD LIKE PRIVACY.
I'D LIKE MY ARM BACK, BUT WE'RE BOTH SHIT OUT OF LUCK.
IF YOU'RE SICK OR WOUNDED, I NEED TO KNOW.
WELL?
AS YOU WISH.
OH. YOU WERE AT CONSTANTINE.

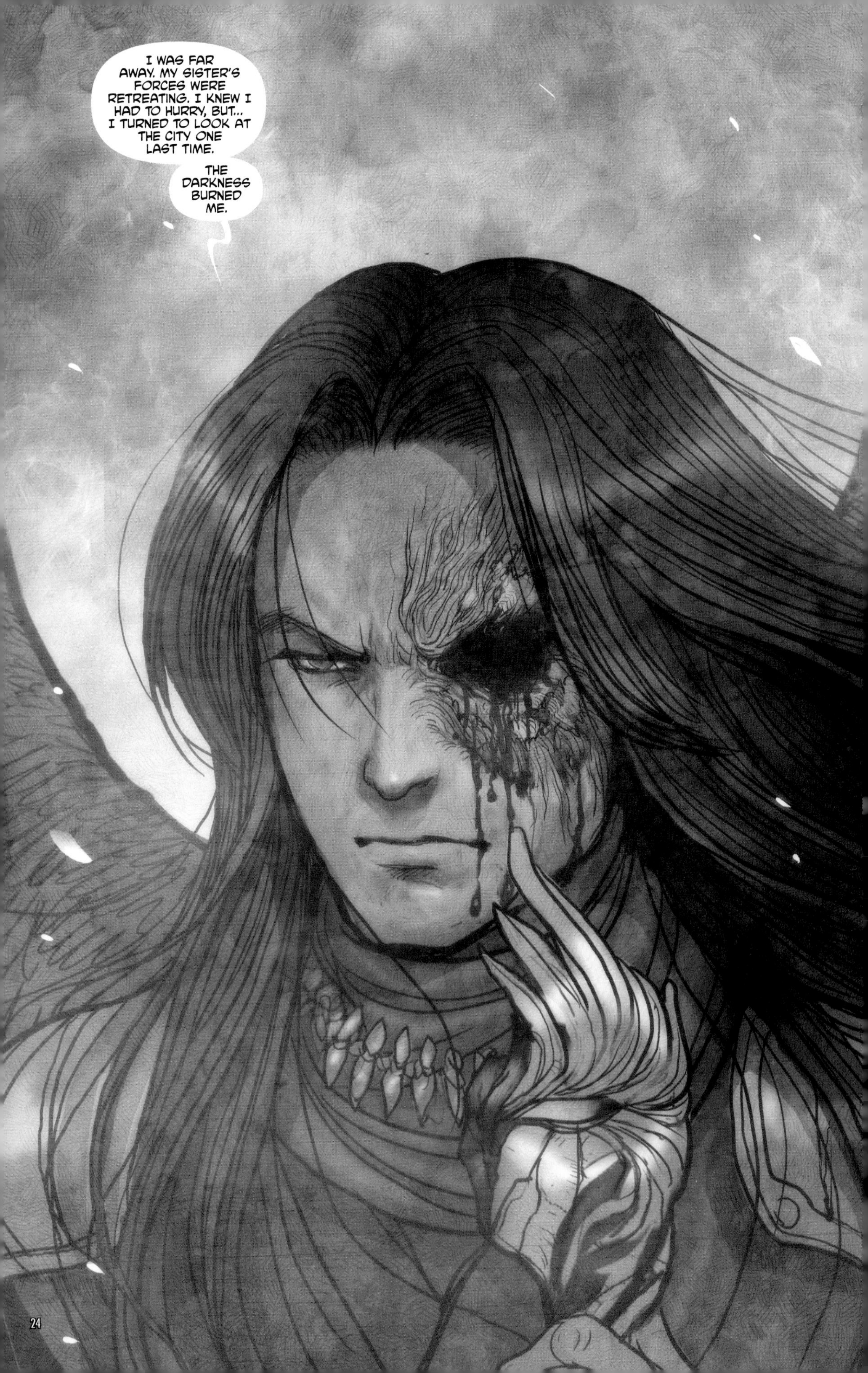
I WAS FAR AWAY. MY SISTER'S FORCES WERE RETREATING. I KNEW I HAD TO HURRY, BUT... I TURNED TO LOOK AT THE CITY ONE LAST TIME.
THE DARKNESS BURNED ME.

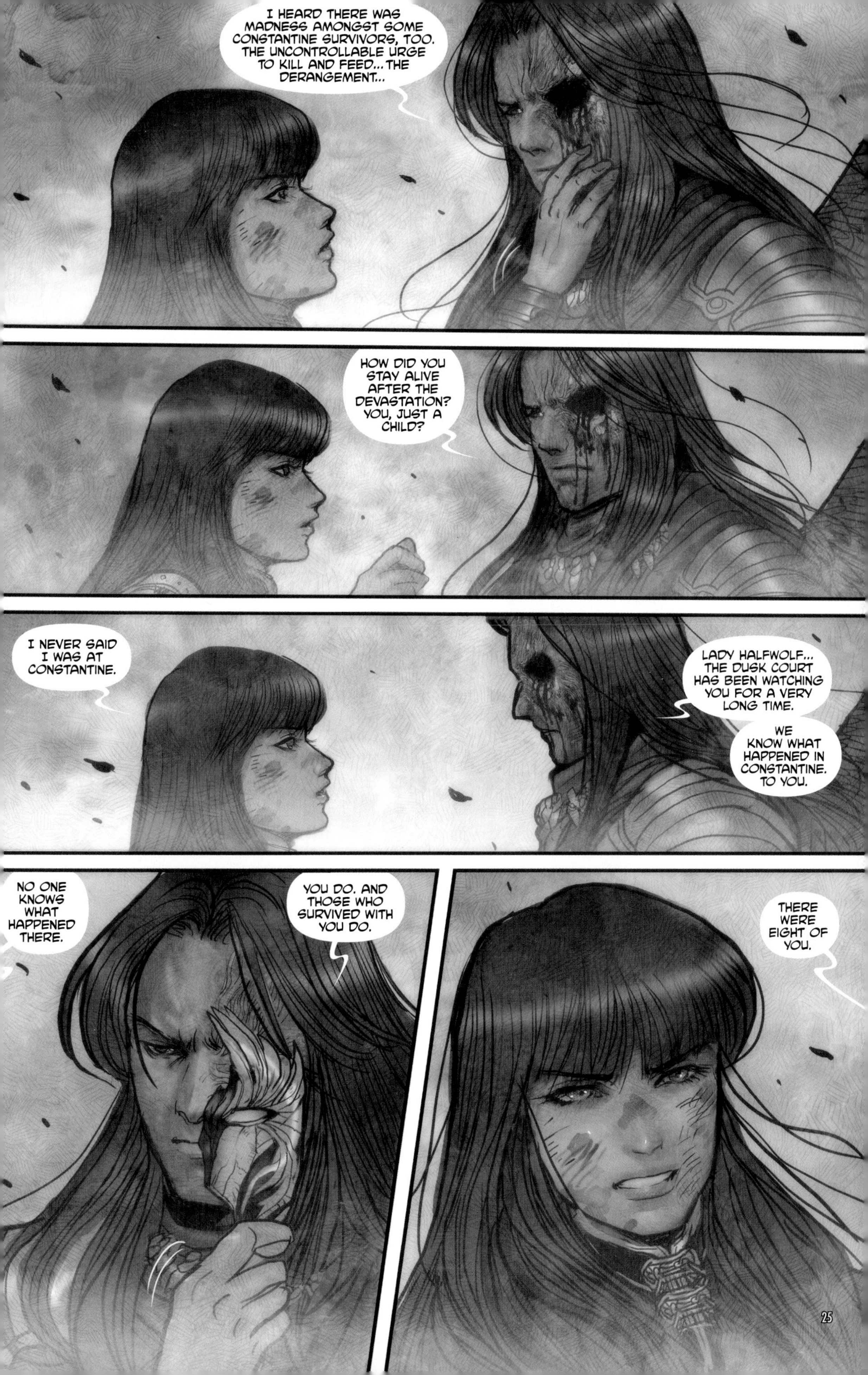
I HEARD THERE WAS MADNESS AMONGST SOME CONSTANTINE SURVIVORS, TOO. THE UNCONTROLLABLE URGE TO KILL AND FEED... THE DERANGEMENT...
HOW DID YOU STAY ALIVE AFTER THE DEVASTATION? YOU, JUST A CHILD?
I NEVER SAID I WAS AT CONSTANTINE.
LADY HALFWOLF... THE DUSK COURT HAS BEEN WATCHING YOU FOR A VERY LONG TIME.
WE KNOW WHAT HAPPENED IN CONSTANTINE. TO YOU.
NO ONE KNOWS WHAT HAPPENED THERE.
YOU DO. AND THOSE WHO SURVIVED WITH YOU DO.
THERE WERE EIGHT OF YOU.

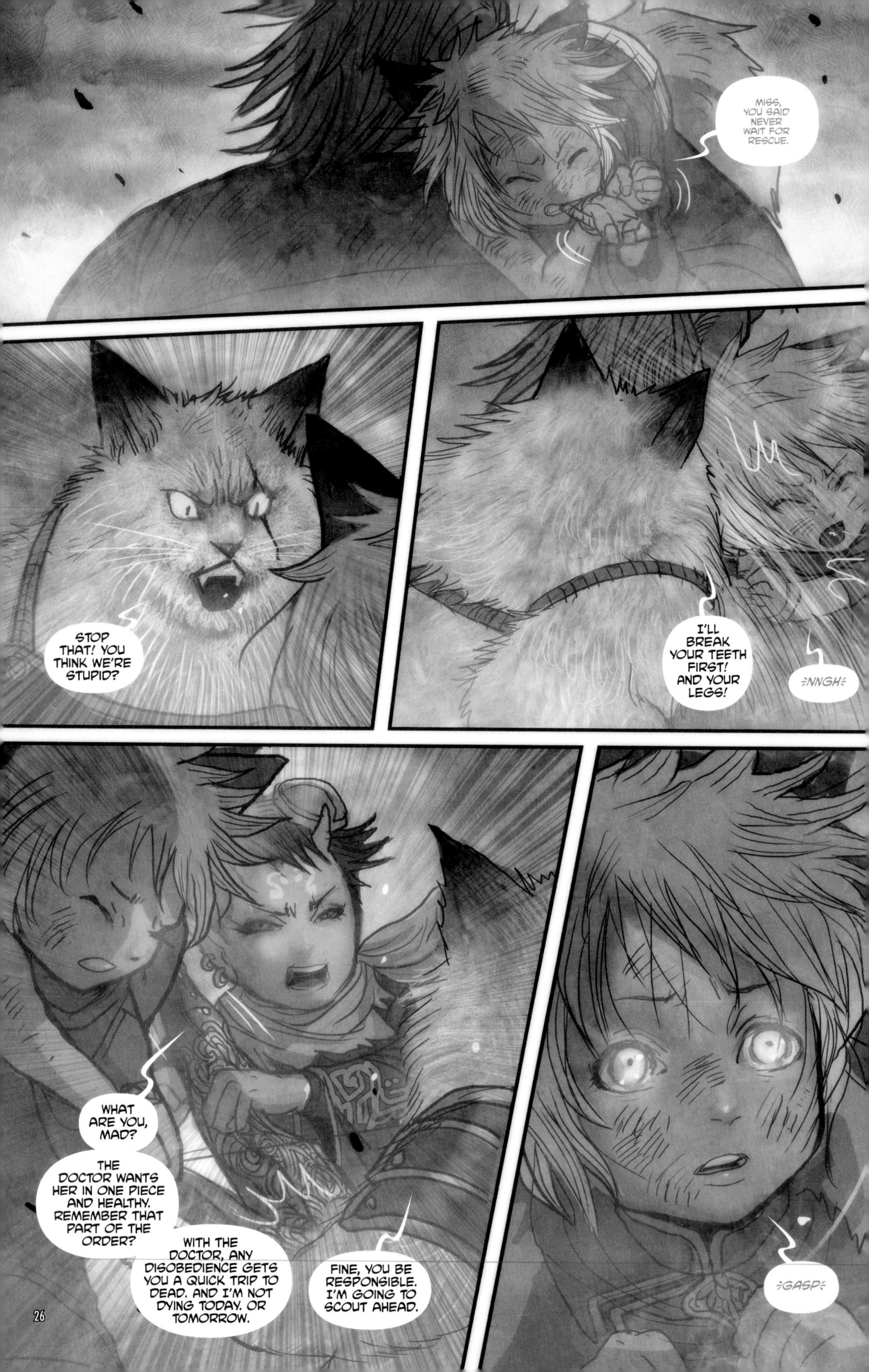
MISS, YOU SAID NEVER WAIT FOR RESCUE.
STOP THAT! YOU THINK WE'RE STUPID?
I'LL BREAK YOUR TEETH FIRST! AND YOUR LEGS!
NNGH
WHAT ARE YOU, MAD?
THE DOCTOR WANTS HER IN ONE PIECE AND HEALTHY. REMEMBER THAT PART OF THE ORDER?
WITH THE DOCTOR, ANY DISOBEDIENCE GETS YOU A QUICK TRIP TO DEAD. AND I'M NOT DYING TODAY. OR TOMORROW.
FINE, YOU BE RESPONSIBLE. I'M GOING TO SCOUT AHEAD.
GASP

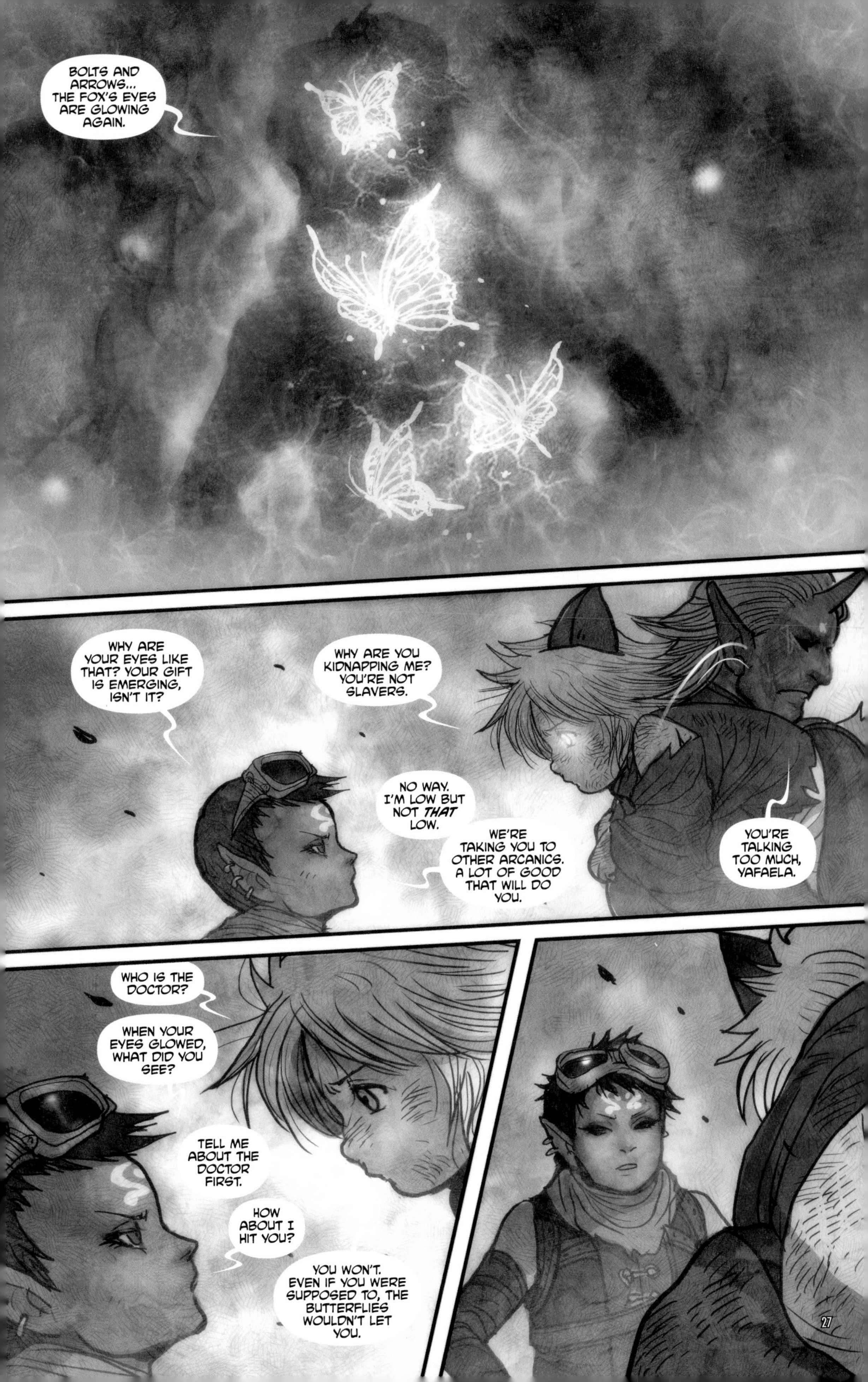
BOLTS AND ARROWS... THE FOX'S EYES ARE GLOWING AGAIN.
WHY ARE YOUR EYES LIKE THAT? YOUR GIFT IS EMERGING, ISN'T IT?
WHY ARE YOU KIDNAPPING ME? YOU'RE NOT SLAVERS.
NO WAY. I'M LOW BUT NOT *THAT* LOW.
WE'RE TAKING YOU TO OTHER ARCANICS. A LOT OF GOOD THAT WILL DO YOU.
YOU'RE TALKING TOO MUCH, YAFAELA.
WHO IS THE DOCTOR?
WHEN YOUR EYES GLOWED, WHAT DID YOU SEE?
TELL ME ABOUT THE DOCTOR FIRST.
HOW ABOUT I HIT YOU?
YOU WON'T. EVEN IF YOU WERE SUPPOSED TO, THE BUTTERFLIES WOULDN'T LET YOU.

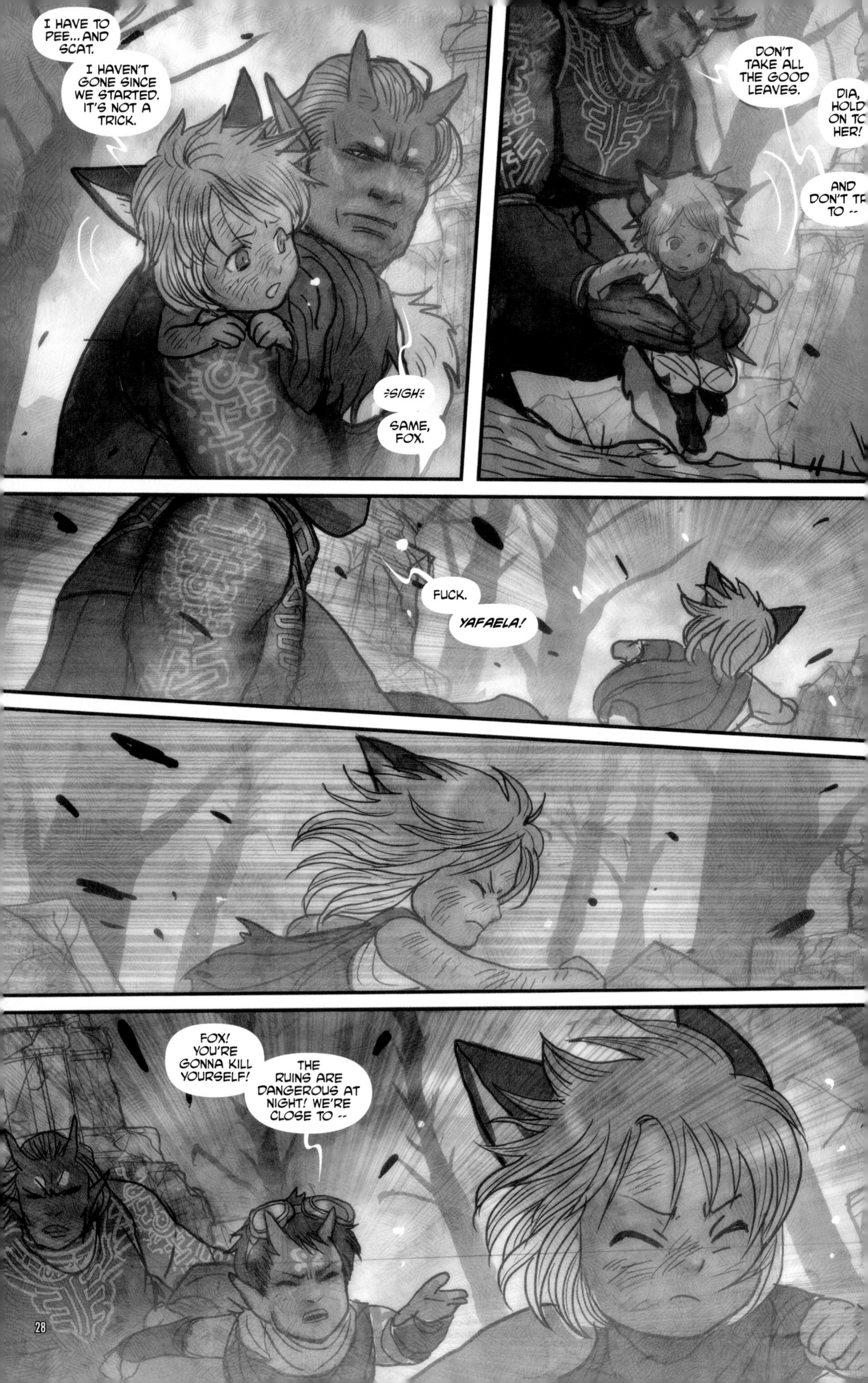

I HAVE TO PEE... AND SCAT.
I HAVEN'T GONE SINCE WE STARTED. IT'S NOT A TRICK.
SIGH
SAME, FOX.
DON'T TAKE ALL THE GOOD LEAVES.
DIA, HOLD ON TO HER!
AND DON'T TR TO --
FUCK.
YAFAELA!
FOX! YOU'RE GONNA KILL YOURSELF!
THE RUINS ARE DANGEROUS AT NIGHT! WE'RE CLOSE TO --

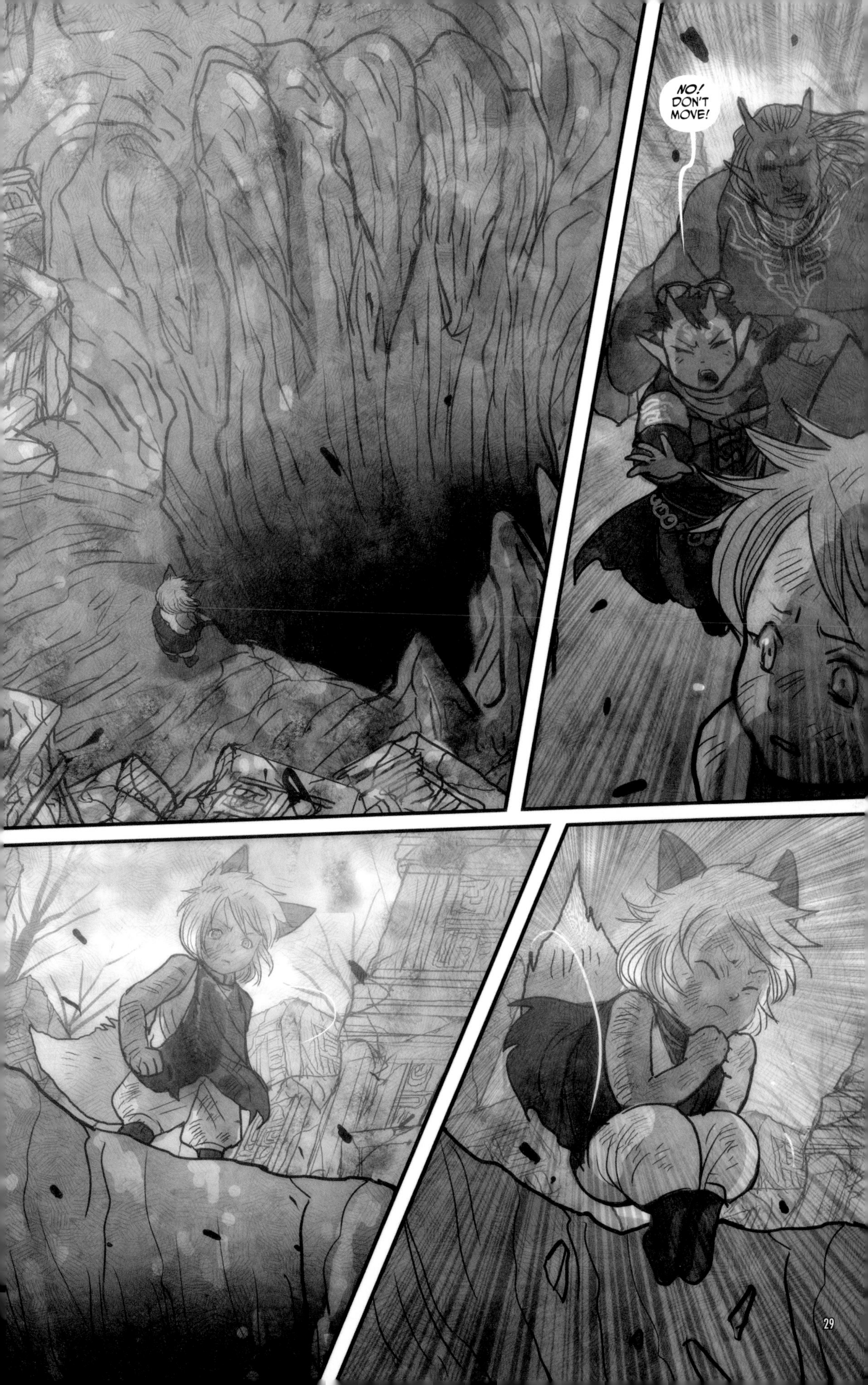
NO! DON'T MOVE!

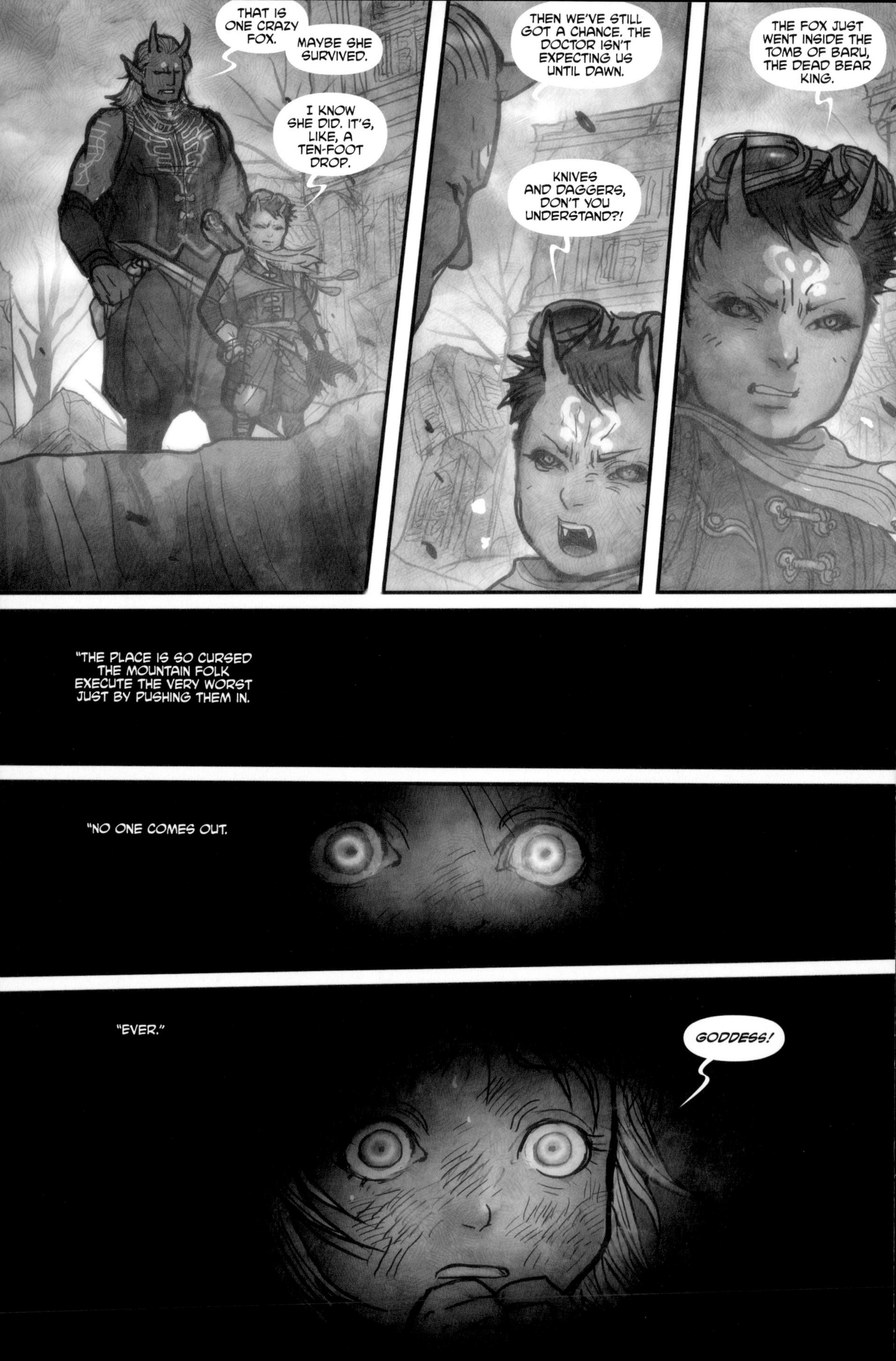
THAT IS ONE CRAZY FOX.
MAYBE SHE SURVIVED.
I KNOW SHE DID. IT'S, LIKE, A TEN-FOOT DROP.
THEN WE'VE STILL GOT A CHANCE. THE DOCTOR ISN'T EXPECTING US UNTIL DAWN.
KNIVES AND DAGGERS, DON'T YOU UNDERSTAND?!
THE FOX JUST WENT INSIDE THE TOMB OF BARU, THE DEAD BEAR KING.
"THE PLACE IS SO CURSED THE MOUNTAIN FOLK EXECUTE THE VERY WORST JUST BY PUSHING THEM IN.
"NO ONE COMES OUT.
"EVER."
GODDESS!

Archival research from the esteemed **Professor Tam Tam,** former First Record-Keeper of the Is'hami Temple, and learned contemporary of Namron Black Claw...

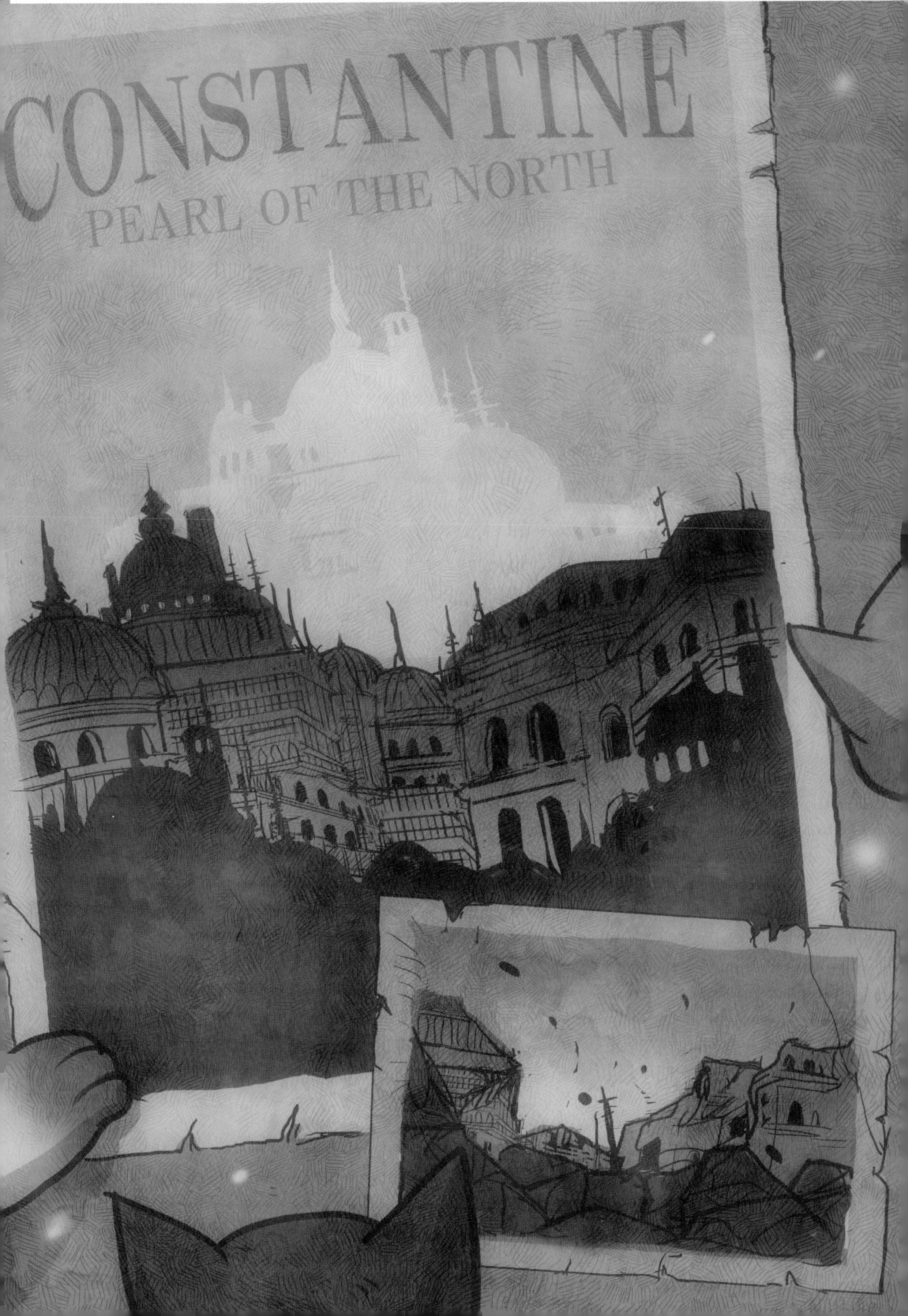
CONSTANTINE
PEARL OF THE NORTH

CHAPTER TWENTY

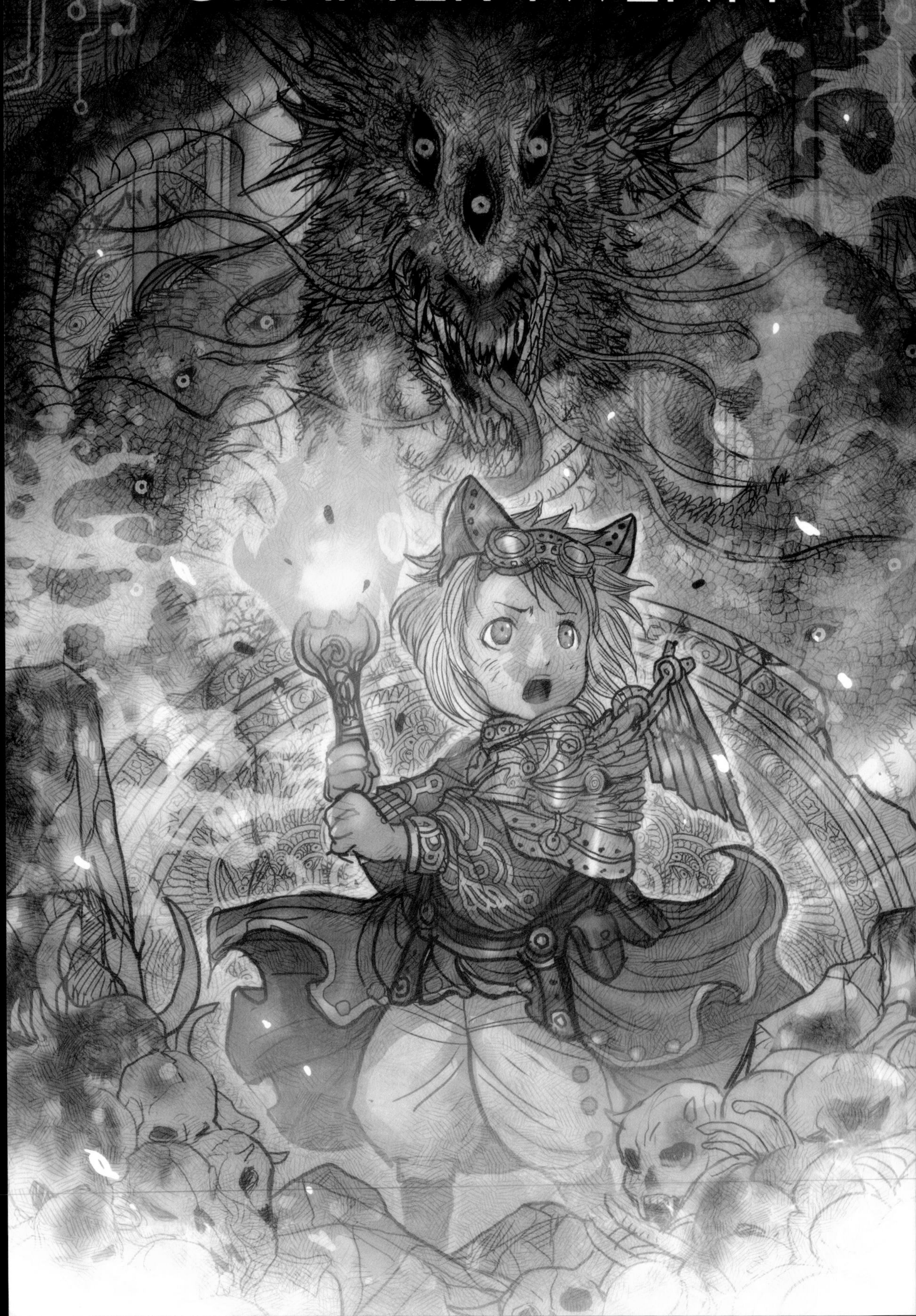

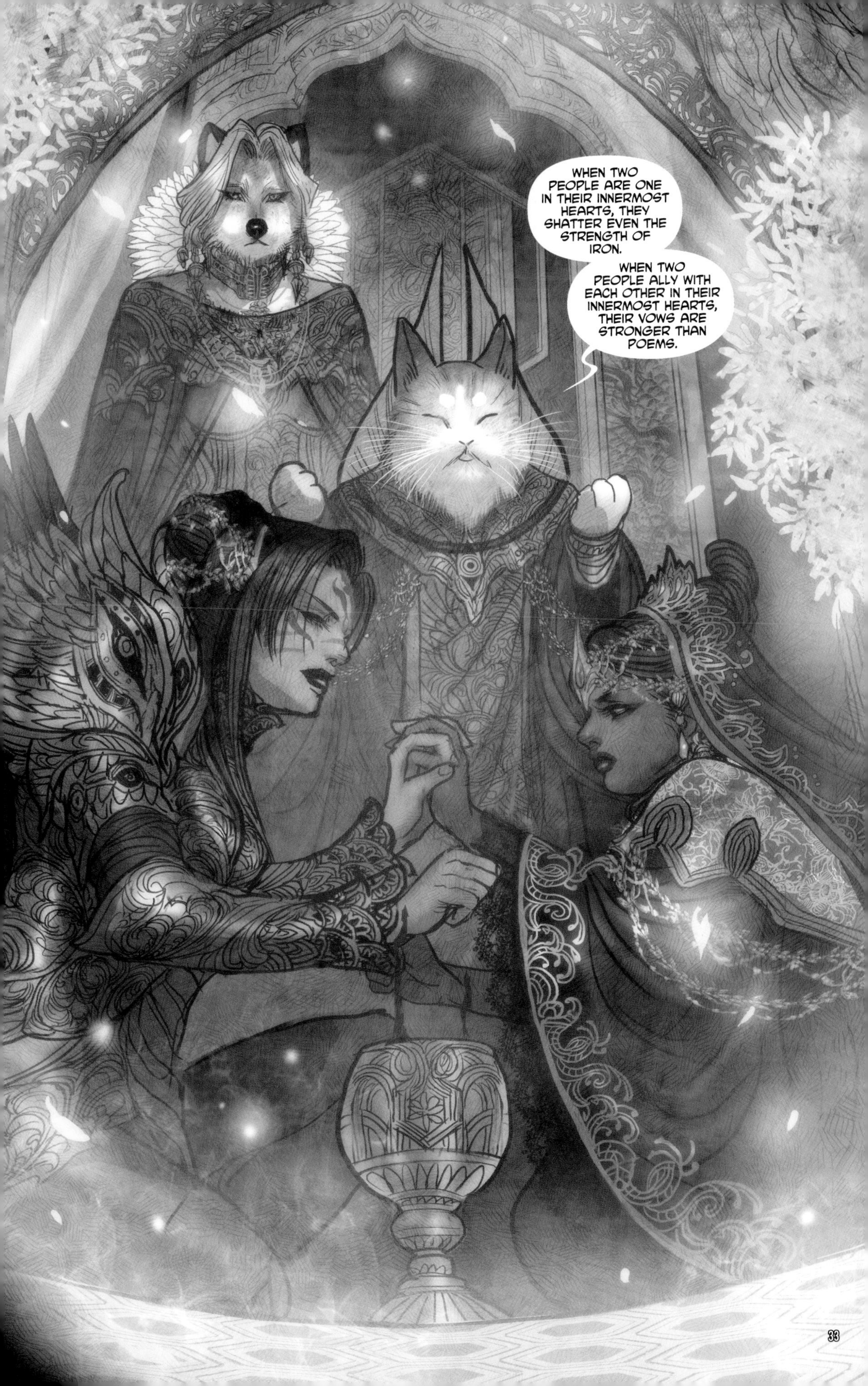
WHEN TWO PEOPLE ARE ONE IN THEIR INNERMOST HEARTS, THEY SHATTER EVEN THE STRENGTH OF IRON.
WHEN TWO PEOPLE ALLY WITH EACH OTHER IN THEIR INNERMOST HEARTS, THEIR VOWS ARE STRONGER THAN POEMS.

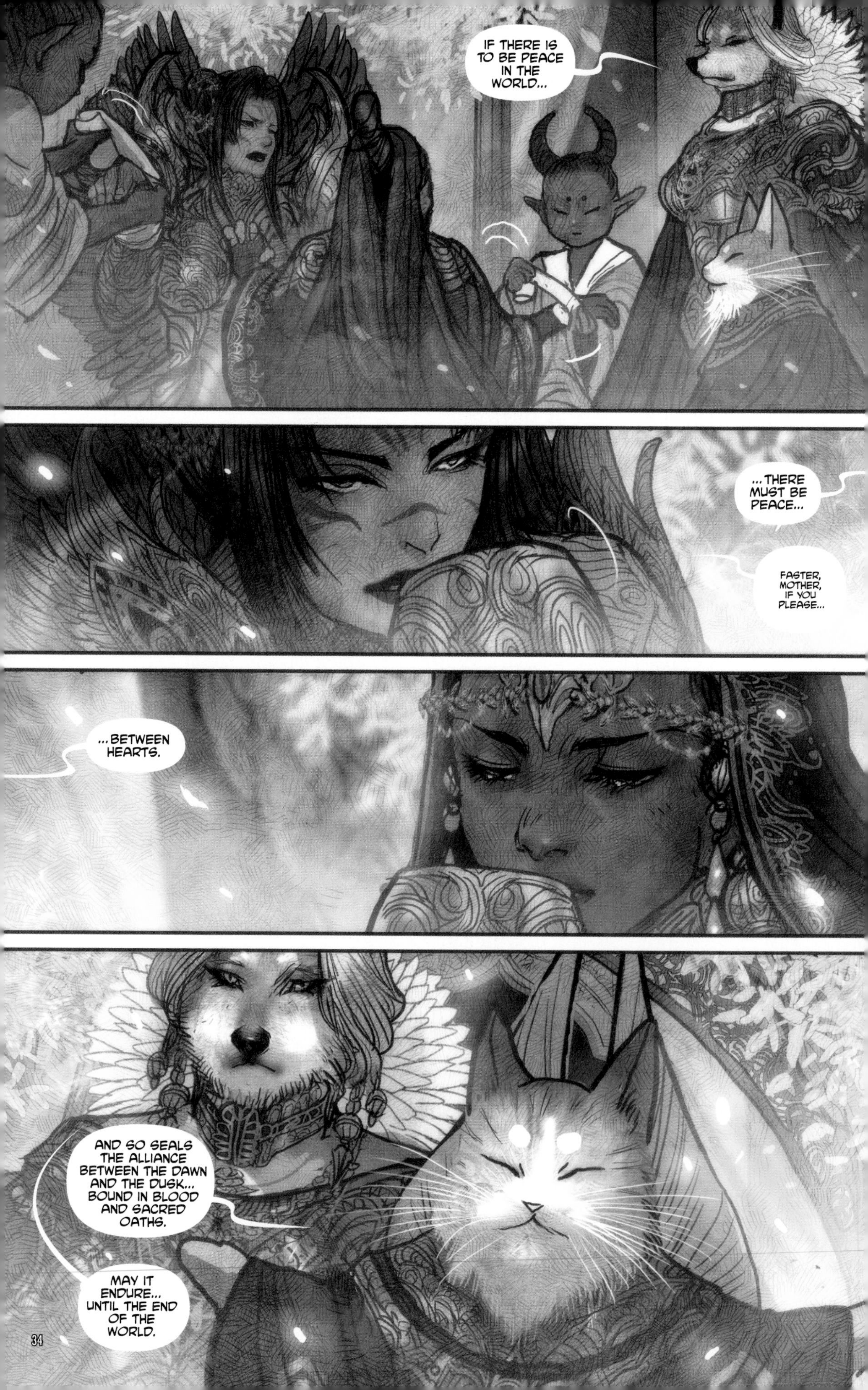
IF THERE IS TO BE PEACE IN THE WORLD...
...THERE MUST BE PEACE...
FASTER, MOTHER, IF YOU PLEASE...
...BETWEEN HEARTS.
AND SO SEALS THE ALLIANCE BETWEEN THE DAWN AND THE DUSK... BOUND IN BLOOD AND SACRED OATHS.
MAY IT ENDURE... UNTIL THE END OF THE WORLD.

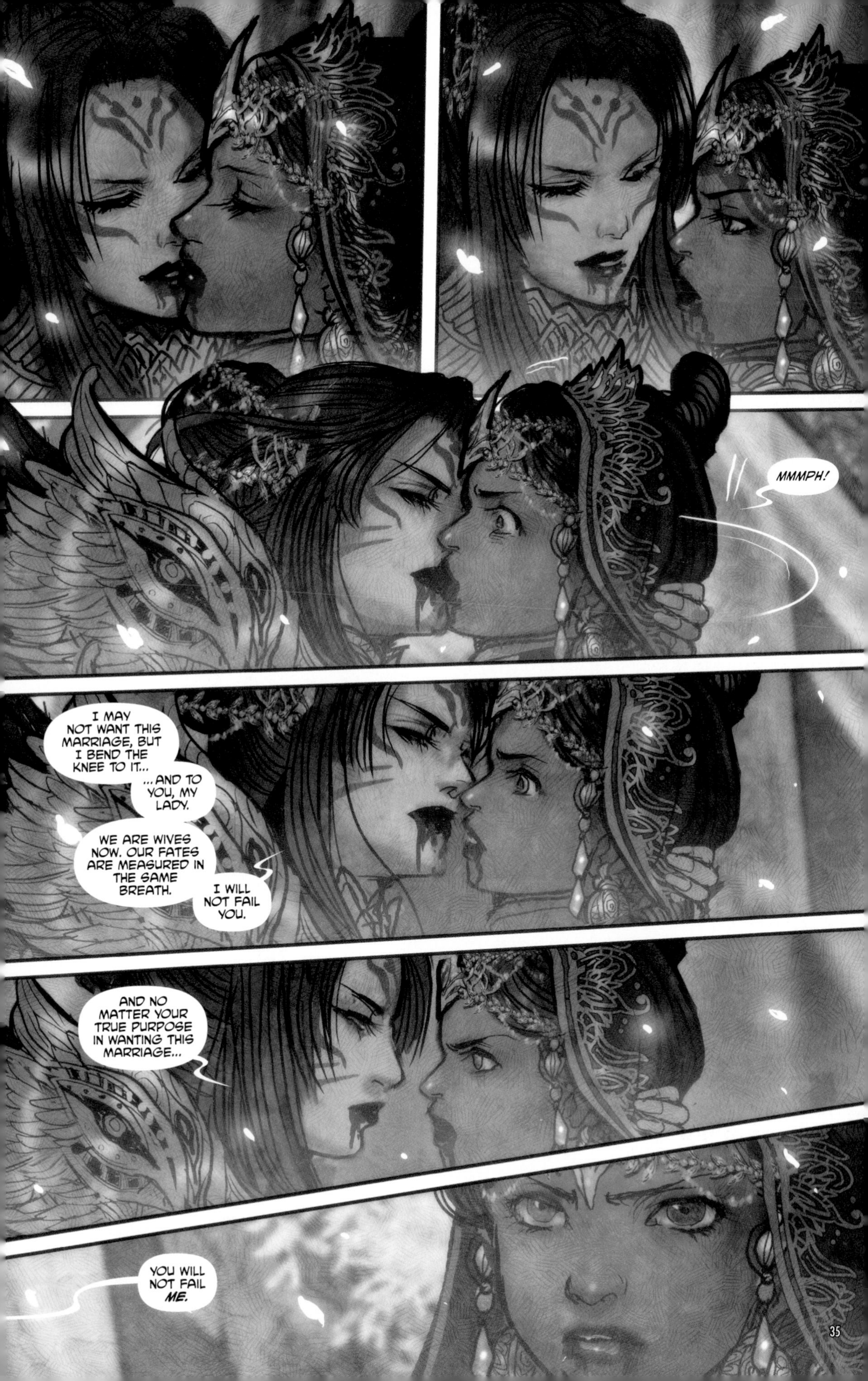
MMMPH!
I MAY NOT WANT THIS MARRIAGE, BUT I BEND THE KNEE TO IT...
...AND TO YOU, MY LADY.
WE ARE WIVES NOW. OUR FATES ARE MEASURED IN THE SAME BREATH.
I WILL NOT FAIL YOU.
AND NO MATTER YOUR TRUE PURPOSE IN WANTING THIS MARRIAGE...
YOU WILL NOT FAIL *ME.*

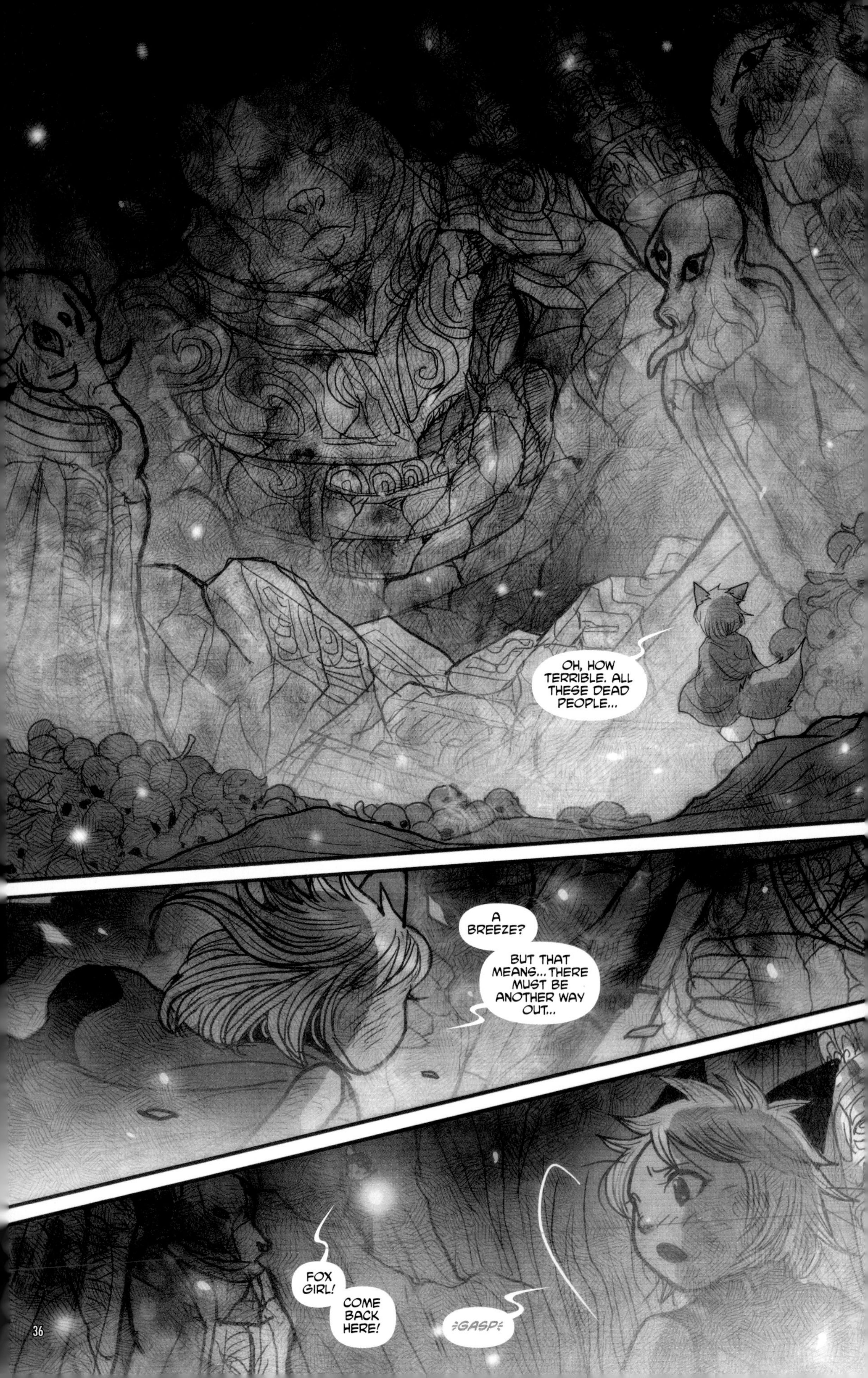
OH, HOW TERRIBLE. ALL THESE DEAD PEOPLE...
A BREEZE?
BUT THAT MEANS... THERE MUST BE ANOTHER WAY OUT...
FOX GIRL!
COME BACK HERE!
GASP

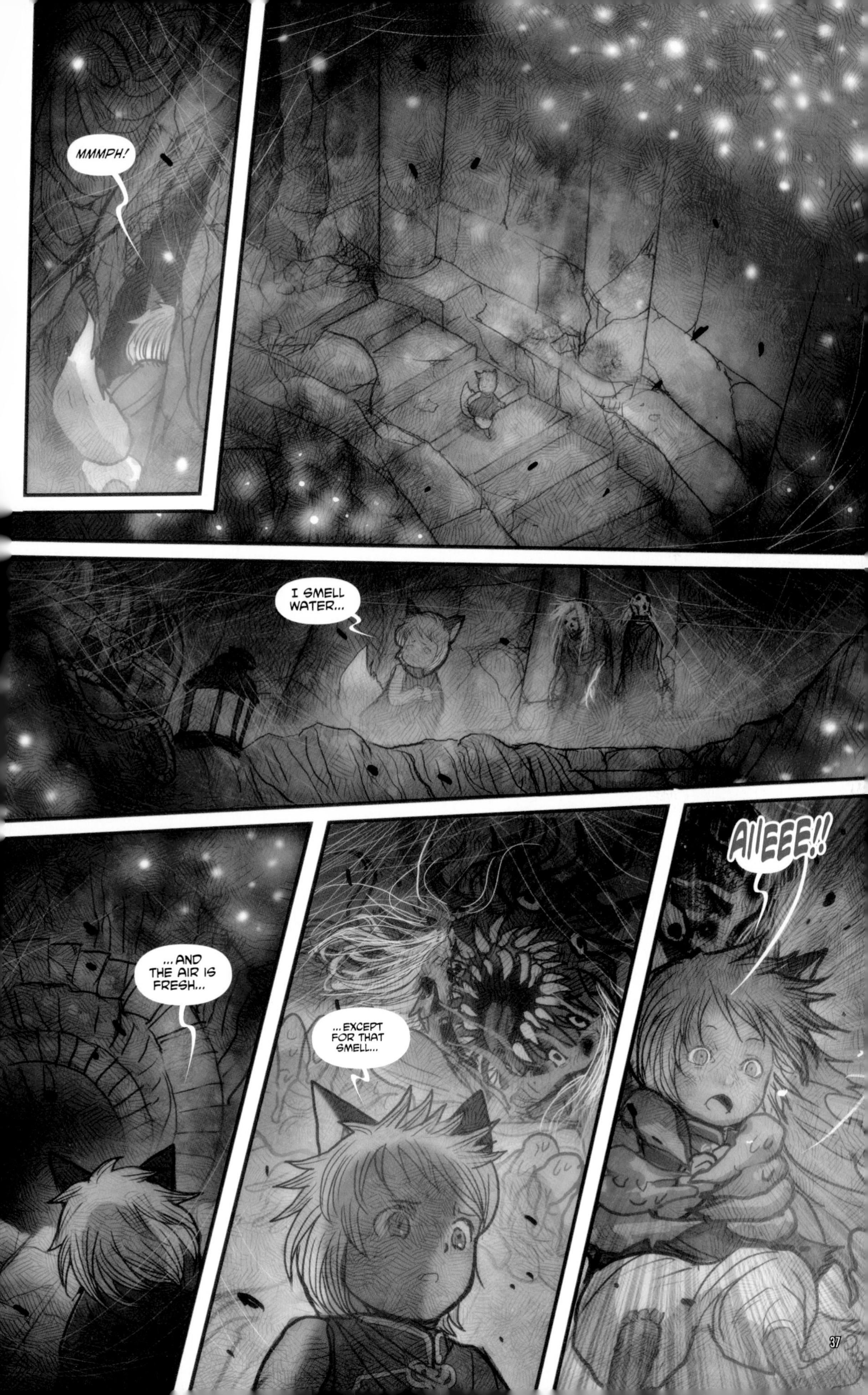
MMMPH!
I SMELL WATER...
...AND THE AIR IS FRESH...
...EXCEPT FOR THAT SMELL...
AIIEEE!!

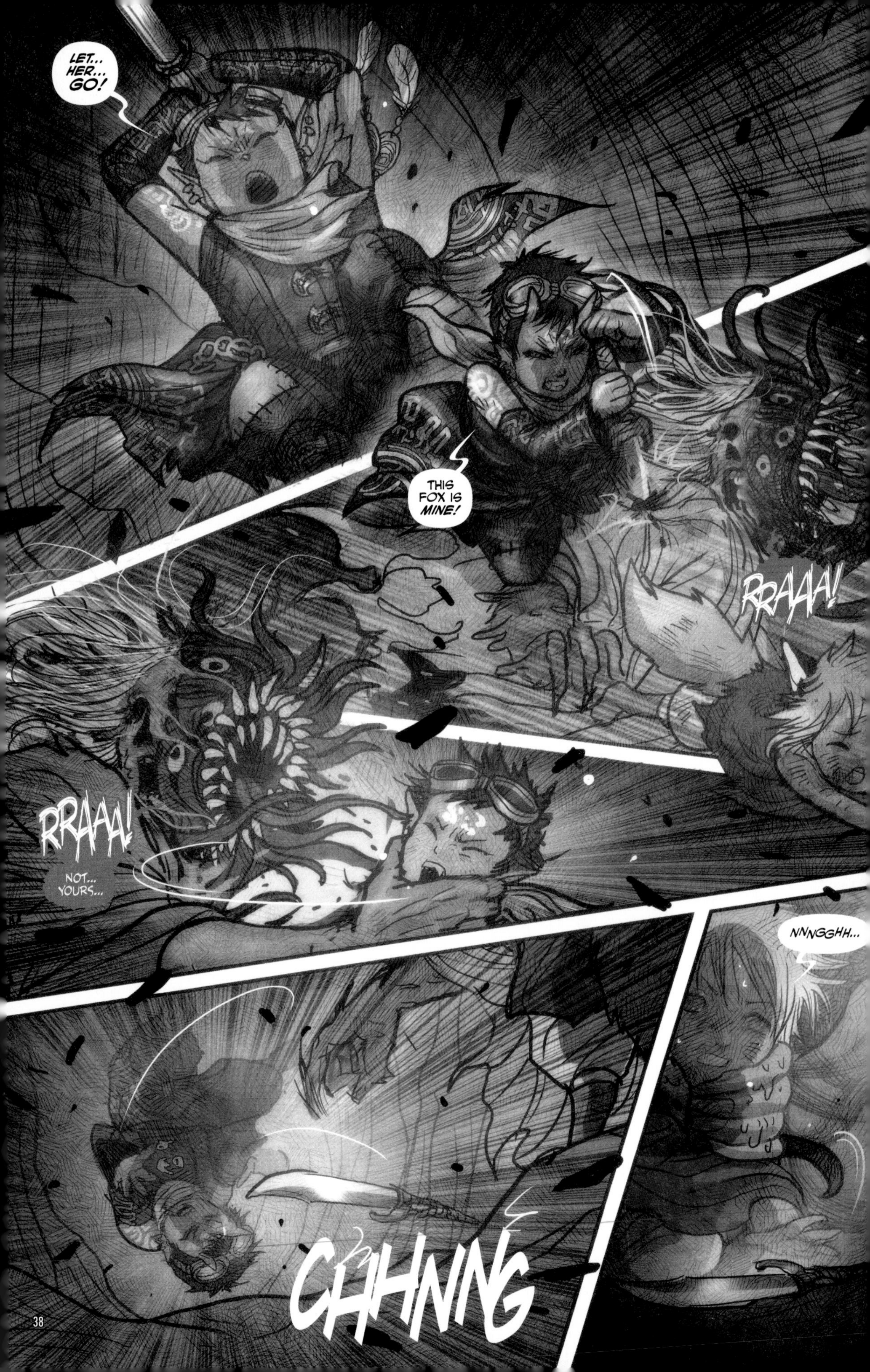
LET... HER... GO!
THIS FOX IS MINE!
RRAAA!
RRAAA!
NOT... YOURS...
NNNGGHH...
CHHNNG

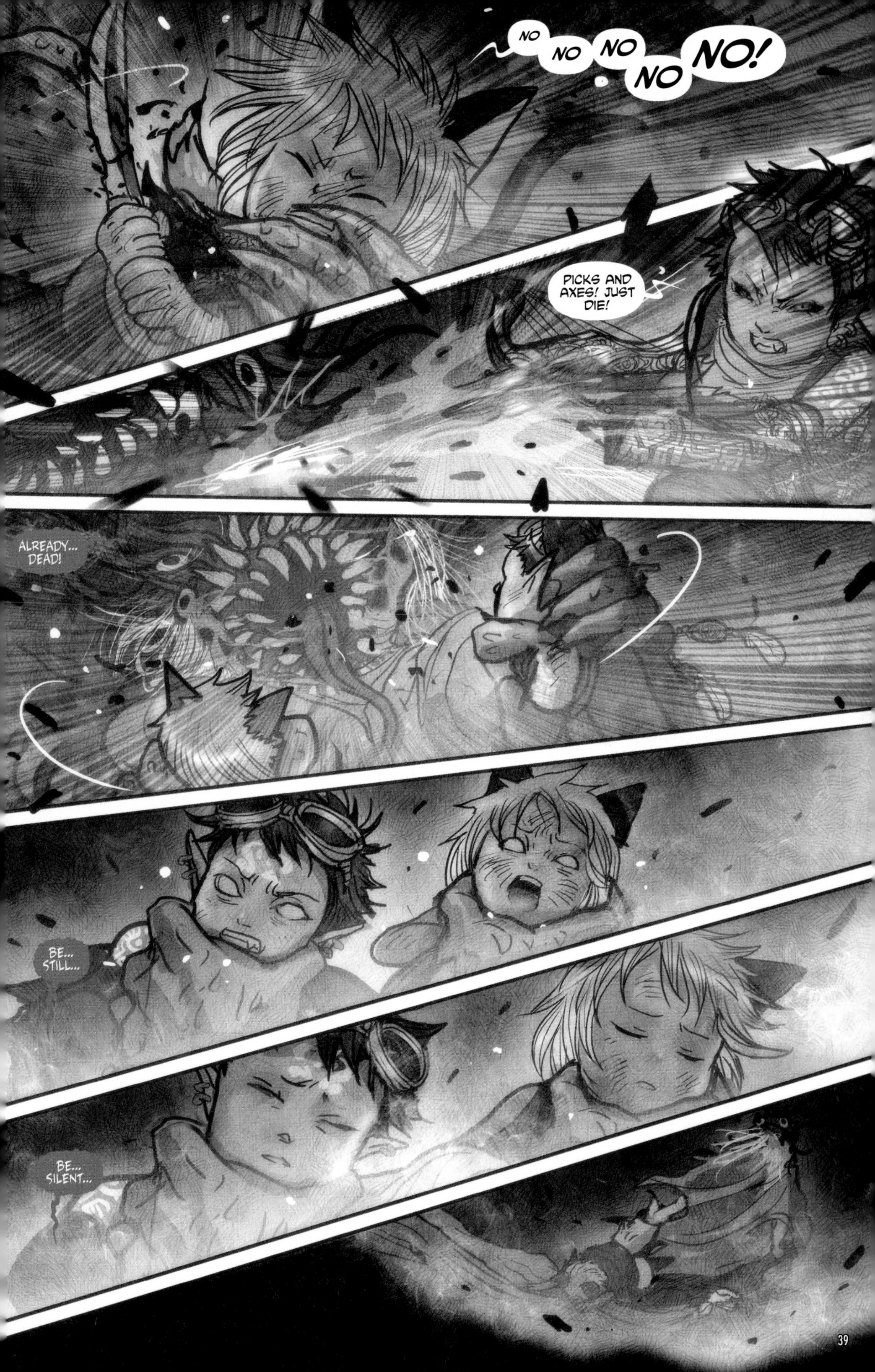
NO
NO
NO
NO
NO!
PICKS AND AXES! JUST DIE!
ALREADY... DEAD!
BE... STILL...
BE... SILENT...

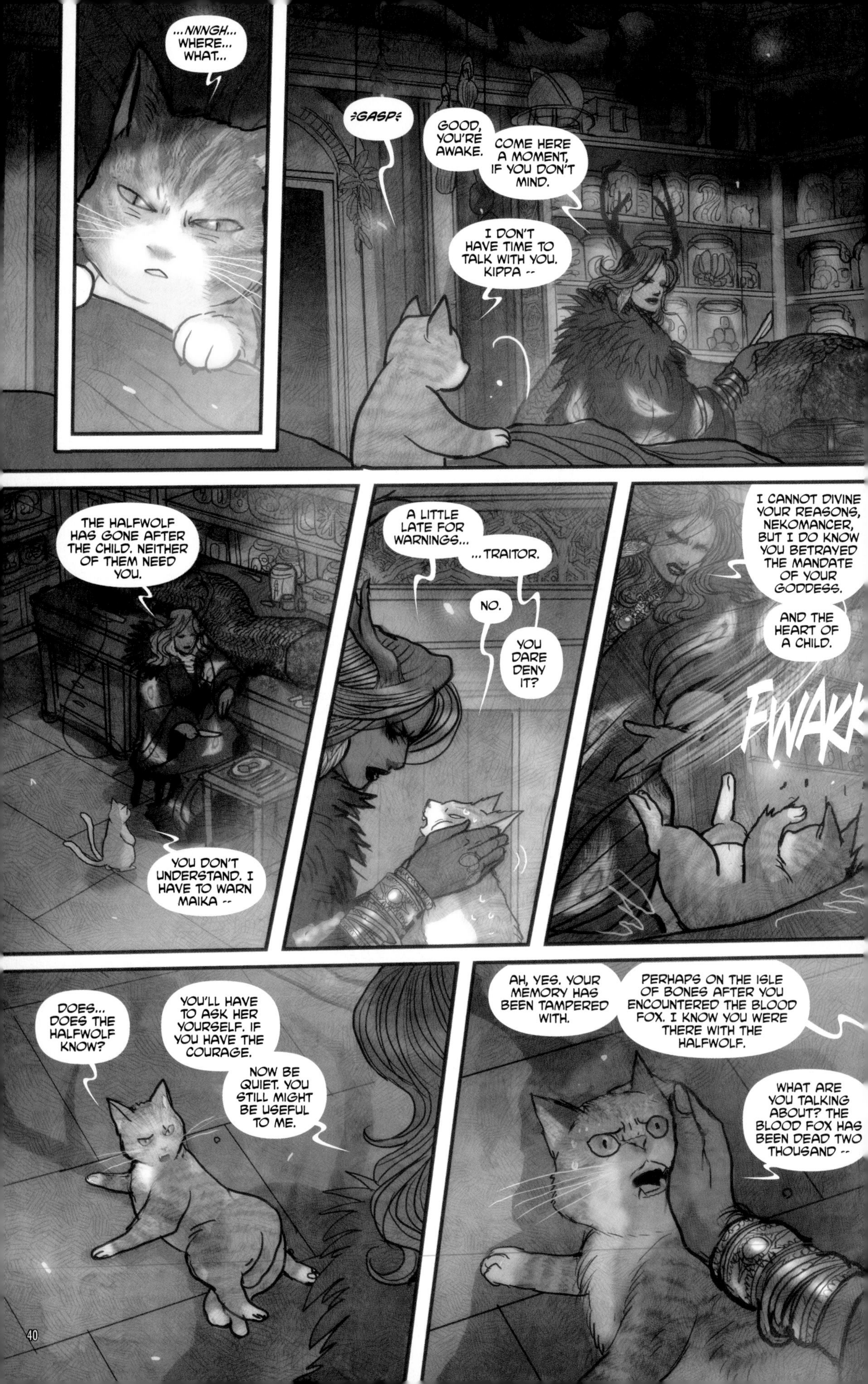
...NNNGH... WHERE... WHAT...
GASP
GOOD, YOU'RE AWAKE.
COME HERE A MOMENT, IF YOU DON'T MIND.
I DON'T HAVE TIME TO TALK WITH YOU. KIPPA --
THE HALFWOLF HAS GONE AFTER THE CHILD. NEITHER OF THEM NEED YOU.
YOU DON'T UNDERSTAND. I HAVE TO WARN MAIKA --
A LITTLE LATE FOR WARNINGS...
...TRAITOR.
NO.
YOU DARE DENY IT?
I CANNOT DIVINE YOUR REASONS, NEKOMANCER, BUT I DO KNOW YOU BETRAYED THE MANDATE OF YOUR GODDESS.
AND THE HEART OF A CHILD.
FWAKK
DOES... DOES THE HALFWOLF KNOW?
YOU'LL HAVE TO ASK HER YOURSELF. IF YOU HAVE THE COURAGE.
NOW BE QUIET. YOU STILL MIGHT BE USEFUL TO ME.
AH, YES. YOUR MEMORY HAS BEEN TAMPERED WITH.
PERHAPS ON THE ISLE OF BONES AFTER YOU ENCOUNTERED THE BLOOD FOX. I KNOW YOU WERE THERE WITH THE HALFWOLF.
WHAT ARE YOU TALKING ABOUT? THE BLOOD FOX HAS BEEN DEAD TWO THOUSAND --

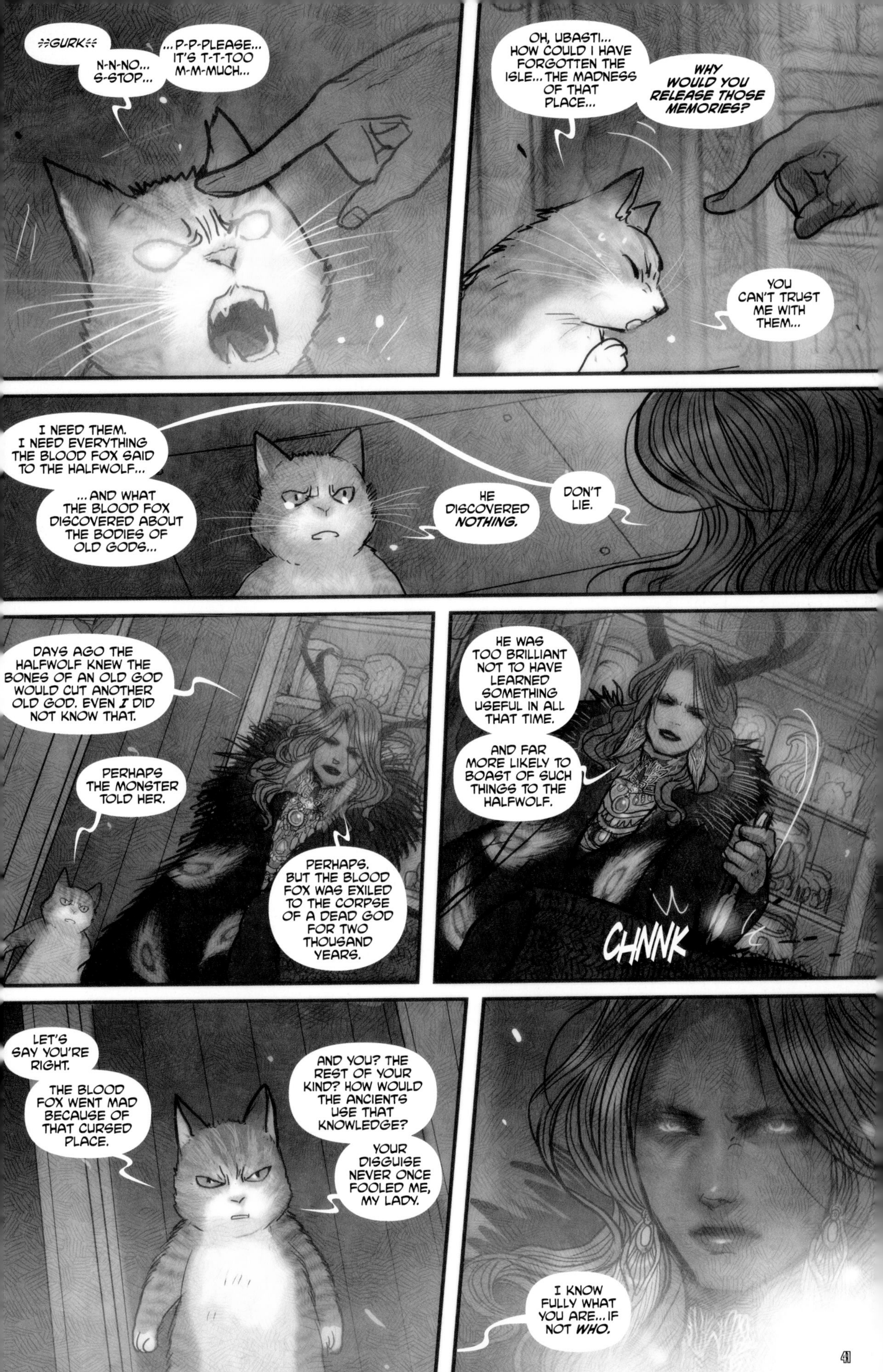
≈GURK≈
N-N-NO... S-STOP...
...P-P-PLEASE... IT'S T-T-TOO M-M-MUCH...
OH, UBASTI... HOW COULD I HAVE FORGOTTEN THE ISLE... THE MADNESS OF THAT PLACE...
WHY WOULD YOU RELEASE THOSE MEMORIES?
YOU CAN'T TRUST ME WITH THEM...
I NEED THEM. I NEED EVERYTHING THE BLOOD FOX SAID TO THE HALFWOLF...
...AND WHAT THE BLOOD FOX DISCOVERED ABOUT THE BODIES OF OLD GODS...
HE DISCOVERED NOTHING.
DON'T LIE.
DAYS AGO THE HALFWOLF KNEW THE BONES OF AN OLD GOD WOULD CUT ANOTHER OLD GOD. EVEN I DID NOT KNOW THAT.
PERHAPS THE MONSTER TOLD HER.
PERHAPS. BUT THE BLOOD FOX WAS EXILED TO THE CORPSE OF A DEAD GOD FOR TWO THOUSAND YEARS.
HE WAS TOO BRILLIANT NOT TO HAVE LEARNED SOMETHING USEFUL IN ALL THAT TIME.
AND FAR MORE LIKELY TO BOAST OF SUCH THINGS TO THE HALFWOLF.
CHNNK
LET'S SAY YOU'RE RIGHT.
THE BLOOD FOX WENT MAD BECAUSE OF THAT CURSED PLACE.
AND YOU? THE REST OF YOUR KIND? HOW WOULD THE ANCIENTS USE THAT KNOWLEDGE?
YOUR DISGUISE NEVER ONCE FOOLED ME, MY LADY.
I KNOW FULLY WHAT YOU ARE... IF NOT WHO.

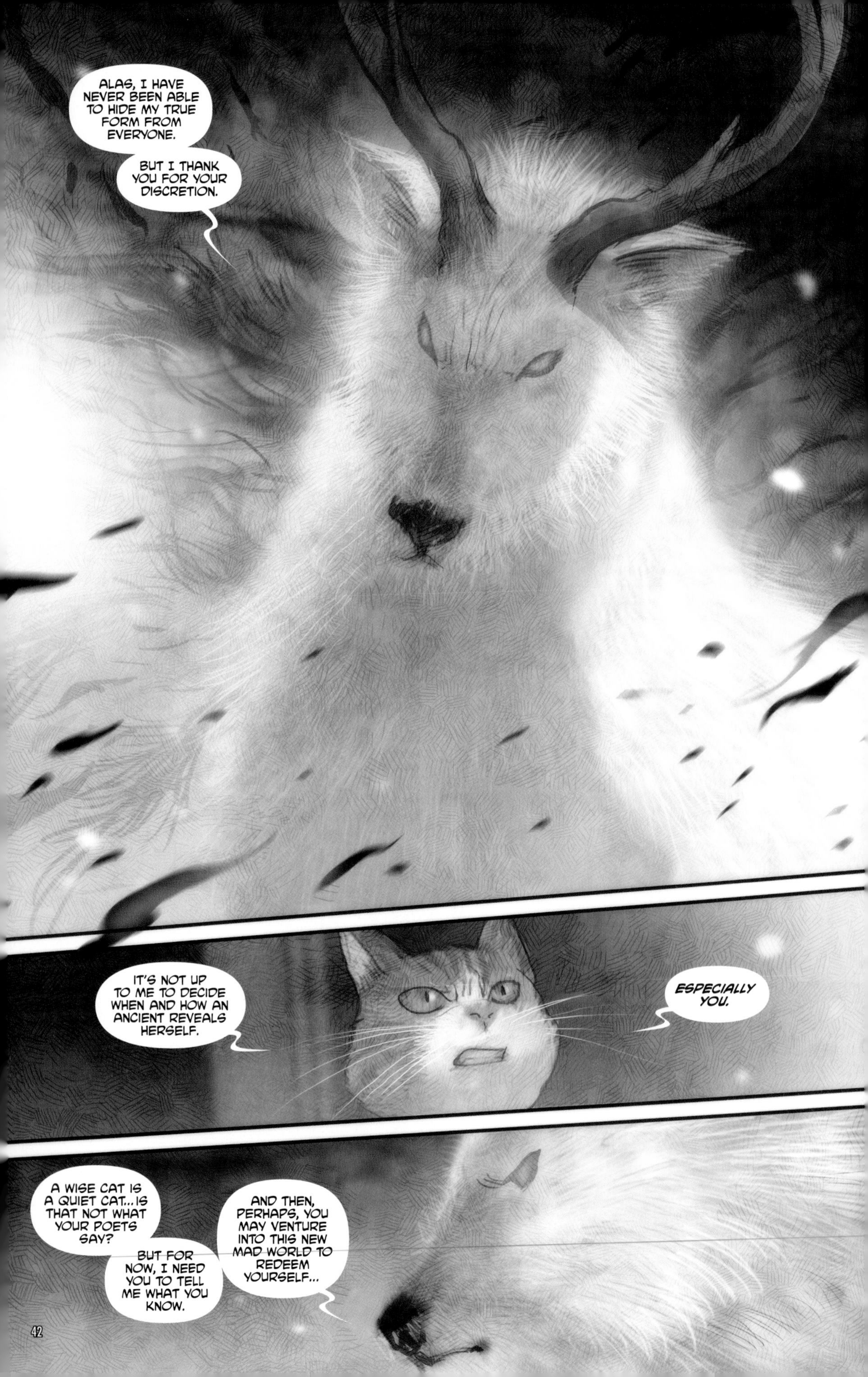
ALAS, I HAVE NEVER BEEN ABLE TO HIDE MY TRUE FORM FROM EVERYONE.
BUT I THANK YOU FOR YOUR DISCRETION.
IT'S NOT UP TO ME TO DECIDE WHEN AND HOW AN ANCIENT REVEALS HERSELF.
ESPECIALLY YOU.
A WISE CAT IS A QUIET CAT...IS THAT NOT WHAT YOUR POETS SAY?
BUT FOR NOW, I NEED YOU TO TELL ME WHAT YOU KNOW.
AND THEN, PERHAPS, YOU MAY VENTURE INTO THIS NEW MAD WORLD TO REDEEM YOURSELF...

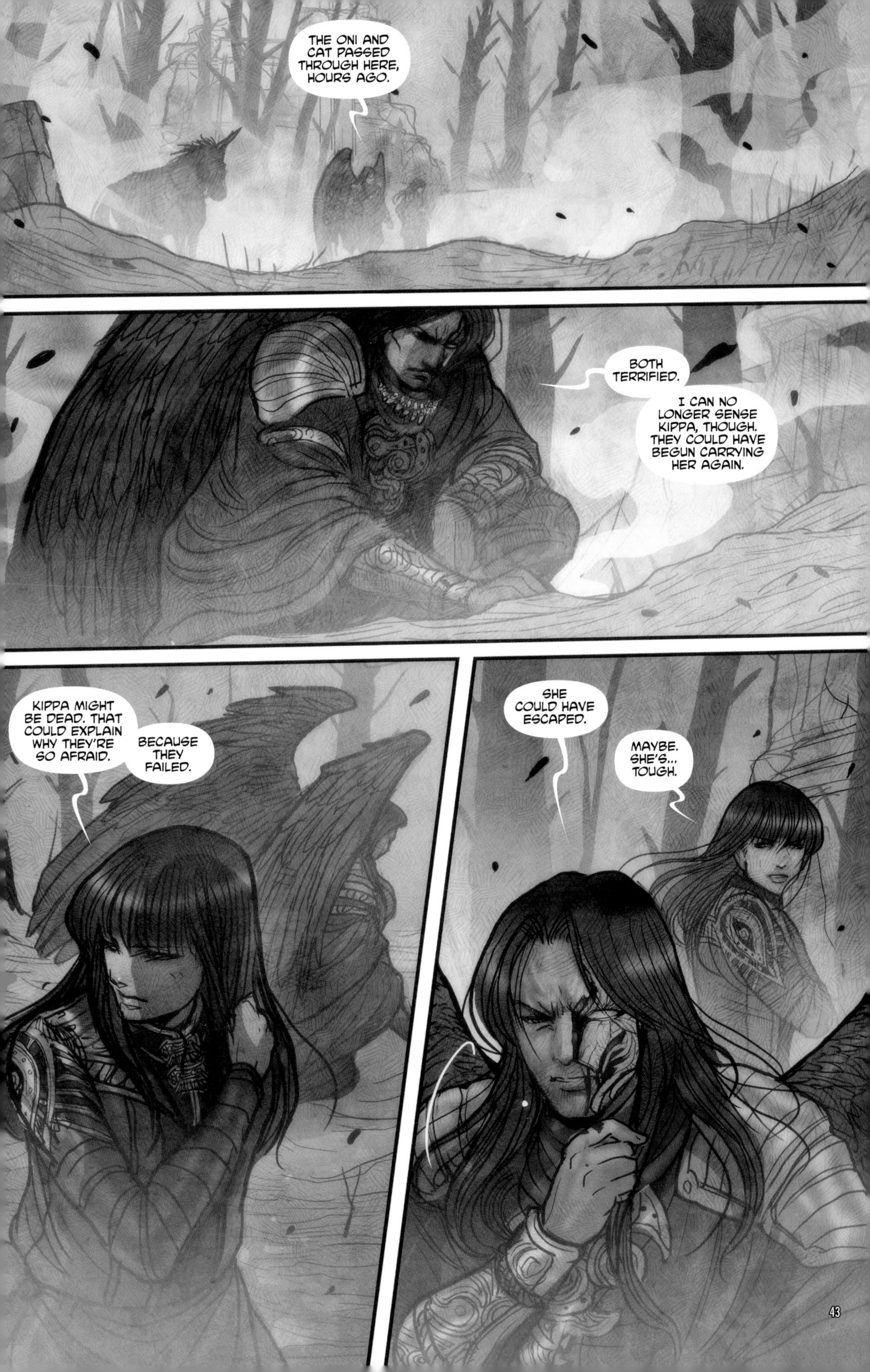
THE ONI AND CAT PASSED THROUGH HERE, HOURS AGO.
BOTH TERRIFIED.
I CAN NO LONGER SENSE KIPPA, THOUGH. THEY COULD HAVE BEGUN CARRYING HER AGAIN.
KIPPA MIGHT BE DEAD. THAT COULD EXPLAIN WHY THEY'RE SO AFRAID.
BECAUSE THEY FAILED.
SHE COULD HAVE ESCAPED.
MAYBE. SHE'S... TOUGH.

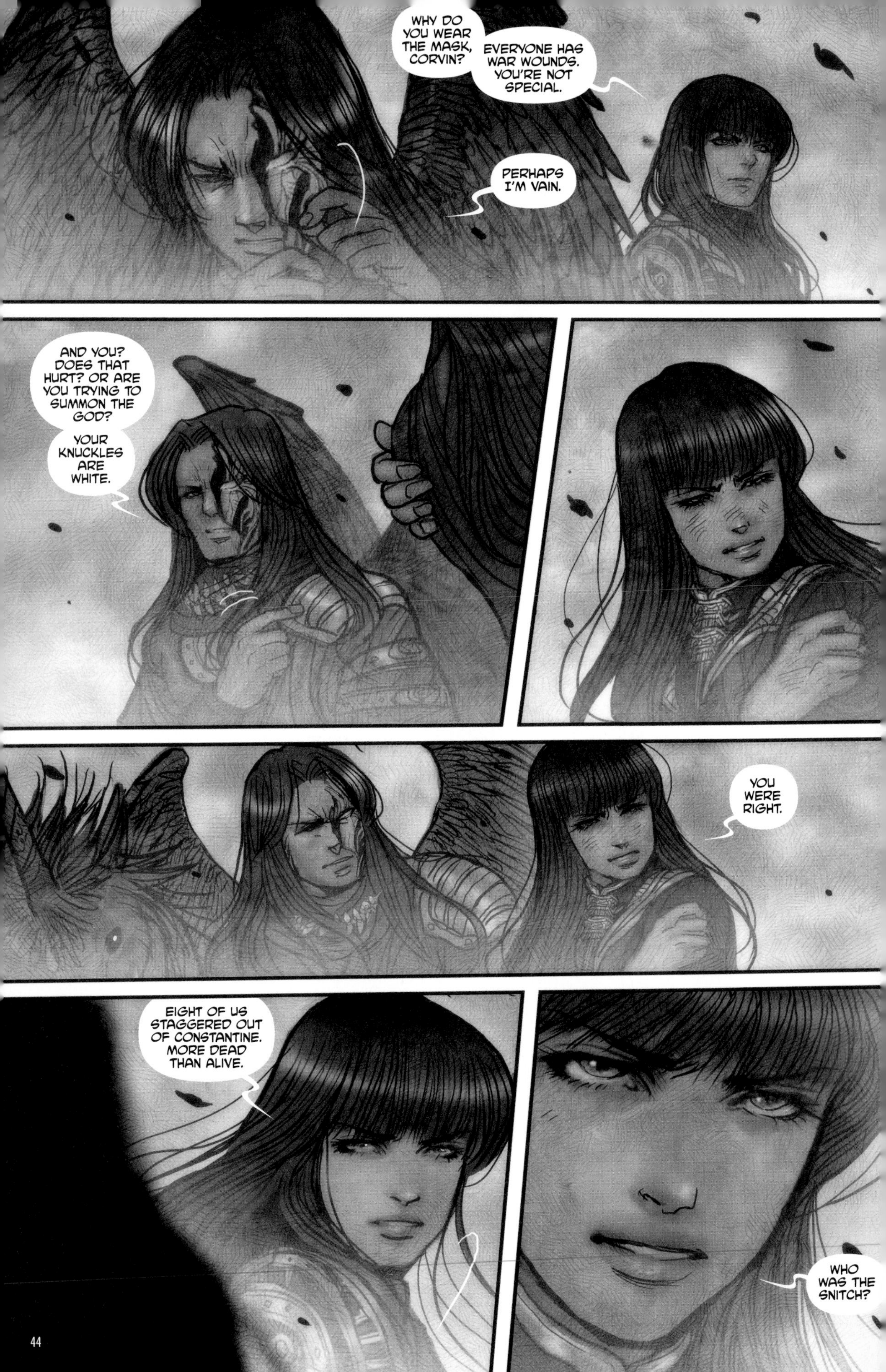
WHY DO YOU WEAR THE MASK, CORVIN?
EVERYONE HAS WAR WOUNDS. YOU'RE NOT SPECIAL.
PERHAPS I'M VAIN.
AND YOU? DOES THAT HURT? OR ARE YOU TRYING TO SUMMON THE GOD?
YOUR KNUCKLES ARE WHITE.
YOU WERE RIGHT.
EIGHT OF US STAGGERED OUT OF CONSTANTINE. MORE DEAD THAN ALIVE.
WHO WAS THE SNITCH?

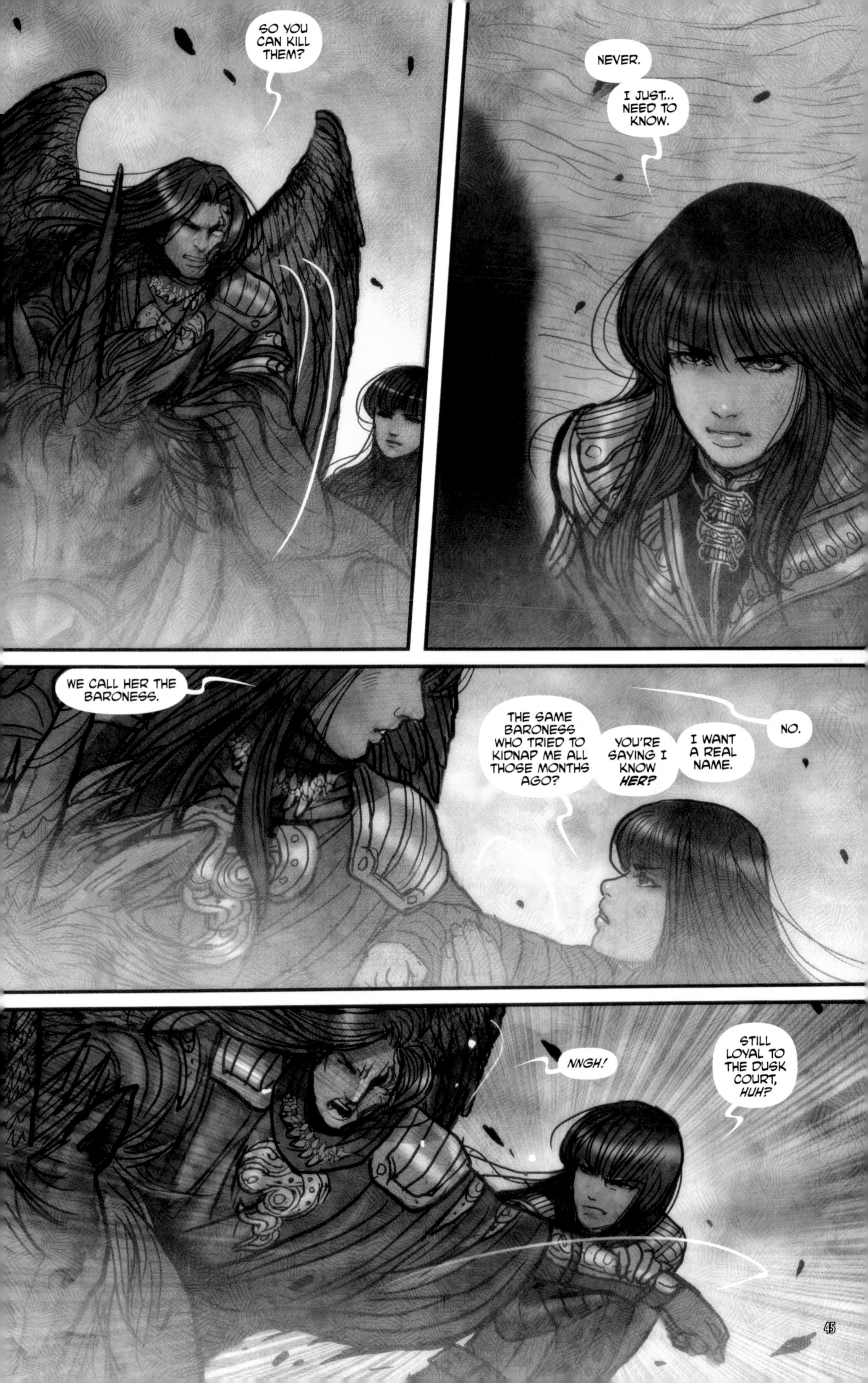
SO YOU CAN KILL THEM?
NEVER.
I JUST... NEED TO KNOW.
WE CALL HER THE BARONESS.
THE SAME BARONESS WHO TRIED TO KIDNAP ME ALL THOSE MONTHS AGO?
YOU'RE SAYING I KNOW *HER?*
I WANT A REAL NAME.
NO.
NNGH!
STILL LOYAL TO THE DUSK COURT, *HUH?*

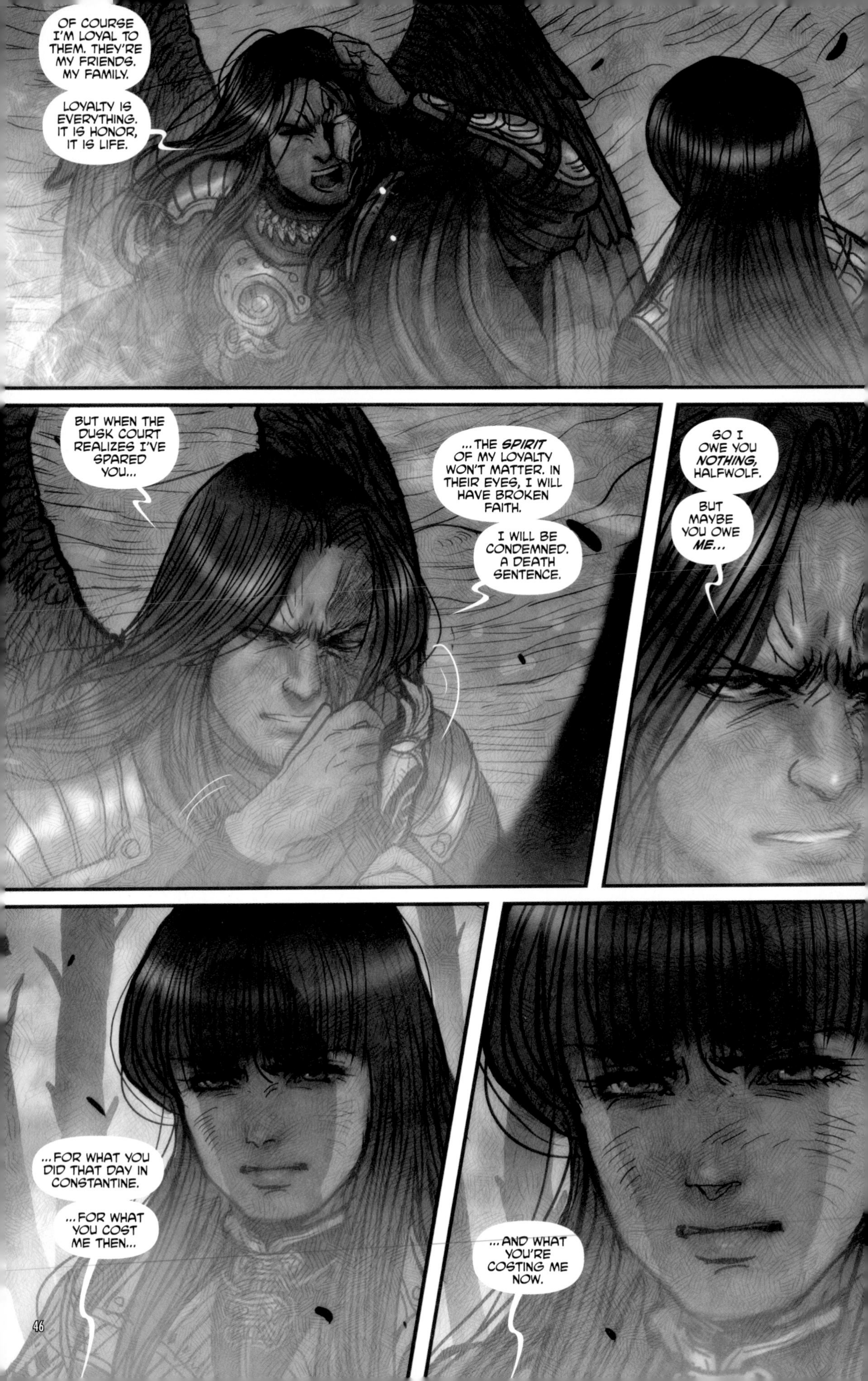
OF COURSE I'M LOYAL TO THEM. THEY'RE MY FRIENDS. MY FAMILY.
LOYALTY IS EVERYTHING. IT IS HONOR, IT IS LIFE.
BUT WHEN THE DUSK COURT REALIZES I'VE SPARED YOU...
...THE *SPIRIT* OF MY LOYALTY WON'T MATTER. IN THEIR EYES, I WILL HAVE BROKEN FAITH.
I WILL BE CONDEMNED. A DEATH SENTENCE.
SO I OWE YOU *NOTHING,* HALFWOLF.
BUT MAYBE YOU OWE *ME...*
...FOR WHAT YOU DID THAT DAY IN CONSTANTINE.
...FOR WHAT YOU COST ME THEN...
...AND WHAT YOU'RE COSTING ME NOW.

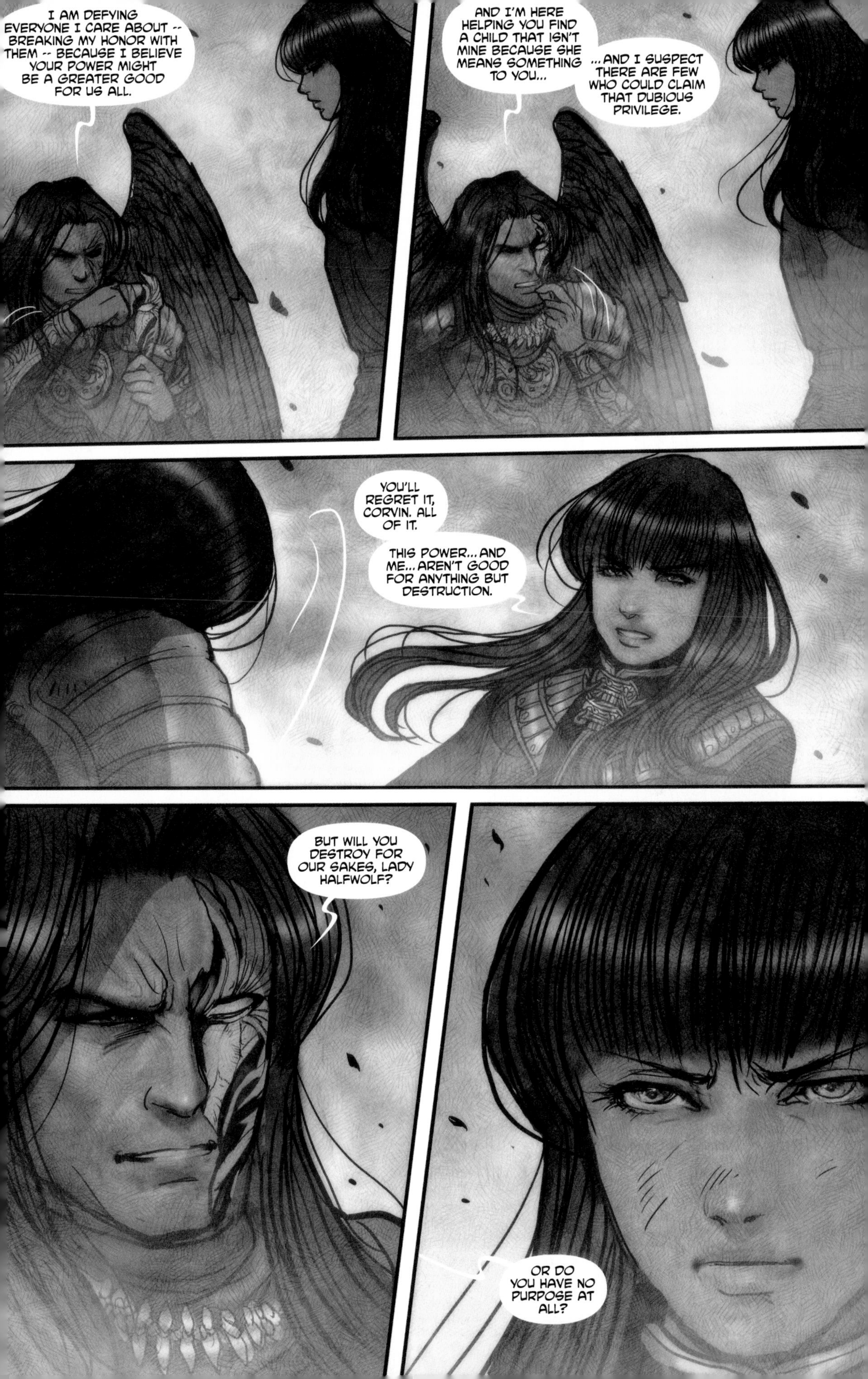
I AM DEFYING EVERYONE I CARE ABOUT -- BREAKING MY HONOR WITH THEM -- BECAUSE I BELIEVE YOUR POWER MIGHT BE A GREATER GOOD FOR US ALL.
AND I'M HERE HELPING YOU FIND A CHILD THAT ISN'T MINE BECAUSE SHE MEANS SOMETHING TO YOU...
...AND I SUSPECT THERE ARE FEW WHO COULD CLAIM THAT DUBIOUS PRIVILEGE.
YOU'LL REGRET IT, CORVIN. ALL OF IT.
THIS POWER...AND ME...AREN'T GOOD FOR ANYTHING BUT DESTRUCTION.
BUT WILL YOU DESTROY FOR OUR SAKES, LADY HALFWOLF?
OR DO YOU HAVE NO PURPOSE AT ALL?

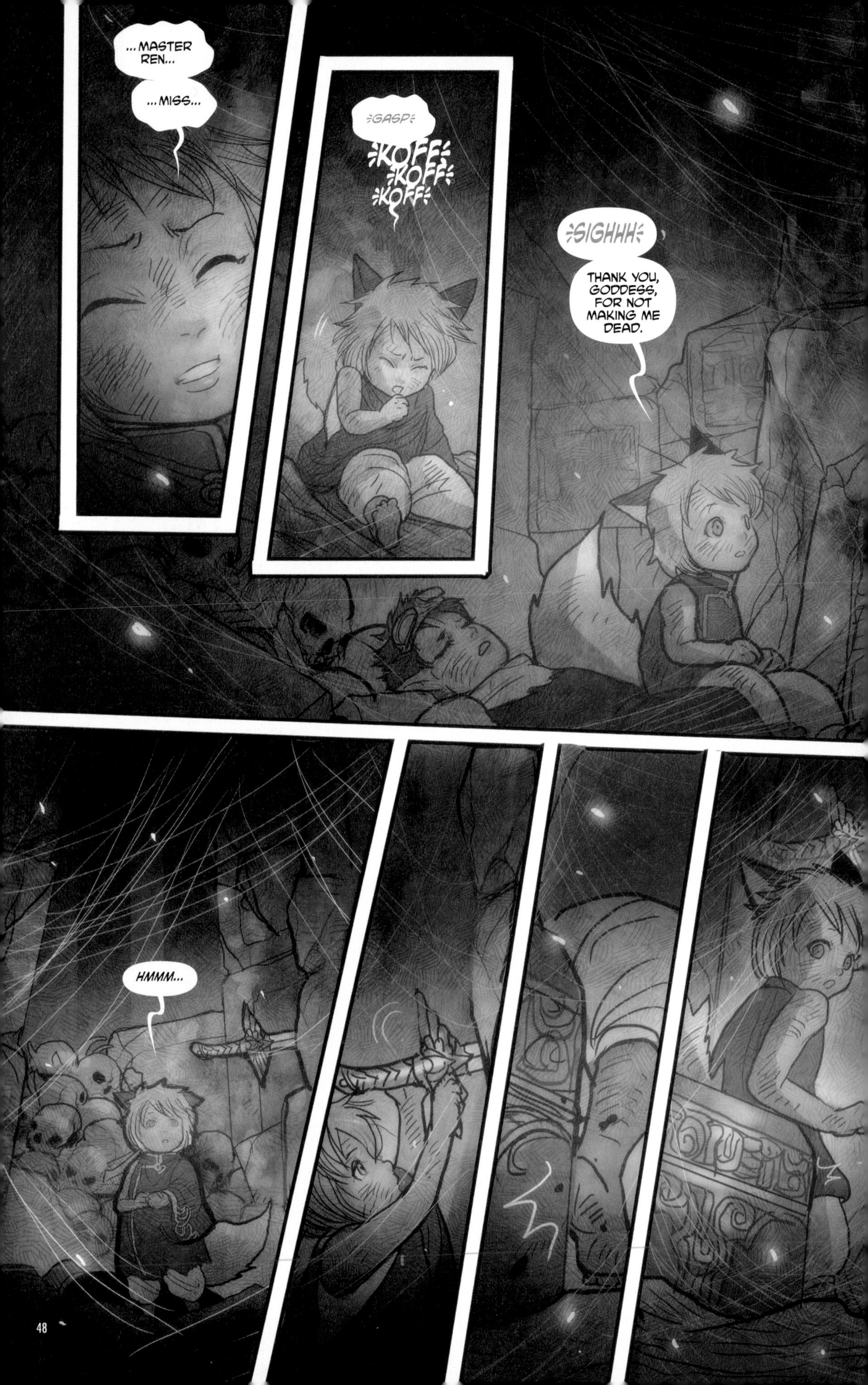
...MASTER REN...
...MISS...
GASP
KOFF KOFF KOFF
SIGHHH
THANK YOU, GODDESS, FOR NOT MAKING ME DEAD.
HMMM...

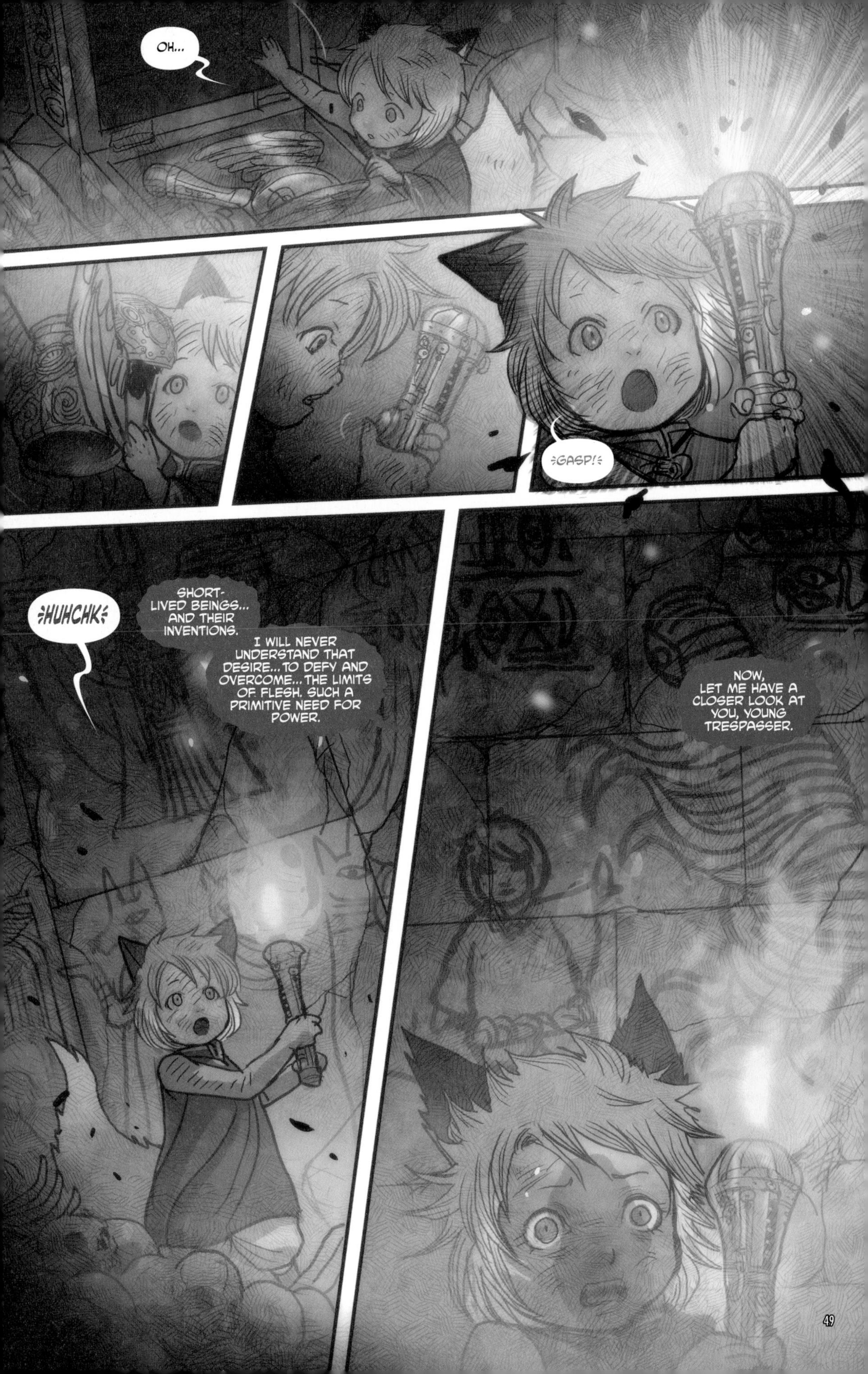
OH...
GASP!
HUHCHK
SHORT-LIVED BEINGS... AND THEIR INVENTIONS.
I WILL NEVER UNDERSTAND THAT DESIRE... TO DEFY AND OVERCOME... THE LIMITS OF FLESH. SUCH A PRIMITIVE NEED FOR POWER.
NOW, LET ME HAVE A CLOSER LOOK AT YOU, YOUNG TRESPASSER.

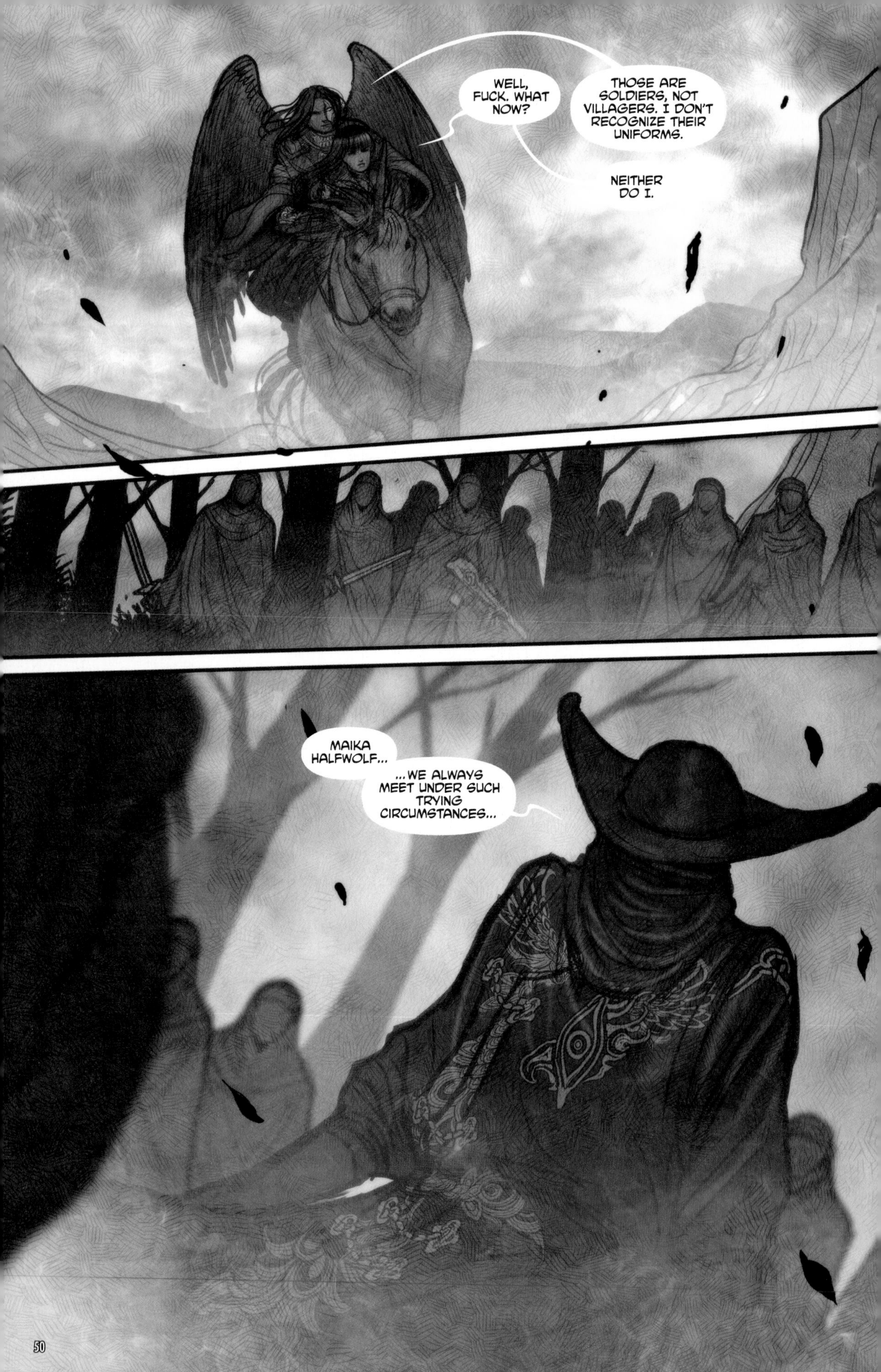
THOSE ARE SOLDIERS, NOT VILLAGERS. I DON'T RECOGNIZE THEIR UNIFORMS.
WELL, FUCK. WHAT NOW?
NEITHER DO I.
MAIKA HALFWOLF...
...WE ALWAYS MEET UNDER SUCH TRYING CIRCUMSTANCES...

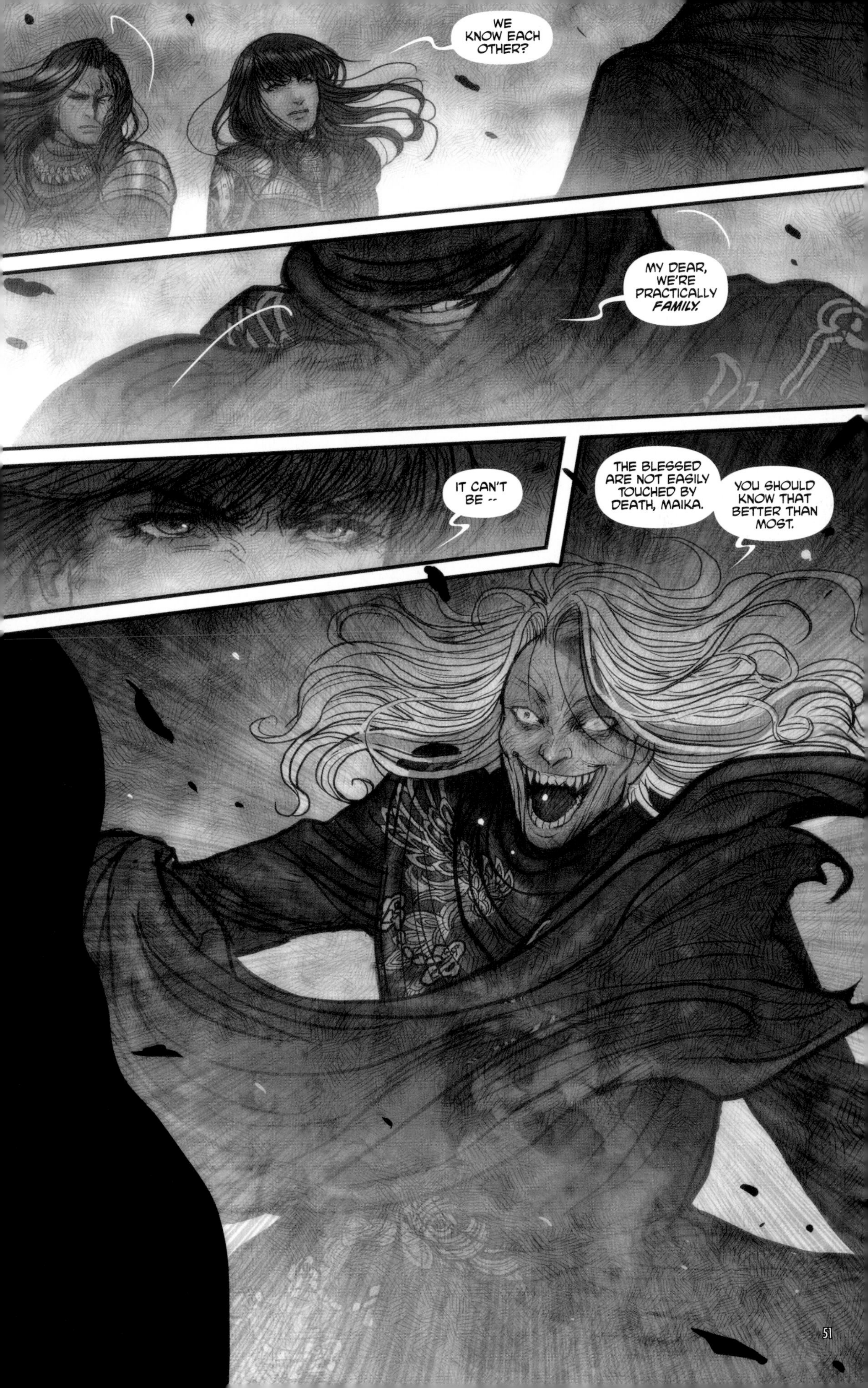
WE KNOW EACH OTHER?
MY DEAR, WE'RE PRACTICALLY *FAMILY.*
IT CAN'T BE --
THE BLESSED ARE NOT EASILY TOUCHED BY DEATH, MAIKA.
YOU SHOULD KNOW THAT BETTER THAN MOST.

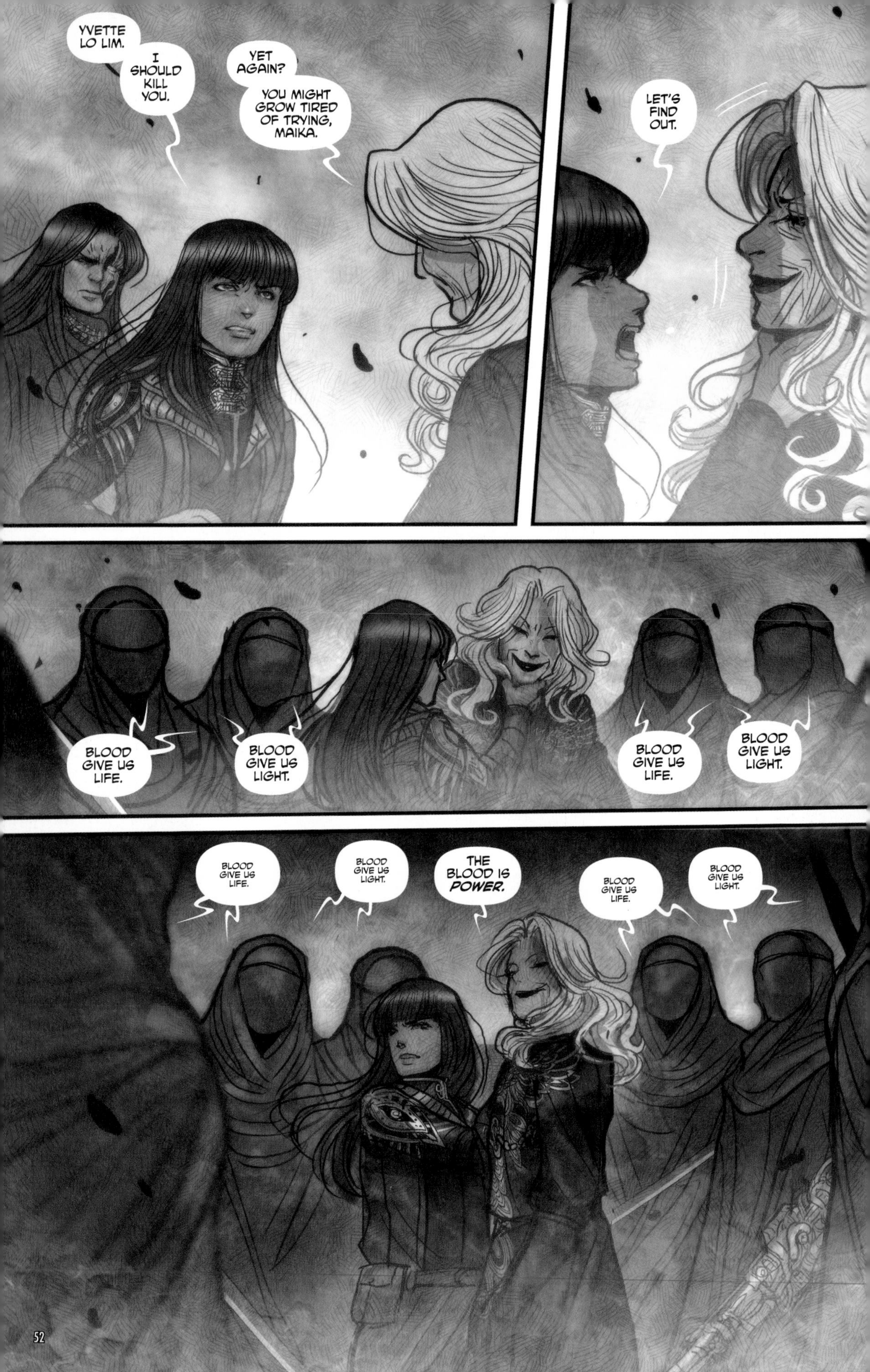
YVETTE LO LIM.
I SHOULD KILL YOU.
YET AGAIN?
YOU MIGHT GROW TIRED OF TRYING, MAIKA.
LET'S FIND OUT.
BLOOD GIVE US LIFE.
BLOOD GIVE US LIGHT.
BLOOD GIVE US LIFE.
BLOOD GIVE US LIGHT.
BLOOD GIVE US LIFE.
BLOOD GIVE US LIGHT.
THE BLOOD IS *POWER.*
BLOOD GIVE US LIFE.
BLOOD GIVE US LIGHT.

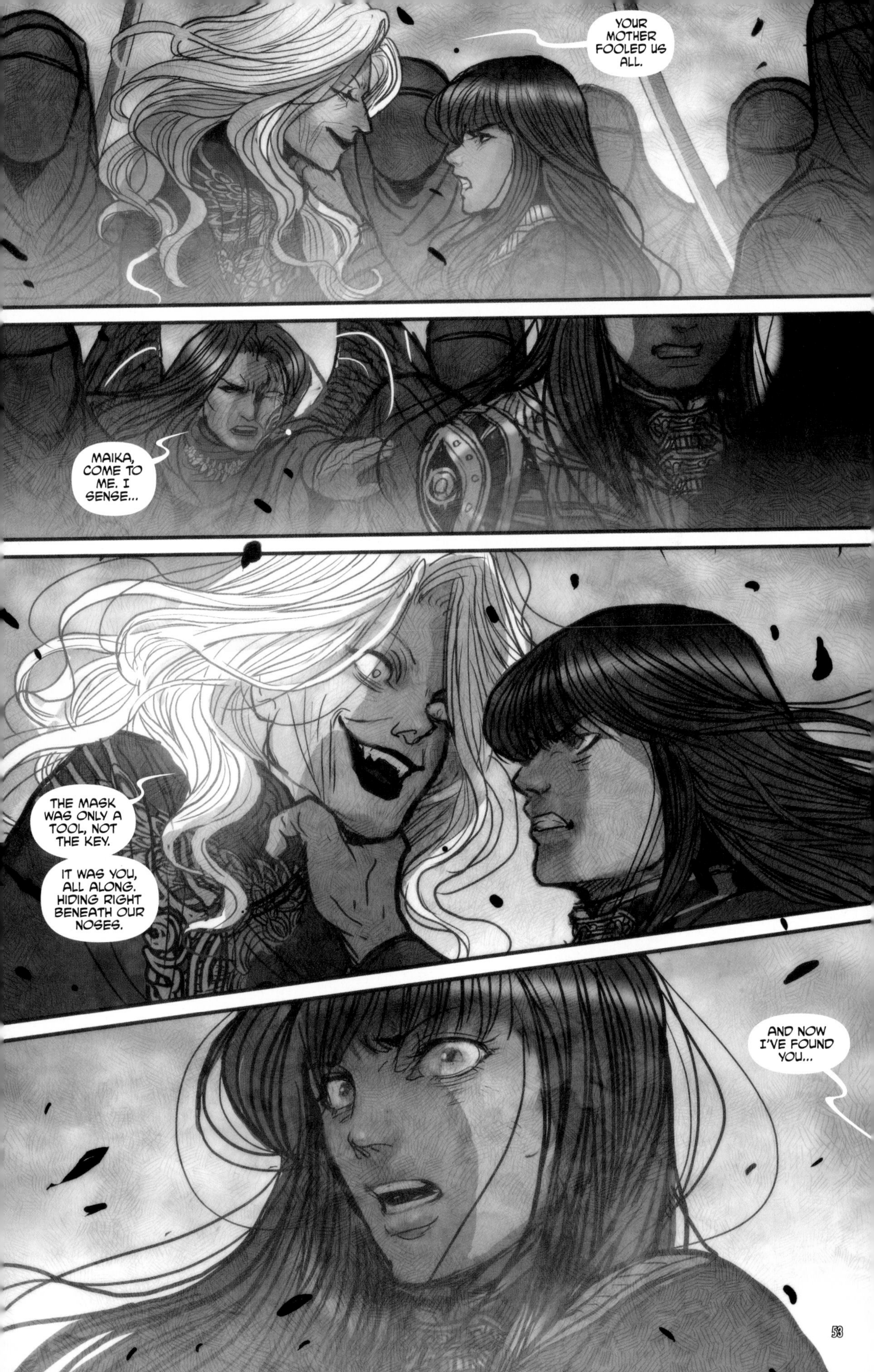
YOUR MOTHER FOOLED US ALL.
MAIKA, COME TO ME. I SENSE...
THE MASK WAS ONLY A TOOL, NOT THE KEY.
IT WAS YOU, ALL ALONG. HIDING RIGHT BENEATH OUR NOSES.
AND NOW I'VE FOUND YOU...

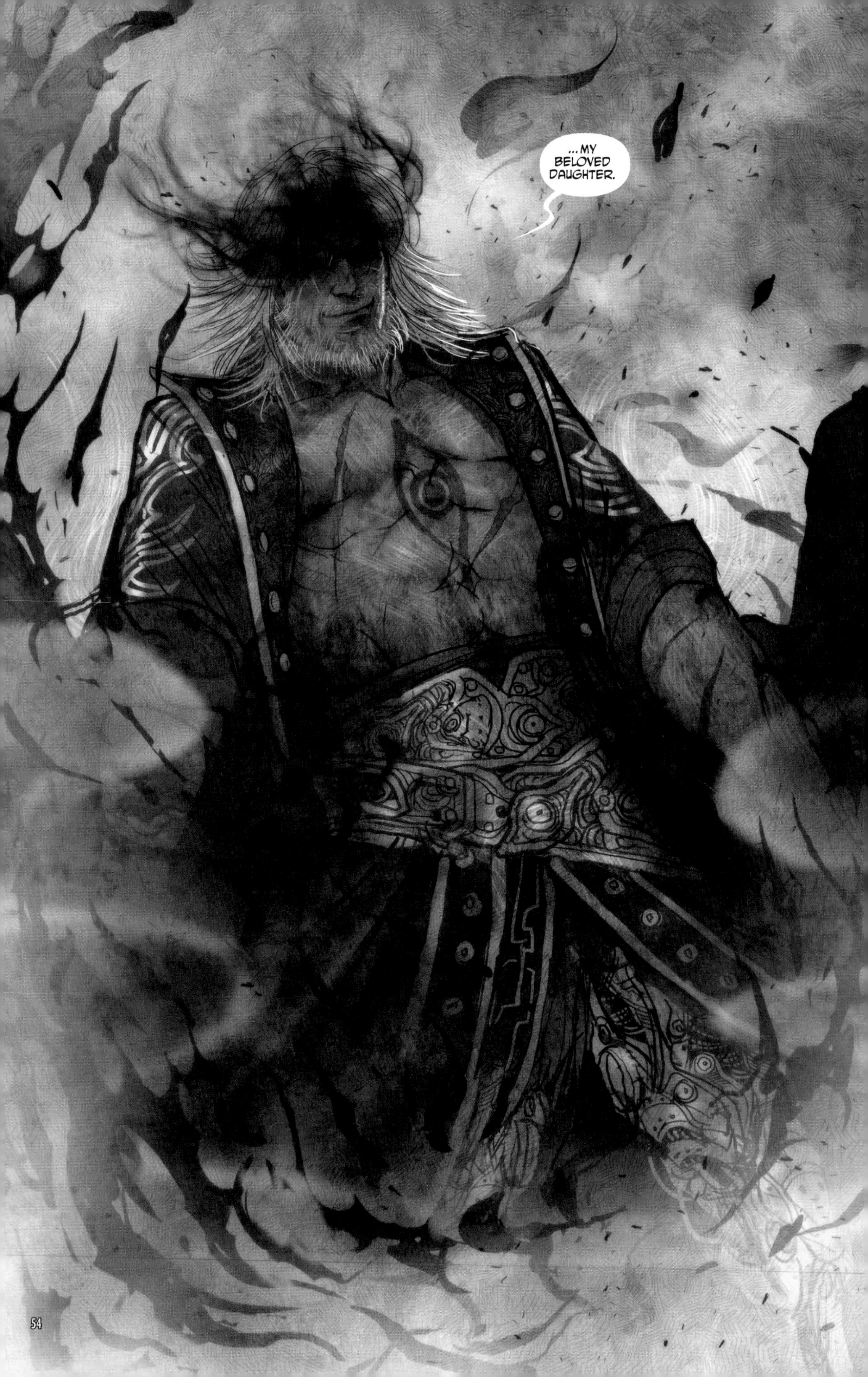
...MY BELOVED DAUGHTER.

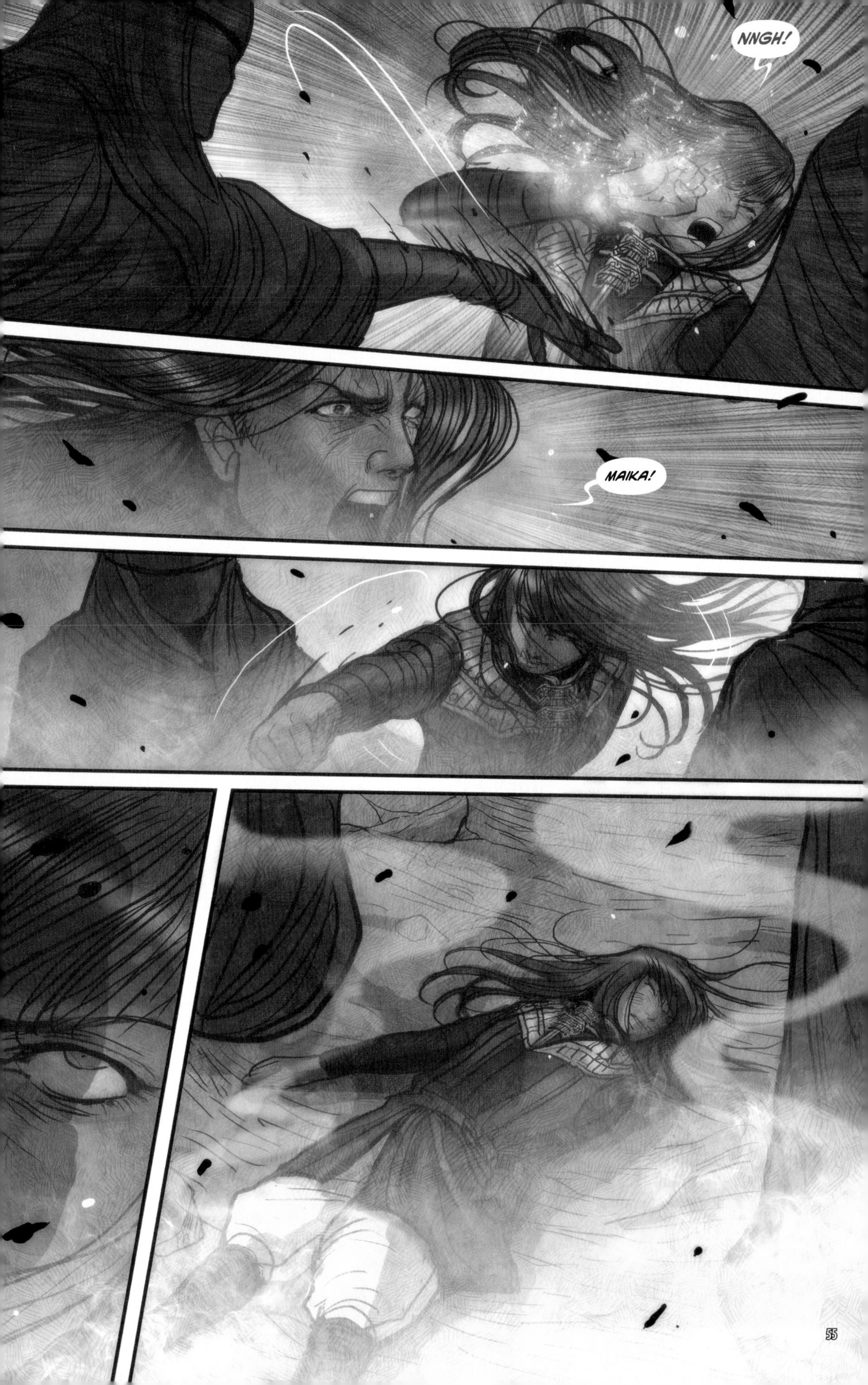
NNGH!
MAIKA!

An excerpt of a lecture from the esteemed **Professor Tam Tam,** former First Record-Keeper of the Is'hami Temple, and learned contemporary of Namron Black Claw...

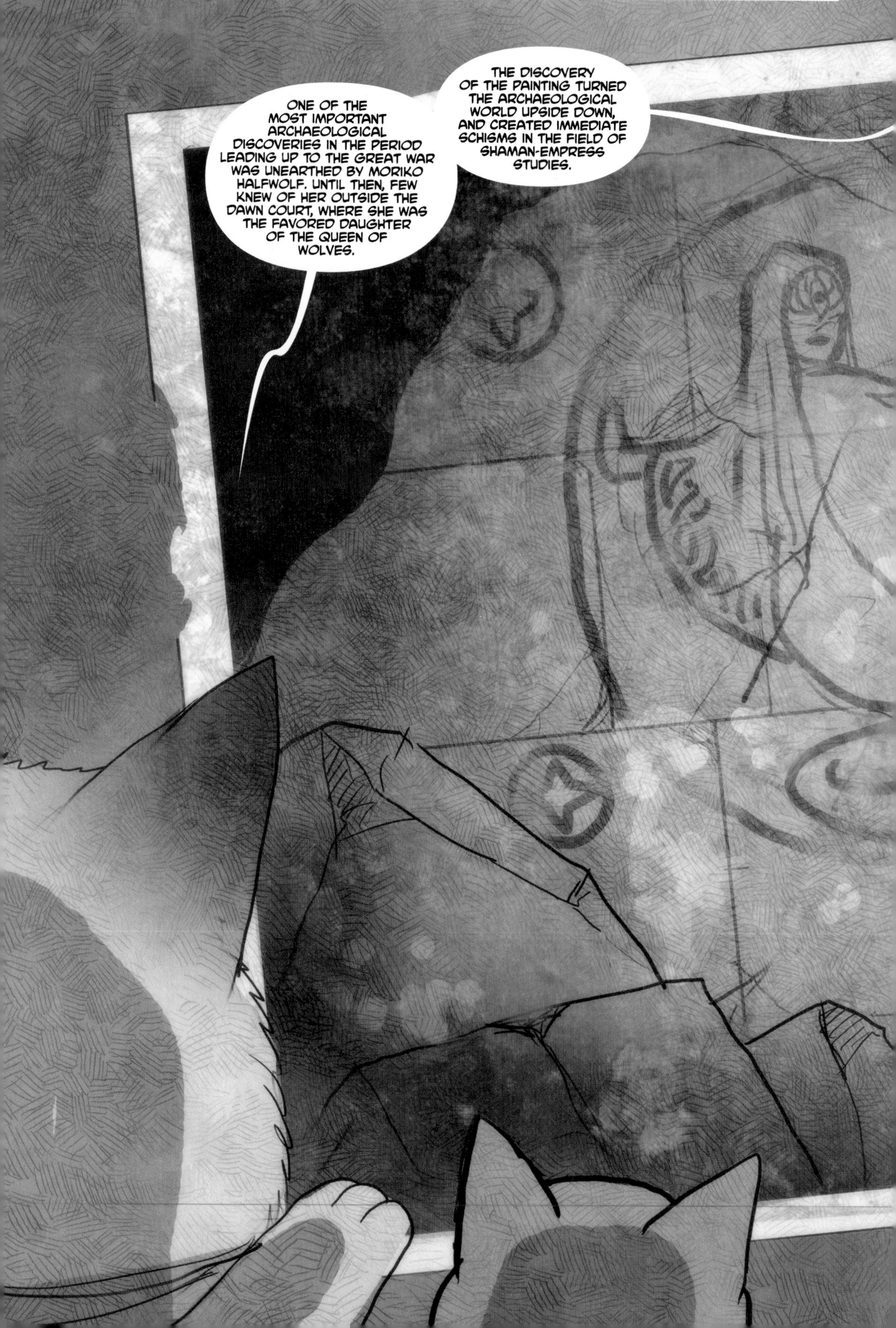
ONE OF THE MOST IMPORTANT ARCHAEOLOGICAL DISCOVERIES IN THE PERIOD LEADING UP TO THE GREAT WAR WAS UNEARTHED BY MORIKO HALFWOLF. UNTIL THEN, FEW KNEW OF HER OUTSIDE THE DAWN COURT, WHERE SHE WAS THE FAVORED DAUGHTER OF THE QUEEN OF WOLVES.
THE DISCOVERY OF THE PAINTING TURNED THE ARCHAEOLOGICAL WORLD UPSIDE DOWN, AND CREATED IMMEDIATE SCHISMS IN THE FIELD OF SHAMAN-EMPRESS STUDIES.

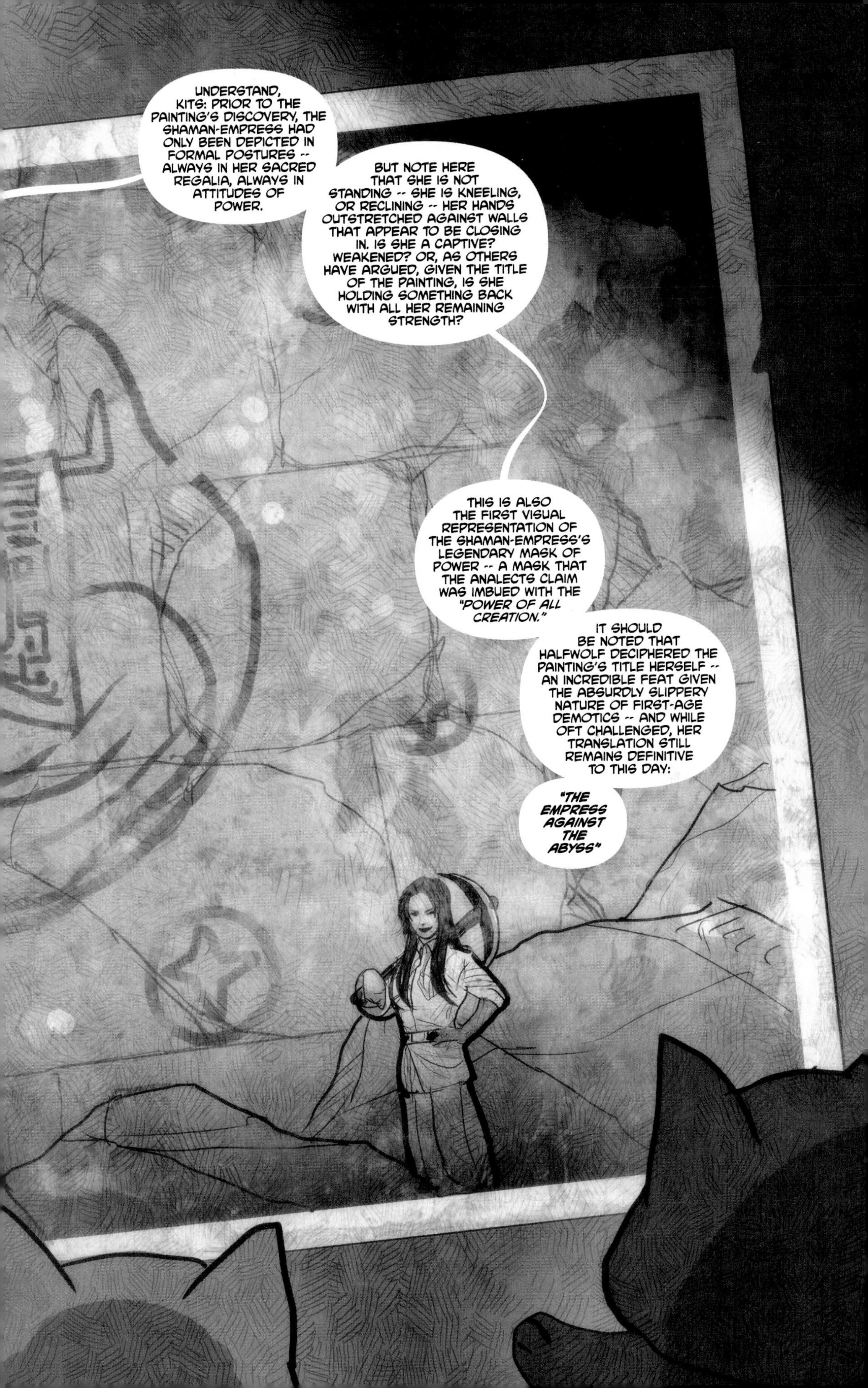
UNDERSTAND, KITS: PRIOR TO THE PAINTING'S DISCOVERY, THE SHAMAN-EMPRESS HAD ONLY BEEN DEPICTED IN FORMAL POSTURES -- ALWAYS IN HER SACRED REGALIA, ALWAYS IN ATTITUDES OF POWER.
BUT NOTE HERE THAT SHE IS NOT STANDING -- SHE IS KNEELING, OR RECLINING -- HER HANDS OUTSTRETCHED AGAINST WALLS THAT APPEAR TO BE CLOSING IN. IS SHE A CAPTIVE? WEAKENED? OR, AS OTHERS HAVE ARGUED, GIVEN THE TITLE OF THE PAINTING, IS SHE HOLDING SOMETHING BACK WITH ALL HER REMAINING STRENGTH?
THIS IS ALSO THE FIRST VISUAL REPRESENTATION OF THE SHAMAN-EMPRESS'S LEGENDARY MASK OF POWER -- A MASK THAT THE ANALECTS CLAIM WAS IMBUED WITH THE *"POWER OF ALL CREATION."*
IT SHOULD BE NOTED THAT HALFWOLF DECIPHERED THE PAINTING'S TITLE HERSELF -- AN INCREDIBLE FEAT GIVEN THE ABSURDLY SLIPPERY NATURE OF FIRST-AGE DEMOTICS -- AND WHILE OFT CHALLENGED, HER TRANSLATION STILL REMAINS DEFINITIVE TO THIS DAY:
"THE EMPRESS AGAINST THE ABYSS"

CHAPTER TWENTY-ONE

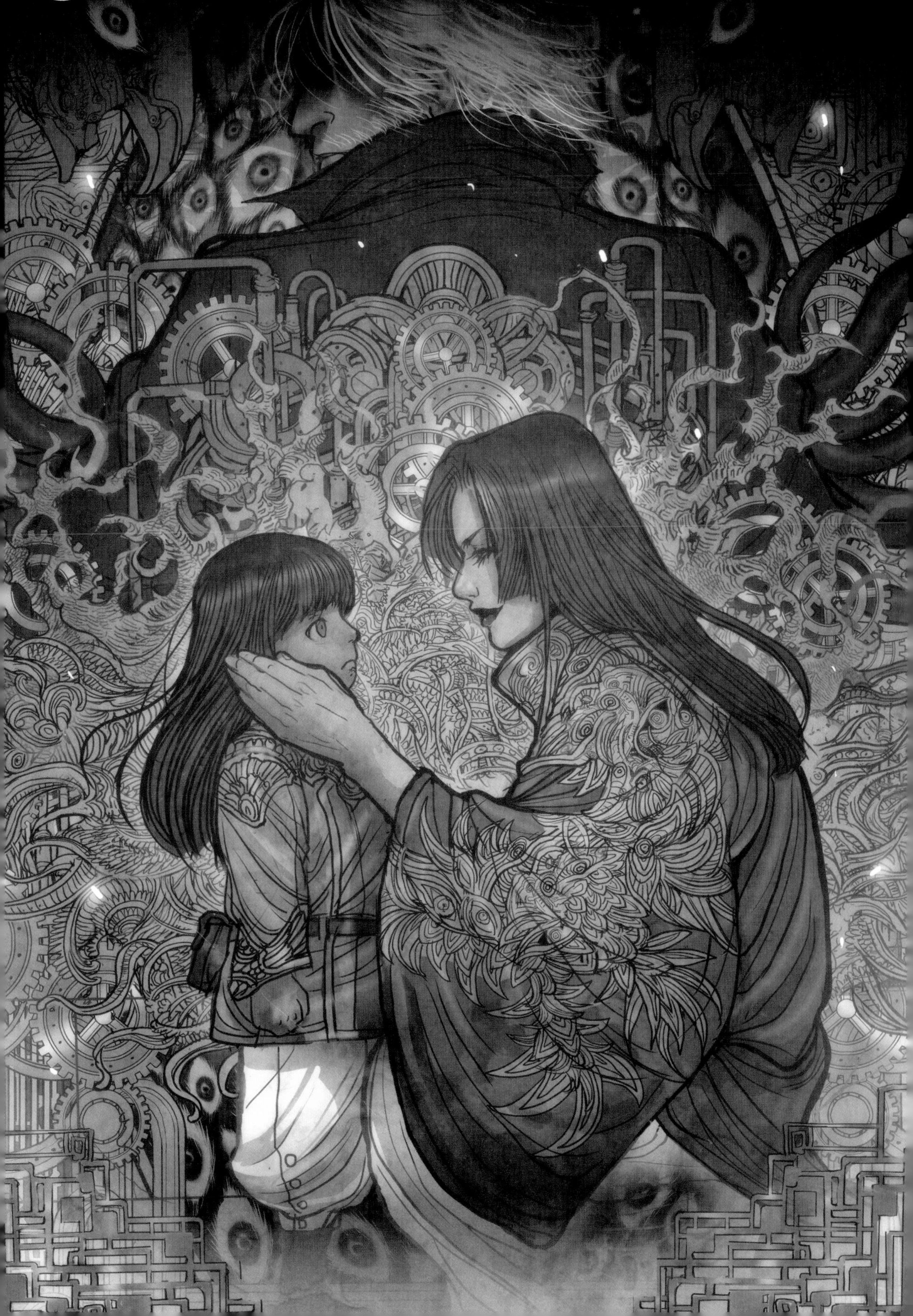

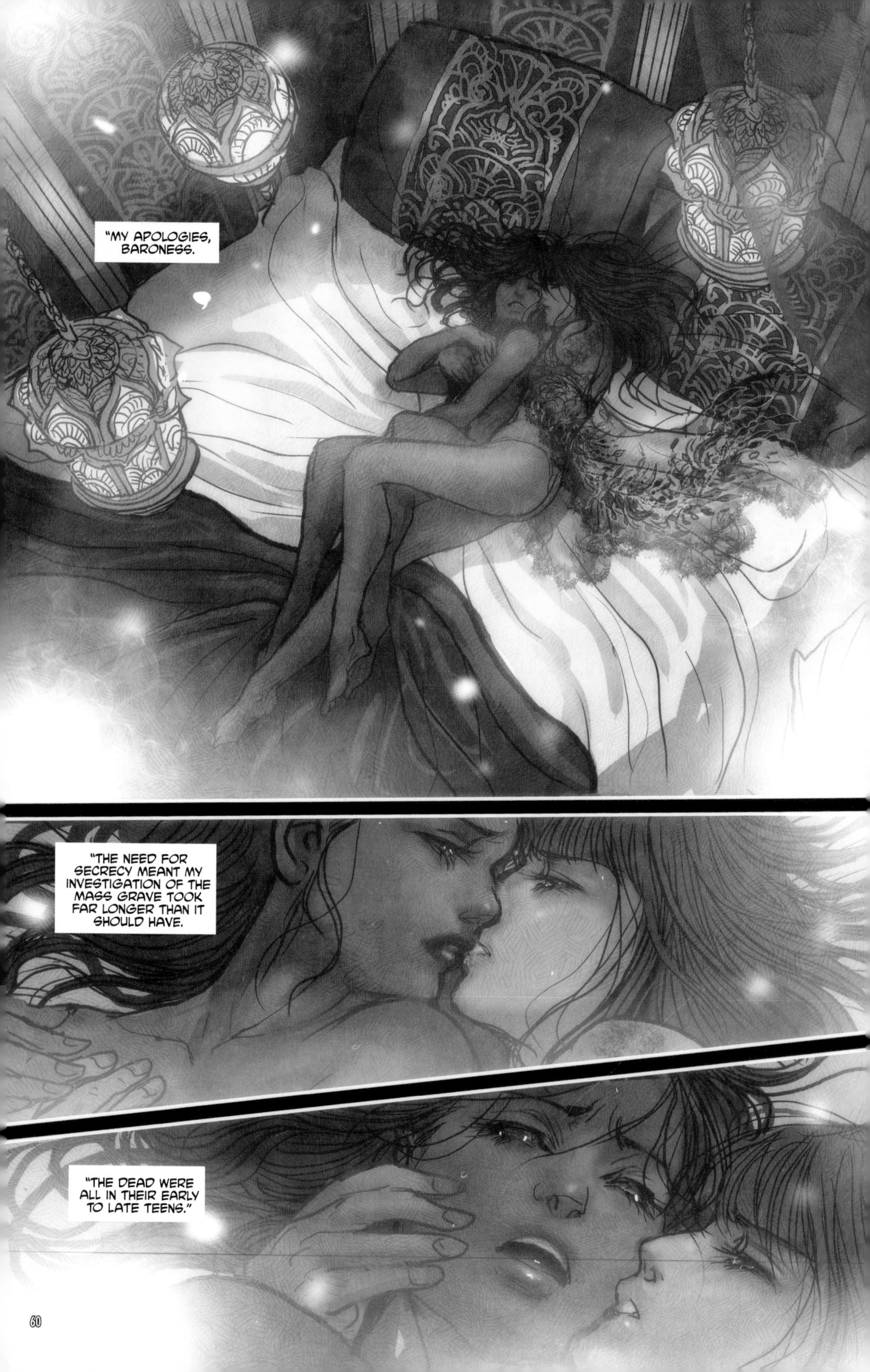
"MY APOLOGIES, BARONESS.
"THE NEED FOR SECRECY MEANT MY INVESTIGATION OF THE MASS GRAVE TOOK FAR LONGER THAN IT SHOULD HAVE.
"THE DEAD WERE ALL IN THEIR EARLY TO LATE TEENS."

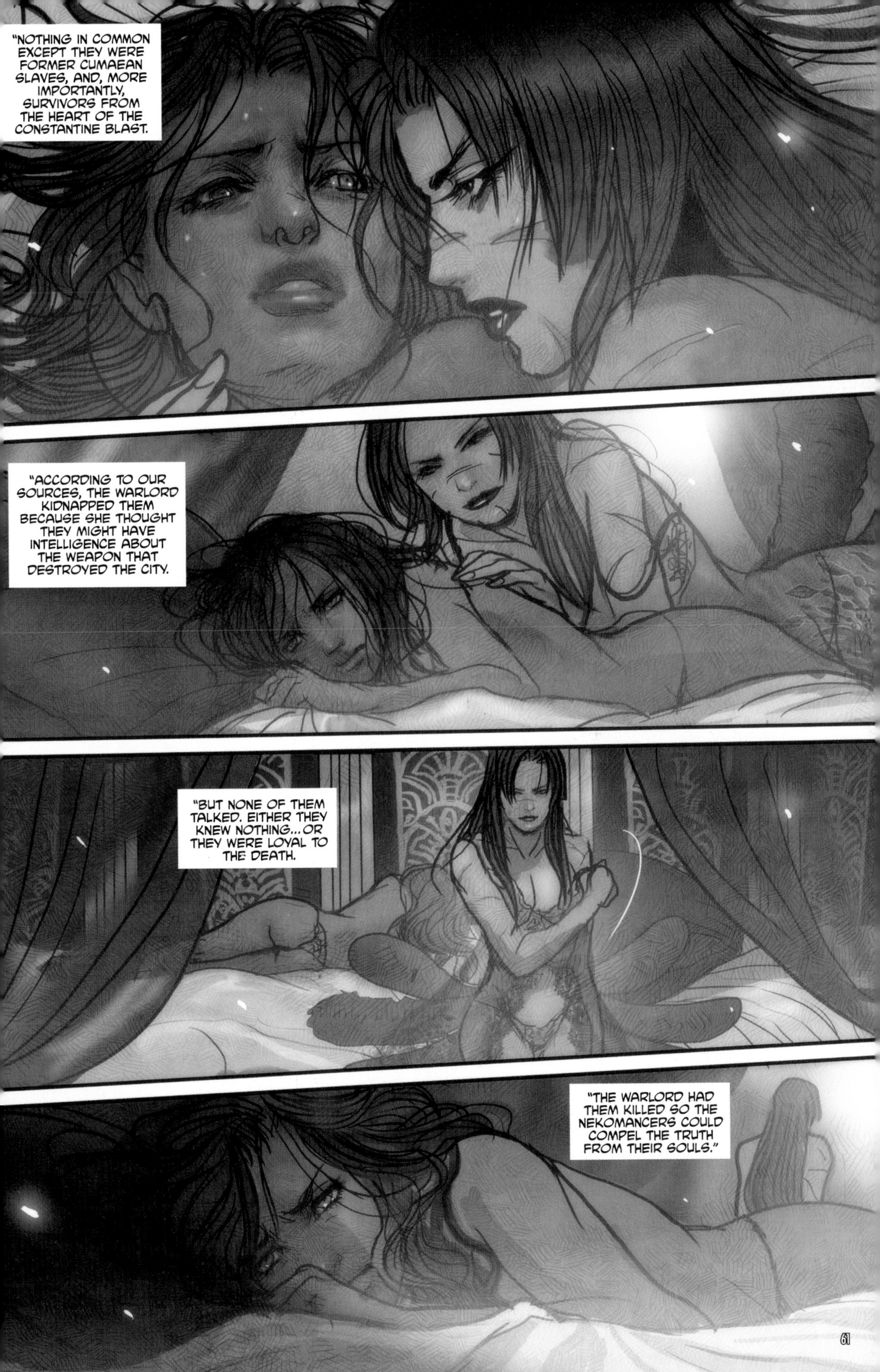
"NOTHING IN COMMON EXCEPT THEY WERE FORMER CUMAEAN SLAVES, AND, MORE IMPORTANTLY, SURVIVORS FROM THE HEART OF THE CONSTANTINE BLAST.
"ACCORDING TO OUR SOURCES, THE WARLORD KIDNAPPED THEM BECAUSE SHE THOUGHT THEY MIGHT HAVE INTELLIGENCE ABOUT THE WEAPON THAT DESTROYED THE CITY.
"BUT NONE OF THEM TALKED. EITHER THEY KNEW NOTHING...OR THEY WERE LOYAL TO THE DEATH.
"THE WARLORD HAD THEM KILLED SO THE NEKOMANCERS COULD COMPEL THE TRUTH FROM THEIR SOULS."

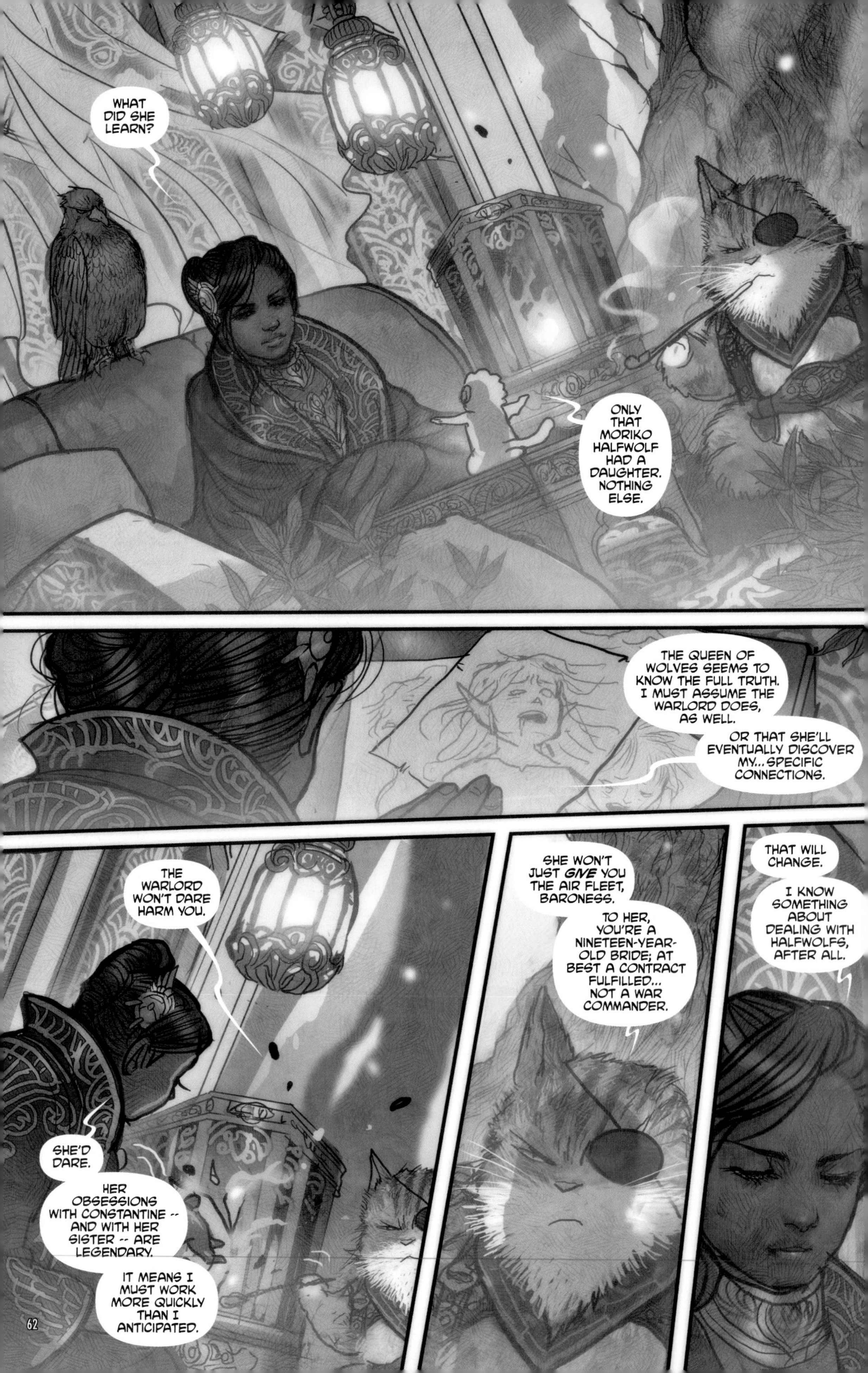
WHAT DID SHE LEARN?
ONLY THAT MORIKO HALFWOLF HAD A DAUGHTER. NOTHING ELSE.
THE QUEEN OF WOLVES SEEMS TO KNOW THE FULL TRUTH. I MUST ASSUME THE WARLORD DOES, AS WELL.
OR THAT SHE'LL EVENTUALLY DISCOVER MY... SPECIFIC CONNECTIONS.
THE WARLORD WON'T DARE HARM YOU.
SHE'D DARE.
HER OBSESSIONS WITH CONSTANTINE -- AND WITH HER SISTER -- ARE LEGENDARY.
IT MEANS I MUST WORK MORE QUICKLY THAN I ANTICIPATED.
SHE WON'T JUST *GIVE* YOU THE AIR FLEET, BARONESS.
TO HER, YOU'RE A NINETEEN-YEAR-OLD BRIDE; AT BEST A CONTRACT FULFILLED... NOT A WAR COMMANDER.
THAT WILL CHANGE.
I KNOW SOMETHING ABOUT DEALING WITH HALFWOLFS, AFTER ALL.

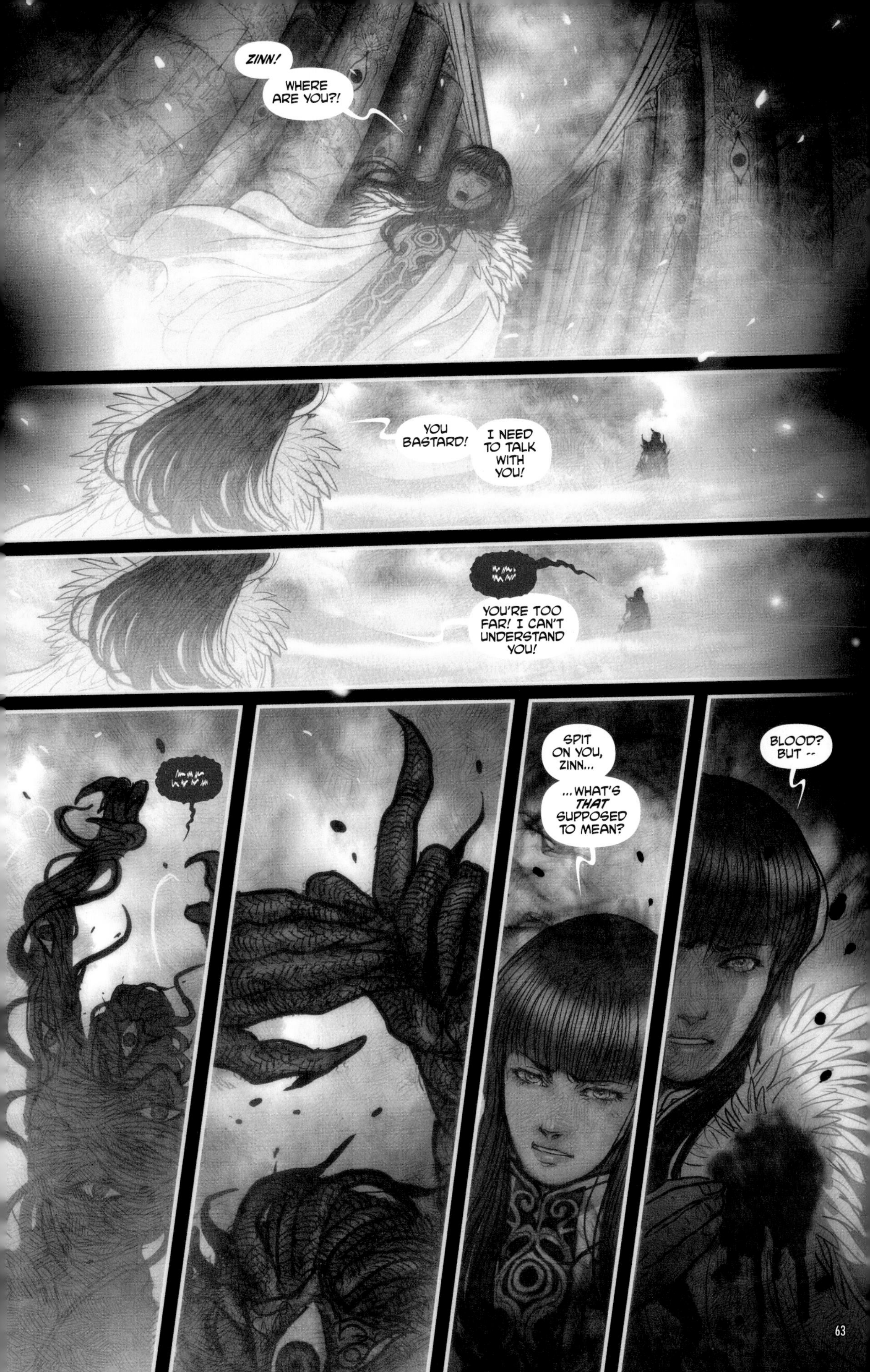
ZINN!
WHERE ARE YOU?!
YOU BASTARD!
I NEED TO TALK WITH YOU!
YOU'RE TOO FAR! I CAN'T UNDERSTAND YOU!
SPIT ON YOU, ZINN...
...WHAT'S *THAT* SUPPOSED TO MEAN?
BLOOD? BUT --

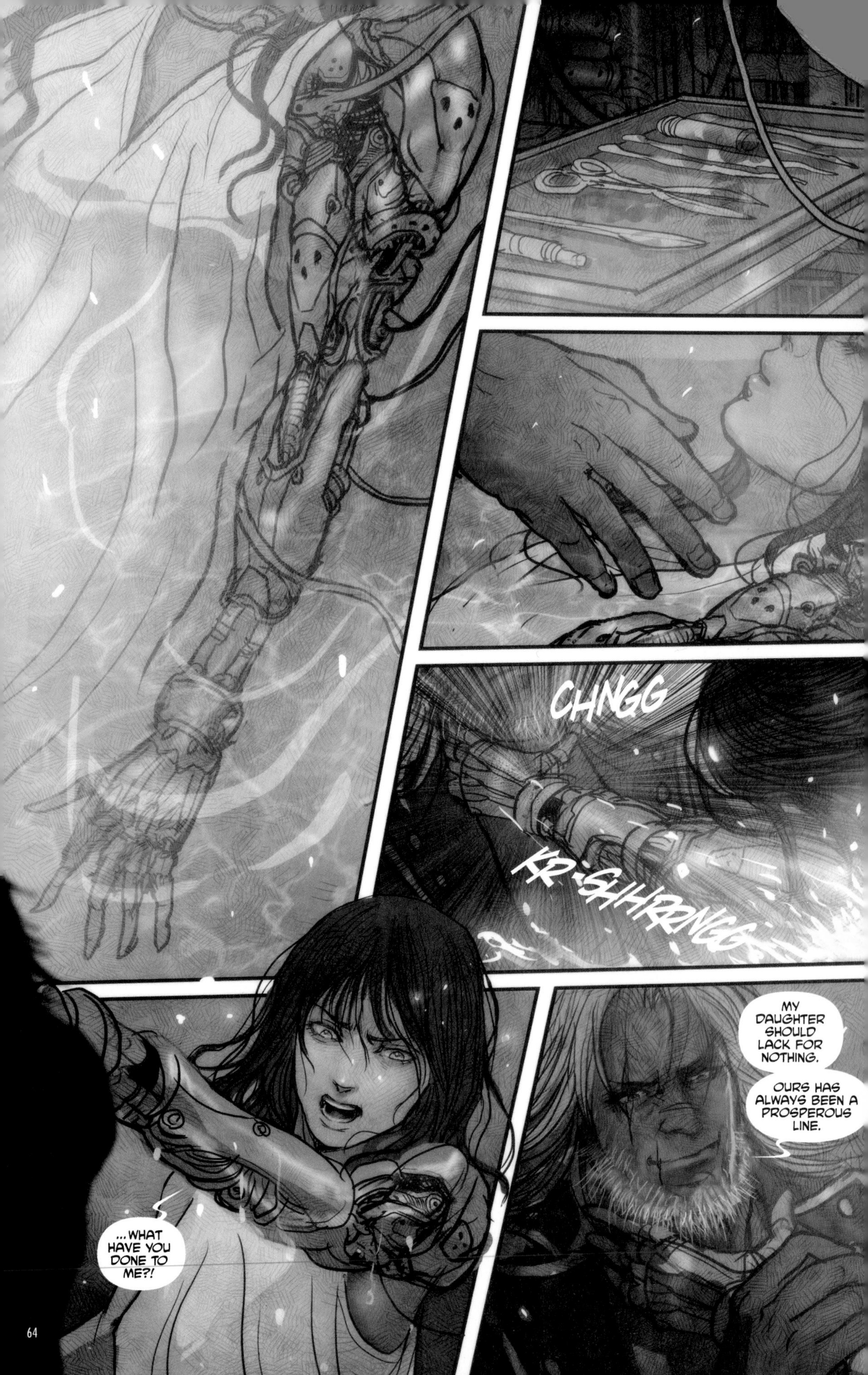
CHNGG
KR-SHHRRNGG
...WHAT HAVE YOU DONE TO ME?!
MY DAUGHTER SHOULD LACK FOR NOTHING.
OURS HAS ALWAYS BEEN A PROSPEROUS LINE.

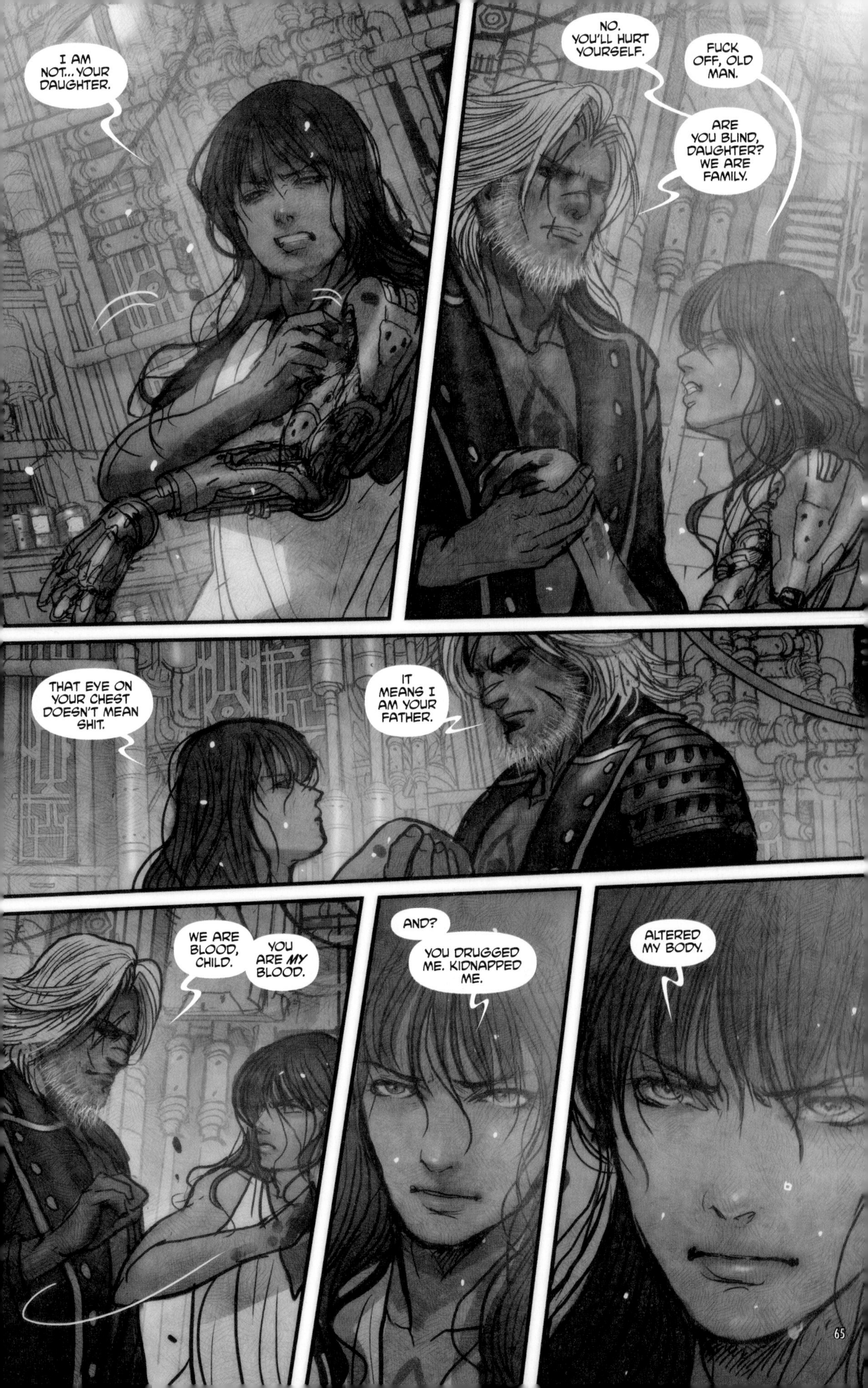
I AM NOT... YOUR DAUGHTER.
NO. YOU'LL HURT YOURSELF.
FUCK OFF, OLD MAN.
ARE YOU BLIND, DAUGHTER? WE ARE FAMILY.
THAT EYE ON YOUR CHEST DOESN'T MEAN SHIT.
IT MEANS I AM YOUR FATHER.
WE ARE BLOOD, CHILD.
YOU ARE *MY* BLOOD.
AND?
YOU DRUGGED ME. KIDNAPPED ME.
ALTERED MY BODY.

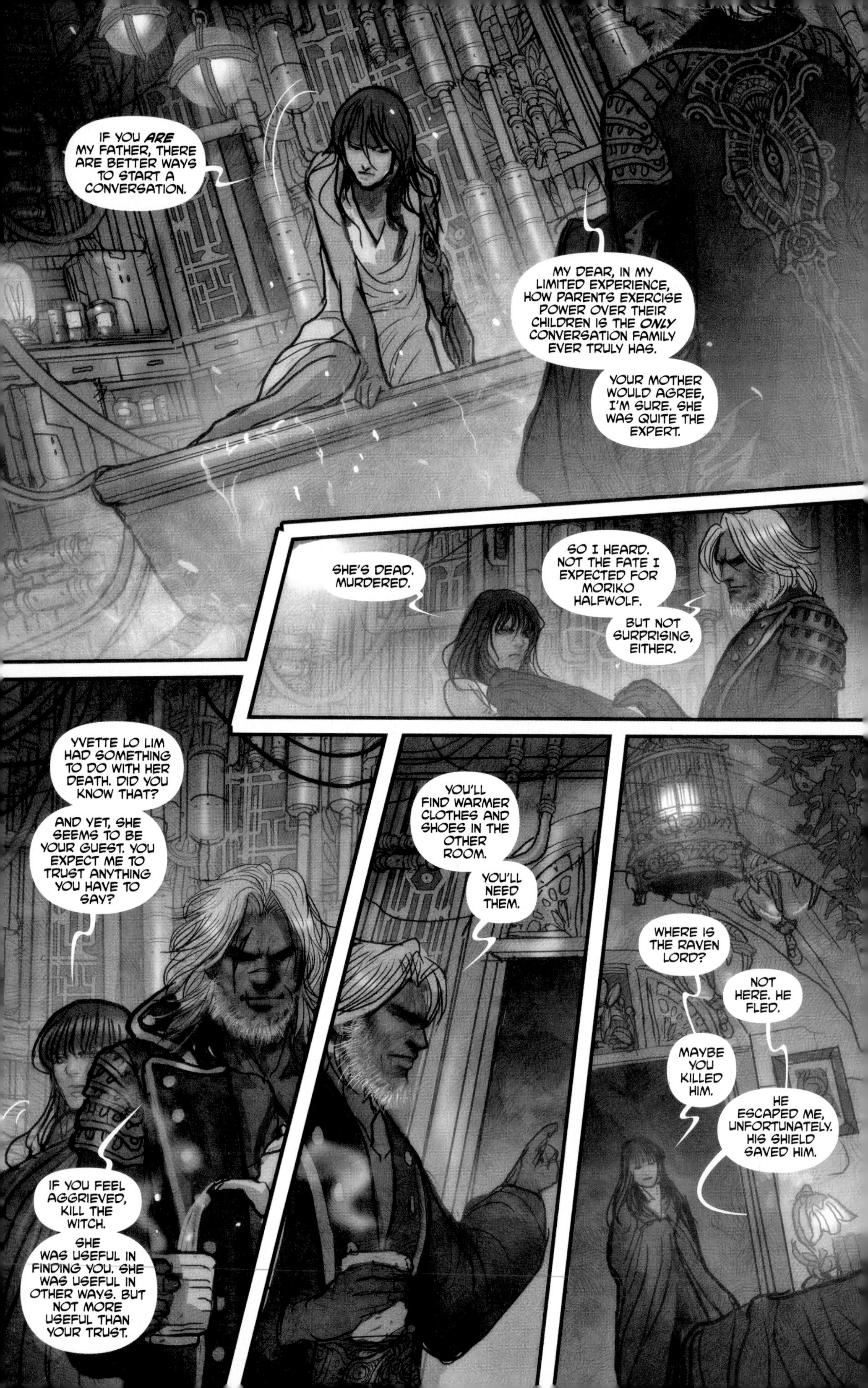

IF YOU *ARE* MY FATHER, THERE ARE BETTER WAYS TO START A CONVERSATION.
MY DEAR, IN MY LIMITED EXPERIENCE, HOW PARENTS EXERCISE POWER OVER THEIR CHILDREN IS THE *ONLY* CONVERSATION FAMILY EVER TRULY HAS.
YOUR MOTHER WOULD AGREE, I'M SURE. SHE WAS QUITE THE EXPERT.
SHE'S DEAD. MURDERED.
SO I HEARD. NOT THE FATE I EXPECTED FOR MORIKO HALFWOLF.
BUT NOT SURPRISING, EITHER.
YVETTE LO LIM HAD SOMETHING TO DO WITH HER DEATH. DID YOU KNOW THAT?
AND YET, SHE SEEMS TO BE YOUR GUEST. YOU EXPECT ME TO TRUST ANYTHING YOU HAVE TO SAY?
IF YOU FEEL AGGRIEVED, KILL THE WITCH.
SHE WAS USEFUL IN FINDING YOU. SHE WAS USEFUL IN OTHER WAYS. BUT NOT MORE USEFUL THAN YOUR TRUST.
YOU'LL FIND WARMER CLOTHES AND SHOES IN THE OTHER ROOM.
YOU'LL NEED THEM.
WHERE IS THE RAVEN LORD?
NOT HERE. HE FLED.
MAYBE YOU KILLED HIM.
HE ESCAPED ME, UNFORTUNATELY. HIS SHIELD SAVED HIM.

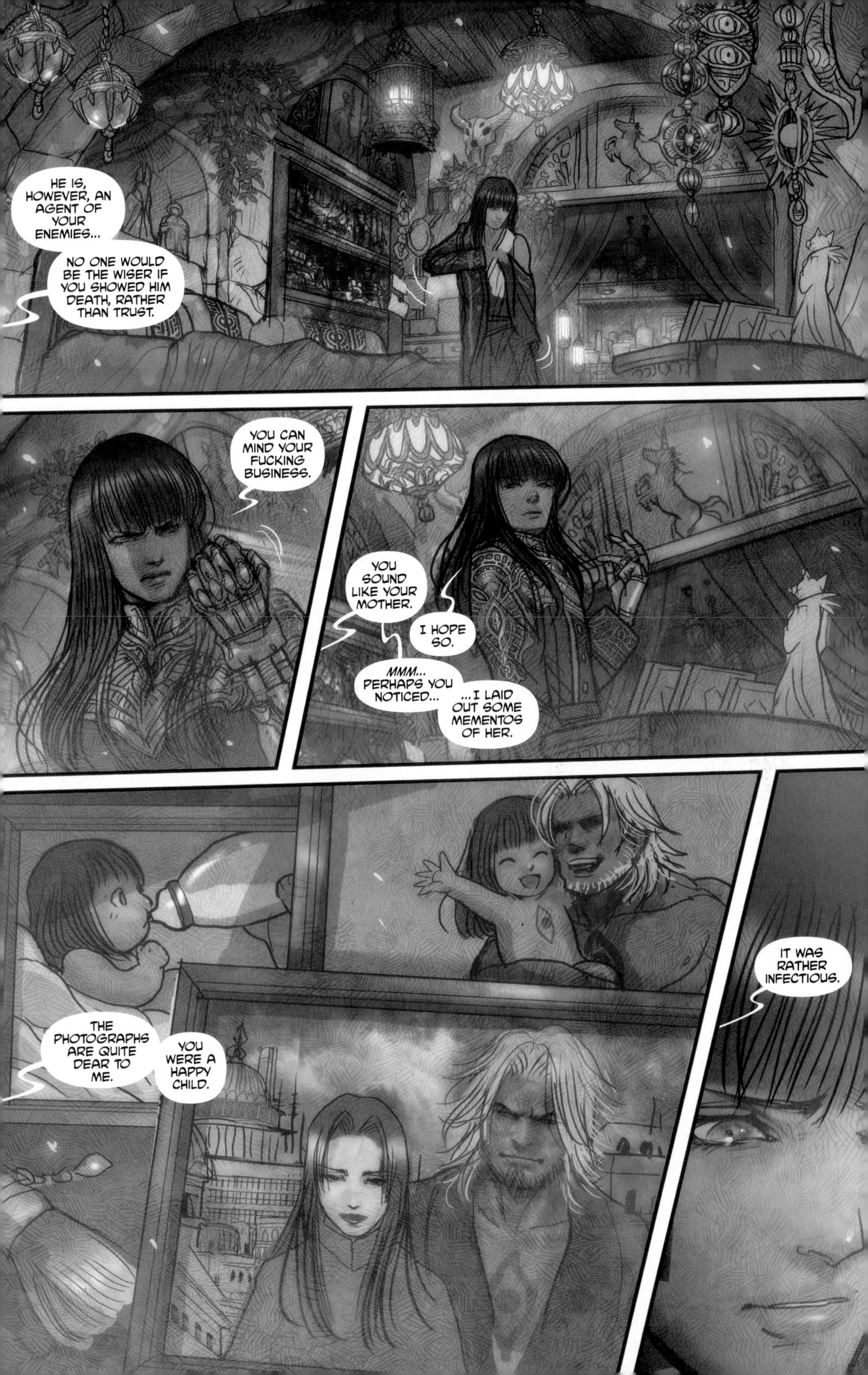
HE IS, HOWEVER, AN AGENT OF YOUR ENEMIES...
NO ONE WOULD BE THE WISER IF YOU SHOWED HIM DEATH, RATHER THAN TRUST.
YOU CAN MIND YOUR FUCKING BUSINESS.
YOU SOUND LIKE YOUR MOTHER.
I HOPE SO.
MMM... PERHAPS YOU NOTICED...
...I LAID OUT SOME MEMENTOS OF HER.
THE PHOTOGRAPHS ARE QUITE DEAR TO ME.
YOU WERE A HAPPY CHILD.
IT WAS RATHER INFECTIOUS.

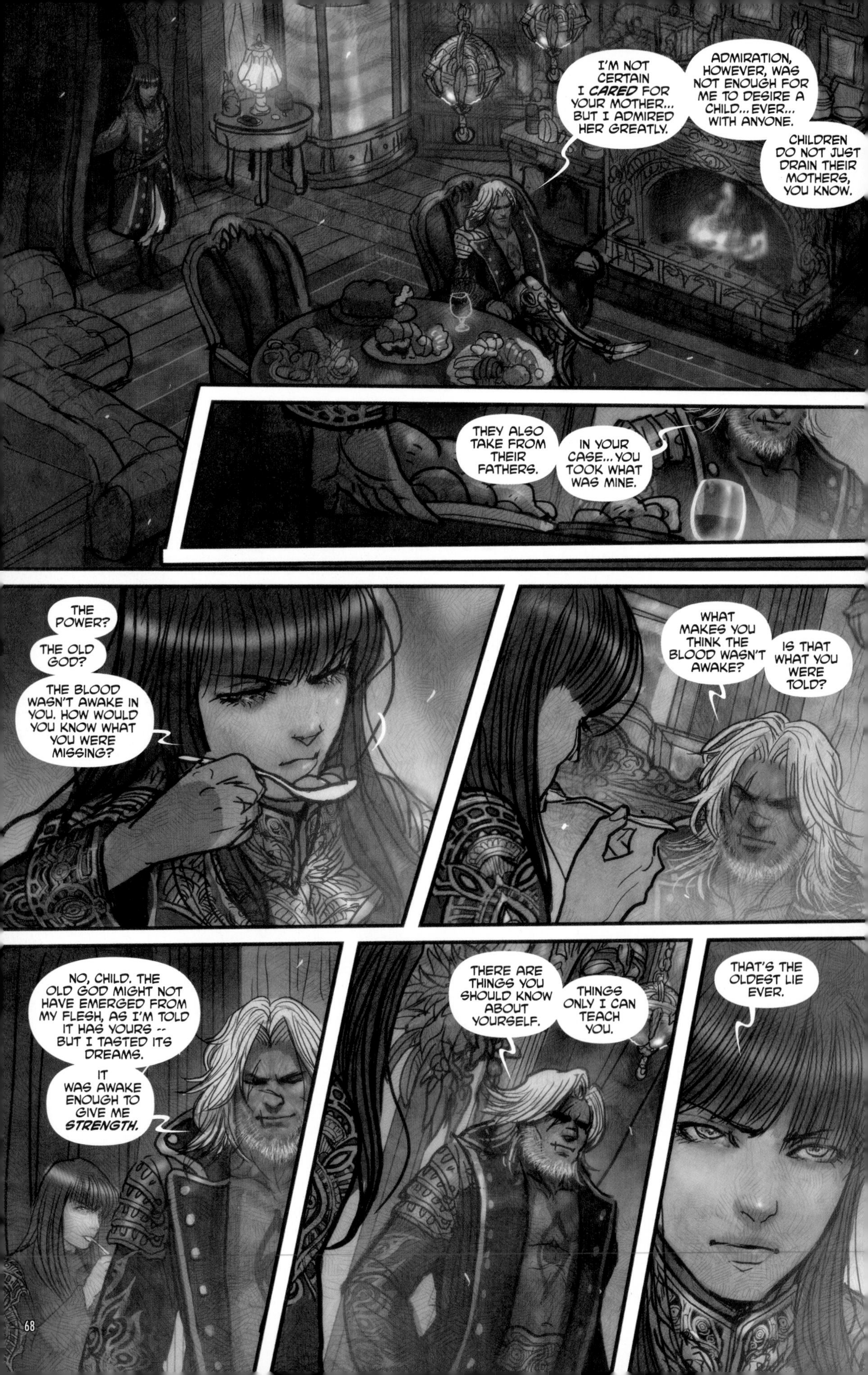
I'M NOT CERTAIN I *CARED* FOR YOUR MOTHER... BUT I ADMIRED HER GREATLY.
ADMIRATION, HOWEVER, WAS NOT ENOUGH FOR ME TO DESIRE A CHILD... EVER... WITH ANYONE.
CHILDREN DO NOT JUST DRAIN THEIR MOTHERS, YOU KNOW.
THEY ALSO TAKE FROM THEIR FATHERS.
IN YOUR CASE... YOU TOOK WHAT WAS MINE.
THE POWER?
THE OLD GOD?
THE BLOOD WASN'T AWAKE IN YOU. HOW WOULD YOU KNOW WHAT YOU WERE MISSING?
WHAT MAKES YOU THINK THE BLOOD WASN'T AWAKE?
IS THAT WHAT YOU WERE TOLD?
NO, CHILD. THE OLD GOD MIGHT NOT HAVE EMERGED FROM MY FLESH, AS I'M TOLD IT HAS YOURS -- BUT I TASTED ITS DREAMS.
IT WAS AWAKE ENOUGH TO GIVE ME *STRENGTH.*
THERE ARE THINGS YOU SHOULD KNOW ABOUT YOURSELF.
THINGS ONLY I CAN TEACH YOU.
THAT'S THE OLDEST LIE EVER.

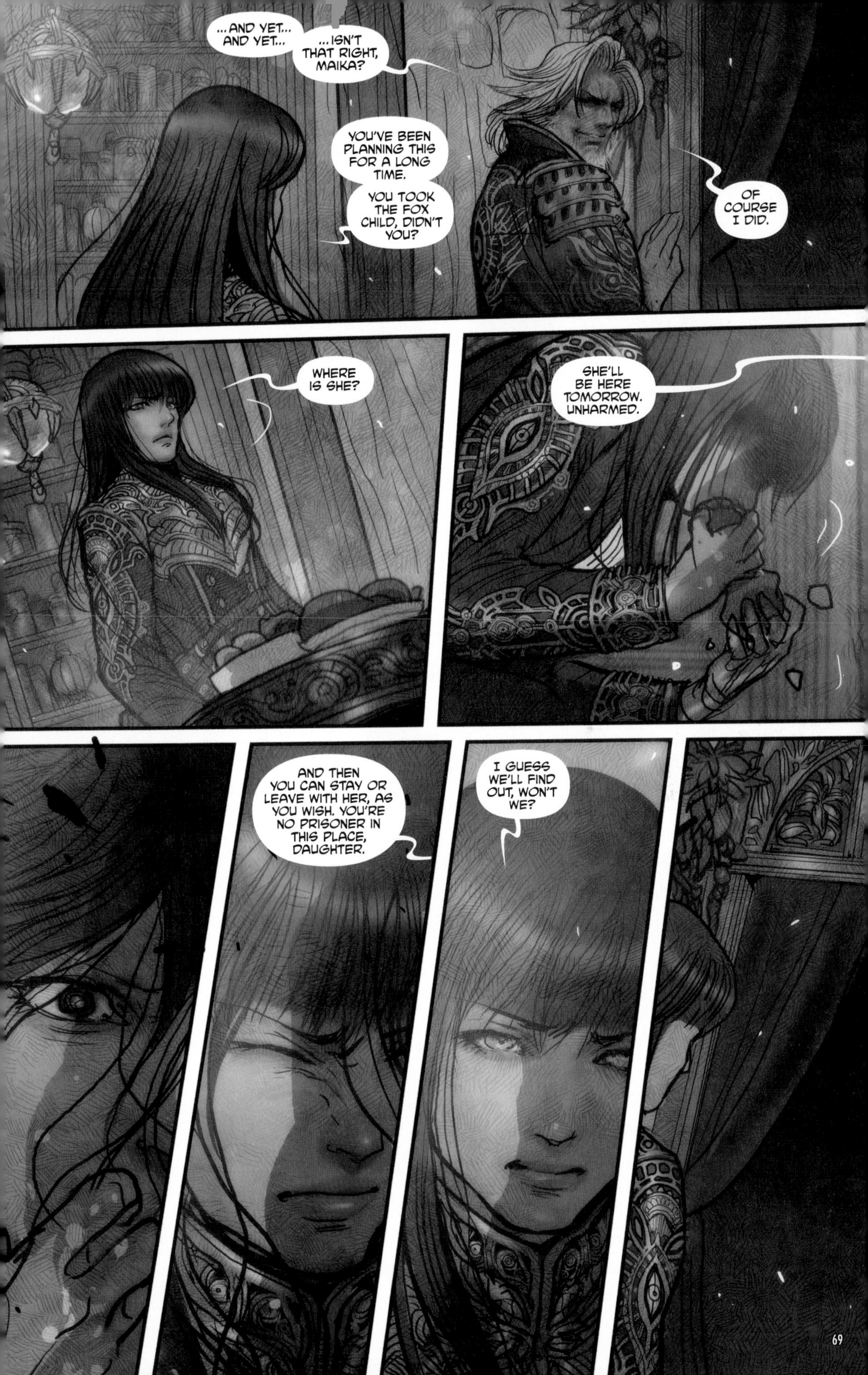
...AND YET... AND YET...
...ISN'T THAT RIGHT, MAIKA?
YOU'VE BEEN PLANNING THIS FOR A LONG TIME.
YOU TOOK THE FOX CHILD, DIDN'T YOU?
OF COURSE I DID.
WHERE IS SHE?
SHE'LL BE HERE TOMORROW. UNHARMED.
AND THEN YOU CAN STAY OR LEAVE WITH HER, AS YOU WISH. YOU'RE NO PRISONER IN THIS PLACE, DAUGHTER.
I GUESS WE'LL FIND OUT, WON'T WE?

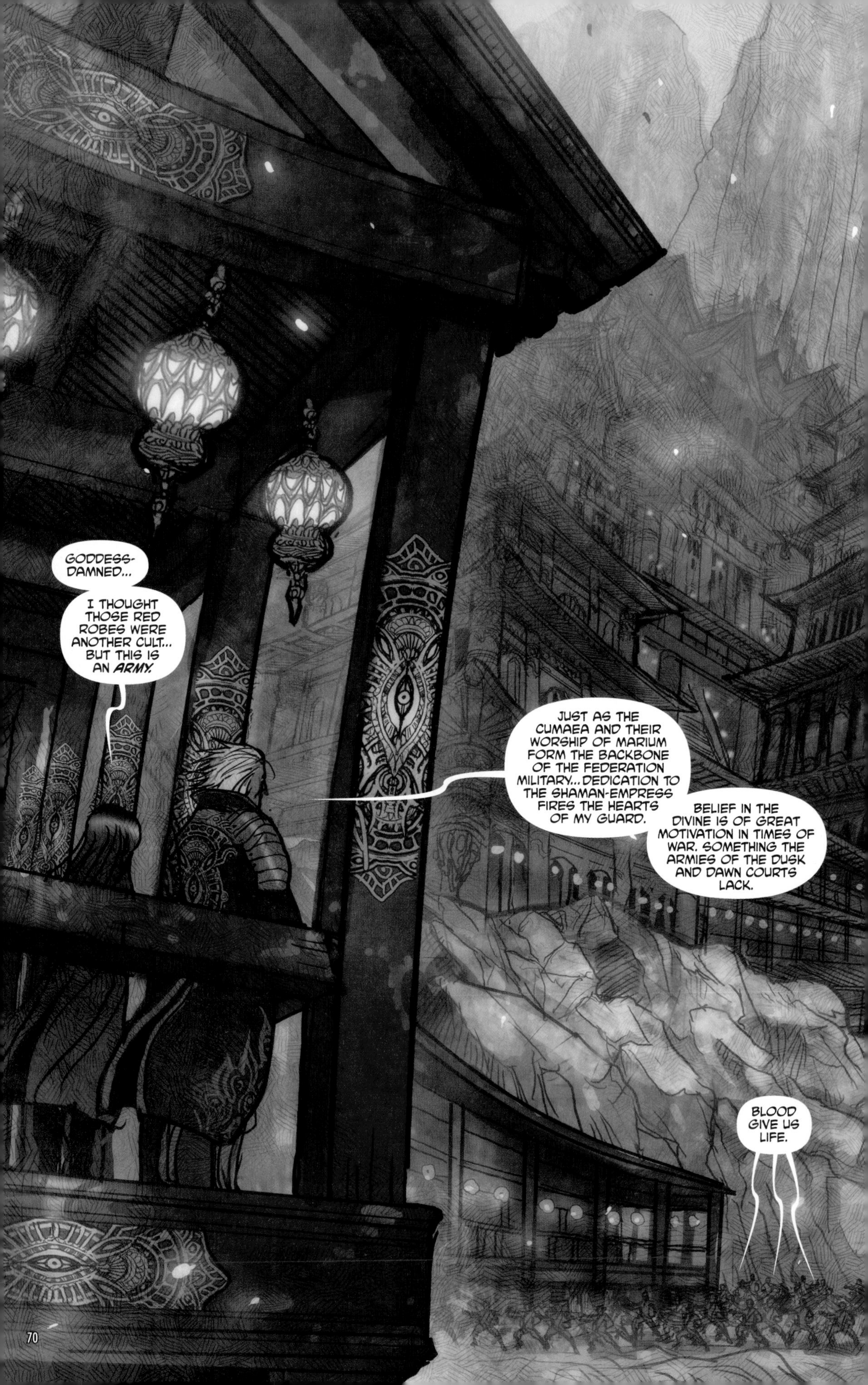
GODDESS-DAMNED...
I THOUGHT THOSE RED ROBES WERE ANOTHER CULT... BUT THIS IS AN *ARMY.*
JUST AS THE CUMAEA AND THEIR WORSHIP OF MARIUM FORM THE BACKBONE OF THE FEDERATION MILITARY... DEDICATION TO THE SHAMAN-EMPRESS FIRES THE HEARTS OF MY GUARD.
BELIEF IN THE DIVINE IS OF GREAT MOTIVATION IN TIMES OF WAR. SOMETHING THE ARMIES OF THE DUSK AND DAWN COURTS LACK.
BLOOD GIVE US LIFE.

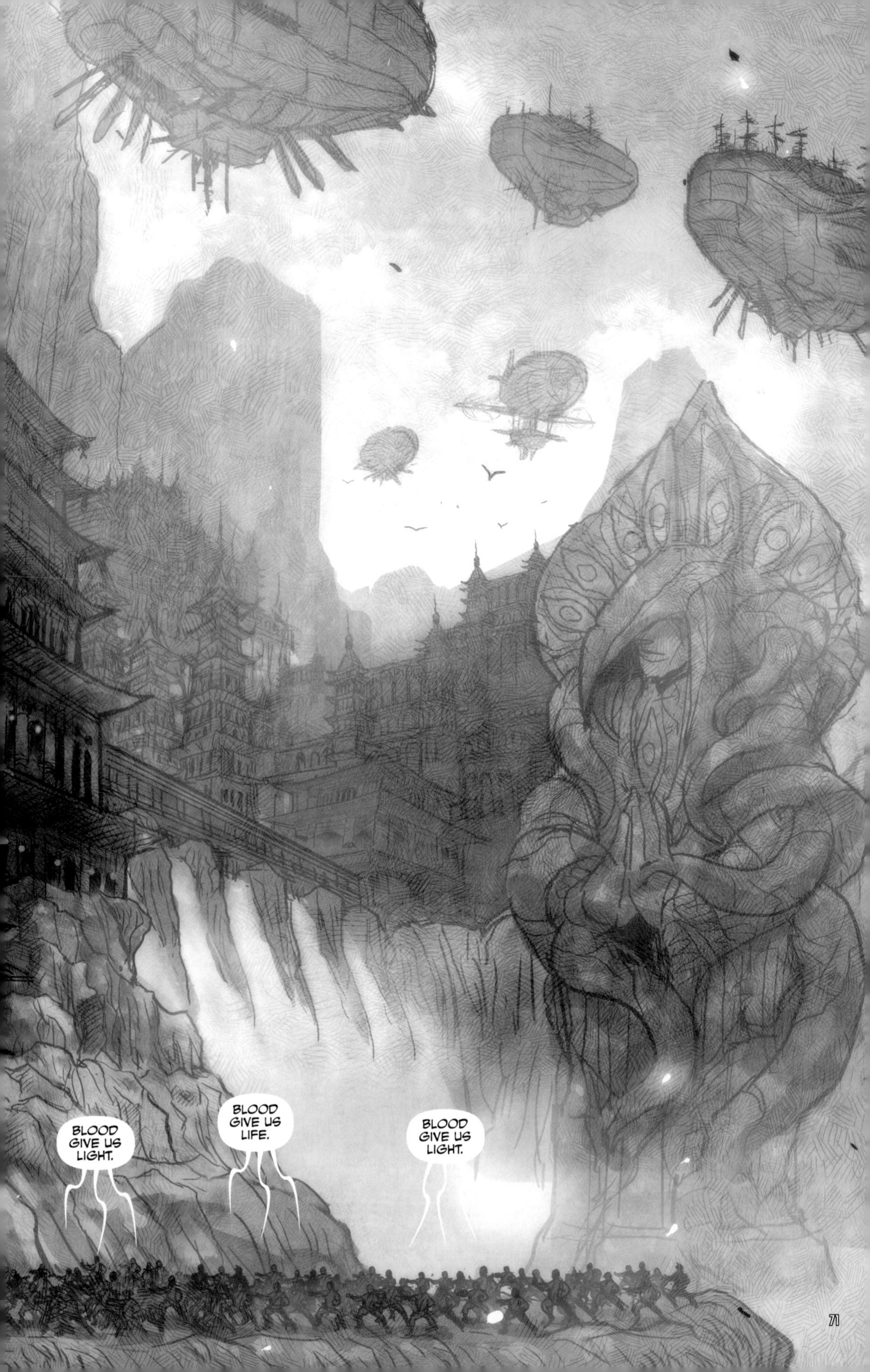
BLOOD GIVE US LIGHT.
BLOOD GIVE US LIFE.
BLOOD GIVE US LIGHT.

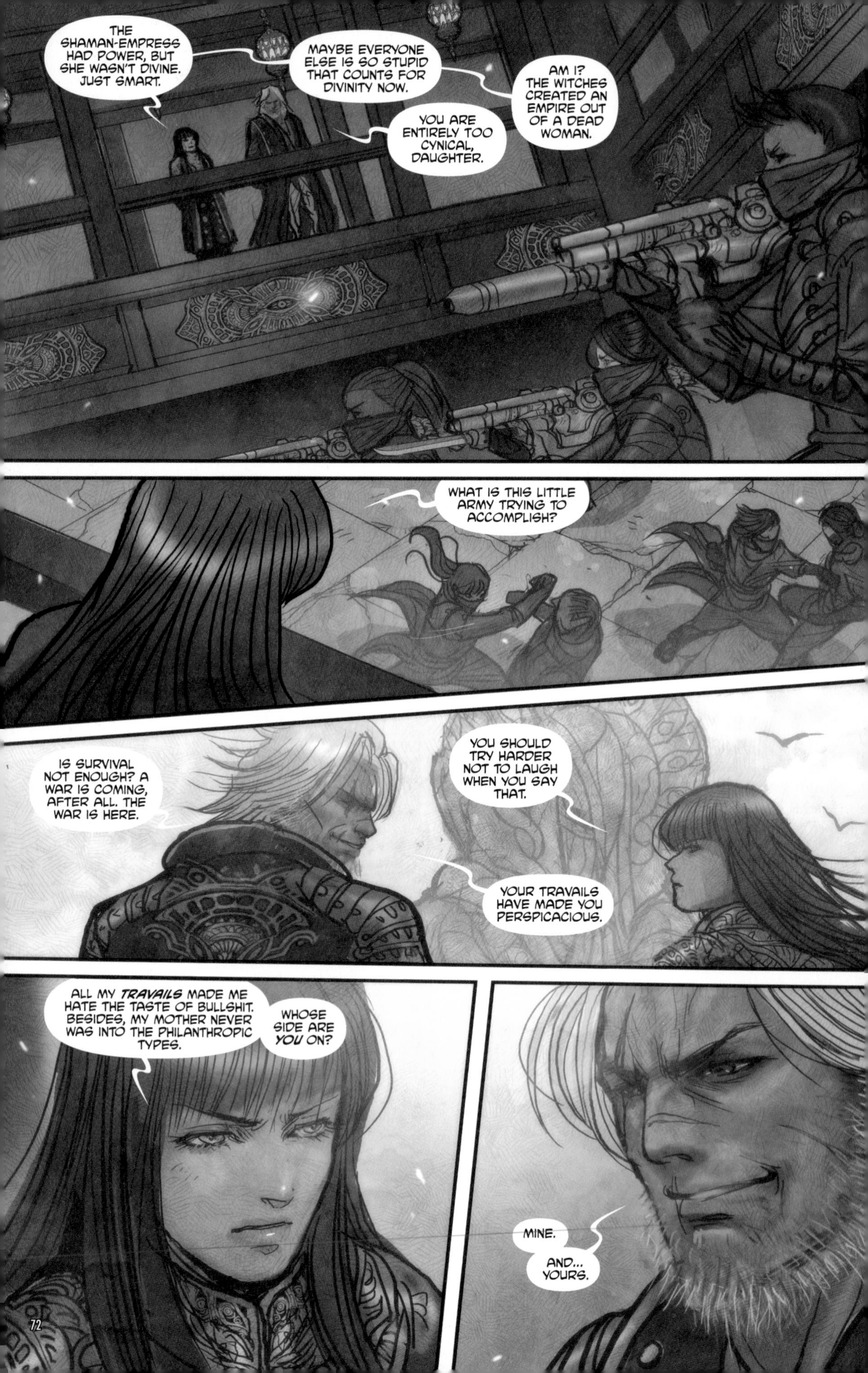
THE SHAMAN-EMPRESS HAD POWER, BUT SHE WASN'T DIVINE. JUST SMART.
MAYBE EVERYONE ELSE IS SO STUPID THAT COUNTS FOR DIVINITY NOW.
YOU ARE ENTIRELY TOO CYNICAL, DAUGHTER.
AM I? THE WITCHES CREATED AN EMPIRE OUT OF A DEAD WOMAN.
WHAT IS THIS LITTLE ARMY TRYING TO ACCOMPLISH?
IS SURVIVAL NOT ENOUGH? A WAR IS COMING, AFTER ALL. THE WAR IS HERE.
YOU SHOULD TRY HARDER NOT TO LAUGH WHEN YOU SAY THAT.
YOUR TRAVAILS HAVE MADE YOU PERSPICACIOUS.
ALL MY *TRAVAILS* MADE ME HATE THE TASTE OF BULLSHIT. BESIDES, MY MOTHER NEVER WAS INTO THE PHILANTHROPIC TYPES.
WHOSE SIDE ARE *YOU* ON?
MINE.
AND... YOURS.

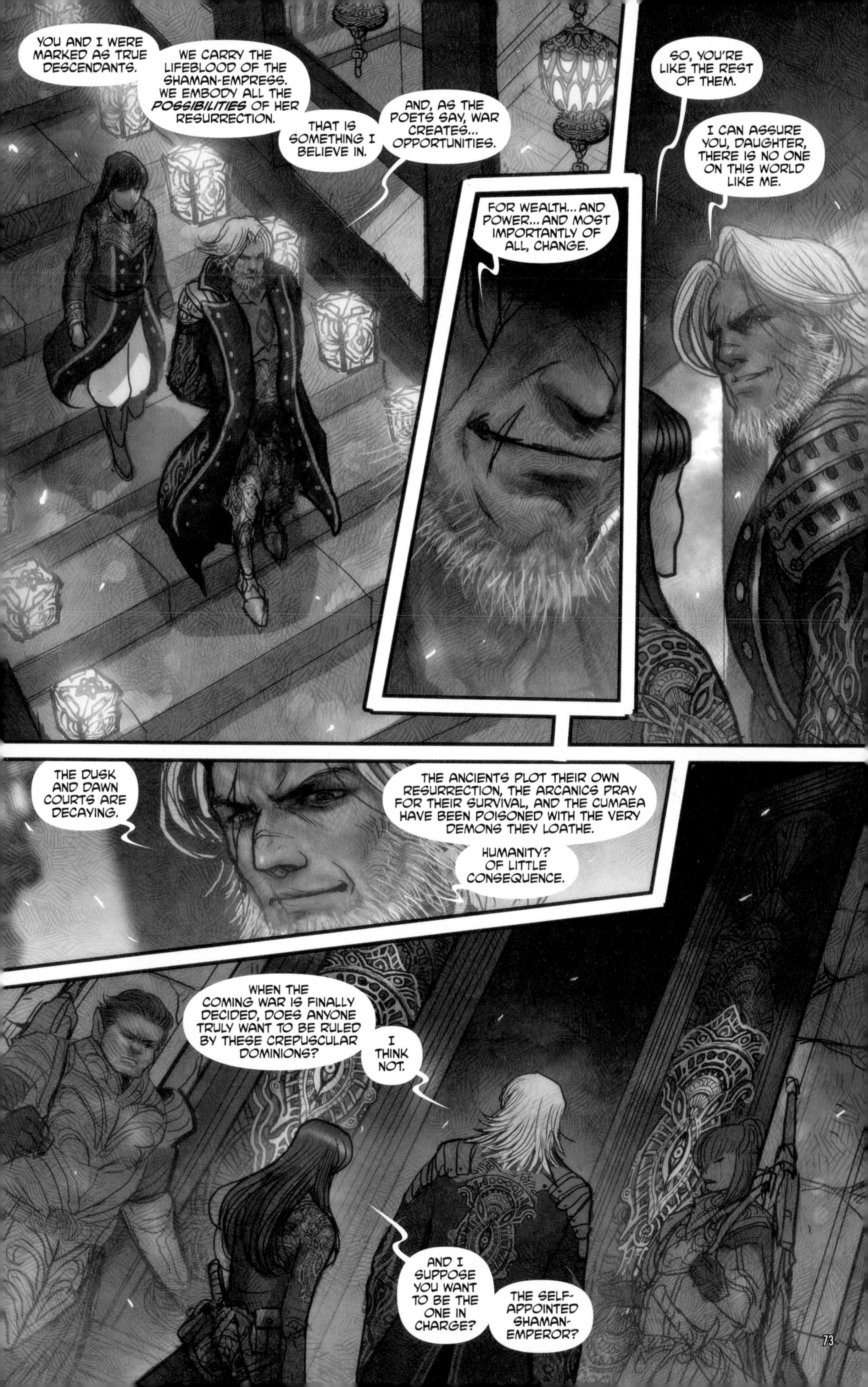

YOU AND I WERE MARKED AS TRUE DESCENDANTS.
WE CARRY THE LIFEBLOOD OF THE SHAMAN-EMPRESS. WE EMBODY ALL THE *POSSIBILITIES* OF HER RESURRECTION.
THAT IS SOMETHING I BELIEVE IN.
AND, AS THE POETS SAY, WAR CREATES... OPPORTUNITIES.
FOR WEALTH... AND POWER... AND MOST IMPORTANTLY OF ALL, CHANGE.
SO, YOU'RE LIKE THE REST OF THEM.
I CAN ASSURE YOU, DAUGHTER, THERE IS NO ONE ON THIS WORLD LIKE ME.
THE DUSK AND DAWN COURTS ARE DECAYING.
THE ANCIENTS PLOT THEIR OWN RESURRECTION, THE ARCANICS PRAY FOR THEIR SURVIVAL, AND THE CUMAEA HAVE BEEN POISONED WITH THE VERY DEMONS THEY LOATHE.
HUMANITY? OF LITTLE CONSEQUENCE.
WHEN THE COMING WAR IS FINALLY DECIDED, DOES ANYONE TRULY WANT TO BE RULED BY THESE CREPUSCULAR DOMINIONS?
I THINK NOT.
AND I SUPPOSE YOU WANT TO BE THE ONE IN CHARGE?
THE SELF-APPOINTED SHAMAN-EMPEROR?

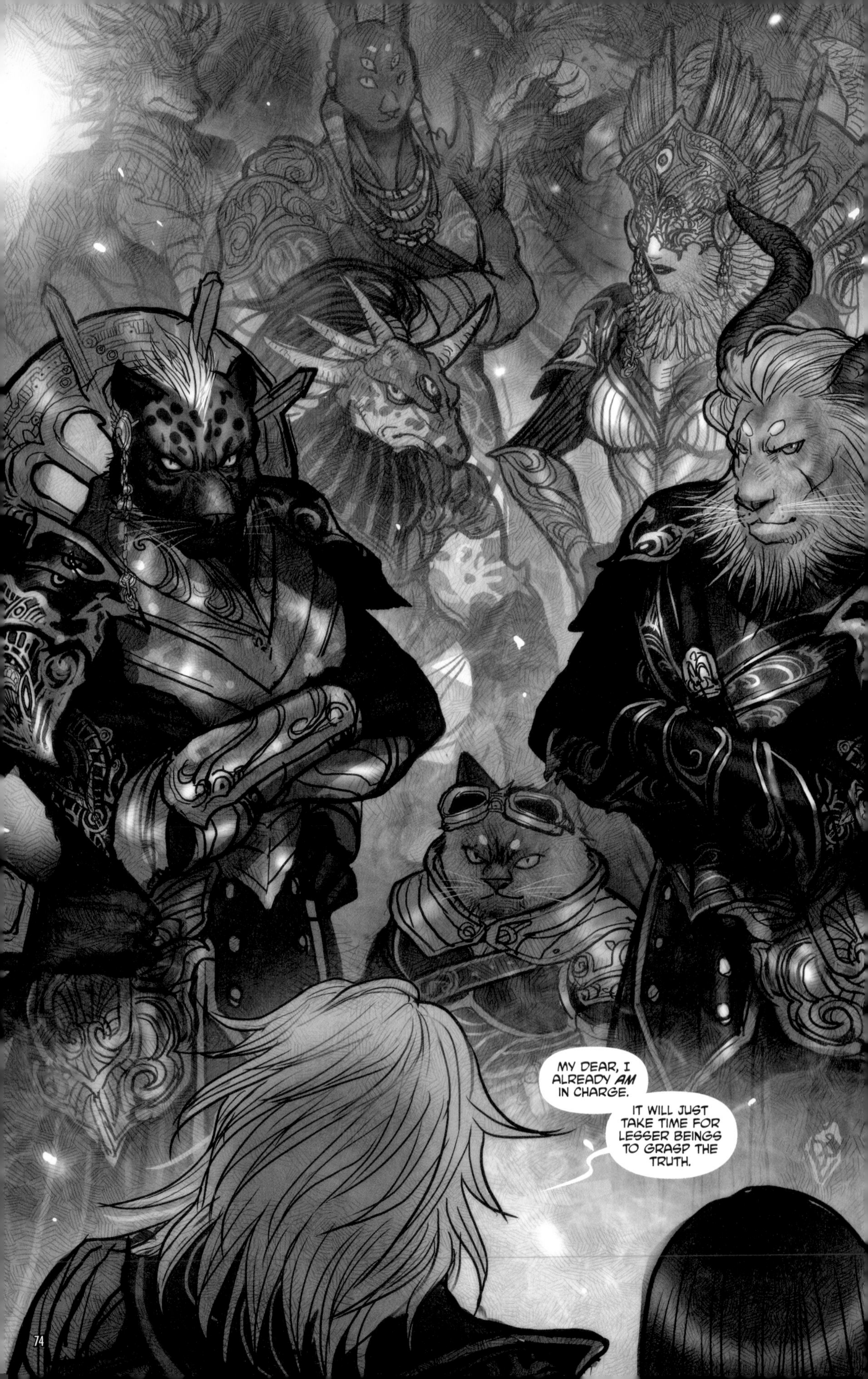
MY DEAR, I ALREADY *AM* IN CHARGE.
IT WILL JUST TAKE TIME FOR LESSER BEINGS TO GRASP THE TRUTH.

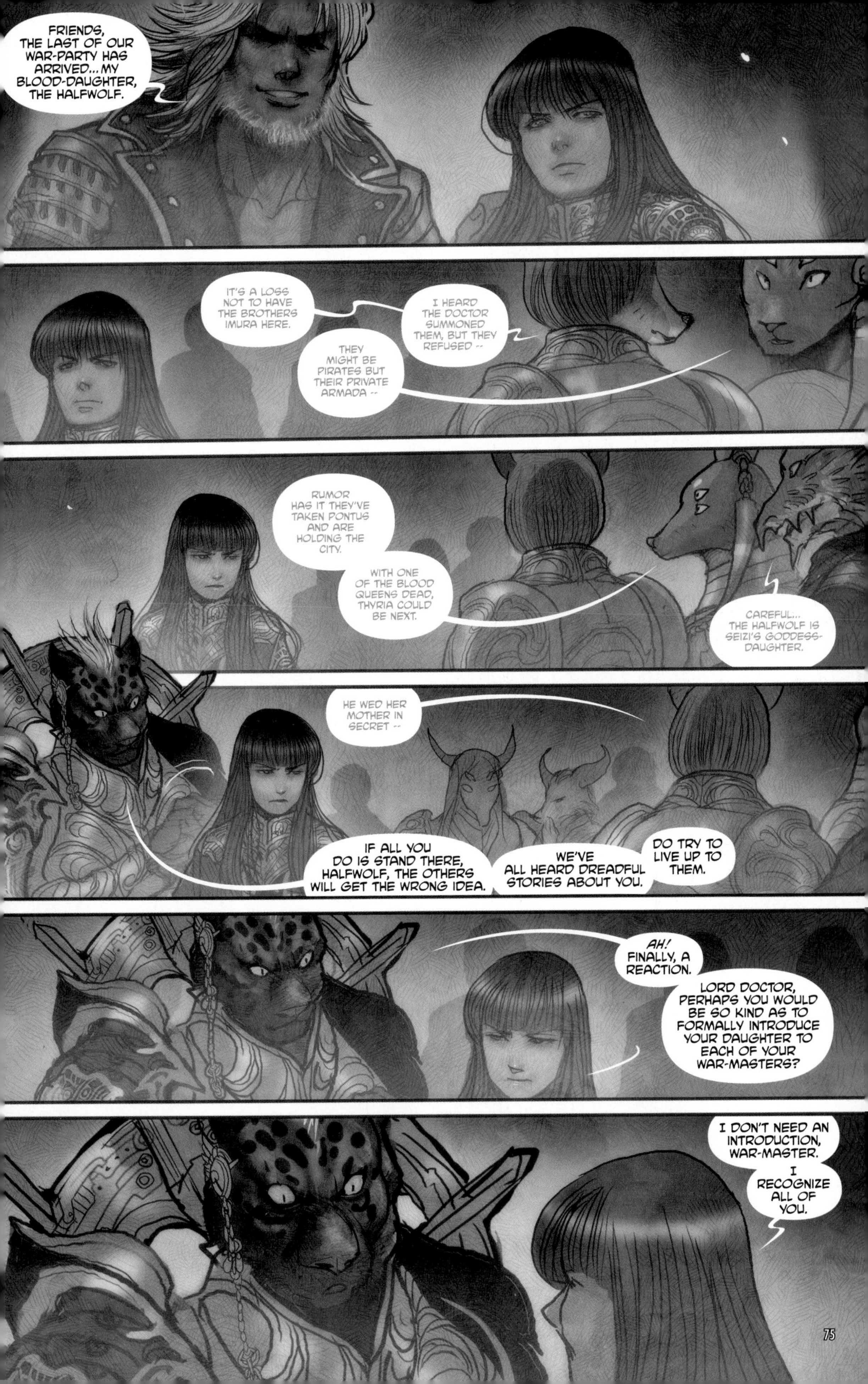
FRIENDS, THE LAST OF OUR WAR-PARTY HAS ARRIVED... MY BLOOD-DAUGHTER, THE HALFWOLF.
IT'S A LOSS NOT TO HAVE THE BROTHERS IMURA HERE.
I HEARD THE DOCTOR SUMMONED THEM, BUT THEY REFUSED --
THEY MIGHT BE PIRATES BUT THEIR PRIVATE ARMADA --
RUMOR HAS IT THEY'VE TAKEN PONTUS AND ARE HOLDING THE CITY.
WITH ONE OF THE BLOOD QUEENS DEAD, THYRIA COULD BE NEXT.
CAREFUL... THE HALFWOLF IS SEIZI'S GODDESS-DAUGHTER.
HE WED HER MOTHER IN SECRET --
IF ALL YOU DO IS STAND THERE, HALFWOLF, THE OTHERS WILL GET THE WRONG IDEA.
WE'VE ALL HEARD DREADFUL STORIES ABOUT YOU.
DO TRY TO LIVE UP TO THEM.
AH! FINALLY, A REACTION.
LORD DOCTOR, PERHAPS YOU WOULD BE SO KIND AS TO FORMALLY INTRODUCE YOUR DAUGHTER TO EACH OF YOUR WAR-MASTERS?
I DON'T NEED AN INTRODUCTION, WAR-MASTER.
I RECOGNIZE ALL OF YOU.

YOU ARE AGATA TONG NAMMA. ALSO CALLED THE DUELIST, FOR BEING UNBEATEN AT PISTOL AND BLADE.

THE GREATEST SWORDSWOMAN OF HER GENERATION, YOU AND YOUR PERSONAL GUARD SINGLE-HANDEDLY HELD OFF FEDERATION SOLDIERS AT NOTCH HALLOW WHILE YOUR SURVIVING TROOPS RETREATED.

ARCANIC GIFT: NONE.

ULIAZA GRIMM, CAPTAIN OF THE GREY LEGION.

AN ELITE UNIT THAT SERVED UNDER THE WARLORD. YOU WERE AT THE FOREFRONT OF EVERY MAJOR ENGAGEMENT IN THE GREAT WAR AND EVEN MANAGED TO ESCAPE THE DESTRUCTION OF CONSTANTINE WITH THE MAJORITY OF YOUR FORCES INTACT.

ARCANIC GIFT: POWER OF ANTICIPATION.

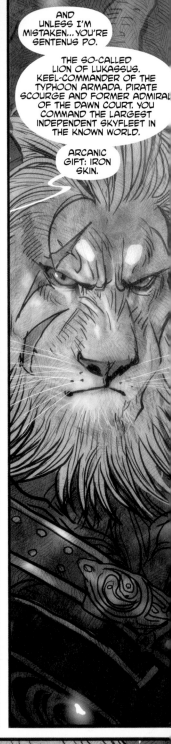

AND UNLESS I'M MISTAKEN...YOU'RE SENTENUS PO.

THE SO-CALLED LION OF LUKASSUS. KEEL-COMMANDER OF THE TYPHOON ARMADA. PIRATE SCOURGE AND FORMER ADMIRAL OF THE DAWN COURT. YOU COMMAND THE LARGEST INDEPENDENT SKYFLEET IN THE KNOWN WORLD.

ARCANIC GIFT: IRON SKIN.

I COULD GO ON?

OH, NO NEED.

YOU'RE A STUDY, DAUGHTER.

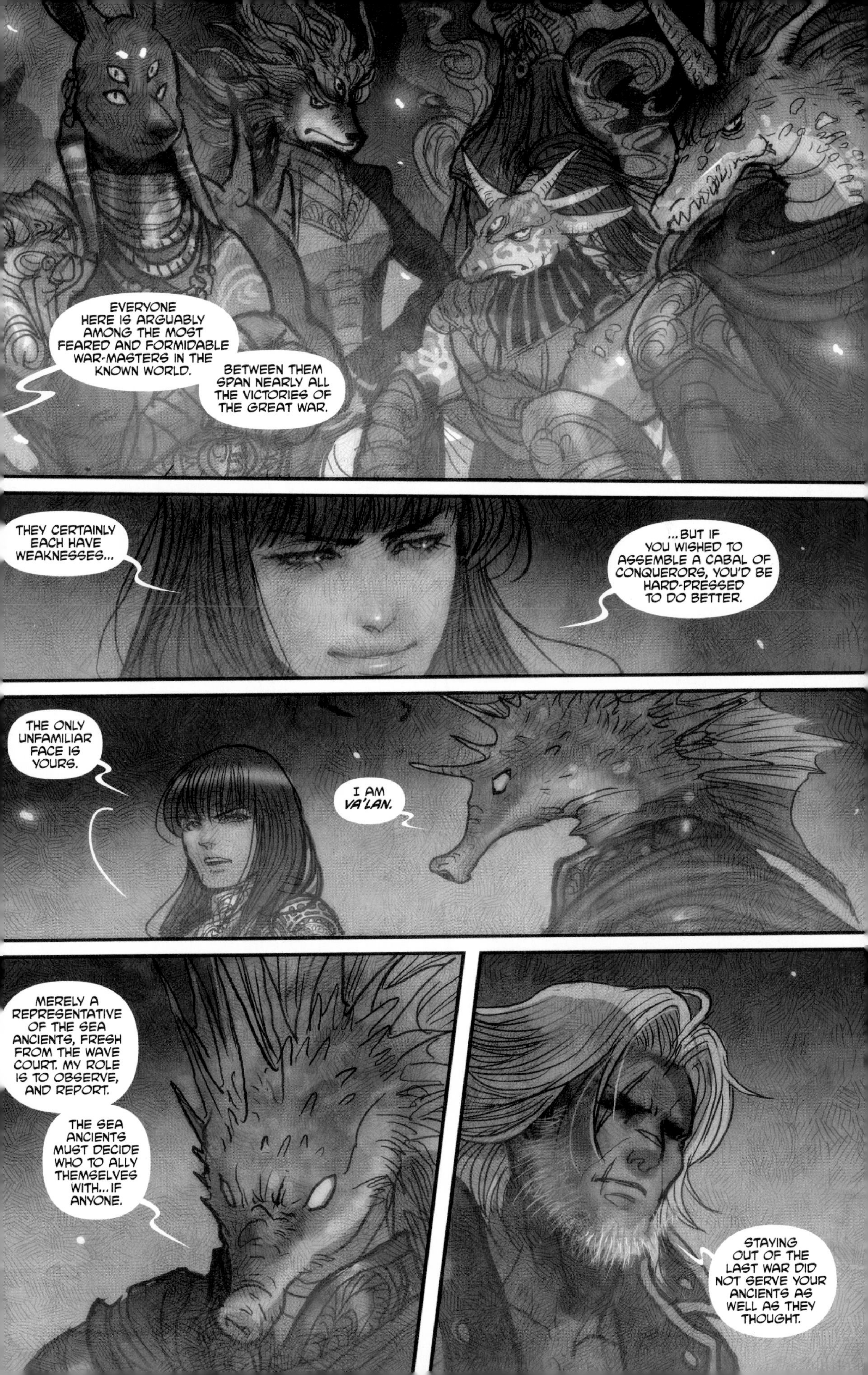
EVERYONE HERE IS ARGUABLY AMONG THE MOST FEARED AND FORMIDABLE WAR-MASTERS IN THE KNOWN WORLD.
BETWEEN THEM SPAN NEARLY ALL THE VICTORIES OF THE GREAT WAR.
THEY CERTAINLY EACH HAVE WEAKNESSES...
...BUT IF YOU WISHED TO ASSEMBLE A CABAL OF CONQUERORS, YOU'D BE HARD-PRESSED TO DO BETTER.
THE ONLY UNFAMILIAR FACE IS YOURS.
I AM *VA'LAN.*
MERELY A REPRESENTATIVE OF THE SEA ANCIENTS, FRESH FROM THE WAVE COURT. MY ROLE IS TO OBSERVE, AND REPORT.
THE SEA ANCIENTS MUST DECIDE WHO TO ALLY THEMSELVES WITH... IF ANYONE.
STAYING OUT OF THE LAST WAR DID NOT SERVE YOUR ANCIENTS AS WELL AS THEY THOUGHT.

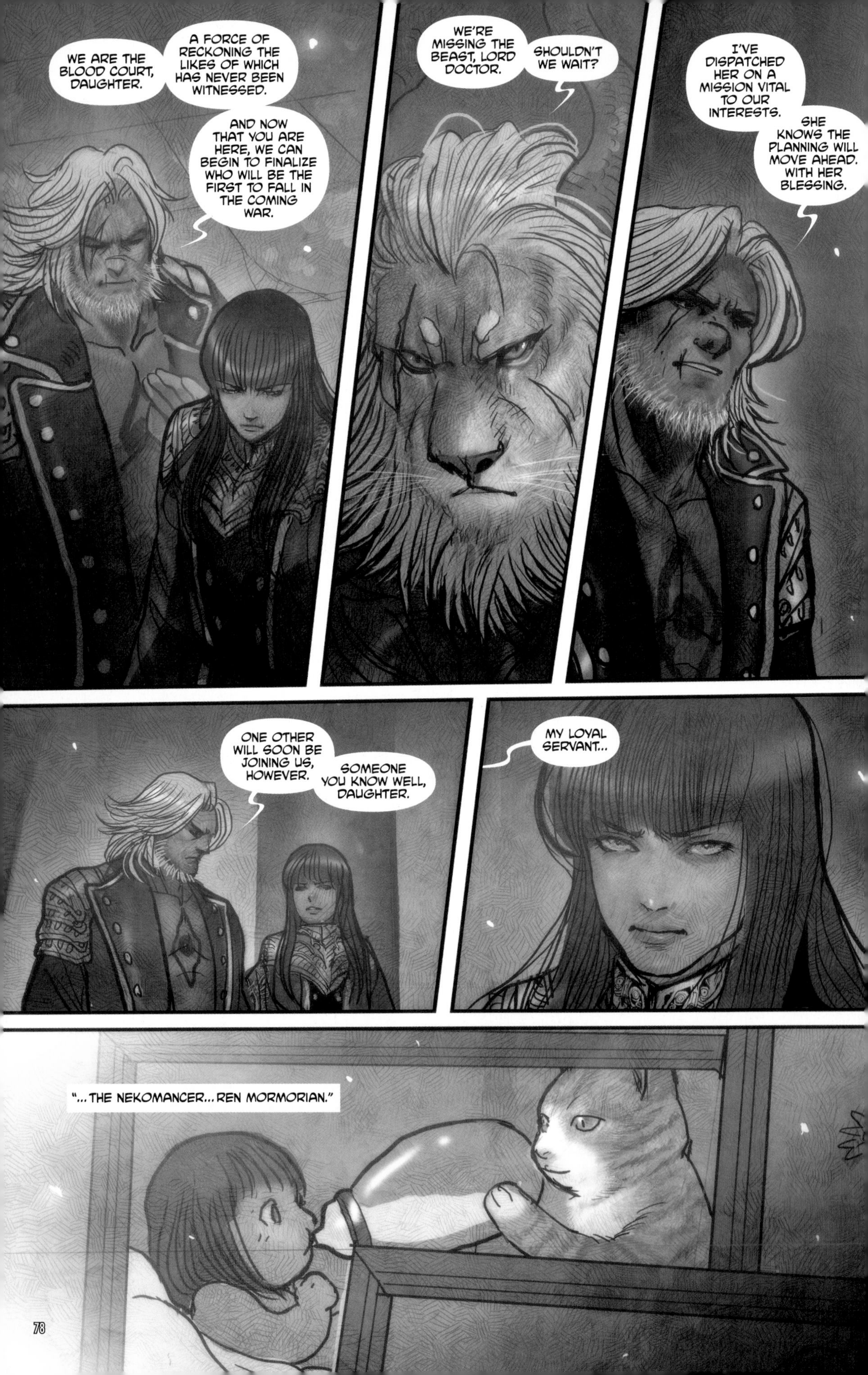
WE ARE THE BLOOD COURT, DAUGHTER.
A FORCE OF RECKONING THE LIKES OF WHICH HAS NEVER BEEN WITNESSED.
AND NOW THAT YOU ARE HERE, WE CAN BEGIN TO FINALIZE WHO WILL BE THE FIRST TO FALL IN THE COMING WAR.
WE'RE MISSING THE BEAST, LORD DOCTOR.
SHOULDN'T WE WAIT?
I'VE DISPATCHED HER ON A MISSION VITAL TO OUR INTERESTS.
SHE KNOWS THE PLANNING WILL MOVE AHEAD. WITH HER BLESSING.
ONE OTHER WILL SOON BE JOINING US, HOWEVER.
SOMEONE YOU KNOW WELL, DAUGHTER.
MY LOYAL SERVANT...
"...THE NEKOMANCER...REN MORMORIAN."

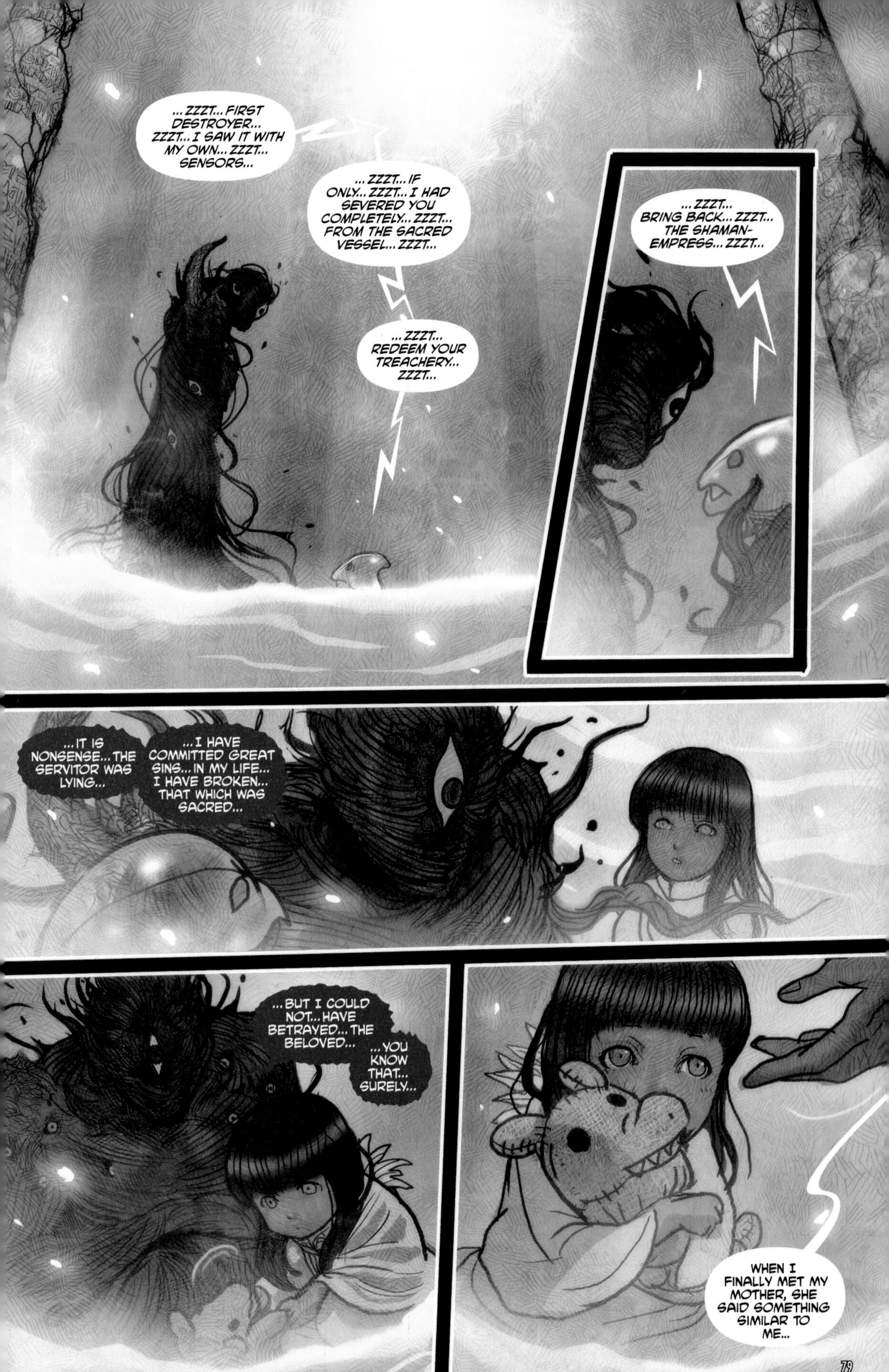
...ZZZT... FIRST DESTROYER... ZZZT... I SAW IT WITH MY OWN... ZZZT... SENSORS...
...ZZZT... IF ONLY... ZZZT... I HAD SEVERED YOU COMPLETELY... ZZZT... FROM THE SACRED VESSEL... ZZZT...
...ZZZT... REDEEM YOUR TREACHERY... ZZZT...
...ZZZT... BRING BACK... ZZZT... THE SHAMAN-EMPRESS... ZZZT...
...IT IS NONSENSE... THE SERVITOR WAS LYING...
...I HAVE COMMITTED GREAT SINS... IN MY LIFE... I HAVE BROKEN... THAT WHICH WAS SACRED...
...BUT I COULD NOT... HAVE BETRAYED... THE BELOVED...
...YOU KNOW THAT... SURELY...
WHEN I FINALLY MET MY MOTHER, SHE SAID SOMETHING SIMILAR TO ME...

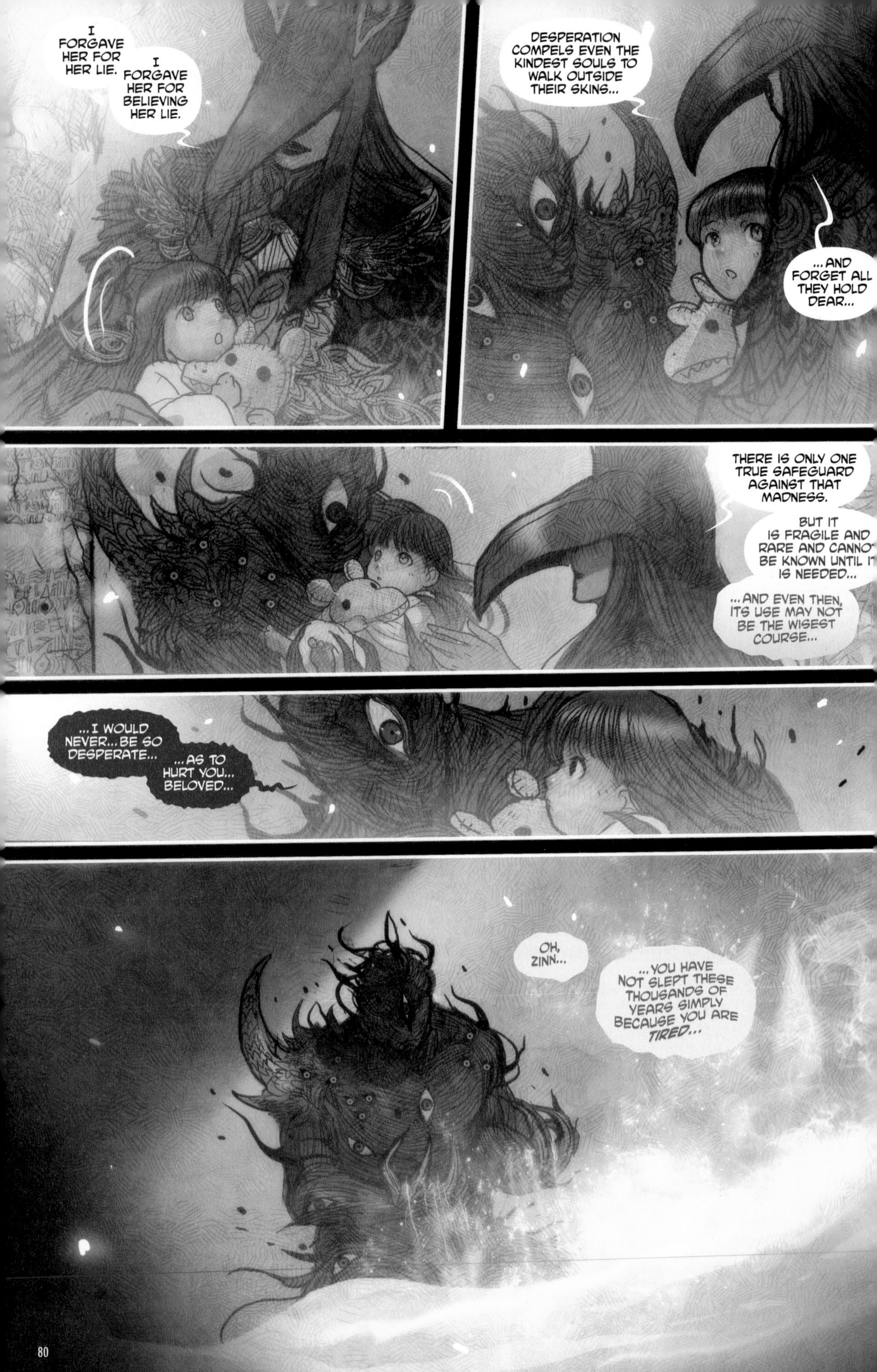
I FORGAVE HER FOR HER LIE.
I FORGAVE HER FOR BELIEVING HER LIE.
DESPERATION COMPELS EVEN THE KINDEST SOULS TO WALK OUTSIDE THEIR SKINS...
...AND FORGET ALL THEY HOLD DEAR...
THERE IS ONLY ONE TRUE SAFEGUARD AGAINST THAT MADNESS.
BUT IT IS FRAGILE AND RARE AND CANNOT BE KNOWN UNTIL IT IS NEEDED...
...AND EVEN THEN, ITS USE MAY NOT BE THE WISEST COURSE...
...I WOULD NEVER...BE SO DESPERATE...
...AS TO HURT YOU... BELOVED...
OH, ZINN...
...YOU HAVE NOT SLEPT THESE THOUSANDS OF YEARS SIMPLY BECAUSE YOU ARE *TIRED*...

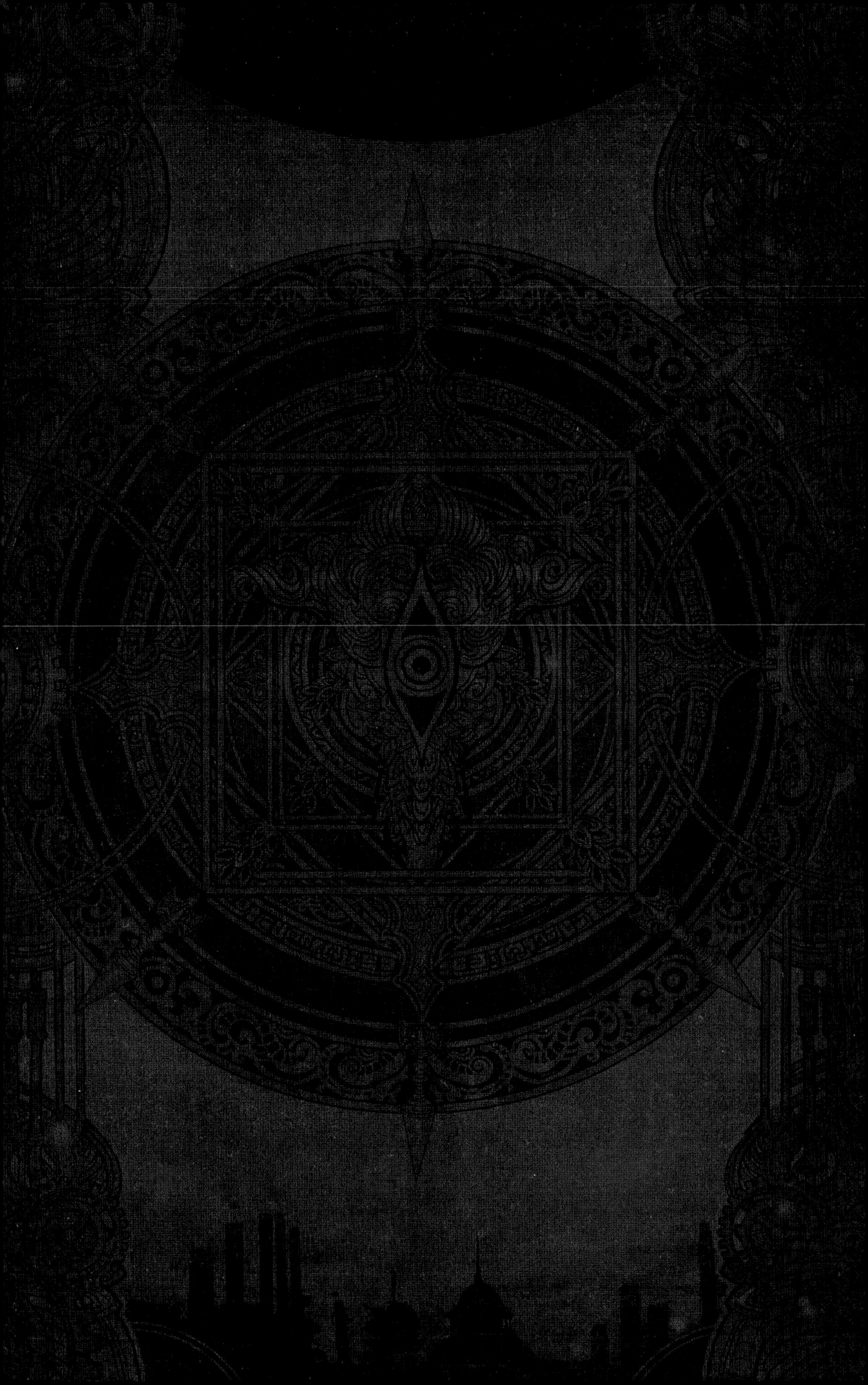

Archival research from the esteemed **Professor Tam Tam,** former First Record-Keeper of the Is'hami Temple, and learned contemporary of Namron Black Claw...

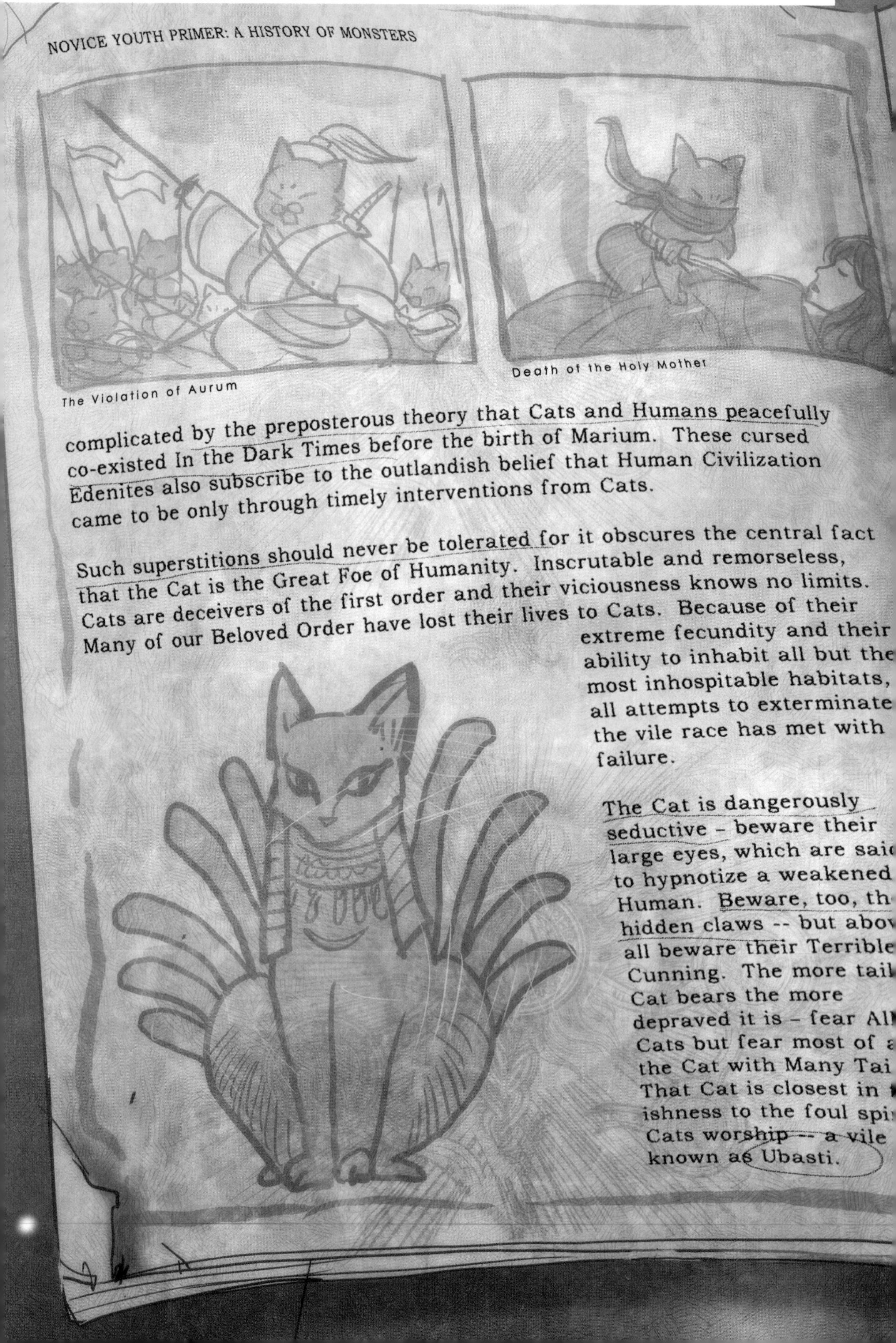

NOVICE YOUTH PRIMER: A HISTORY OF MONSTERS

The Violation of Aurum

Death of the Holy Mother

complicated by the preposterous theory that Cats and Humans peacefully co-existed In the Dark Times before the birth of Marium. These cursed Edenites also subscribe to the outlandish belief that Human Civilization came to be only through timely interventions from Cats.

Such superstitions should never be tolerated for it obscures the central fact that the Cat is the Great Foe of Humanity. Inscrutable and remorseless, Cats are deceivers of the first order and their viciousness knows no limits. Many of our Beloved Order have lost their lives to Cats. Because of their extreme fecundity and their ability to inhabit all but the most inhospitable habitats, all attempts to exterminate the vile race has met with failure.

The Cat is dangerously seductive – beware their large eyes, which are sai
to hypnotize a weakened
Human. Beware, too, th
hidden claws -- but abo
all beware their Terrible
Cunning. The more tai
Cat bears the more
depraved it is – fear Al
Cats but fear most of
the Cat with Many Tai
That Cat is closest in
ishness to the foul spi
Cats worship -- a vile
known as Ubasti.

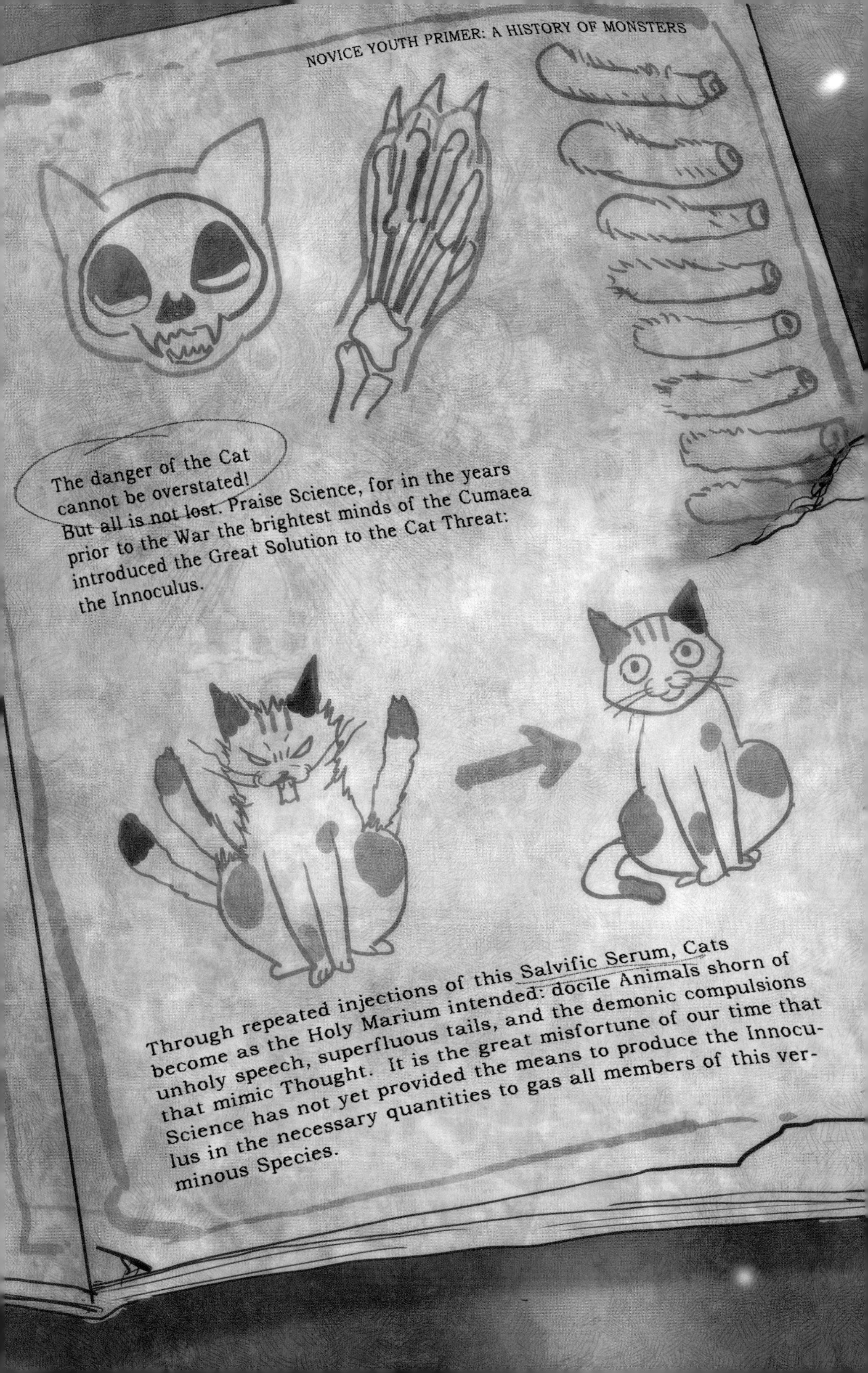
NOVICE YOUTH PRIMER: A HISTORY OF MONSTERS
The danger of the Cat cannot be overstated!
But all is not lost. Praise Science, for in the years prior to the War the brightest minds of the Cumaea introduced the Great Solution to the Cat Threat: the Innoculus.
Through repeated injections of this Salvific Serum, Cats become as the Holy Marium intended: docile Animals shorn of unholy speech, superfluous tails, and the demonic compulsions that mimic Thought. It is the great misfortune of our time that Science has not yet provided the means to produce the Innoculus in the necessary quantities to gas all members of this verminous Species.

CHAPTER TWENTY-TWO

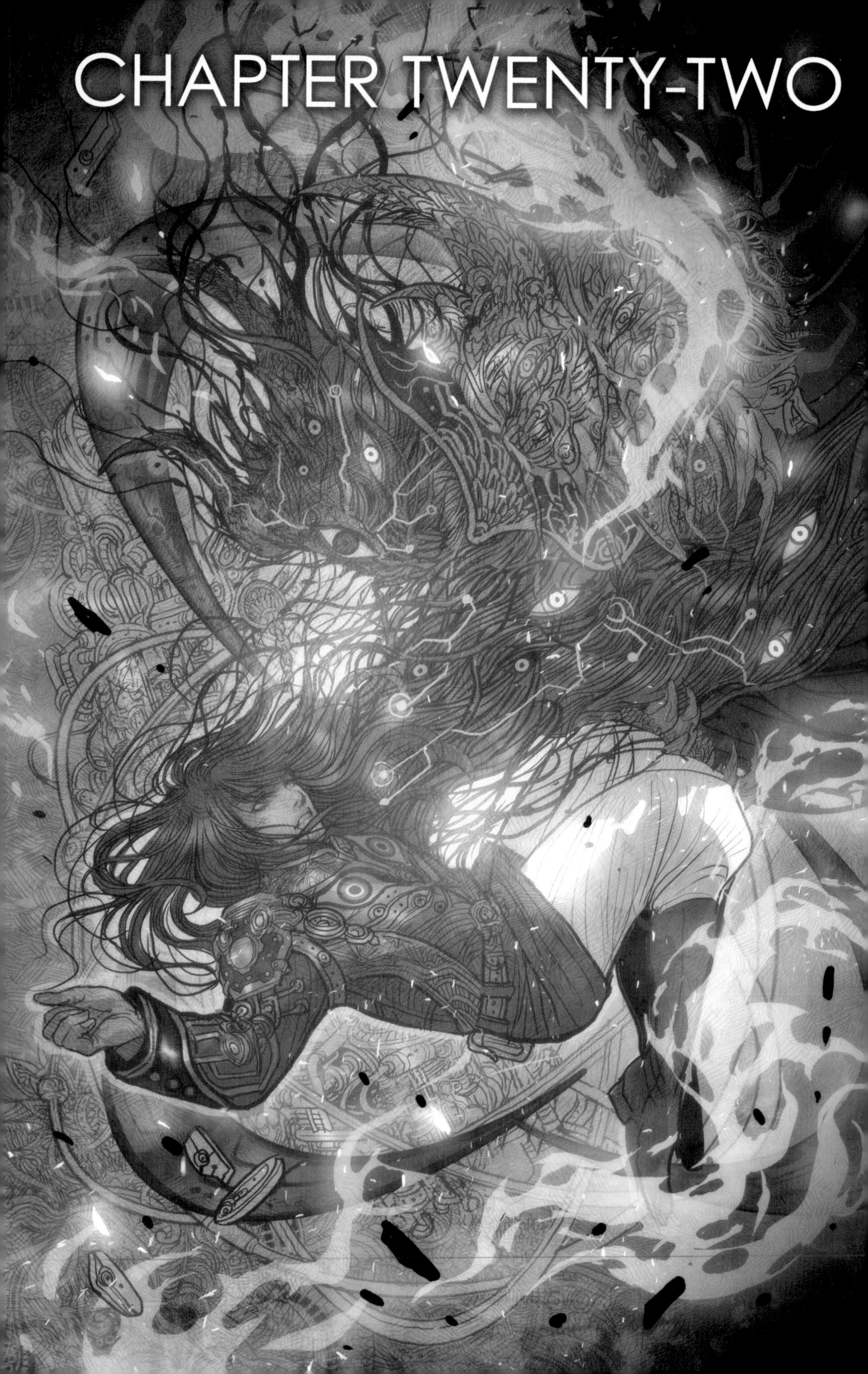

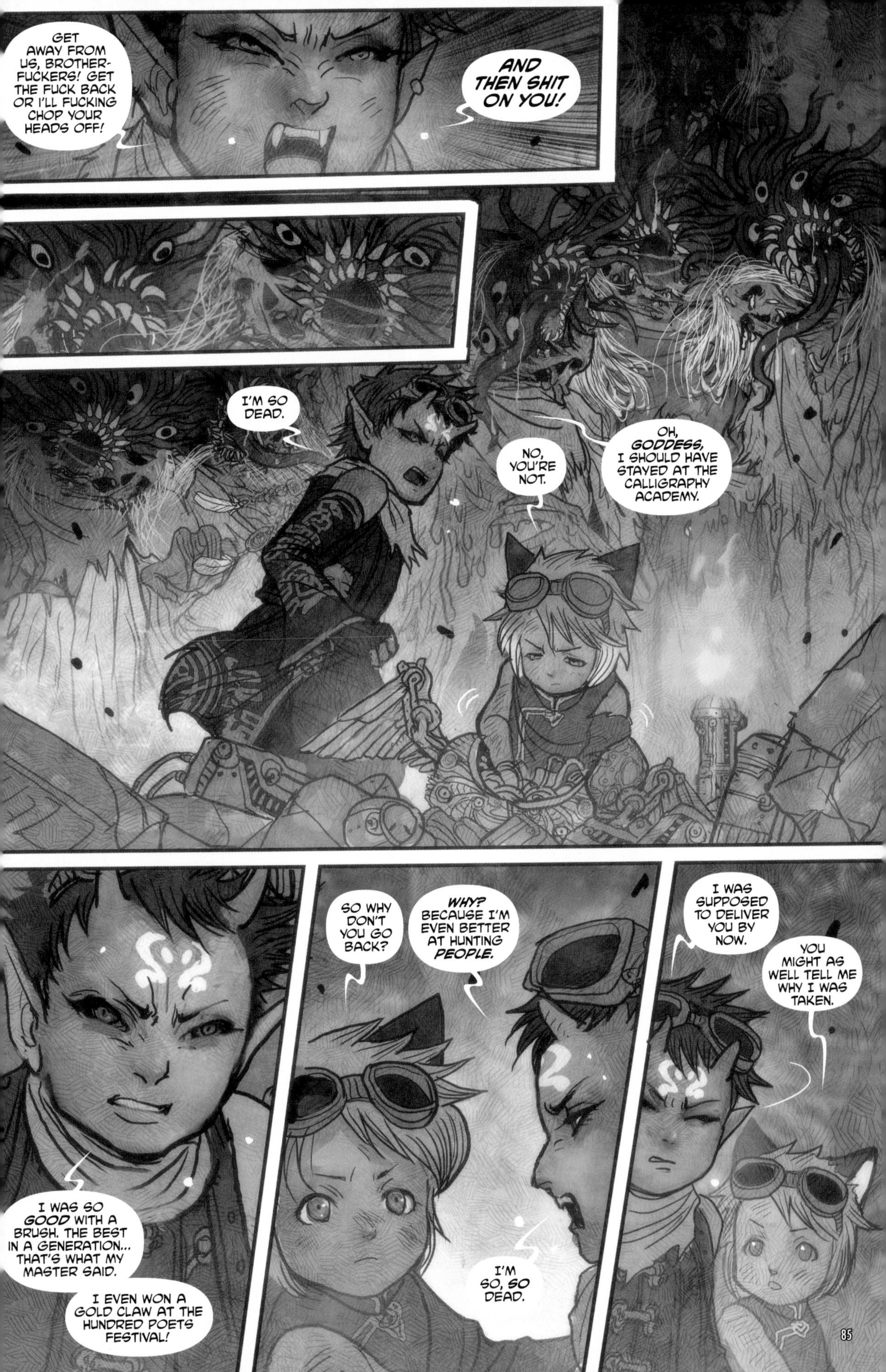
GET AWAY FROM US, BROTHER-FUCKERS! GET THE FUCK BACK OR I'LL FUCKING CHOP YOUR HEADS OFF!
AND THEN SHIT ON YOU!
I'M SO DEAD.
NO, YOU'RE NOT.
OH, GODDESS, I SHOULD HAVE STAYED AT THE CALLIGRAPHY ACADEMY.
I WAS SO GOOD WITH A BRUSH. THE BEST IN A GENERATION... THAT'S WHAT MY MASTER SAID.
I EVEN WON A GOLD CLAW AT THE HUNDRED POETS FESTIVAL!
SO WHY DON'T YOU GO BACK?
WHY? BECAUSE I'M EVEN BETTER AT HUNTING PEOPLE.
I'M SO, SO DEAD.
I WAS SUPPOSED TO DELIVER YOU BY NOW.
YOU MIGHT AS WELL TELL ME WHY I WAS TAKEN.

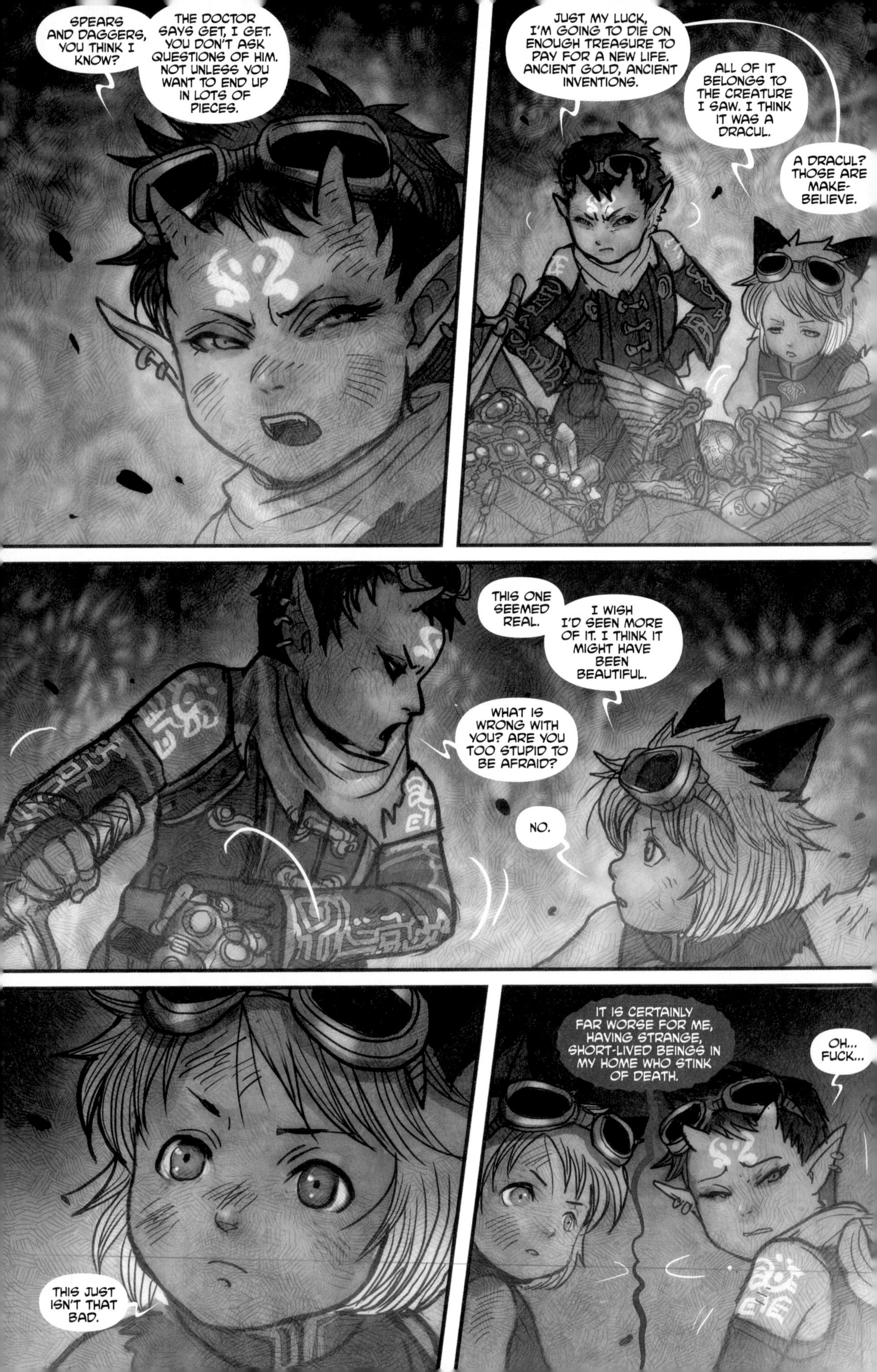
SPEARS AND DAGGERS, YOU THINK I KNOW?
THE DOCTOR SAYS GET, I GET. YOU DON'T ASK QUESTIONS OF HIM. NOT UNLESS YOU WANT TO END UP IN LOTS OF PIECES.
JUST MY LUCK, I'M GOING TO DIE ON ENOUGH TREASURE TO PAY FOR A NEW LIFE. ANCIENT GOLD, ANCIENT INVENTIONS.
ALL OF IT BELONGS TO THE CREATURE I SAW. I THINK IT WAS A DRACUL.
A DRACUL? THOSE ARE MAKE-BELIEVE.
THIS ONE SEEMED REAL.
I WISH I'D SEEN MORE OF IT. I THINK IT MIGHT HAVE BEEN BEAUTIFUL.
WHAT IS WRONG WITH YOU? ARE YOU TOO STUPID TO BE AFRAID?
NO.
THIS JUST ISN'T THAT BAD.
IT IS CERTAINLY FAR WORSE FOR ME, HAVING STRANGE, SHORT-LIVED BEINGS IN MY HOME WHO STINK OF DEATH.
OH... FUCK...

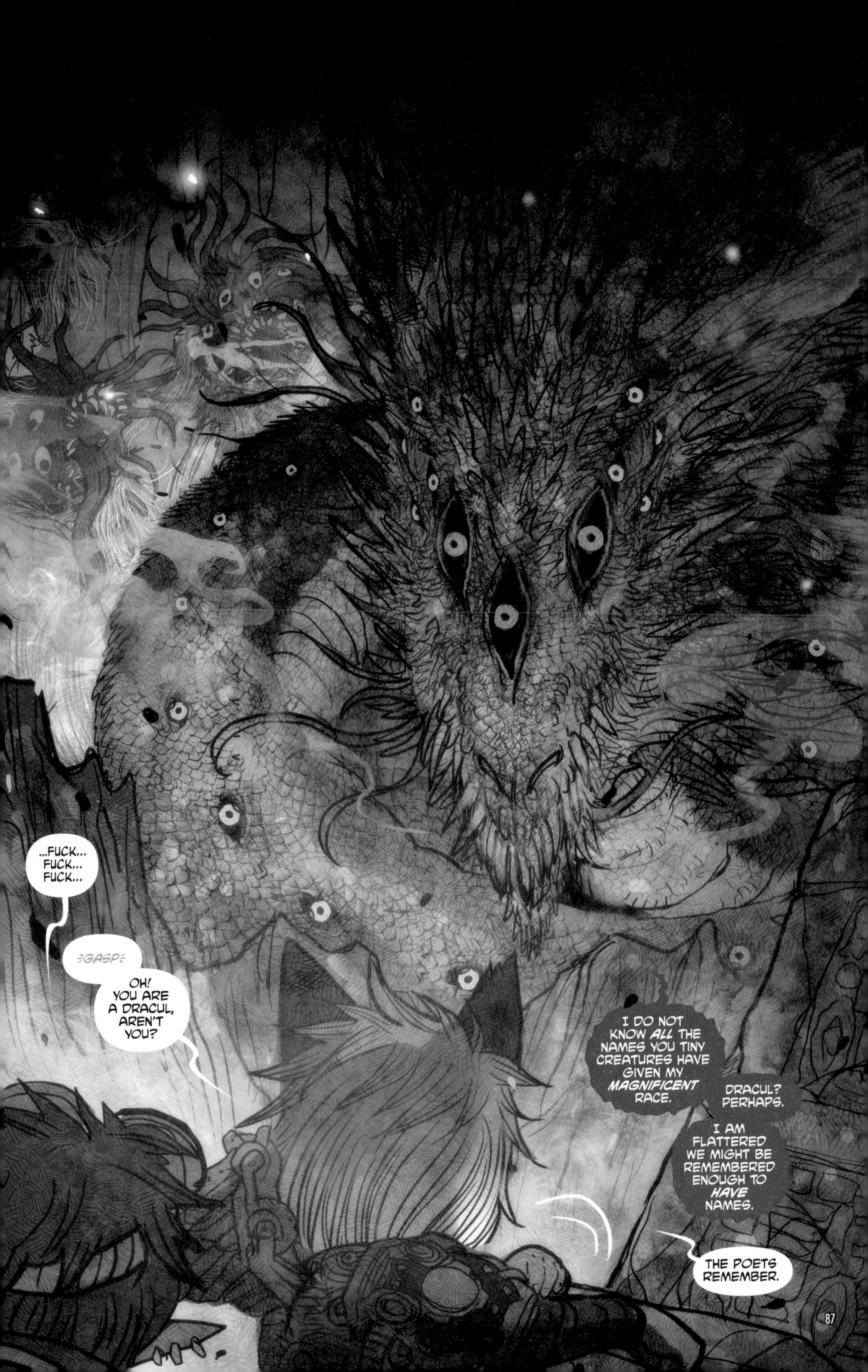
...FUCK... FUCK... FUCK...
GASP
OH! YOU ARE A DRACUL, AREN'T YOU?
I DO NOT KNOW ALL THE NAMES YOU TINY CREATURES HAVE GIVEN MY MAGNIFICENT RACE.
DRACUL? PERHAPS.
I AM FLATTERED WE MIGHT BE REMEMBERED ENOUGH TO HAVE NAMES.
THE POETS REMEMBER.

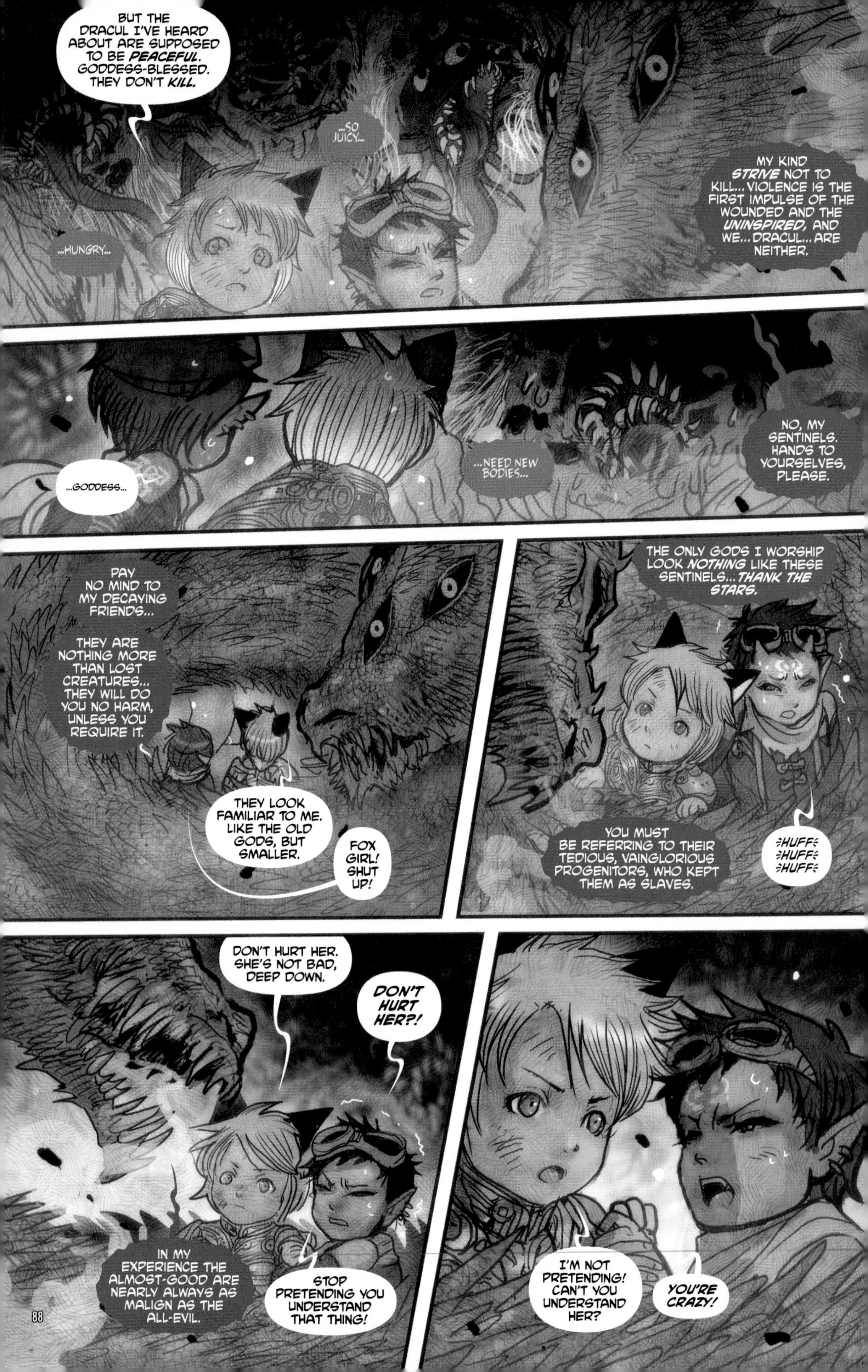
BUT THE DRACUL I'VE HEARD ABOUT ARE SUPPOSED TO BE PEACEFUL. GODDESS-BLESSED. THEY DON'T KILL.
...SO JUICY...
...HUNGRY...
MY KIND STRIVE NOT TO KILL... VIOLENCE IS THE FIRST IMPULSE OF THE WOUNDED AND THE UNINSPIRED, AND WE... DRACUL... ARE NEITHER.
...GODDESS...
...NEED NEW BODIES...
NO, MY SENTINELS. HANDS TO YOURSELVES, PLEASE.
PAY NO MIND TO MY DECAYING FRIENDS...
THEY ARE NOTHING MORE THAN LOST CREATURES... THEY WILL DO YOU NO HARM, UNLESS YOU REQUIRE IT.
THEY LOOK FAMILIAR TO ME. LIKE THE OLD GODS, BUT SMALLER.
FOX GIRL! SHUT UP!
THE ONLY GODS I WORSHIP LOOK NOTHING LIKE THESE SENTINELS... THANK THE STARS.
YOU MUST BE REFERRING TO THEIR TEDIOUS, VAINGLORIOUS PROGENITORS, WHO KEPT THEM AS SLAVES.
HUFF HUFF HUFF
DON'T HURT HER. SHE'S NOT BAD, DEEP DOWN.
DON'T HURT HER?!
IN MY EXPERIENCE THE ALMOST-GOOD ARE NEARLY ALWAYS AS MALIGN AS THE ALL-EVIL.
STOP PRETENDING YOU UNDERSTAND THAT THING!
I'M NOT PRETENDING! CAN'T YOU UNDERSTAND HER?
YOU'RE CRAZY!

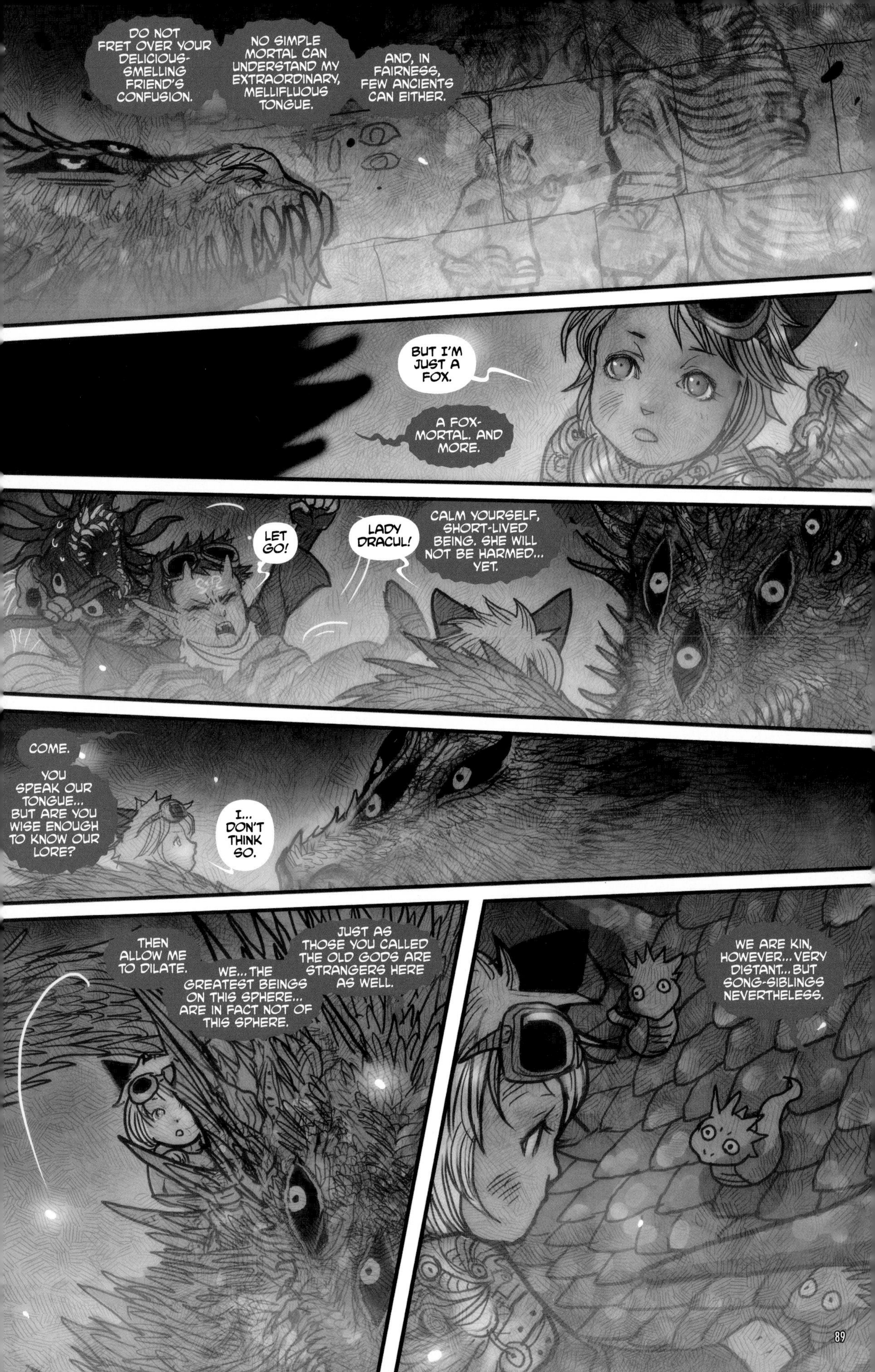
DO NOT FRET OVER YOUR DELICIOUS-SMELLING FRIEND'S CONFUSION.
NO SIMPLE MORTAL CAN UNDERSTAND MY EXTRAORDINARY, MELLIFLUOUS TONGUE.
AND, IN FAIRNESS, FEW ANCIENTS CAN EITHER.
BUT I'M JUST A FOX.
A FOX-MORTAL. AND MORE.
LET GO!
LADY DRACUL!
CALM YOURSELF, SHORT-LIVED BEING. SHE WILL NOT BE HARMED... YET.
COME.
YOU SPEAK OUR TONGUE... BUT ARE YOU WISE ENOUGH TO KNOW OUR LORE?
I... DON'T THINK SO.
THEN ALLOW ME TO DILATE.
WE... THE GREATEST BEINGS ON THIS SPHERE... ARE IN FACT NOT OF THIS SPHERE.
JUST AS THOSE YOU CALLED THE OLD GODS ARE STRANGERS HERE AS WELL.
WE ARE KIN, HOWEVER... VERY DISTANT... BUT SONG-SIBLINGS NEVERTHELESS.

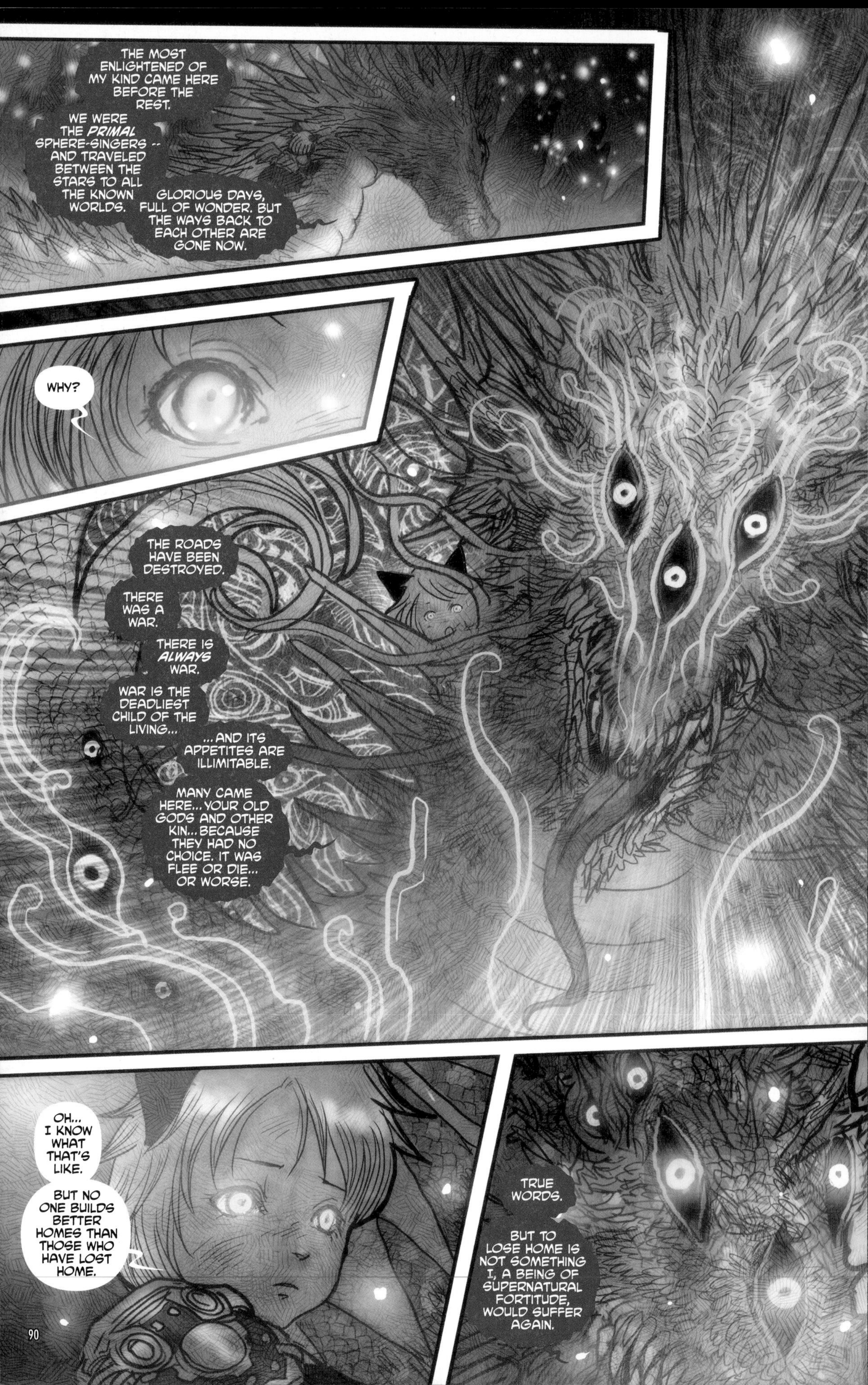
THE MOST ENLIGHTENED OF MY KIND CAME HERE BEFORE THE REST.
WE WERE THE PRIMAL SPHERE-SINGERS -- AND TRAVELED BETWEEN THE STARS TO ALL THE KNOWN WORLDS.
GLORIOUS DAYS, FULL OF WONDER. BUT THE WAYS BACK TO EACH OTHER ARE GONE NOW.
WHY?
THE ROADS HAVE BEEN DESTROYED.
THERE WAS A WAR.
THERE IS ALWAYS WAR.
WAR IS THE DEADLIEST CHILD OF THE LIVING...
...AND ITS APPETITES ARE ILLIMITABLE.
MANY CAME HERE... YOUR OLD GODS AND OTHER KIN... BECAUSE THEY HAD NO CHOICE. IT WAS FLEE OR DIE... OR WORSE.
OH... I KNOW WHAT THAT'S LIKE.
BUT NO ONE BUILDS BETTER HOMES THAN THOSE WHO HAVE LOST HOME.
TRUE WORDS.
BUT TO LOSE HOME IS NOT SOMETHING I, A BEING OF SUPERNATURAL FORTITUDE, WOULD SUFFER AGAIN.

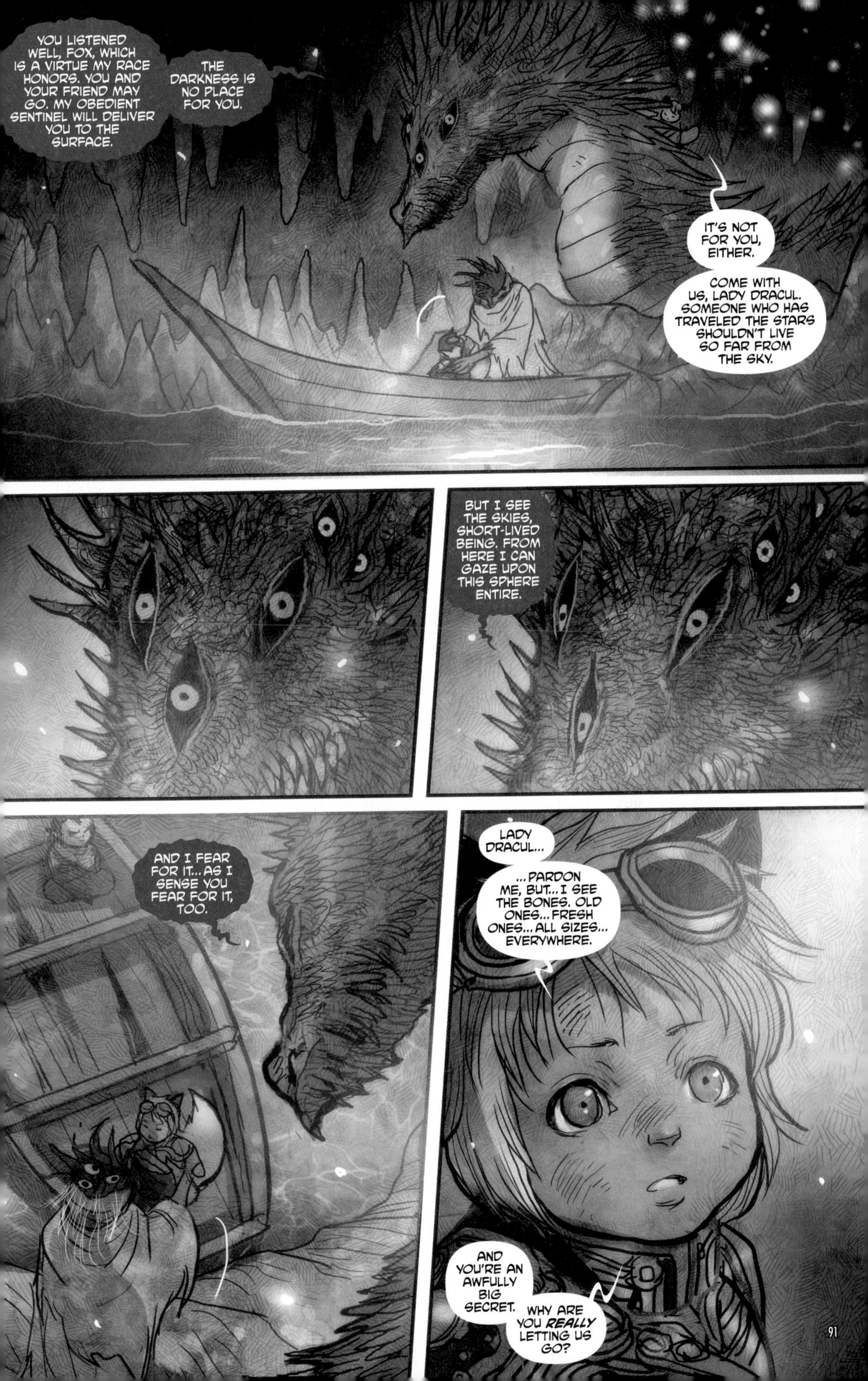
YOU LISTENED WELL, FOX, WHICH IS A VIRTUE MY RACE HONORS. YOU AND YOUR FRIEND MAY GO. MY OBEDIENT SENTINEL WILL DELIVER YOU TO THE SURFACE.
THE DARKNESS IS NO PLACE FOR YOU.
IT'S NOT FOR YOU, EITHER.
COME WITH US, LADY DRACUL. SOMEONE WHO HAS TRAVELED THE STARS SHOULDN'T LIVE SO FAR FROM THE SKY.
BUT I SEE THE SKIES, SHORT-LIVED BEING. FROM HERE I CAN GAZE UPON THIS SPHERE ENTIRE.
AND I FEAR FOR IT... AS I SENSE YOU FEAR FOR IT, TOO.
LADY DRACUL...
...PARDON ME, BUT... I SEE THE BONES. OLD ONES... FRESH ONES... ALL SIZES... EVERYWHERE.
AND YOU'RE AN AWFULLY BIG SECRET.
WHY ARE YOU *REALLY* LETTING US GO?

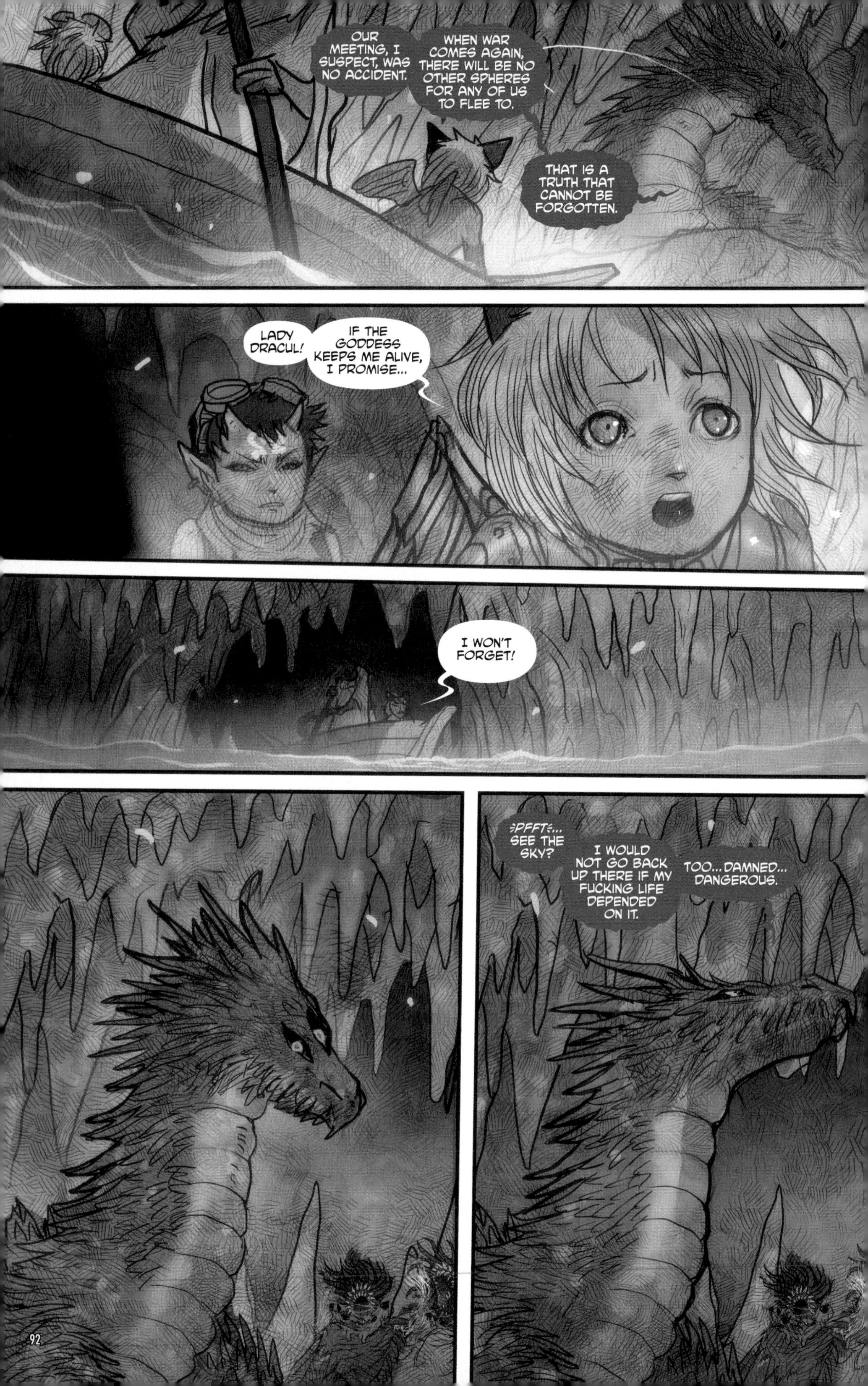
OUR MEETING, I SUSPECT, WAS NO ACCIDENT.
WHEN WAR COMES AGAIN, THERE WILL BE NO OTHER SPHERES FOR ANY OF US TO FLEE TO.
THAT IS A TRUTH THAT CANNOT BE FORGOTTEN.
LADY DRACUL!
IF THE GODDESS KEEPS ME ALIVE, I PROMISE...
I WON'T FORGET!
PFFT... SEE THE SKY?
I WOULD NOT GO BACK UP THERE IF MY FUCKING LIFE DEPENDED ON IT.
TOO...DAMNED... DANGEROUS.

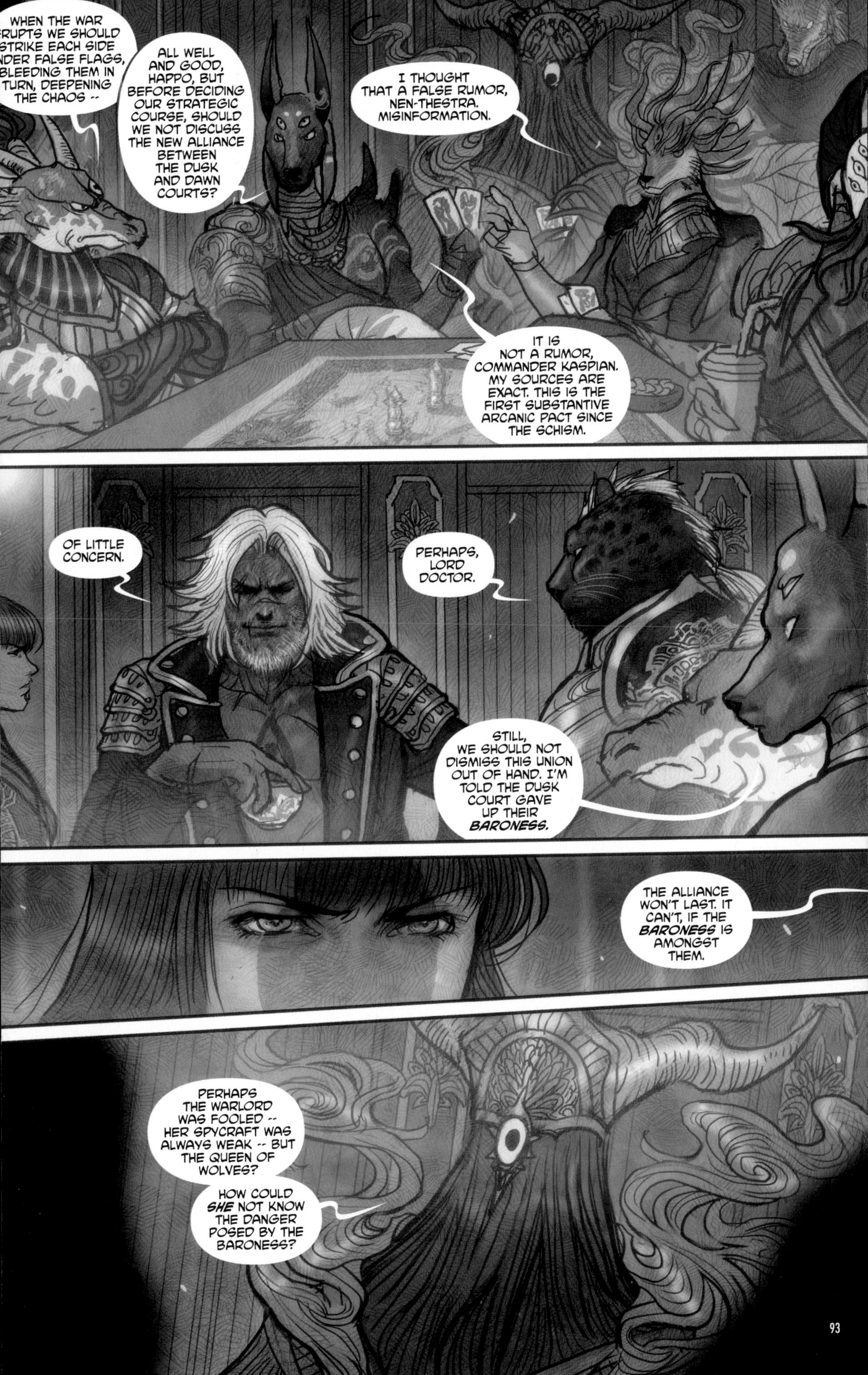
WHEN THE WAR ERUPTS WE SHOULD STRIKE EACH SIDE UNDER FALSE FLAGS, BLEEDING THEM IN TURN, DEEPENING THE CHAOS --
ALL WELL AND GOOD, HAPPO, BUT BEFORE DECIDING OUR STRATEGIC COURSE, SHOULD WE NOT DISCUSS THE NEW ALLIANCE BETWEEN THE DUSK AND DAWN COURTS?
I THOUGHT THAT A FALSE RUMOR, NEN-THESTRA. MISINFORMATION.
IT IS NOT A RUMOR, COMMANDER KASPIAN. MY SOURCES ARE EXACT. THIS IS THE FIRST SUBSTANTIVE ARCANIC PACT SINCE THE SCHISM.
OF LITTLE CONCERN.
PERHAPS, LORD DOCTOR.
STILL, WE SHOULD NOT DISMISS THIS UNION OUT OF HAND. I'M TOLD THE DUSK COURT GAVE UP THEIR BARONESS.
THE ALLIANCE WON'T LAST. IT CAN'T, IF THE BARONESS IS AMONGST THEM.
PERHAPS THE WARLORD WAS FOOLED -- HER SPYCRAFT WAS ALWAYS WEAK -- BUT THE QUEEN OF WOLVES?
HOW COULD SHE NOT KNOW THE DANGER POSED BY THE BARONESS?

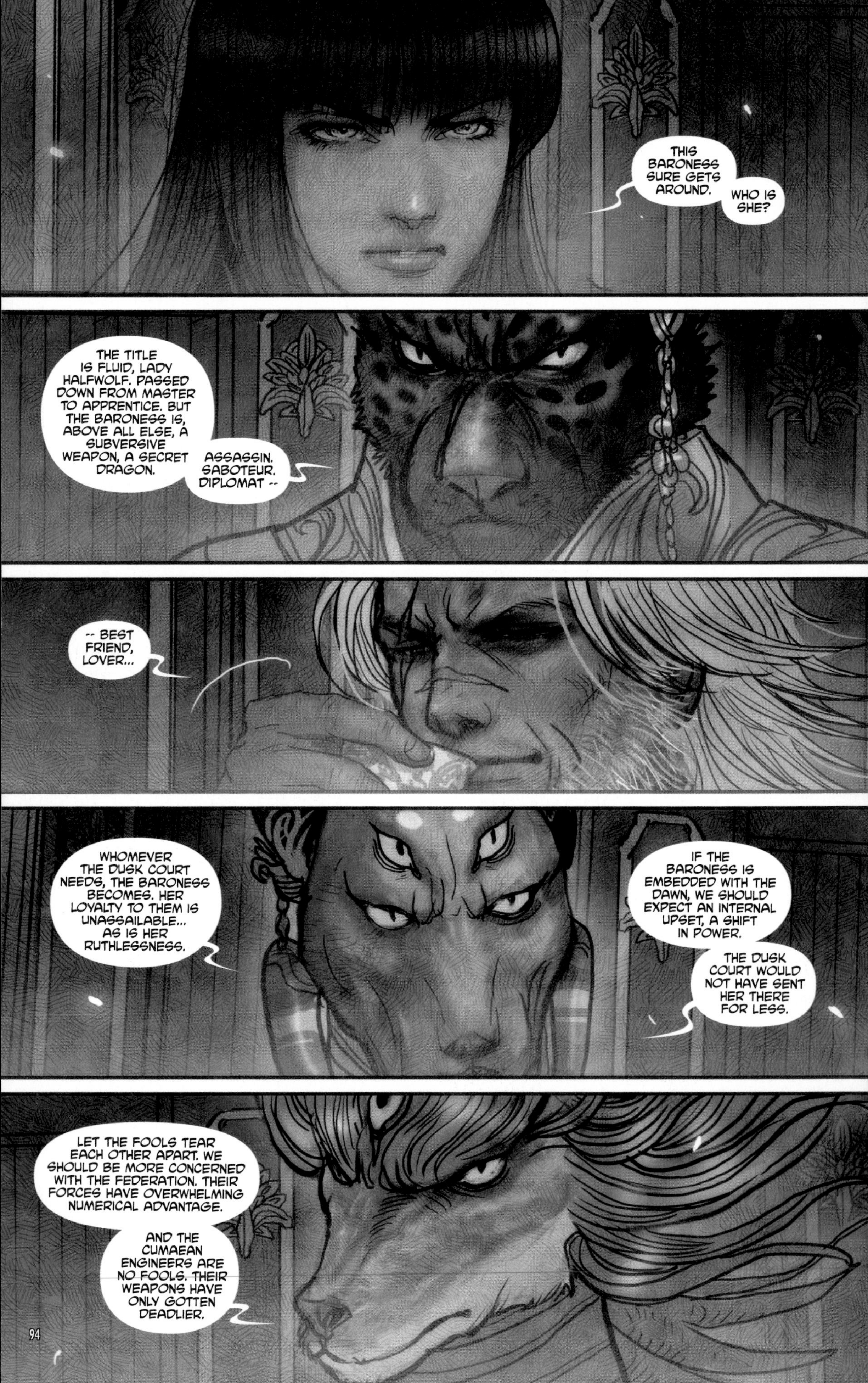
THIS BARONESS SURE GETS AROUND.
WHO IS SHE?
THE TITLE IS FLUID, LADY HALFWOLF. PASSED DOWN FROM MASTER TO APPRENTICE. BUT THE BARONESS IS, ABOVE ALL ELSE, A SUBVERSIVE WEAPON, A SECRET DRAGON.
ASSASSIN. SABOTEUR. DIPLOMAT --
-- BEST FRIEND, LOVER...
WHOMEVER THE DUSK COURT NEEDS, THE BARONESS BECOMES. HER LOYALTY TO THEM IS UNASSAILABLE... AS IS HER RUTHLESSNESS.
IF THE BARONESS IS EMBEDDED WITH THE DAWN, WE SHOULD EXPECT AN INTERNAL UPSET, A SHIFT IN POWER.
THE DUSK COURT WOULD NOT HAVE SENT HER THERE FOR LESS.
LET THE FOOLS TEAR EACH OTHER APART. WE SHOULD BE MORE CONCERNED WITH THE FEDERATION. THEIR FORCES HAVE OVERWHELMING NUMERICAL ADVANTAGE.
AND THE CUMAEAN ENGINEERS ARE NO FOOLS. THEIR WEAPONS HAVE ONLY GOTTEN DEADLIER.

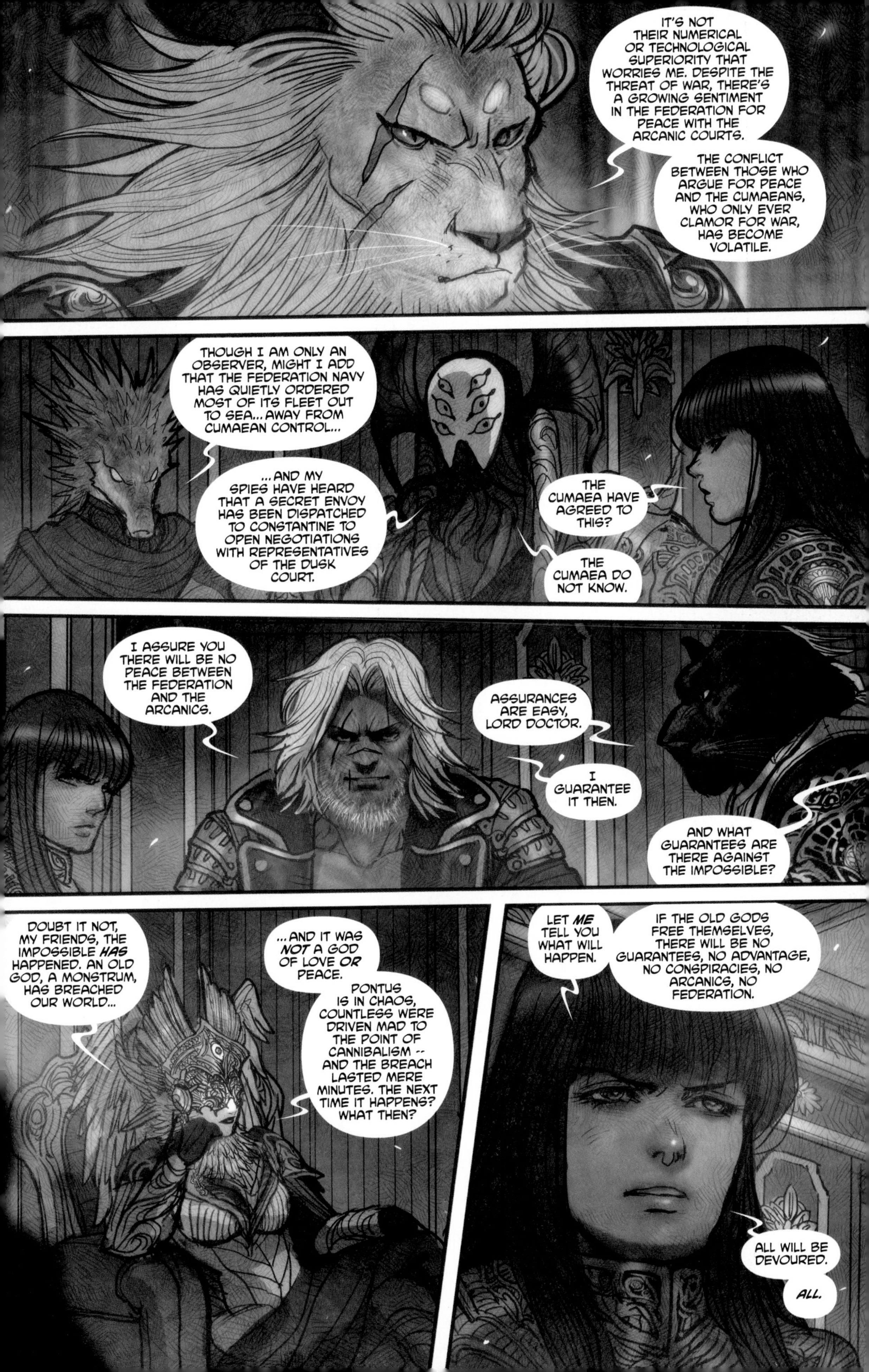

IT'S NOT THEIR NUMERICAL OR TECHNOLOGICAL SUPERIORITY THAT WORRIES ME. DESPITE THE THREAT OF WAR, THERE'S A GROWING SENTIMENT IN THE FEDERATION FOR PEACE WITH THE ARCANIC COURTS.
THE CONFLICT BETWEEN THOSE WHO ARGUE FOR PEACE AND THE CUMAEANS, WHO ONLY EVER CLAMOR FOR WAR, HAS BECOME VOLATILE.
THOUGH I AM ONLY AN OBSERVER, MIGHT I ADD THAT THE FEDERATION NAVY HAS QUIETLY ORDERED MOST OF ITS FLEET OUT TO SEA...AWAY FROM CUMAEAN CONTROL...
...AND MY SPIES HAVE HEARD THAT A SECRET ENVOY HAS BEEN DISPATCHED TO CONSTANTINE TO OPEN NEGOTIATIONS WITH REPRESENTATIVES OF THE DUSK COURT.
THE CUMAEA HAVE AGREED TO THIS?
THE CUMAEA DO NOT KNOW.
I ASSURE YOU THERE WILL BE NO PEACE BETWEEN THE FEDERATION AND THE ARCANICS.
ASSURANCES ARE EASY, LORD DOCTOR.
I GUARANTEE IT THEN.
AND WHAT GUARANTEES ARE THERE AGAINST THE IMPOSSIBLE?
DOUBT IT NOT, MY FRIENDS, THE IMPOSSIBLE *HAS* HAPPENED. AN OLD GOD, A MONSTRUM, HAS BREACHED OUR WORLD...
...AND IT WAS *NOT* A GOD OF LOVE *OR* PEACE.
PONTUS IS IN CHAOS, COUNTLESS WERE DRIVEN MAD TO THE POINT OF CANNIBALISM -- AND THE BREACH LASTED MERE MINUTES. THE NEXT TIME IT HAPPENS? WHAT THEN?
LET *ME* TELL YOU WHAT WILL HAPPEN.
IF THE OLD GODS FREE THEMSELVES, THERE WILL BE NO GUARANTEES, NO ADVANTAGE, NO CONSPIRACIES, NO ARCANICS, NO FEDERATION.
ALL WILL BE DEVOURED.
ALL.

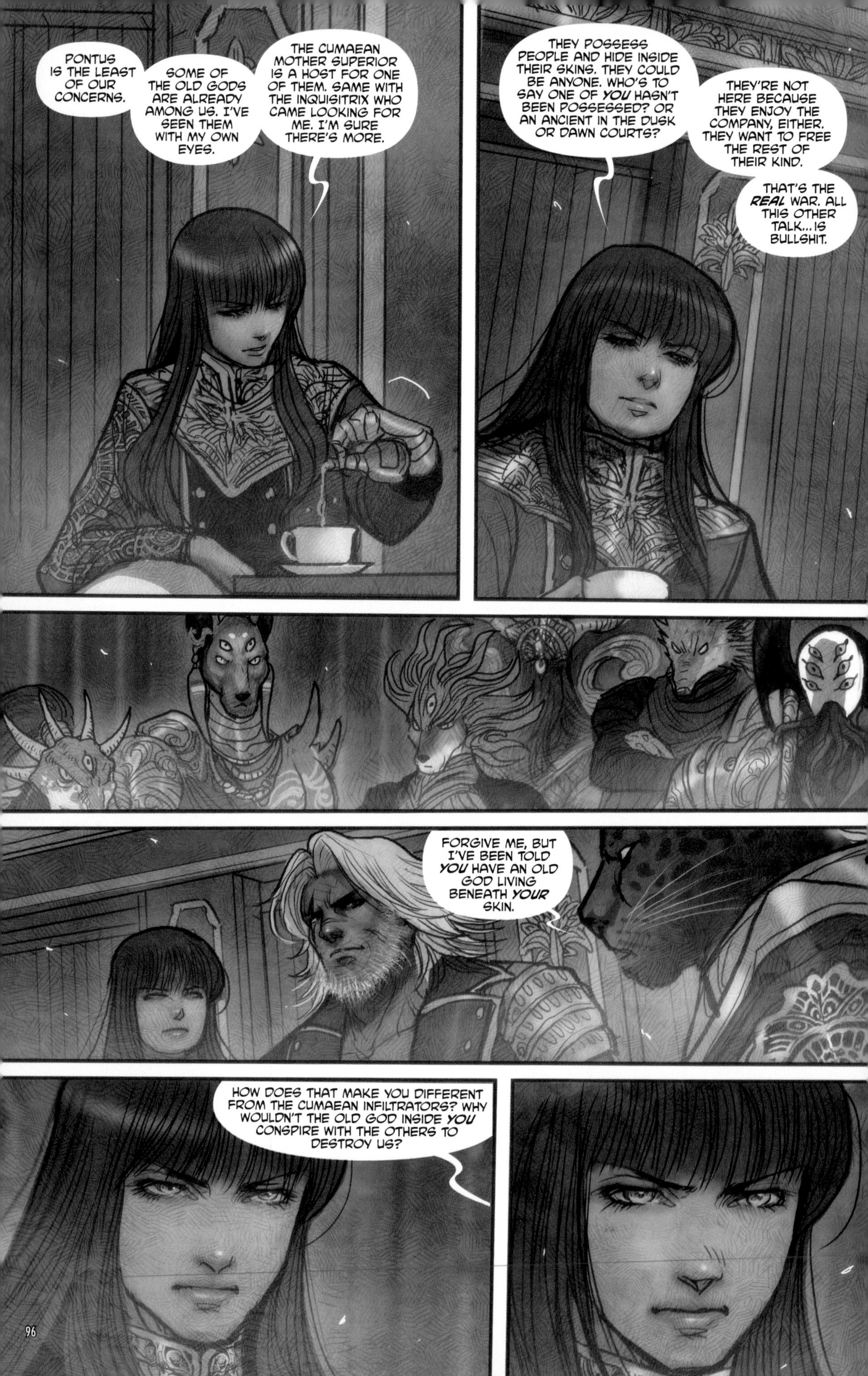
PONTUS IS THE LEAST OF OUR CONCERNS.
SOME OF THE OLD GODS ARE ALREADY AMONG US. I'VE SEEN THEM WITH MY OWN EYES.
THE CUMAEAN MOTHER SUPERIOR IS A HOST FOR ONE OF THEM. SAME WITH THE INQUISITRIX WHO CAME LOOKING FOR ME. I'M SURE THERE'S MORE.
THEY POSSESS PEOPLE AND HIDE INSIDE THEIR SKINS. THEY COULD BE ANYONE. WHO'S TO SAY ONE OF *YOU* HASN'T BEEN POSSESSED? OR AN ANCIENT IN THE DUSK OR DAWN COURTS?
THEY'RE NOT HERE BECAUSE THEY ENJOY THE COMPANY, EITHER. THEY WANT TO FREE THE REST OF THEIR KIND.
THAT'S THE ***REAL*** WAR. ALL THIS OTHER TALK... IS BULLSHIT.
FORGIVE ME, BUT I'VE BEEN TOLD *YOU* HAVE AN OLD GOD LIVING BENEATH *YOUR* SKIN.
HOW DOES THAT MAKE YOU DIFFERENT FROM THE CUMAEAN INFILTRATORS? WHY WOULDN'T THE OLD GOD INSIDE *YOU* CONSPIRE WITH THE OTHERS TO DESTROY US?

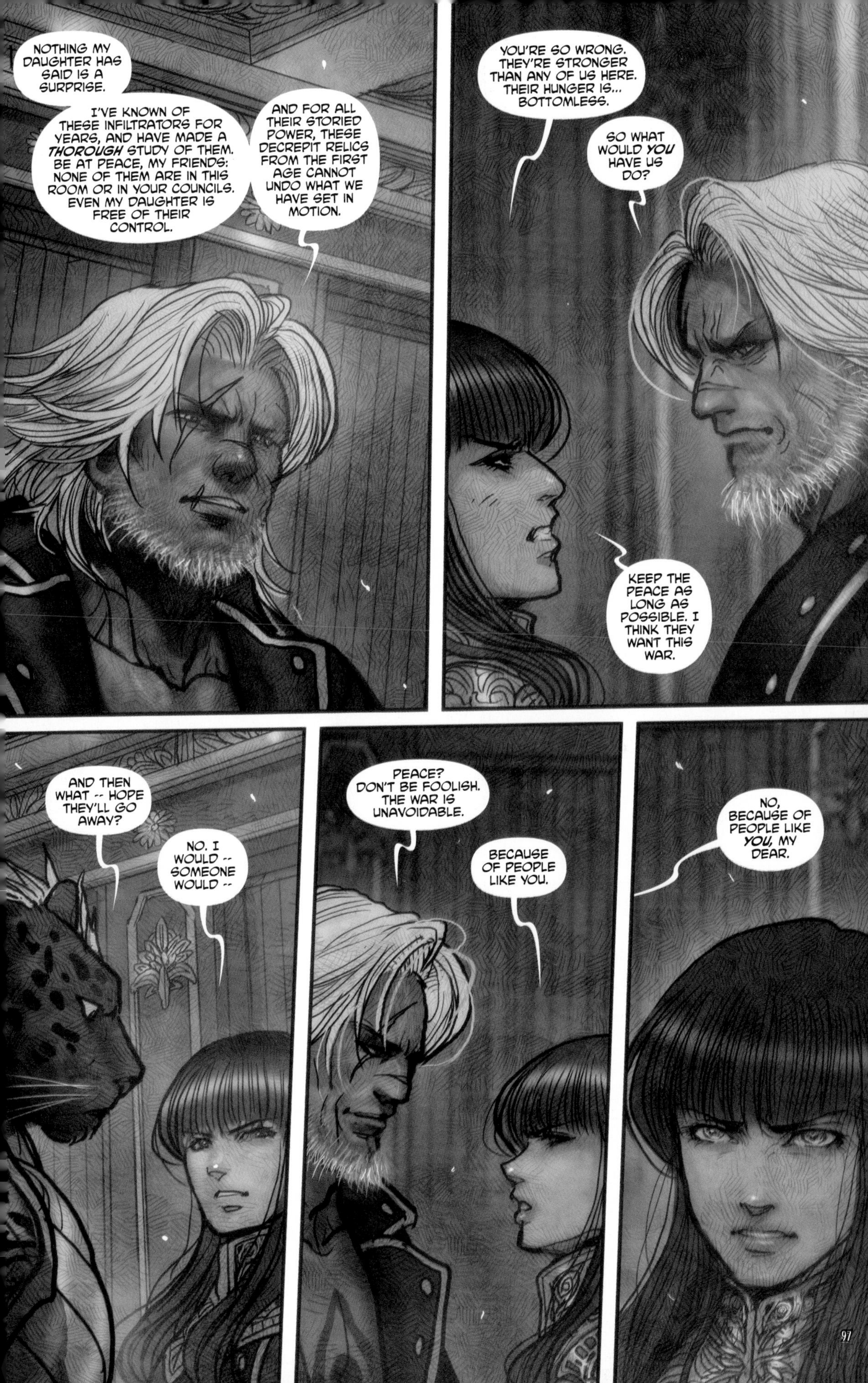
NOTHING MY DAUGHTER HAS SAID IS A SURPRISE.
I'VE KNOWN OF THESE INFILTRATORS FOR YEARS, AND HAVE MADE A *THOROUGH* STUDY OF THEM. BE AT PEACE, MY FRIENDS: NONE OF THEM ARE IN THIS ROOM OR IN YOUR COUNCILS. EVEN MY DAUGHTER IS FREE OF THEIR CONTROL.
AND FOR ALL THEIR STORIED POWER, THESE DECREPIT RELICS FROM THE FIRST AGE CANNOT UNDO WHAT WE HAVE SET IN MOTION.
YOU'RE SO WRONG. THEY'RE STRONGER THAN ANY OF US HERE. THEIR HUNGER IS... BOTTOMLESS.
SO WHAT WOULD *YOU* HAVE US DO?
KEEP THE PEACE AS LONG AS POSSIBLE. I THINK THEY WANT THIS WAR.
AND THEN WHAT -- HOPE THEY'LL GO AWAY?
NO. I WOULD -- SOMEONE WOULD --
PEACE? DON'T BE FOOLISH. THE WAR IS UNAVOIDABLE.
BECAUSE OF PEOPLE LIKE YOU.
NO, BECAUSE OF PEOPLE LIKE *YOU,* MY DEAR.

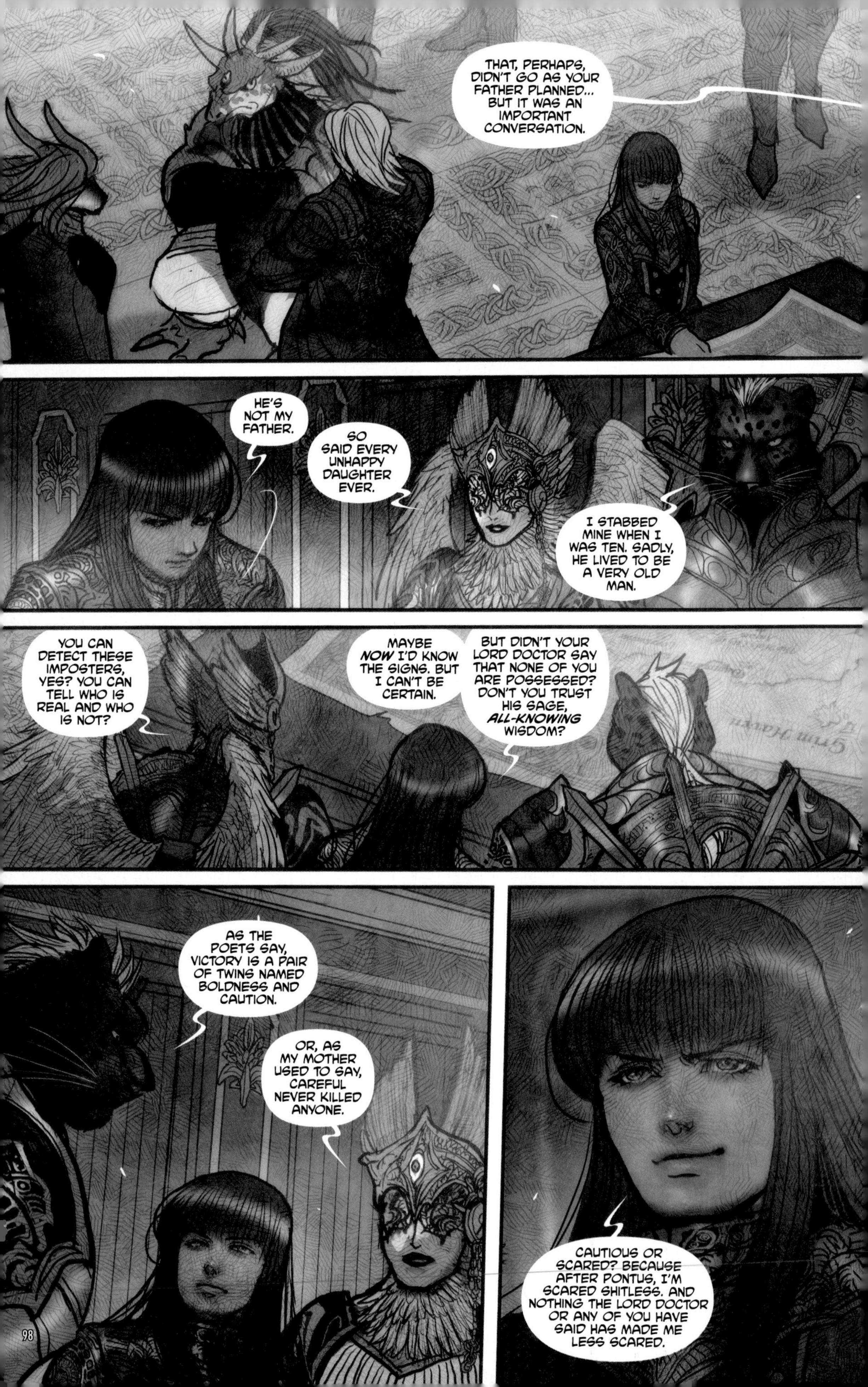
THAT, PERHAPS, DIDN'T GO AS YOUR FATHER PLANNED... BUT IT WAS AN IMPORTANT CONVERSATION.
HE'S NOT MY FATHER.
SO SAID EVERY UNHAPPY DAUGHTER EVER.
I STABBED MINE WHEN I WAS TEN. SADLY, HE LIVED TO BE A VERY OLD MAN.
YOU CAN DETECT THESE IMPOSTERS, YES? YOU CAN TELL WHO IS REAL AND WHO IS NOT?
MAYBE *NOW* I'D KNOW THE SIGNS. BUT I CAN'T BE CERTAIN.
BUT DIDN'T YOUR LORD DOCTOR SAY THAT NONE OF YOU ARE POSSESSED? DON'T YOU TRUST HIS SAGE, *ALL-KNOWING* WISDOM?
AS THE POETS SAY, VICTORY IS A PAIR OF TWINS NAMED BOLDNESS AND CAUTION.
OR, AS MY MOTHER USED TO SAY, CAREFUL NEVER KILLED ANYONE.
CAUTIOUS OR SCARED? BECAUSE AFTER PONTUS, I'M SCARED SHITLESS. AND NOTHING THE LORD DOCTOR OR ANY OF YOU HAVE SAID HAS MADE ME LESS SCARED.

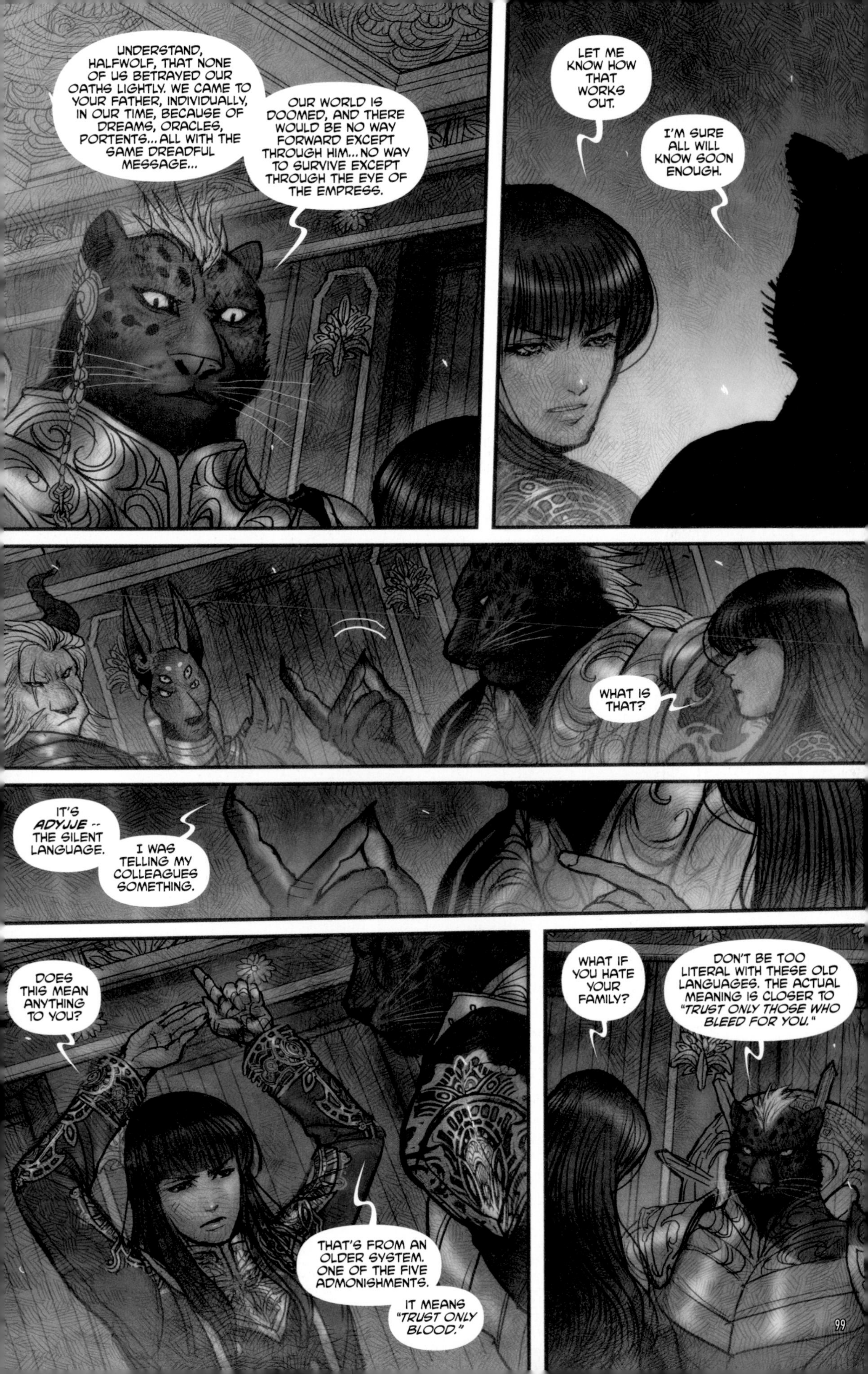
UNDERSTAND, HALFWOLF, THAT NONE OF US BETRAYED OUR OATHS LIGHTLY. WE CAME TO YOUR FATHER, INDIVIDUALLY, IN OUR TIME, BECAUSE OF DREAMS, ORACLES, PORTENTS... ALL WITH THE SAME DREADFUL MESSAGE...
OUR WORLD IS DOOMED, AND THERE WOULD BE NO WAY FORWARD EXCEPT THROUGH HIM... NO WAY TO SURVIVE EXCEPT THROUGH THE EYE OF THE EMPRESS.
LET ME KNOW HOW THAT WORKS OUT.
I'M SURE ALL WILL KNOW SOON ENOUGH.
WHAT IS THAT?
IT'S *ADYJJE* -- THE SILENT LANGUAGE.
I WAS TELLING MY COLLEAGUES SOMETHING.
DOES THIS MEAN ANYTHING TO YOU?
THAT'S FROM AN OLDER SYSTEM. ONE OF THE FIVE ADMONISHMENTS.
IT MEANS "*TRUST ONLY BLOOD.*"
WHAT IF YOU HATE YOUR FAMILY?
DON'T BE TOO LITERAL WITH THESE OLD LANGUAGES. THE ACTUAL MEANING IS CLOSER TO "*TRUST ONLY THOSE WHO BLEED FOR YOU.*"

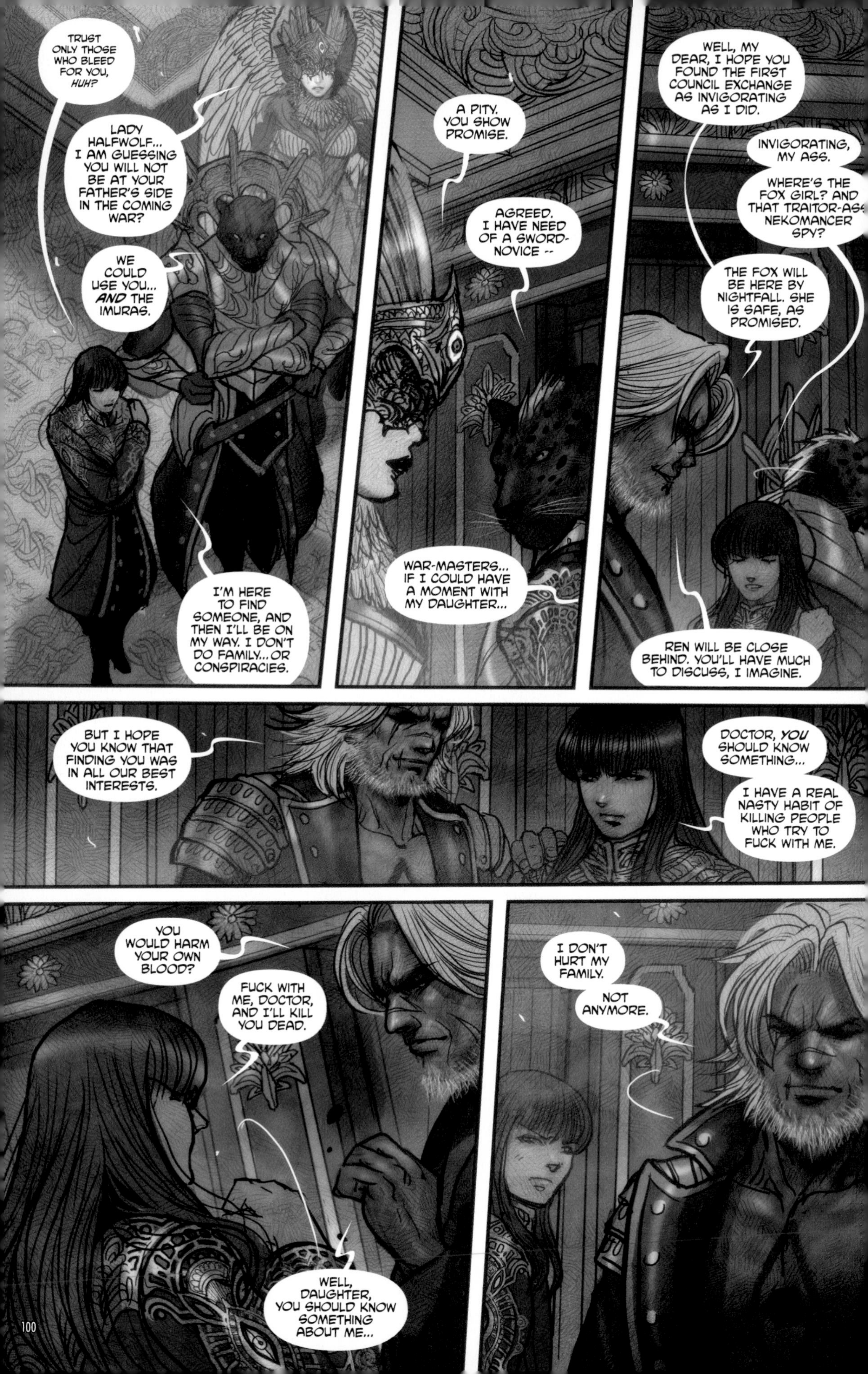
TRUST ONLY THOSE WHO BLEED FOR YOU, HUH?
LADY HALFWOLF... I AM GUESSING YOU WILL NOT BE AT YOUR FATHER'S SIDE IN THE COMING WAR?
WE COULD USE YOU... AND THE IMURAS.
I'M HERE TO FIND SOMEONE, AND THEN I'LL BE ON MY WAY. I DON'T DO FAMILY...OR CONSPIRACIES.
A PITY. YOU SHOW PROMISE.
AGREED. I HAVE NEED OF A SWORD-NOVICE --
WAR-MASTERS... IF I COULD HAVE A MOMENT WITH MY DAUGHTER...
WELL, MY DEAR, I HOPE YOU FOUND THE FIRST COUNCIL EXCHANGE AS INVIGORATING AS I DID.
INVIGORATING, MY ASS.
WHERE'S THE FOX GIRL? AND THAT TRAITOR-ASS NEKOMANCER SPY?
THE FOX WILL BE HERE BY NIGHTFALL. SHE IS SAFE, AS PROMISED.
REN WILL BE CLOSE BEHIND. YOU'LL HAVE MUCH TO DISCUSS, I IMAGINE.
BUT I HOPE YOU KNOW THAT FINDING YOU WAS IN ALL OUR BEST INTERESTS.
DOCTOR, YOU SHOULD KNOW SOMETHING...
I HAVE A REAL NASTY HABIT OF KILLING PEOPLE WHO TRY TO FUCK WITH ME.
YOU WOULD HARM YOUR OWN BLOOD?
FUCK WITH ME, DOCTOR, AND I'LL KILL YOU DEAD.
WELL, DAUGHTER, YOU SHOULD KNOW SOMETHING ABOUT ME...
I DON'T HURT MY FAMILY.
NOT ANYMORE.

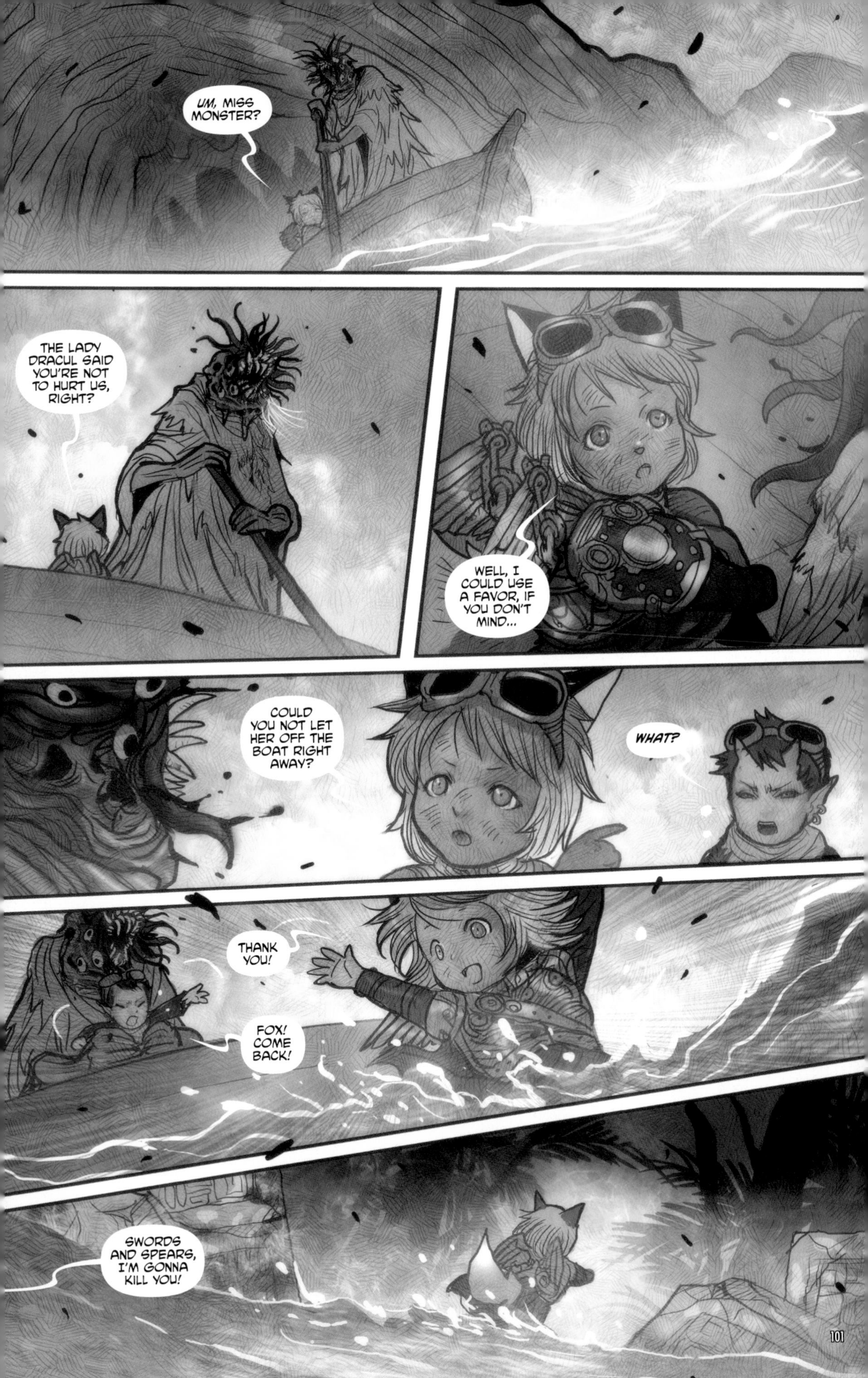
UM, MISS MONSTER?
THE LADY DRACUL SAID YOU'RE NOT TO HURT US, RIGHT?
WELL, I COULD USE A FAVOR, IF YOU DON'T MIND...
COULD YOU NOT LET HER OFF THE BOAT RIGHT AWAY?
WHAT?
THANK YOU!
FOX! COME BACK!
SWORDS AND SPEARS, I'M GONNA KILL YOU!

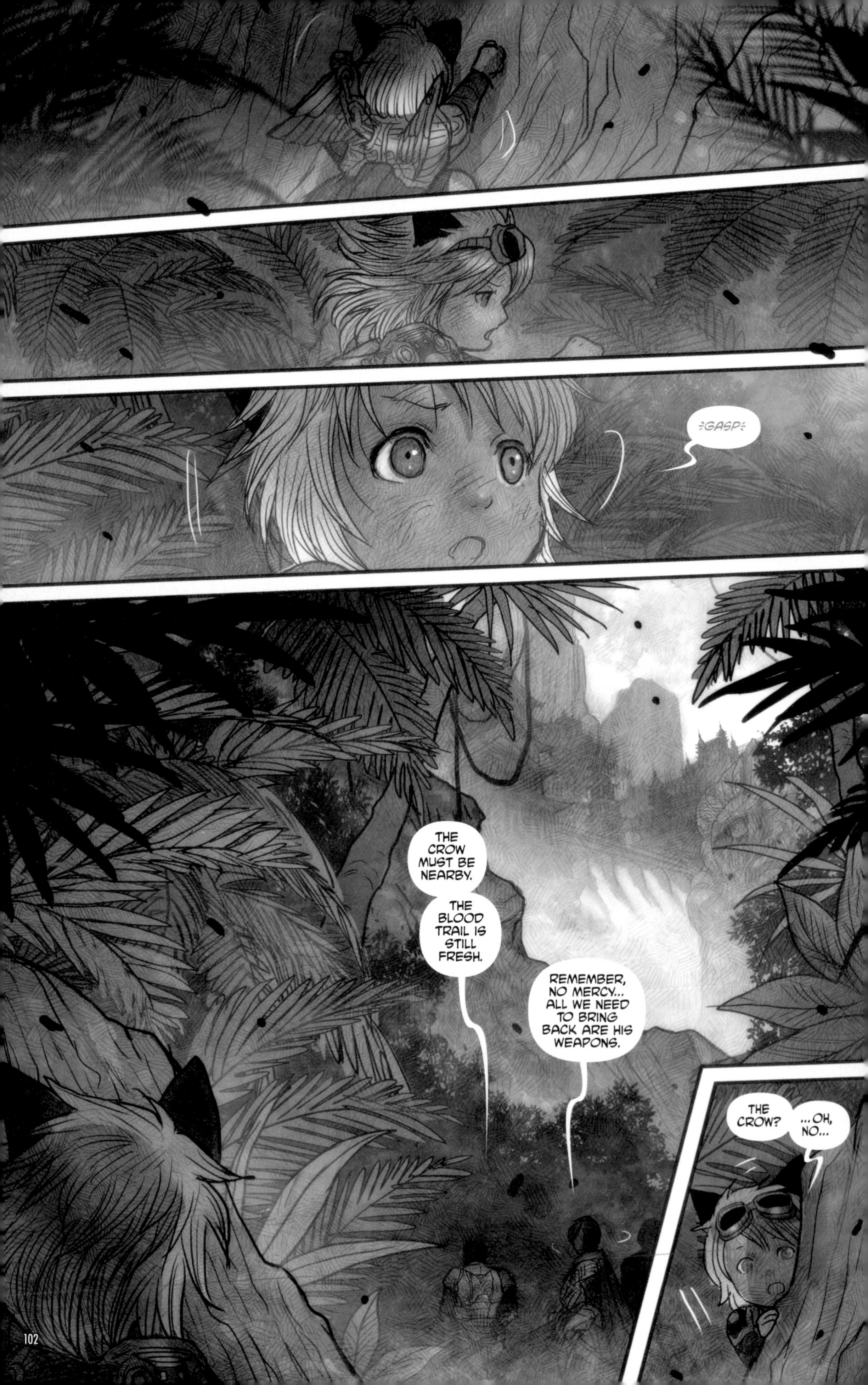
GASP
THE CROW MUST BE NEARBY.
THE BLOOD TRAIL IS STILL FRESH.
REMEMBER, NO MERCY... ALL WE NEED TO BRING BACK ARE HIS WEAPONS.
THE CROW?
...OH, NO...

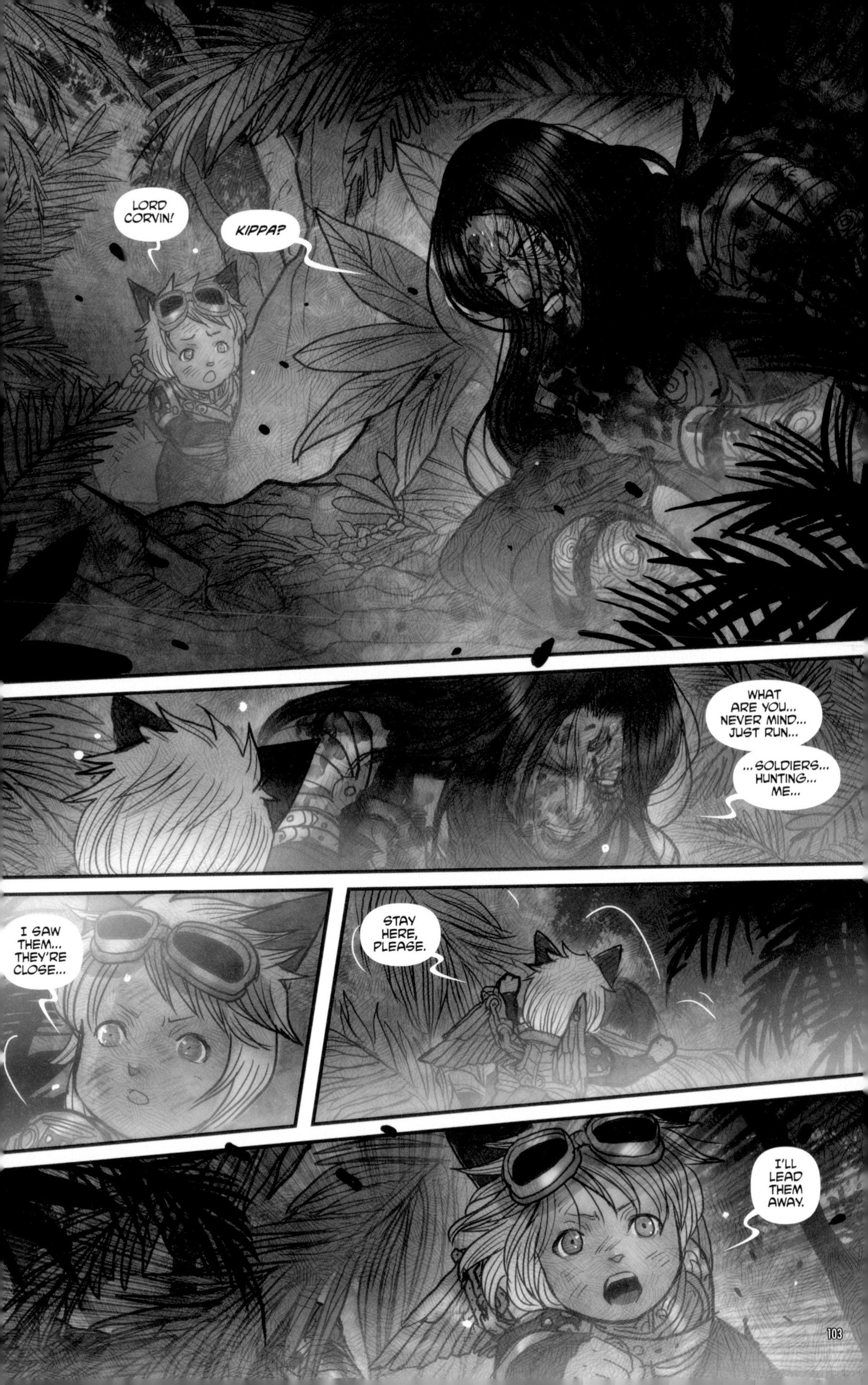
LORD CORVIN!
KIPPA?
WHAT ARE YOU... NEVER MIND... JUST RUN...
...SOLDIERS... HUNTING... ME...
I SAW THEM... THEY'RE CLOSE...
STAY HERE, PLEASE.
I'LL LEAD THEM AWAY.

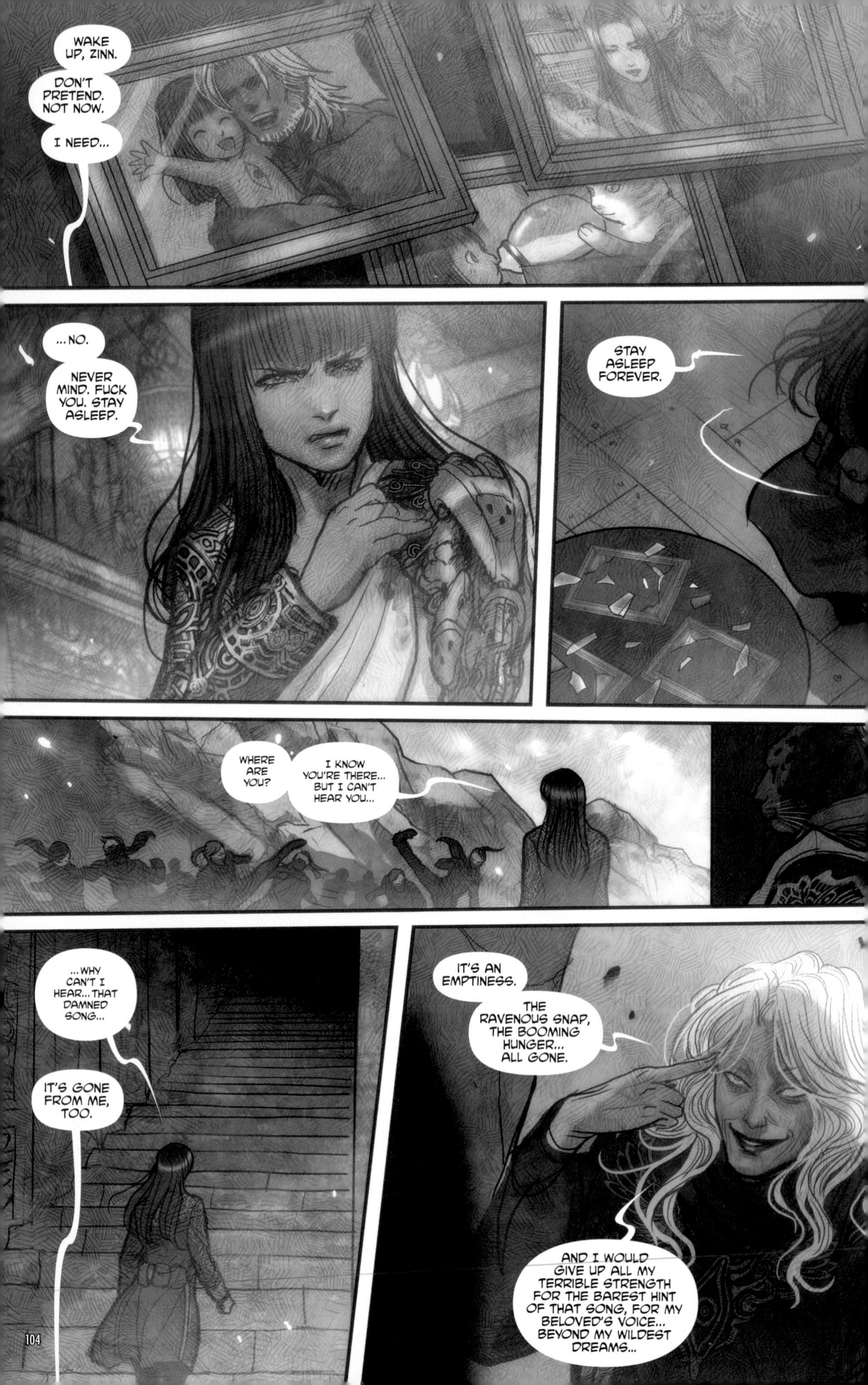
WAKE UP, ZINN.
DON'T PRETEND. NOT NOW.
I NEED...
...NO.
NEVER MIND. FUCK YOU. STAY ASLEEP.
STAY ASLEEP FOREVER.
WHERE ARE YOU?
I KNOW YOU'RE THERE... BUT I CAN'T HEAR YOU...
...WHY CAN'T I HEAR...THAT DAMNED SONG...
IT'S GONE FROM ME, TOO.
IT'S AN EMPTINESS.
THE RAVENOUS SNAP, THE BOOMING HUNGER... ALL GONE.
AND I WOULD GIVE UP ALL MY TERRIBLE STRENGTH FOR THE BAREST HINT OF THAT SONG, FOR MY BELOVED'S VOICE... BEYOND MY WILDEST DREAMS...

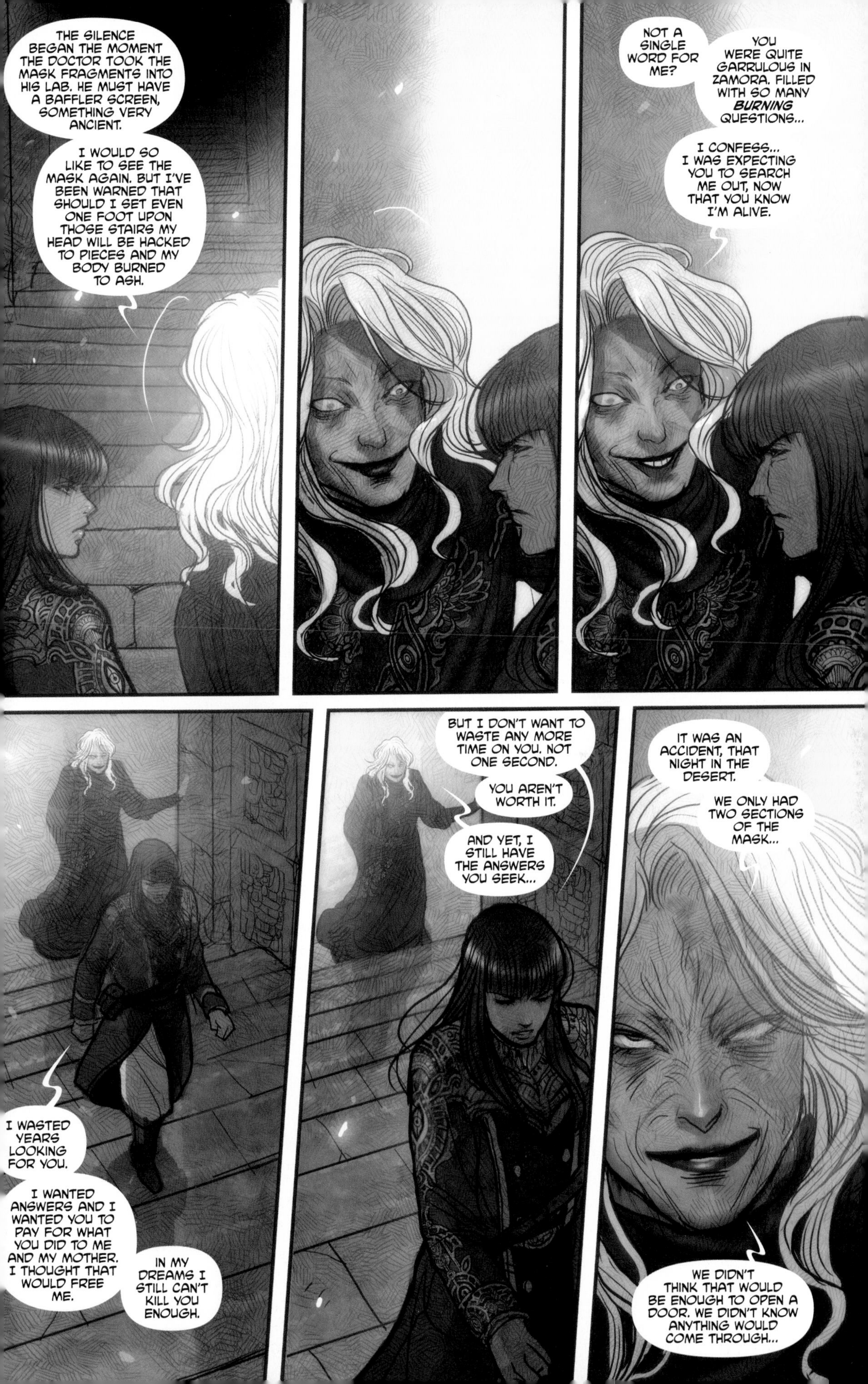
THE SILENCE BEGAN THE MOMENT THE DOCTOR TOOK THE MASK FRAGMENTS INTO HIS LAB. HE MUST HAVE A BAFFLER SCREEN, SOMETHING VERY ANCIENT.
I WOULD SO LIKE TO SEE THE MASK AGAIN. BUT I'VE BEEN WARNED THAT SHOULD I SET EVEN ONE FOOT UPON THOSE STAIRS MY HEAD WILL BE HACKED TO PIECES AND MY BODY BURNED TO ASH.
NOT A SINGLE WORD FOR ME?
YOU WERE QUITE GARRULOUS IN ZAMORA. FILLED WITH SO MANY ***BURNING*** QUESTIONS...
I CONFESS... I WAS EXPECTING YOU TO SEARCH ME OUT, NOW THAT YOU KNOW I'M ALIVE.
I WASTED YEARS LOOKING FOR YOU.
I WANTED ANSWERS AND I WANTED YOU TO PAY FOR WHAT YOU DID TO ME AND MY MOTHER. I THOUGHT THAT WOULD FREE ME.
IN MY DREAMS I STILL CAN'T KILL YOU ENOUGH.
BUT I DON'T WANT TO WASTE ANY MORE TIME ON YOU. NOT ONE SECOND.
YOU AREN'T WORTH IT.
AND YET, I STILL HAVE THE ANSWERS YOU SEEK...
IT WAS AN ACCIDENT, THAT NIGHT IN THE DESERT.
WE ONLY HAD TWO SECTIONS OF THE MASK...
WE DIDN'T THINK THAT WOULD BE ENOUGH TO OPEN A DOOR. WE DIDN'T KNOW ANYTHING WOULD COME THROUGH...

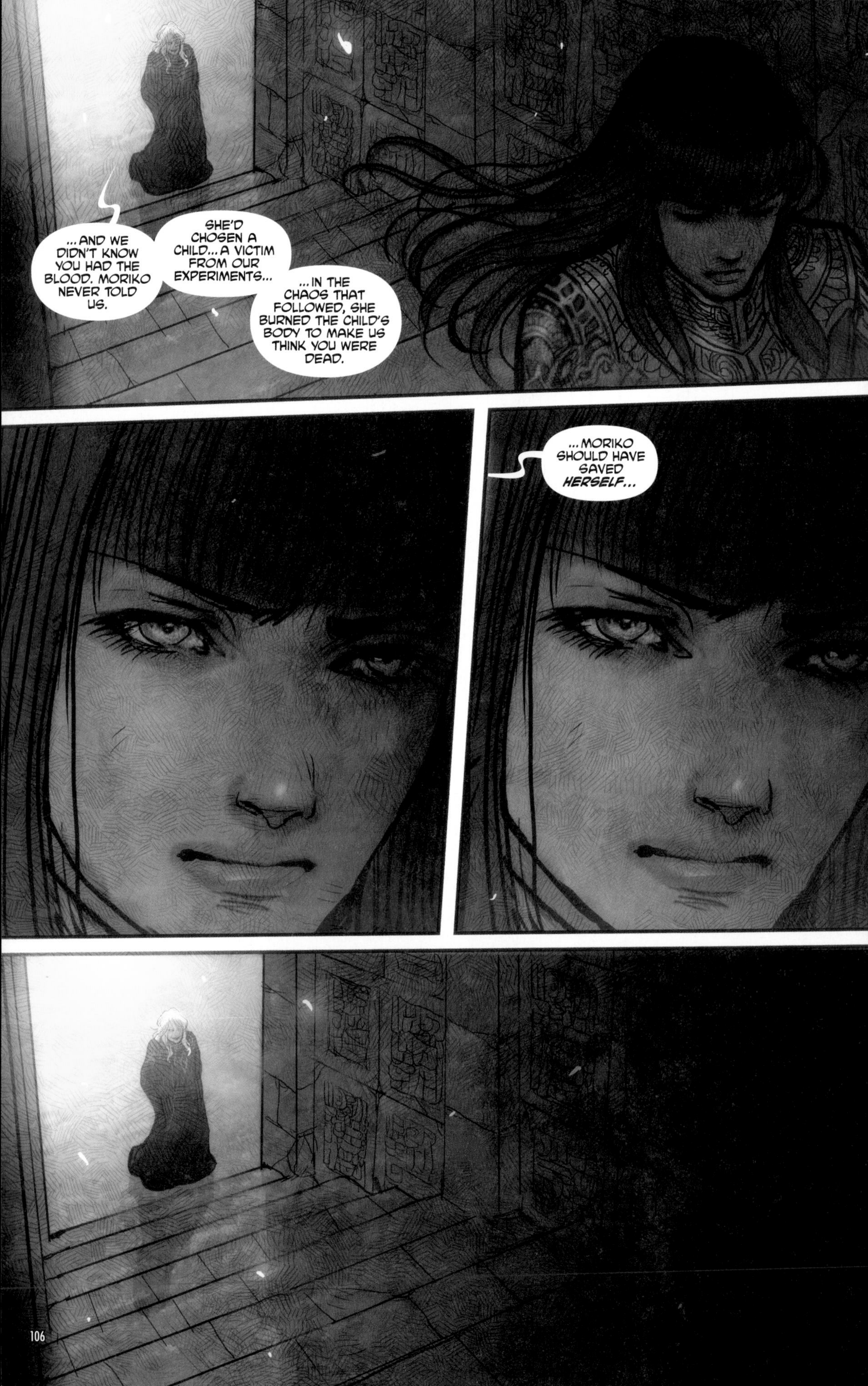
...AND WE DIDN'T KNOW YOU HAD THE BLOOD. MORIKO NEVER TOLD US.
SHE'D CHOSEN A CHILD... A VICTIM FROM OUR EXPERIMENTS...
...IN THE CHAOS THAT FOLLOWED, SHE BURNED THE CHILD'S BODY TO MAKE US THINK YOU WERE DEAD.
...MORIKO SHOULD HAVE SAVED *HERSELF*...

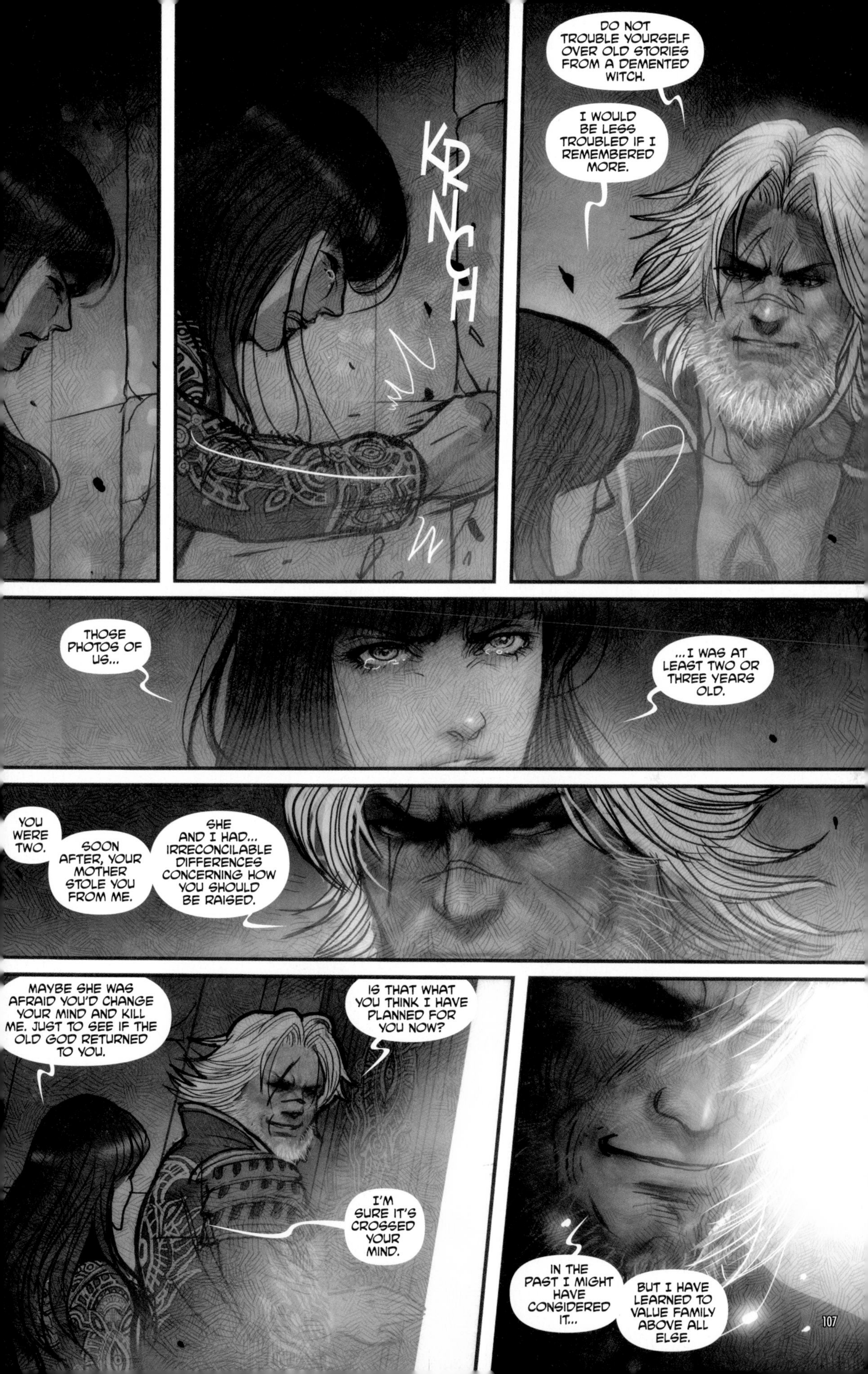
KRNCH
DO NOT TROUBLE YOURSELF OVER OLD STORIES FROM A DEMENTED WITCH.
I WOULD BE LESS TROUBLED IF I REMEMBERED MORE.
THOSE PHOTOS OF US...
...I WAS AT LEAST TWO OR THREE YEARS OLD.
YOU WERE TWO.
SOON AFTER, YOUR MOTHER STOLE YOU FROM ME.
SHE AND I HAD... IRRECONCILABLE DIFFERENCES CONCERNING HOW YOU SHOULD BE RAISED.
MAYBE SHE WAS AFRAID YOU'D CHANGE YOUR MIND AND KILL ME. JUST TO SEE IF THE OLD GOD RETURNED TO YOU.
IS THAT WHAT YOU THINK I HAVE PLANNED FOR YOU NOW?
I'M SURE IT'S CROSSED YOUR MIND.
IN THE PAST I MIGHT HAVE CONSIDERED IT...
BUT I HAVE LEARNED TO VALUE FAMILY ABOVE ALL ELSE.

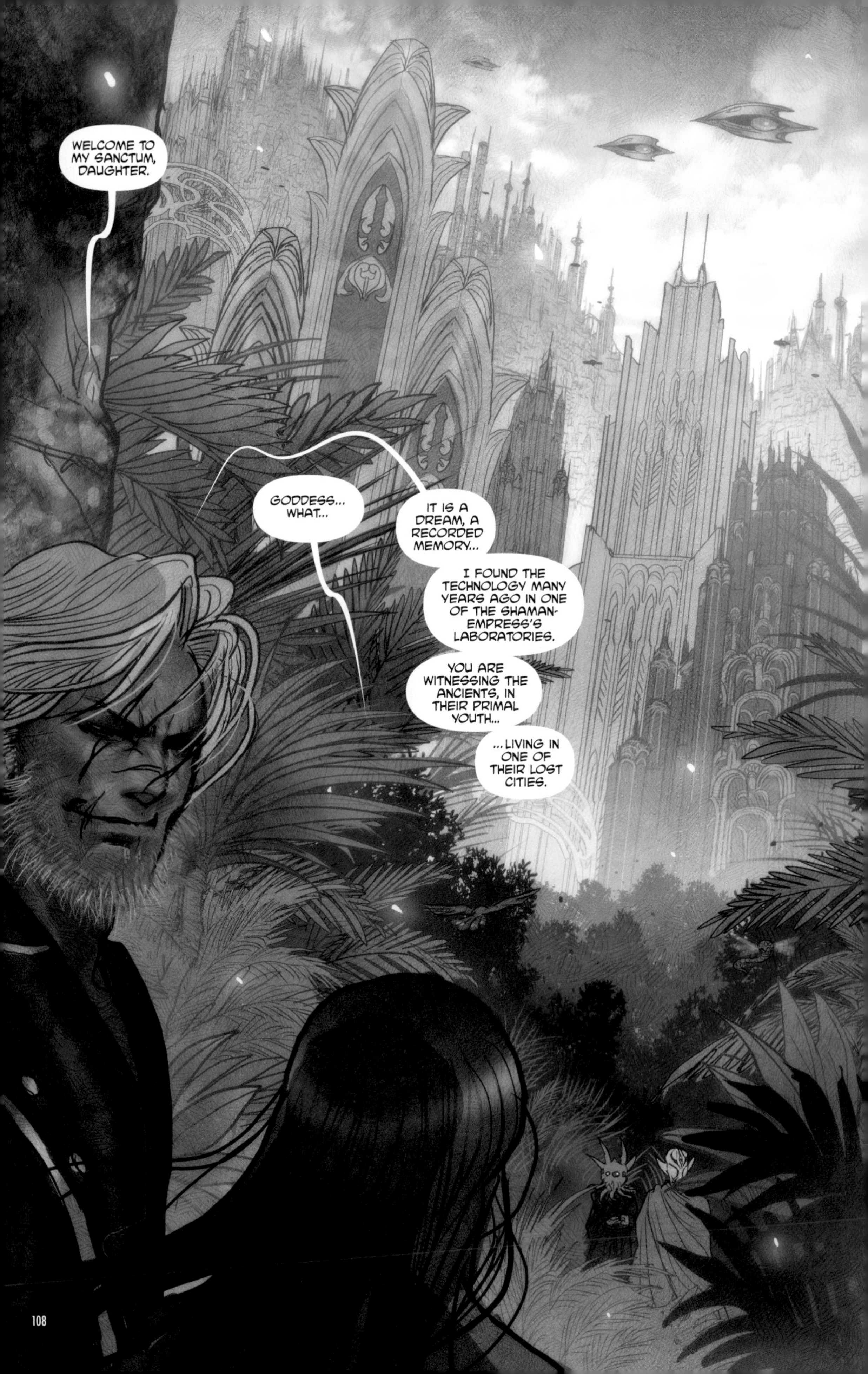
WELCOME TO MY SANCTUM, DAUGHTER.
GODDESS... WHAT...
IT IS A DREAM, A RECORDED MEMORY...
I FOUND THE TECHNOLOGY MANY YEARS AGO IN ONE OF THE SHAMAN-EMPRESS'S LABORATORIES.
YOU ARE WITNESSING THE ANCIENTS, IN THEIR PRIMAL YOUTH...
...LIVING IN ONE OF THEIR LOST CITIES.

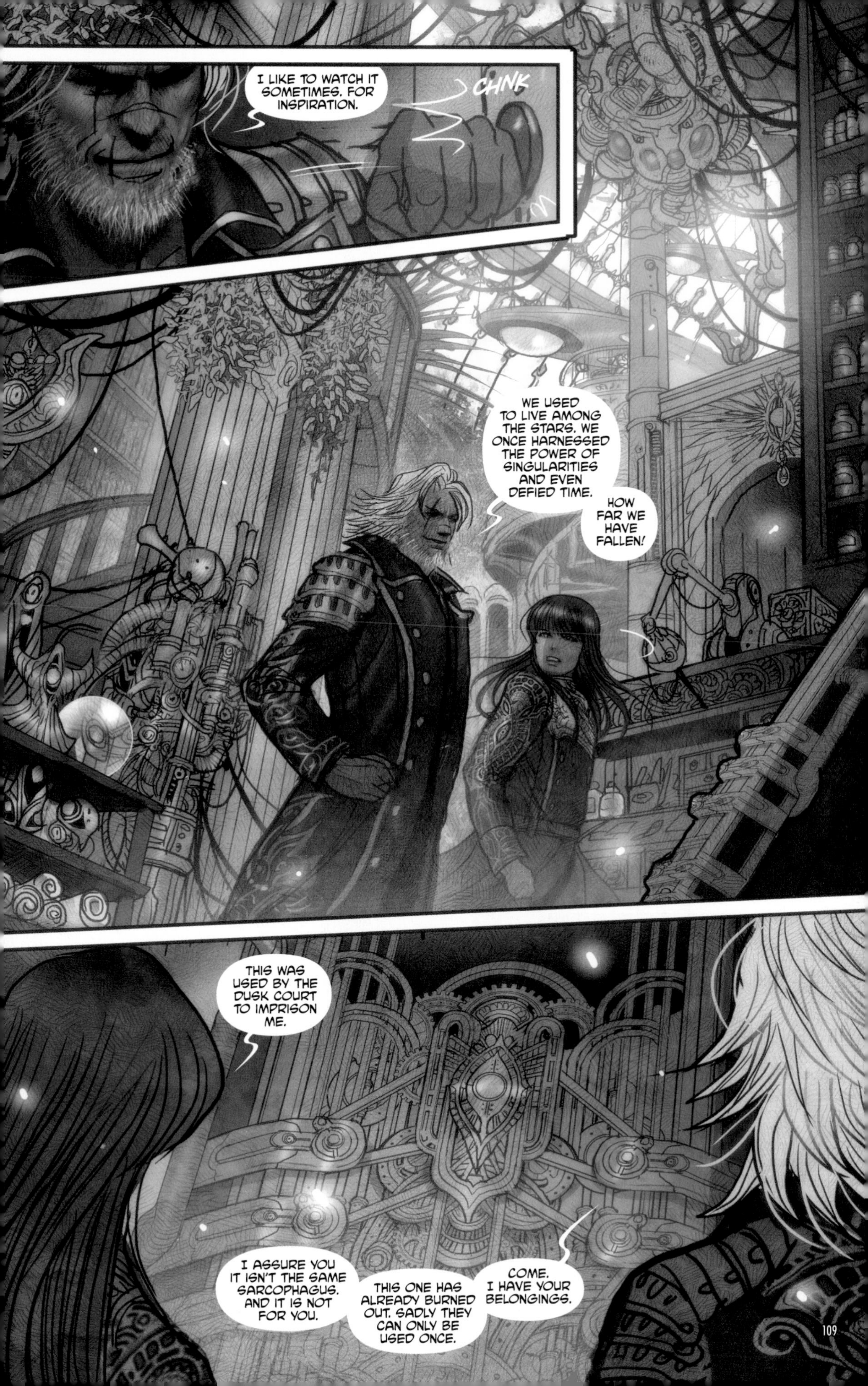
I LIKE TO WATCH IT SOMETIMES. FOR INSPIRATION.
CHNK
WE USED TO LIVE AMONG THE STARS. WE ONCE HARNESSED THE POWER OF SINGULARITIES AND EVEN DEFIED TIME.
HOW FAR WE HAVE FALLEN!
THIS WAS USED BY THE DUSK COURT TO IMPRISON ME.
I ASSURE YOU IT ISN'T THE SAME SARCOPHAGUS. AND IT IS NOT FOR YOU.
THIS ONE HAS ALREADY BURNED OUT. SADLY THEY CAN ONLY BE USED ONCE.
COME. I HAVE YOUR BELONGINGS.

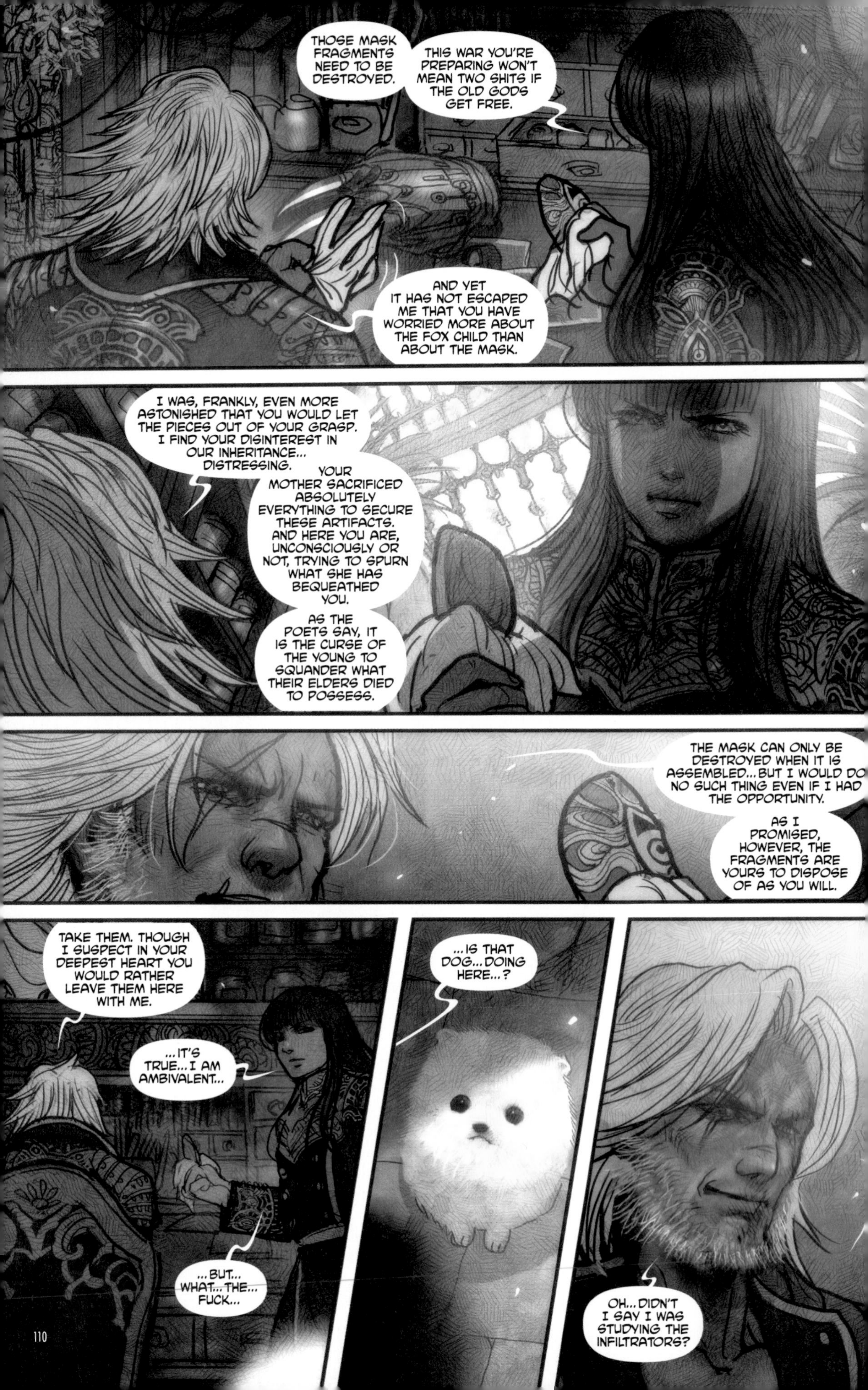
THOSE MASK FRAGMENTS NEED TO BE DESTROYED.
THIS WAR YOU'RE PREPARING WON'T MEAN TWO SHITS IF THE OLD GODS GET FREE.
AND YET IT HAS NOT ESCAPED ME THAT YOU HAVE WORRIED MORE ABOUT THE FOX CHILD THAN ABOUT THE MASK.
I WAS, FRANKLY, EVEN MORE ASTONISHED THAT YOU WOULD LET THE PIECES OUT OF YOUR GRASP. I FIND YOUR DISINTEREST IN OUR INHERITANCE... DISTRESSING.
YOUR MOTHER SACRIFICED ABSOLUTELY EVERYTHING TO SECURE THESE ARTIFACTS. AND HERE YOU ARE, UNCONSCIOUSLY OR NOT, TRYING TO SPURN WHAT SHE HAS BEQUEATHED YOU.
AS THE POETS SAY, IT IS THE CURSE OF THE YOUNG TO SQUANDER WHAT THEIR ELDERS DIED TO POSSESS.
THE MASK CAN ONLY BE DESTROYED WHEN IT IS ASSEMBLED... BUT I WOULD DO NO SUCH THING EVEN IF I HAD THE OPPORTUNITY.
AS I PROMISED, HOWEVER, THE FRAGMENTS ARE YOURS TO DISPOSE OF AS YOU WILL.
TAKE THEM. THOUGH I SUSPECT IN YOUR DEEPEST HEART YOU WOULD RATHER LEAVE THEM HERE WITH ME.
...IT'S TRUE... I AM AMBIVALENT...
...BUT... WHAT... THE... FUCK...
...IS THAT DOG... DOING HERE...?
OH... DIDN'T I SAY I WAS STUDYING THE INFILTRATORS?

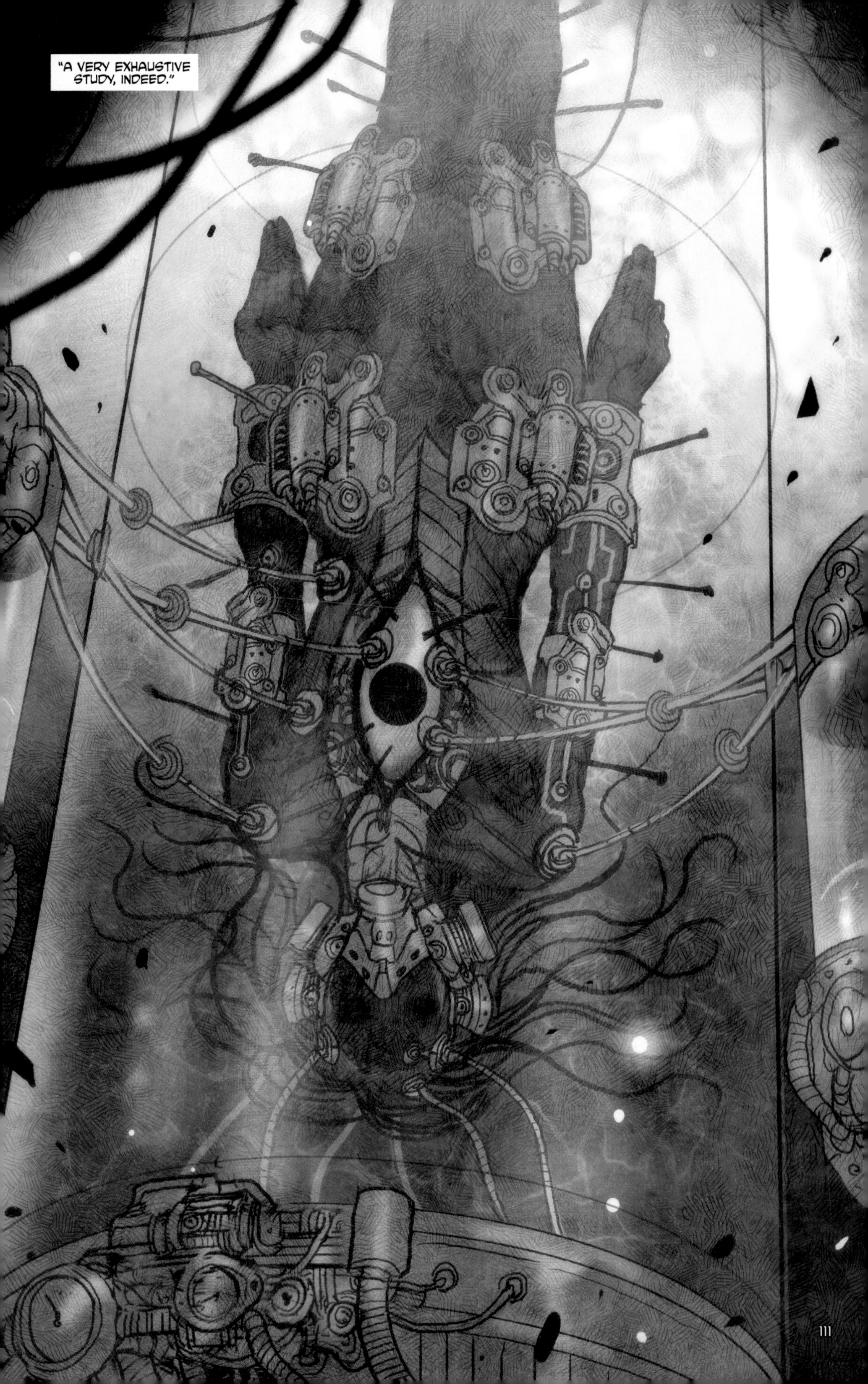
"A VERY EXHAUSTIVE STUDY, INDEED."

CHAPTER TWENTY-THREE

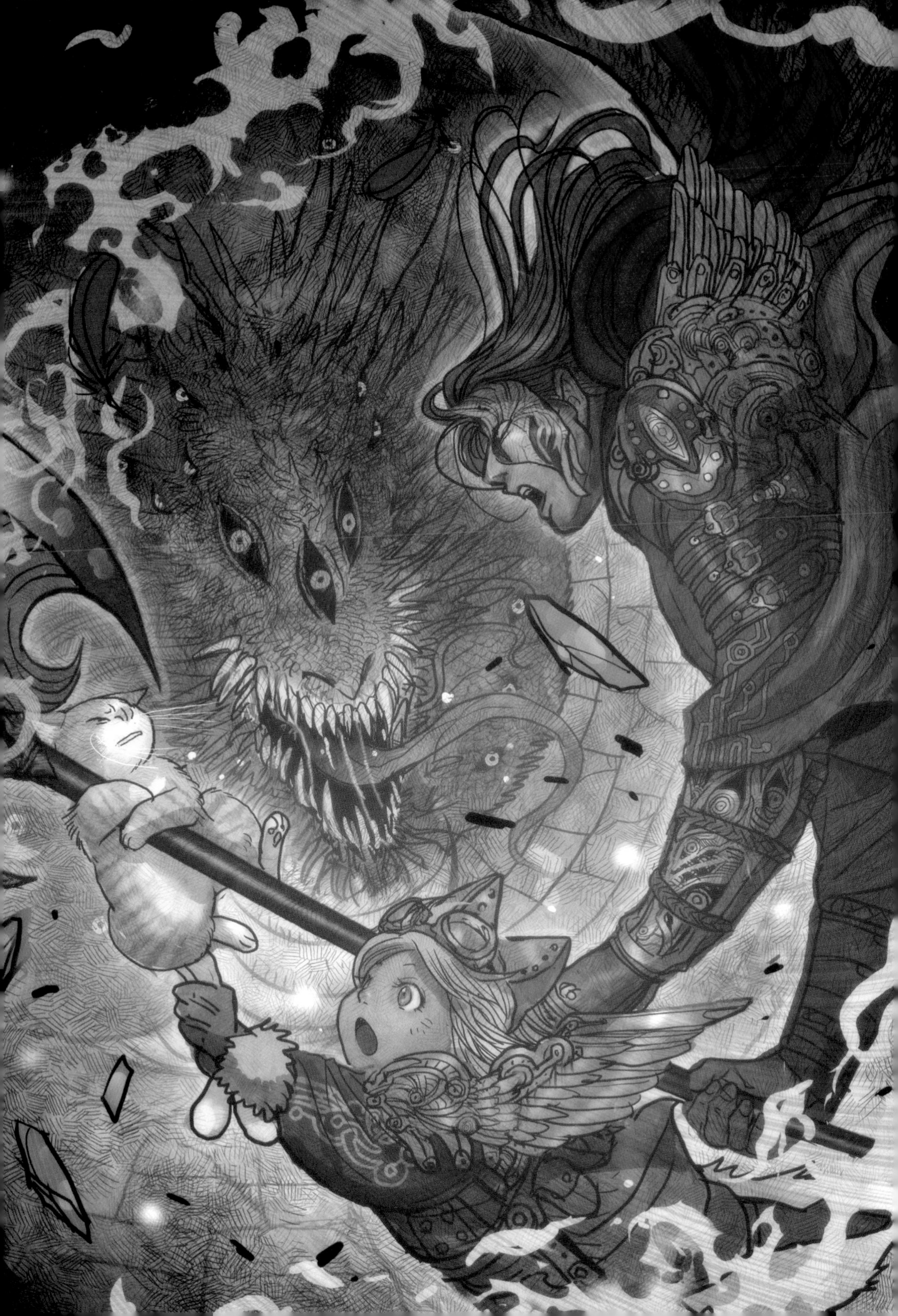

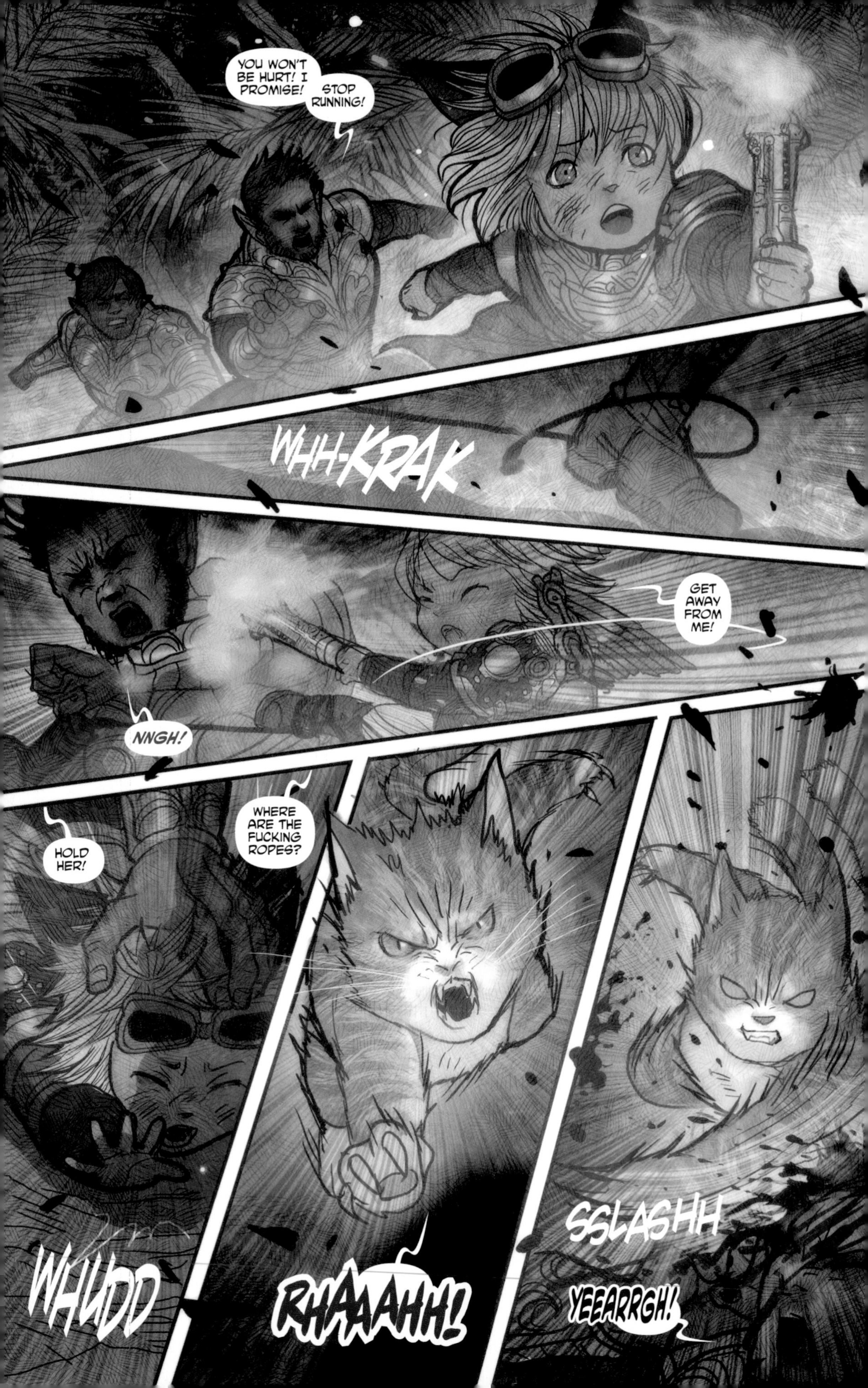
YOU WON'T BE HURT! I PROMISE!
STOP RUNNING!
WHH-KRAK
GET AWAY FROM ME!
NNGH!
HOLD HER!
WHERE ARE THE FUCKING ROPES?
WHUDD
RHAAAHH!
SSLASHH
YEEARRGH!

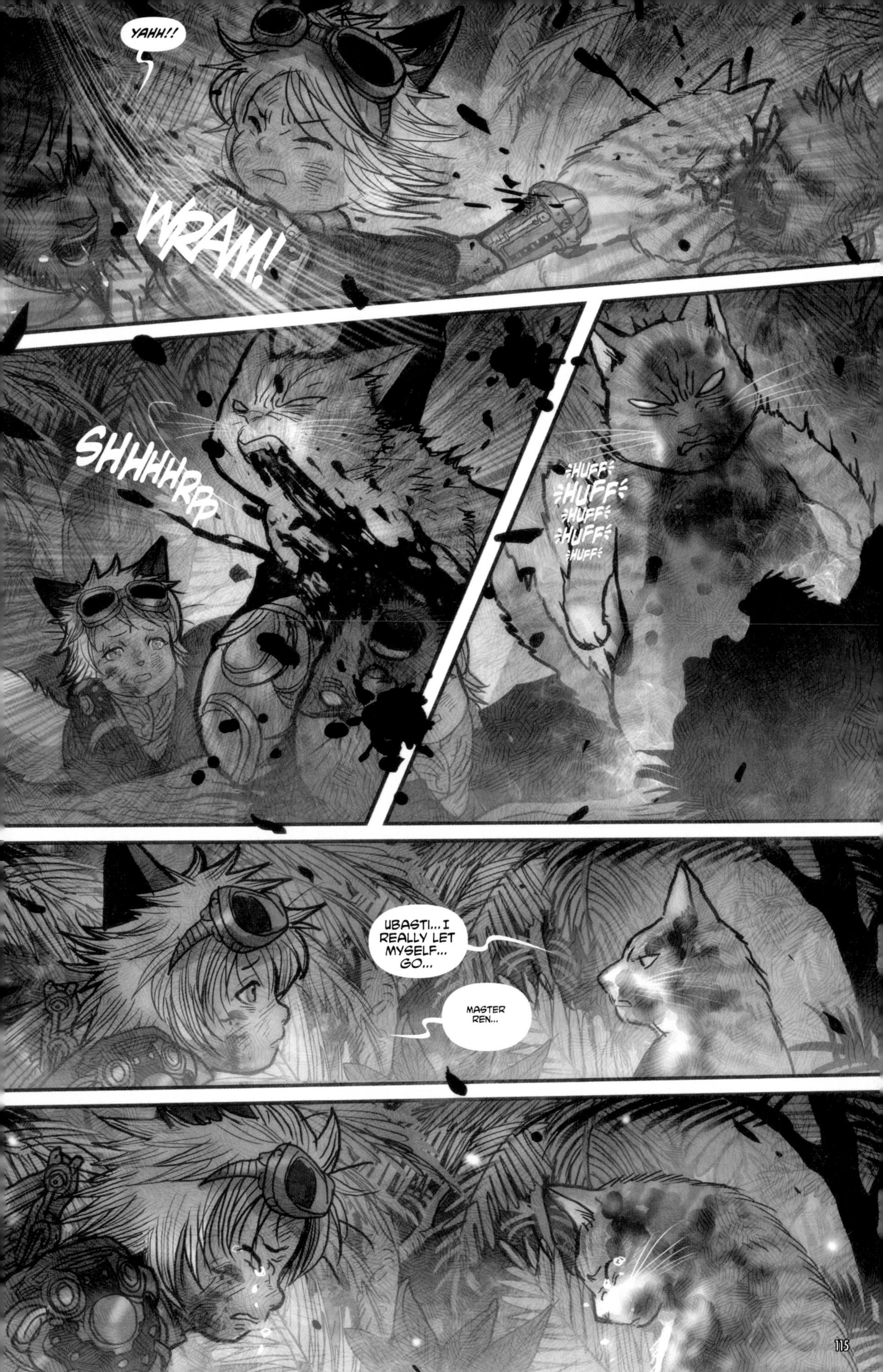
YAHH!!
WRAM!
SHHHHRPP
HUFF
HUFF
HUFF
HUFF
HUFF
UBASTI... I REALLY LET MYSELF... GO...
MASTER REN...

WHAT ARE YOU DOING?

MEDITATING. REVIEWING MY RECESSED MEMORIES...

AN INDISPENSABLE SKILL, FOR ONES SUCH AS WE, WHO HAVE SO MUCH... BURIED DEEP INSIDE.

WE CANNOT AFFORD SECRETS FROM OURSELVES, DAUGHTER.

YOU SHOULD LET ME TEACH YOU.

UH-HUH. MY ARM DOESN'T COME OFF.

BECAUSE YOU WOULD DISCARD IT.

BECAUSE I DIDN'T WANT A NEW LIMB.

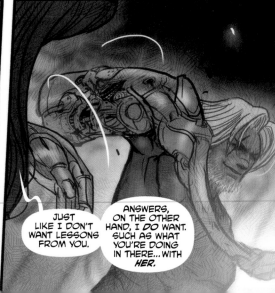

JUST LIKE I DON'T WANT LESSONS FROM YOU.

ANSWERS, ON THE OTHER HAND, I *DO* WANT. SUCH AS WHAT YOU'RE DOING IN THERE... WITH *HER.*

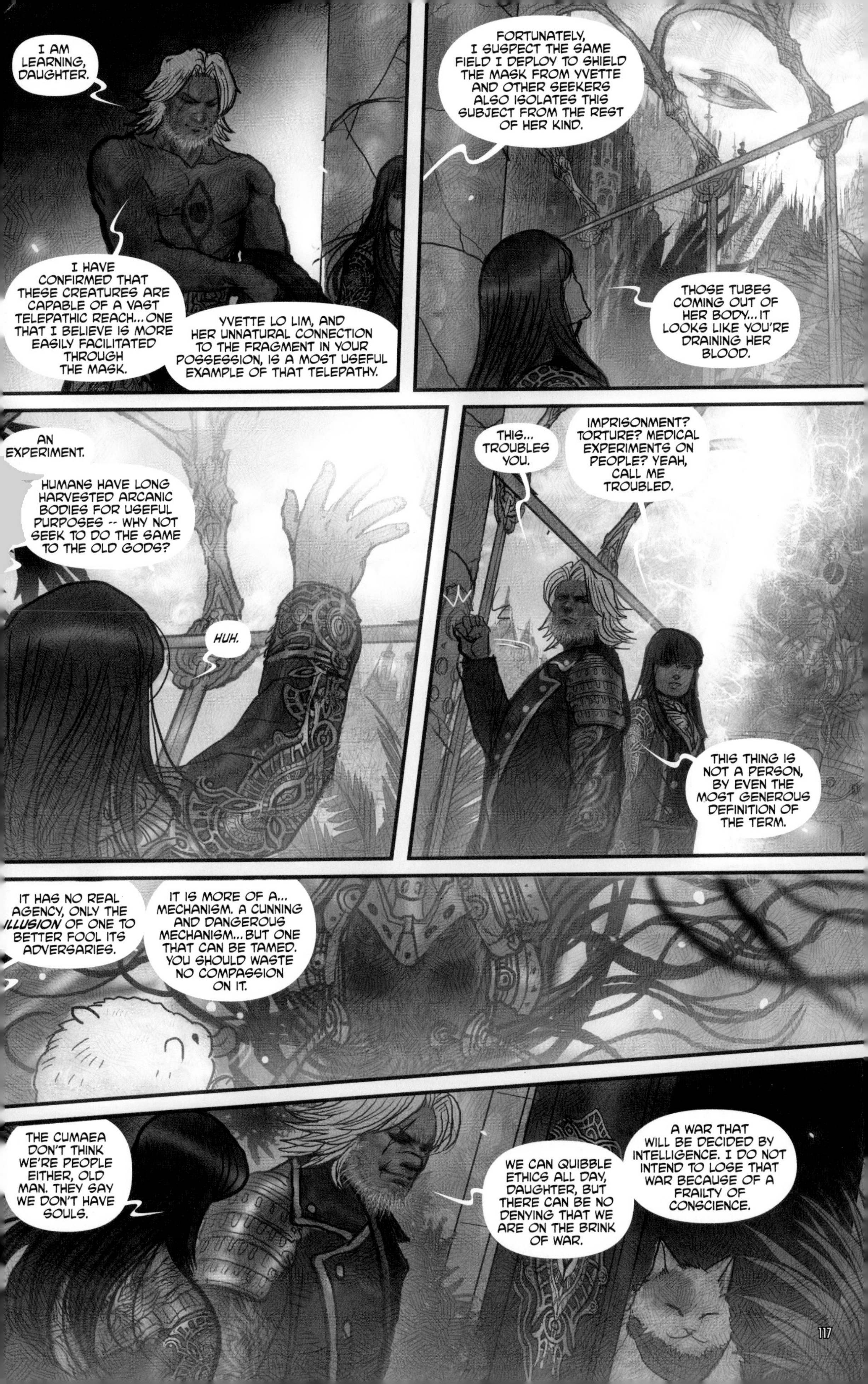
I AM LEARNING, DAUGHTER.
I HAVE CONFIRMED THAT THESE CREATURES ARE CAPABLE OF A VAST TELEPATHIC REACH... ONE THAT I BELIEVE IS MORE EASILY FACILITATED THROUGH THE MASK.
YVETTE LO LIM, AND HER UNNATURAL CONNECTION TO THE FRAGMENT IN YOUR POSSESSION, IS A MOST USEFUL EXAMPLE OF THAT TELEPATHY.
FORTUNATELY, I SUSPECT THE SAME FIELD I DEPLOY TO SHIELD THE MASK FROM YVETTE AND OTHER SEEKERS ALSO ISOLATES THIS SUBJECT FROM THE REST OF HER KIND.
THOSE TUBES COMING OUT OF HER BODY... IT LOOKS LIKE YOU'RE DRAINING HER BLOOD.
AN EXPERIMENT.
HUMANS HAVE LONG HARVESTED ARCANIC BODIES FOR USEFUL PURPOSES -- WHY NOT SEEK TO DO THE SAME TO THE OLD GODS?
HUH.
THIS... TROUBLES YOU.
IMPRISONMENT? TORTURE? MEDICAL EXPERIMENTS ON PEOPLE? YEAH, CALL ME TROUBLED.
THIS THING IS NOT A PERSON, BY EVEN THE MOST GENEROUS DEFINITION OF THE TERM.
IT HAS NO REAL AGENCY, ONLY THE *ILLUSION* OF ONE TO BETTER FOOL ITS ADVERSARIES.
IT IS MORE OF A... MECHANISM. A CUNNING AND DANGEROUS MECHANISM... BUT ONE THAT CAN BE TAMED. YOU SHOULD WASTE NO COMPASSION ON IT.
THE CUMAEA DON'T THINK WE'RE PEOPLE EITHER, OLD MAN. THEY SAY WE DON'T HAVE SOULS.
WE CAN QUIBBLE ETHICS ALL DAY, DAUGHTER, BUT THERE CAN BE NO DENYING THAT WE ARE ON THE BRINK OF WAR.
A WAR THAT WILL BE DECIDED BY INTELLIGENCE. I DO NOT INTEND TO LOSE THAT WAR BECAUSE OF A FRAILTY OF CONSCIENCE.

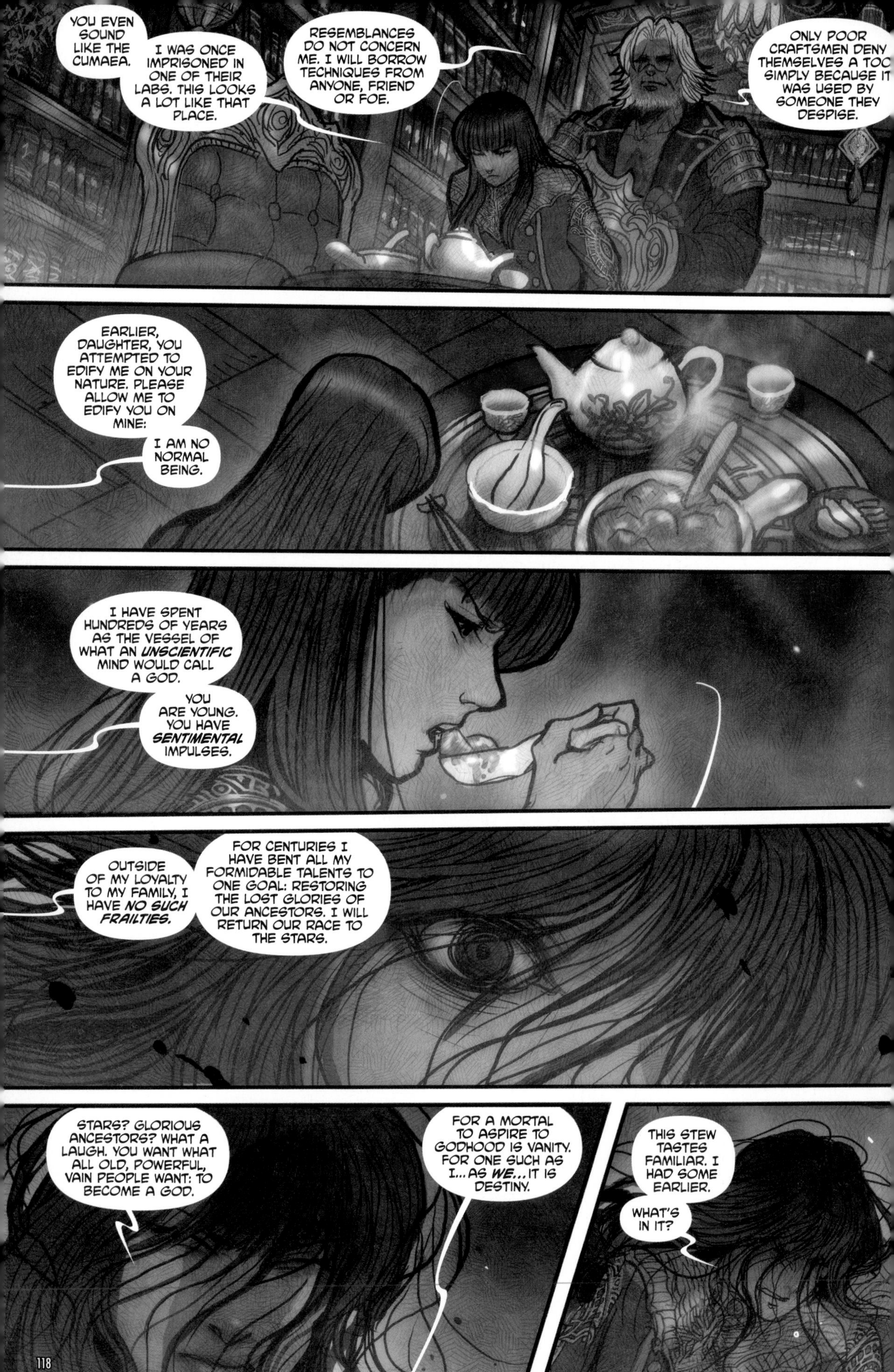
YOU EVEN SOUND LIKE THE CUMAEA.
I WAS ONCE IMPRISONED IN ONE OF THEIR LABS. THIS LOOKS A LOT LIKE THAT PLACE.
RESEMBLANCES DO NOT CONCERN ME. I WILL BORROW TECHNIQUES FROM ANYONE, FRIEND OR FOE.
ONLY POOR CRAFTSMEN DENY THEMSELVES A TOO SIMPLY BECAUSE IT WAS USED BY SOMEONE THEY DESPISE.
EARLIER, DAUGHTER, YOU ATTEMPTED TO EDIFY ME ON YOUR NATURE. PLEASE ALLOW ME TO EDIFY YOU ON MINE:
I AM NO NORMAL BEING.
I HAVE SPENT HUNDREDS OF YEARS AS THE VESSEL OF WHAT AN UNSCIENTIFIC MIND WOULD CALL A GOD.
YOU ARE YOUNG. YOU HAVE SENTIMENTAL IMPULSES.
OUTSIDE OF MY LOYALTY TO MY FAMILY, I HAVE NO SUCH FRAILTIES.
FOR CENTURIES I HAVE BENT ALL MY FORMIDABLE TALENTS TO ONE GOAL: RESTORING THE LOST GLORIES OF OUR ANCESTORS. I WILL RETURN OUR RACE TO THE STARS.
STARS? GLORIOUS ANCESTORS? WHAT A LAUGH. YOU WANT WHAT ALL OLD, POWERFUL, VAIN PEOPLE WANT: TO BECOME A GOD.
FOR A MORTAL TO ASPIRE TO GODHOOD IS VANITY. FOR ONE SUCH AS I... AS WE... IT IS DESTINY.
THIS STEW TASTES FAMILIAR. I HAD SOME EARLIER.
WHAT'S IN IT?

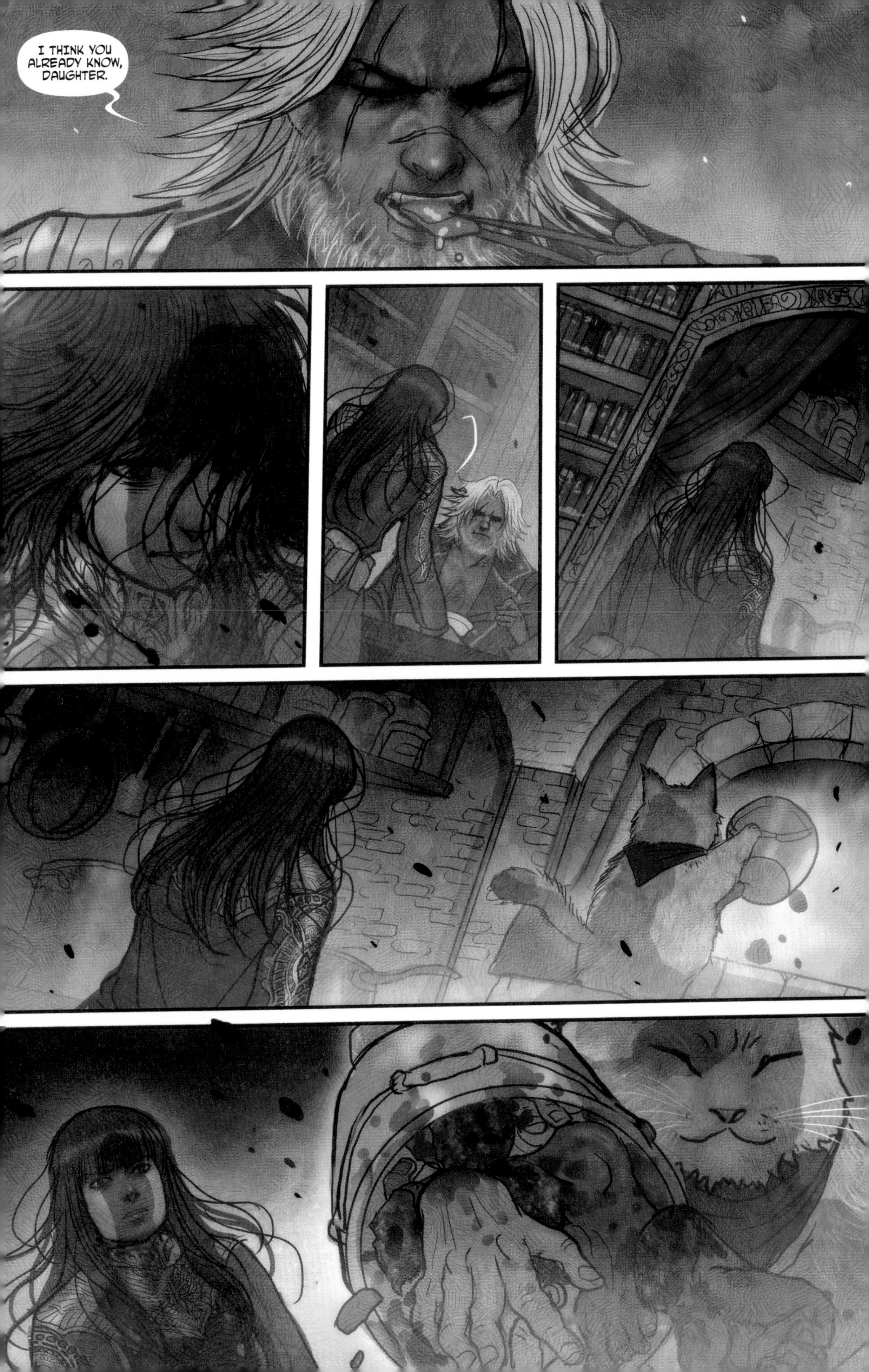
I THINK YOU ALREADY KNOW, DAUGHTER.

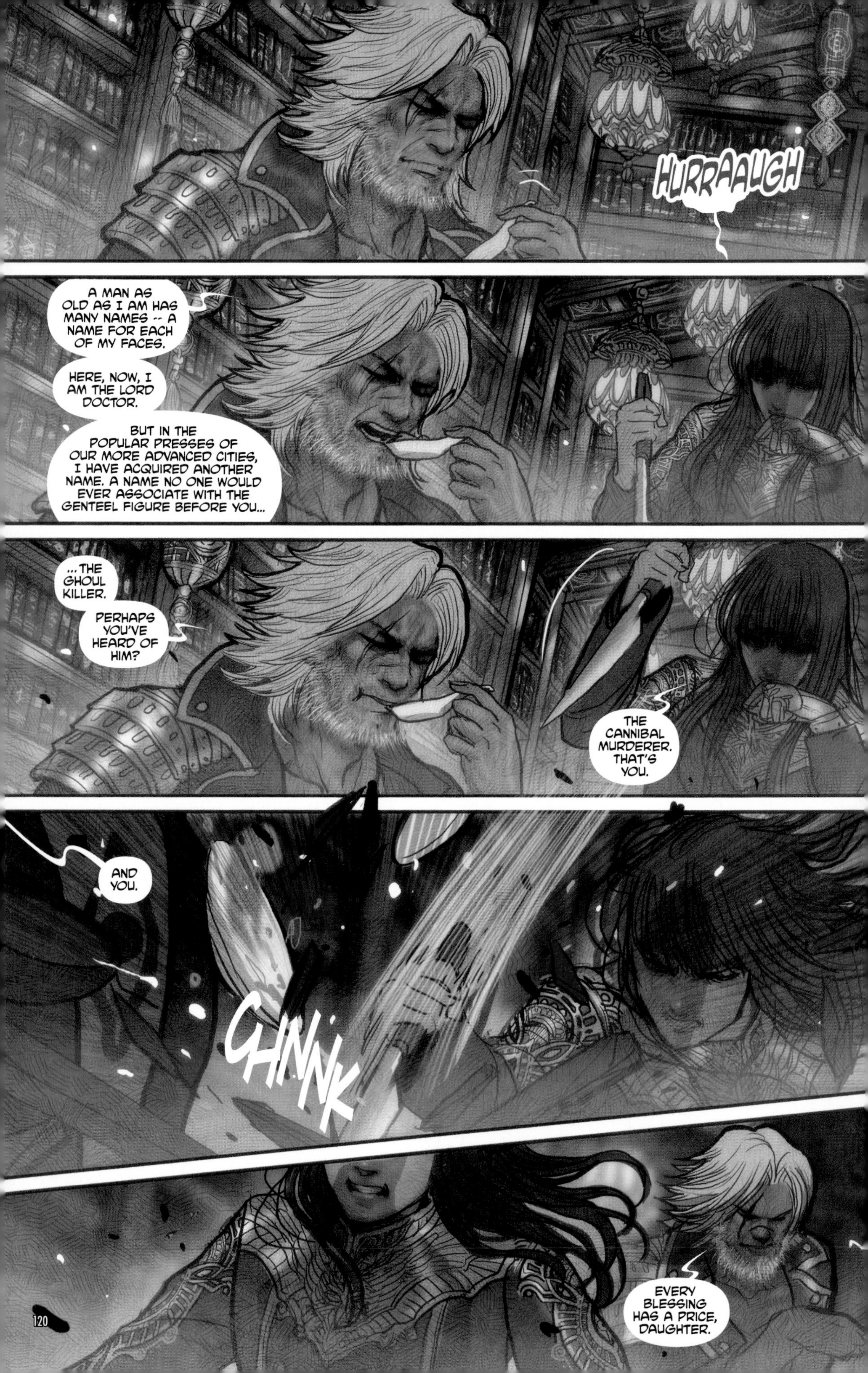

HURRAAUGH
A MAN AS OLD AS I AM HAS MANY NAMES -- A NAME FOR EACH OF MY FACES.
HERE, NOW, I AM THE LORD DOCTOR.
BUT IN THE POPULAR PRESSES OF OUR MORE ADVANCED CITIES, I HAVE ACQUIRED ANOTHER NAME. A NAME NO ONE WOULD EVER ASSOCIATE WITH THE GENTEEL FIGURE BEFORE YOU...
...THE GHOUL KILLER.
PERHAPS YOU'VE HEARD OF HIM?
THE CANNIBAL MURDERER. THAT'S YOU.
AND YOU.
CHINNK
EVERY BLESSING HAS A PRICE, DAUGHTER.

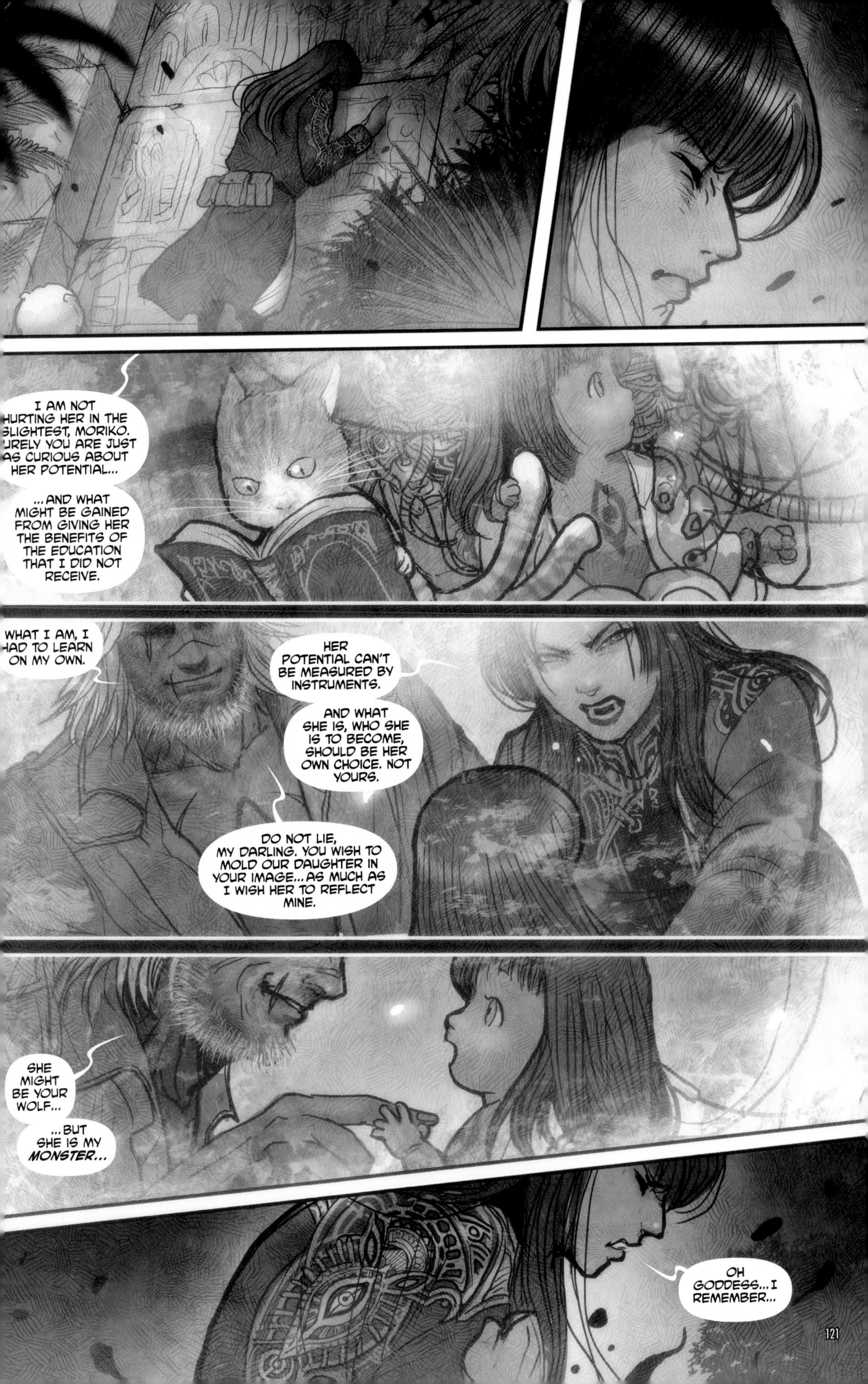
I AM NOT HURTING HER IN THE SLIGHTEST, MORIKO. URELY YOU ARE JUST AS CURIOUS ABOUT HER POTENTIAL...
...AND WHAT MIGHT BE GAINED FROM GIVING HER THE BENEFITS OF THE EDUCATION THAT I DID NOT RECEIVE.
WHAT I AM, I HAD TO LEARN ON MY OWN.
HER POTENTIAL CAN'T BE MEASURED BY INSTRUMENTS.
AND WHAT SHE IS, WHO SHE IS TO BECOME, SHOULD BE HER OWN CHOICE. NOT YOURS.
DO NOT LIE, MY DARLING. YOU WISH TO MOLD OUR DAUGHTER IN YOUR IMAGE...AS MUCH AS I WISH HER TO REFLECT MINE.
SHE MIGHT BE YOUR WOLF...
...BUT SHE IS MY *MONSTER*...
OH GODDESS...I REMEMBER...

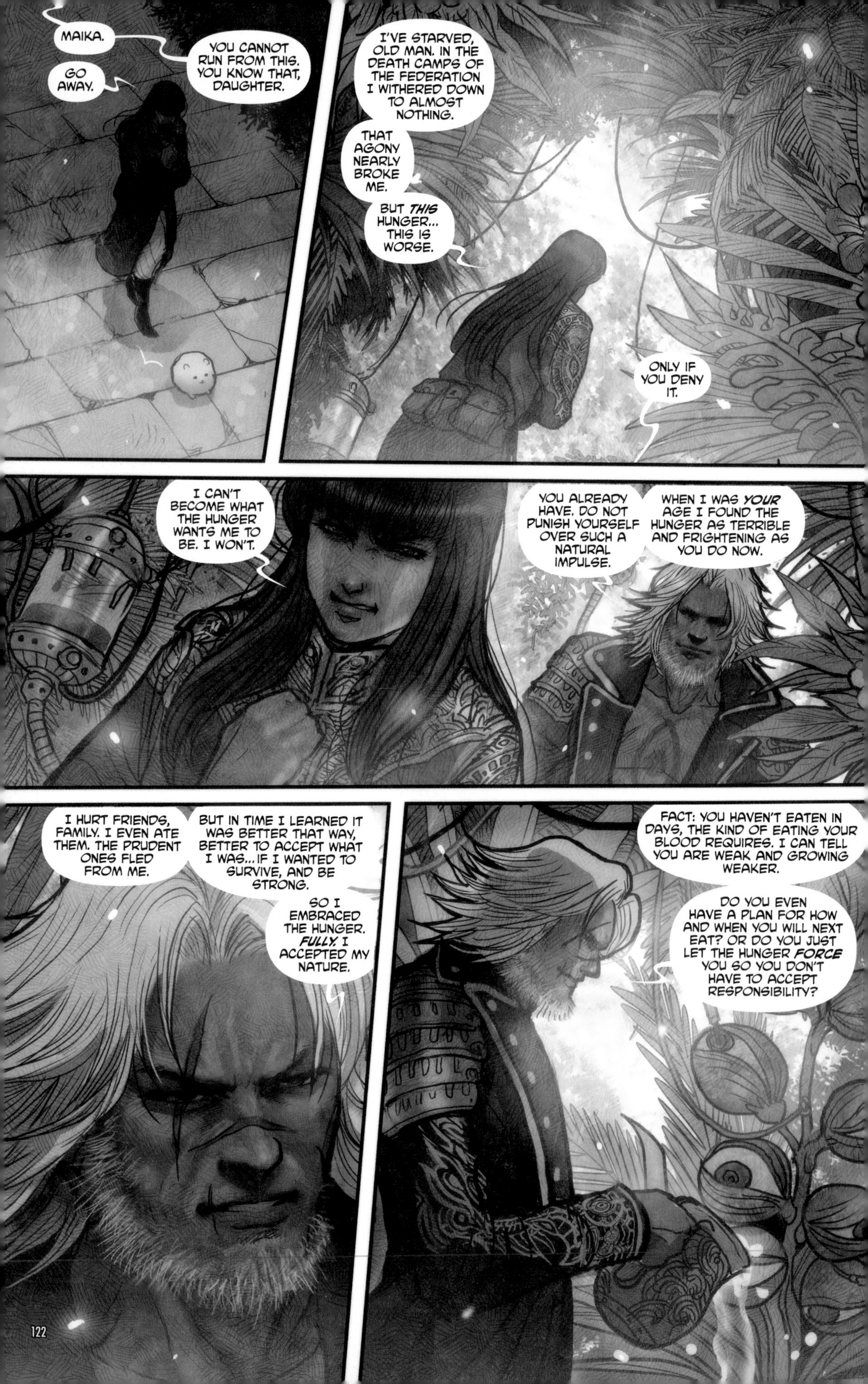
MAIKA.
YOU CANNOT RUN FROM THIS. YOU KNOW THAT, DAUGHTER.
GO AWAY.
I'VE STARVED, OLD MAN. IN THE DEATH CAMPS OF THE FEDERATION I WITHERED DOWN TO ALMOST NOTHING.
THAT AGONY NEARLY BROKE ME.
BUT *THIS* HUNGER... THIS IS WORSE.
ONLY IF YOU DENY IT.
I CAN'T BECOME WHAT THE HUNGER WANTS ME TO BE. I WON'T.
YOU ALREADY HAVE. DO NOT PUNISH YOURSELF OVER SUCH A NATURAL IMPULSE.
WHEN I WAS *YOUR* AGE I FOUND THE HUNGER AS TERRIBLE AND FRIGHTENING AS YOU DO NOW.
I HURT FRIENDS, FAMILY. I EVEN ATE THEM. THE PRUDENT ONES FLED FROM ME.
BUT IN TIME I LEARNED IT WAS BETTER THAT WAY, BETTER TO ACCEPT WHAT I WAS... IF I WANTED TO SURVIVE, AND BE STRONG.
SO I EMBRACED THE HUNGER. *FULLY.* I ACCEPTED MY NATURE.
FACT: YOU HAVEN'T EATEN IN DAYS, THE KIND OF EATING YOUR BLOOD REQUIRES. I CAN TELL YOU ARE WEAK AND GROWING WEAKER.
DO YOU EVEN HAVE A PLAN FOR HOW AND WHEN YOU WILL NEXT EAT? OR DO YOU JUST LET THE HUNGER *FORCE* YOU SO YOU DON'T HAVE TO ACCEPT RESPONSIBILITY?

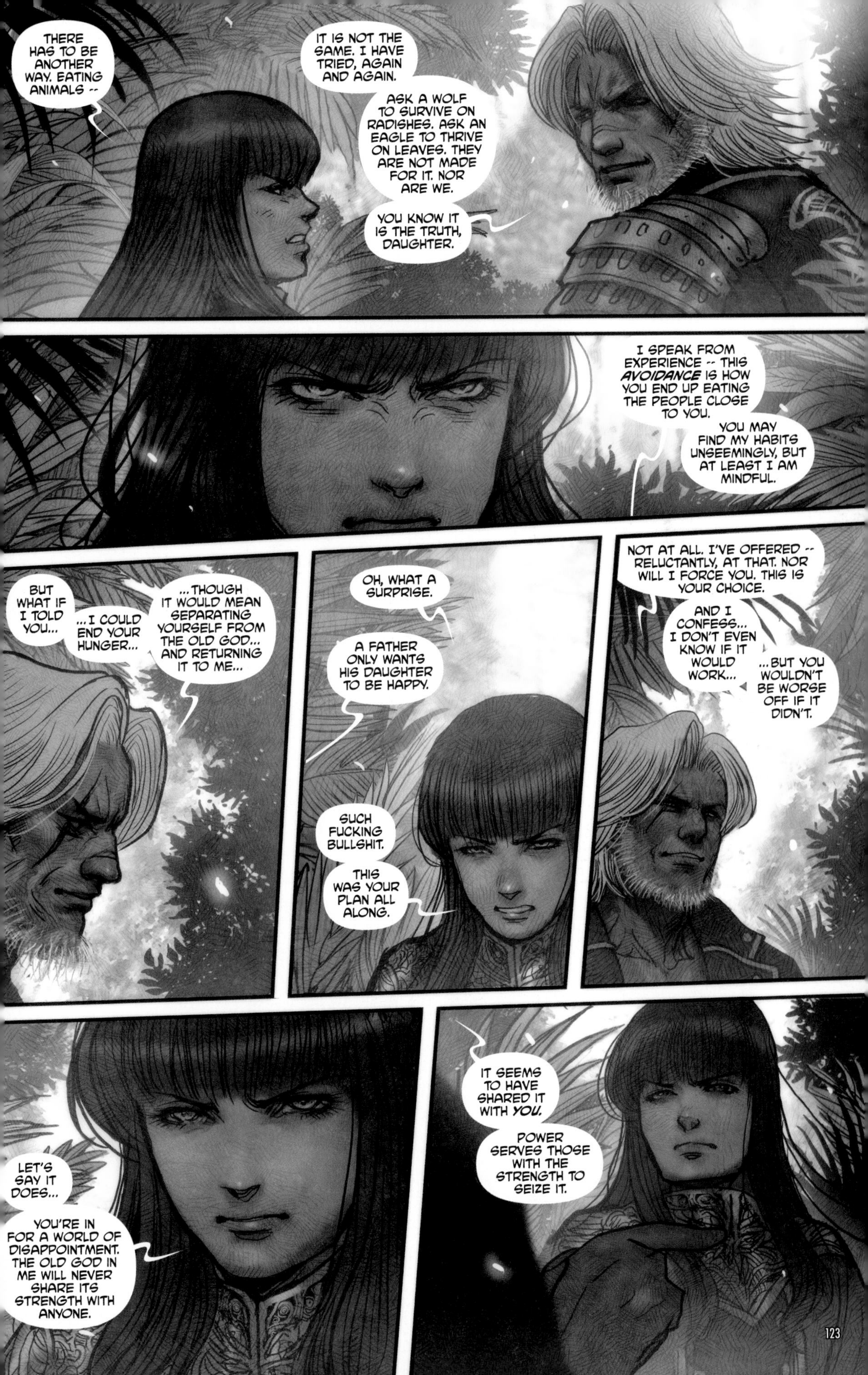
THERE HAS TO BE ANOTHER WAY. EATING ANIMALS --
IT IS NOT THE SAME. I HAVE TRIED, AGAIN AND AGAIN.
ASK A WOLF TO SURVIVE ON RADISHES. ASK AN EAGLE TO THRIVE ON LEAVES. THEY ARE NOT MADE FOR IT. NOR ARE WE.
YOU KNOW IT IS THE TRUTH, DAUGHTER.
I SPEAK FROM EXPERIENCE -- THIS AVOIDANCE IS HOW YOU END UP EATING THE PEOPLE CLOSE TO YOU.
YOU MAY FIND MY HABITS UNSEEMINGLY, BUT AT LEAST I AM MINDFUL.
BUT WHAT IF I TOLD YOU...
...I COULD END YOUR HUNGER...
...THOUGH IT WOULD MEAN SEPARATING YOURSELF FROM THE OLD GOD... AND RETURNING IT TO ME...
OH, WHAT A SURPRISE.
A FATHER ONLY WANTS HIS DAUGHTER TO BE HAPPY.
SUCH FUCKING BULLSHIT.
THIS WAS YOUR PLAN ALL ALONG.
NOT AT ALL. I'VE OFFERED -- RELUCTANTLY, AT THAT. NOR WILL I FORCE YOU. THIS IS YOUR CHOICE.
AND I CONFESS... I DON'T EVEN KNOW IF IT WOULD WORK...
...BUT YOU WOULDN'T BE WORSE OFF IF IT DIDN'T.
LET'S SAY IT DOES...
YOU'RE IN FOR A WORLD OF DISAPPOINTMENT. THE OLD GOD IN ME WILL NEVER SHARE ITS STRENGTH WITH ANYONE.
IT SEEMS TO HAVE SHARED IT WITH YOU.
POWER SERVES THOSE WITH THE STRENGTH TO SEIZE IT.

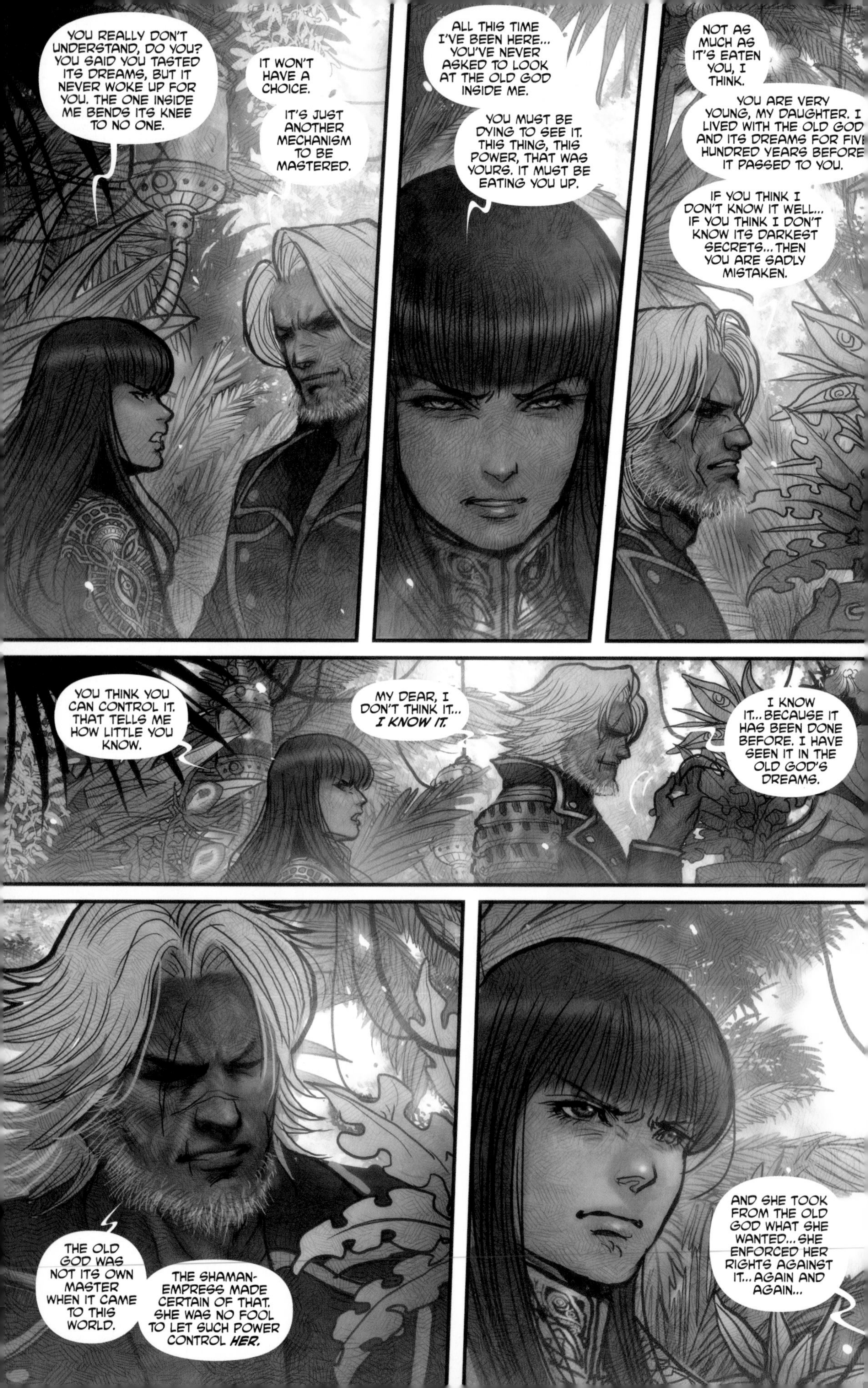
YOU REALLY DON'T UNDERSTAND, DO YOU? YOU SAID YOU TASTED ITS DREAMS, BUT IT NEVER WOKE UP FOR YOU. THE ONE INSIDE ME BENDS ITS KNEE TO NO ONE.
IT WON'T HAVE A CHOICE.
IT'S JUST ANOTHER MECHANISM TO BE MASTERED.
ALL THIS TIME I'VE BEEN HERE... YOU'VE NEVER ASKED TO LOOK AT THE OLD GOD INSIDE ME.
YOU MUST BE DYING TO SEE IT. THIS THING, THIS POWER, THAT WAS YOURS. IT MUST BE EATING YOU UP.
NOT AS MUCH AS IT'S EATEN YOU, I THINK.
YOU ARE VERY YOUNG, MY DAUGHTER. I LIVED WITH THE OLD GOD AND ITS DREAMS FOR FIVE HUNDRED YEARS BEFORE IT PASSED TO YOU.
IF YOU THINK I DON'T KNOW IT WELL... IF YOU THINK I DON'T KNOW ITS DARKEST SECRETS... THEN YOU ARE SADLY MISTAKEN.
YOU THINK YOU CAN CONTROL IT. THAT TELLS ME HOW LITTLE YOU KNOW.
MY DEAR, I DON'T THINK IT... *I KNOW IT.*
I KNOW IT... BECAUSE IT HAS BEEN DONE BEFORE. I HAVE SEEN IT IN THE OLD GOD'S DREAMS.
THE OLD GOD WAS NOT ITS OWN MASTER WHEN IT CAME TO THIS WORLD.
THE SHAMAN-EMPRESS MADE CERTAIN OF THAT. SHE WAS NO FOOL TO LET SUCH POWER CONTROL *HER.*
AND SHE TOOK FROM THE OLD GOD WHAT SHE WANTED... SHE ENFORCED HER RIGHTS AGAINST IT... AGAIN AND AGAIN...

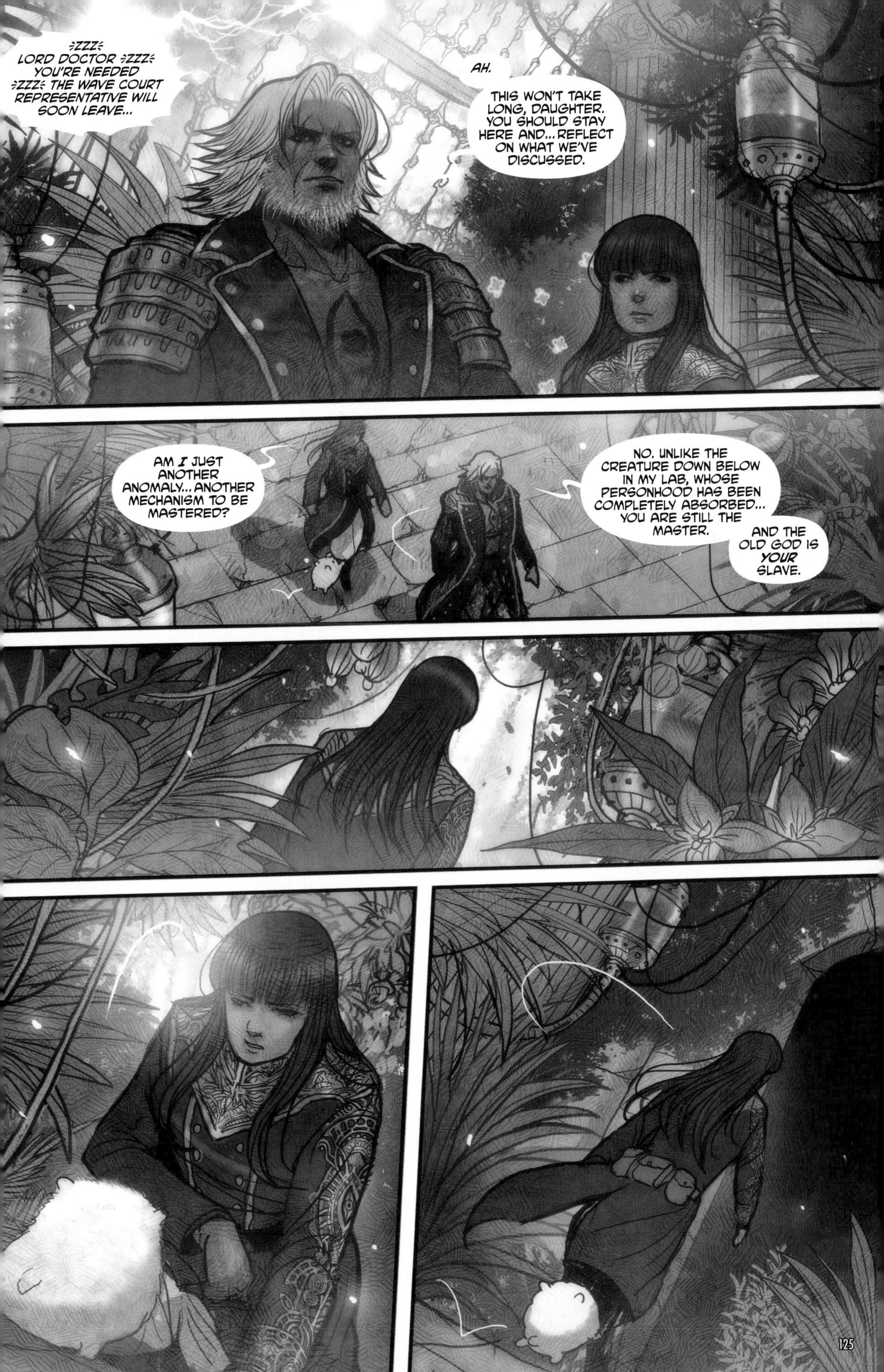

⚡ZZZ⚡ LORD DOCTOR ⚡ZZZ⚡ YOU'RE NEEDED ⚡ZZZ⚡ THE WAVE COURT REPRESENTATIVE WILL SOON LEAVE...
AH.
THIS WON'T TAKE LONG, DAUGHTER. YOU SHOULD STAY HERE AND... REFLECT ON WHAT WE'VE DISCUSSED.
AM I JUST ANOTHER ANOMALY... ANOTHER MECHANISM TO BE MASTERED?
NO. UNLIKE THE CREATURE DOWN BELOW IN MY LAB, WHOSE PERSONHOOD HAS BEEN COMPLETELY ABSORBED... YOU ARE STILL THE MASTER.
AND THE OLD GOD IS YOUR SLAVE.

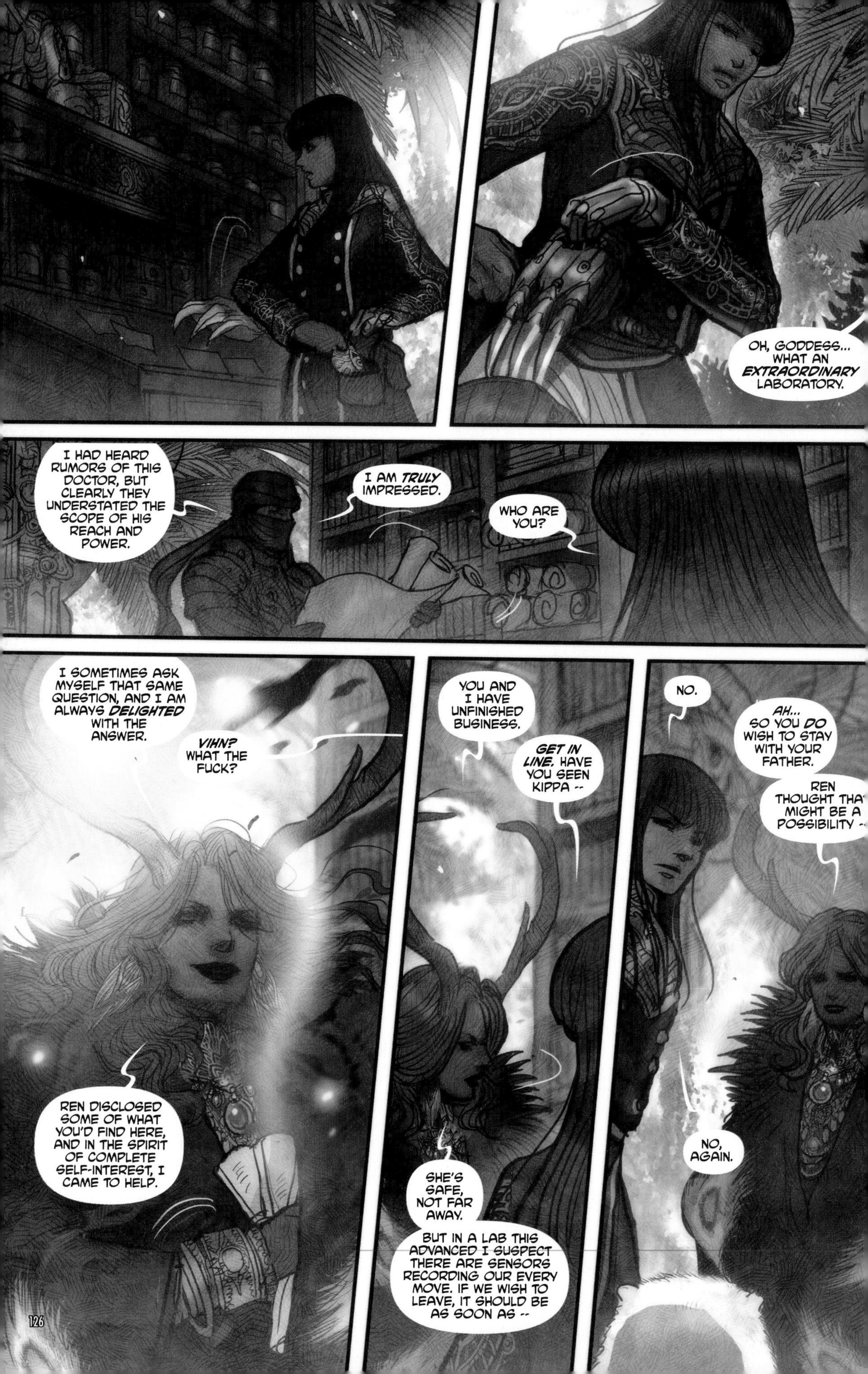
OH, GODDESS... WHAT AN EXTRAORDINARY LABORATORY.
I HAD HEARD RUMORS OF THIS DOCTOR, BUT CLEARLY THEY UNDERSTATED THE SCOPE OF HIS REACH AND POWER.
I AM TRULY IMPRESSED.
WHO ARE YOU?
I SOMETIMES ASK MYSELF THAT SAME QUESTION, AND I AM ALWAYS DELIGHTED WITH THE ANSWER.
VIHN? WHAT THE FUCK?
REN DISCLOSED SOME OF WHAT YOU'D FIND HERE, AND IN THE SPIRIT OF COMPLETE SELF-INTEREST, I CAME TO HELP.
YOU AND I HAVE UNFINISHED BUSINESS.
GET IN LINE. HAVE YOU SEEN KIPPA --
SHE'S SAFE, NOT FAR AWAY.
BUT IN A LAB THIS ADVANCED I SUSPECT THERE ARE SENSORS RECORDING OUR EVERY MOVE. IF WE WISH TO LEAVE, IT SHOULD BE AS SOON AS --
NO.
AH... SO YOU DO WISH TO STAY WITH YOUR FATHER.
REN THOUGHT THAT MIGHT BE A POSSIBILITY --
NO, AGAIN.

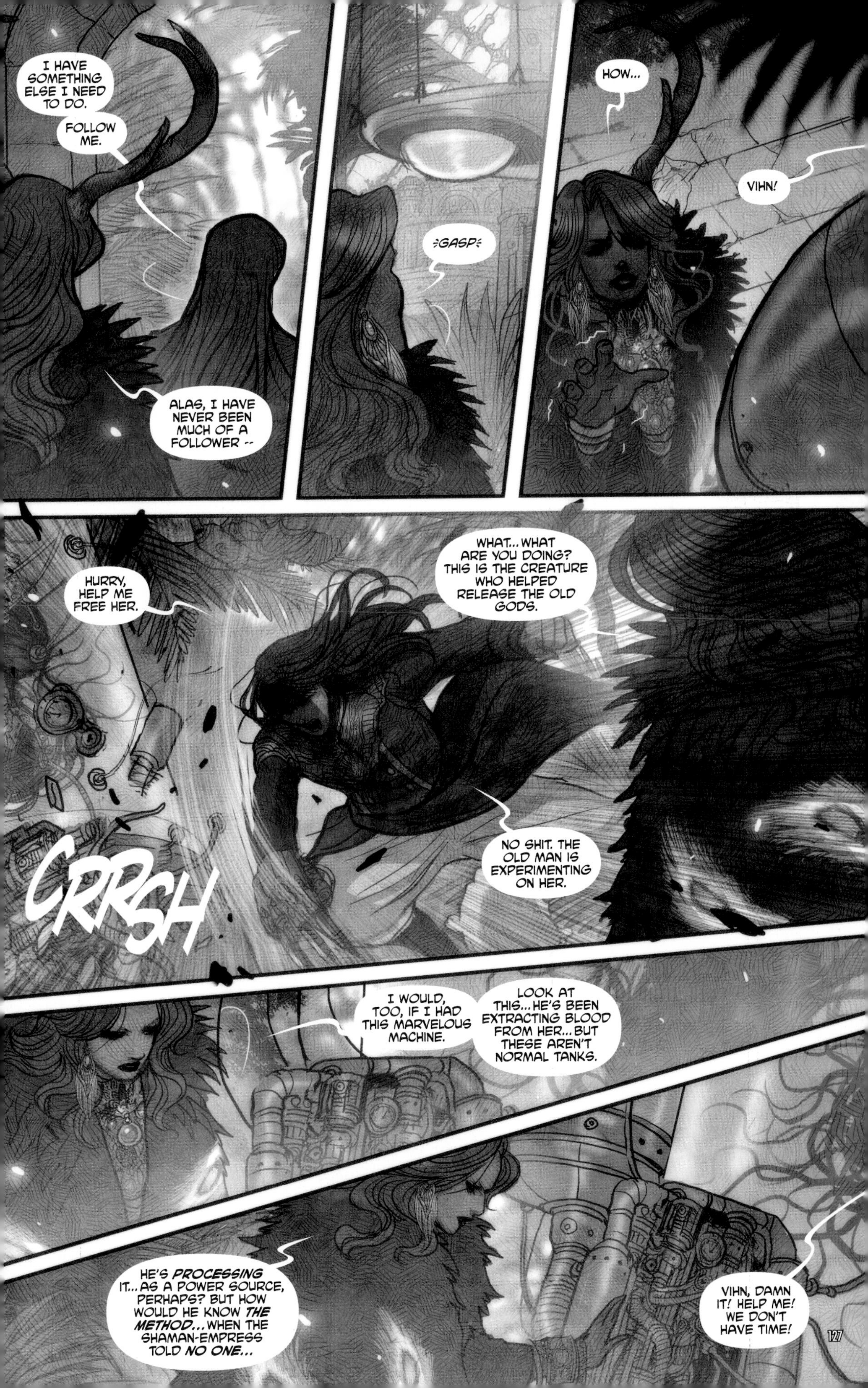
I HAVE SOMETHING ELSE I NEED TO DO.
FOLLOW ME.
ALAS, I HAVE NEVER BEEN MUCH OF A FOLLOWER --
GASP
HOW...
VIHN!
HURRY, HELP ME FREE HER.
WHAT... WHAT ARE YOU DOING? THIS IS THE CREATURE WHO HELPED RELEASE THE OLD GODS.
NO SHIT. THE OLD MAN IS EXPERIMENTING ON HER.
CRRSH
I WOULD, TOO, IF I HAD THIS MARVELOUS MACHINE.
LOOK AT THIS... HE'S BEEN EXTRACTING BLOOD FROM HER... BUT THESE AREN'T NORMAL TANKS.
HE'S *PROCESSING* IT... AS A POWER SOURCE, PERHAPS? BUT HOW WOULD HE KNOW *THE METHOD...* WHEN THE SHAMAN-EMPRESS TOLD *NO ONE...*
VIHN, DAMN IT! HELP ME! WE DON'T HAVE TIME!

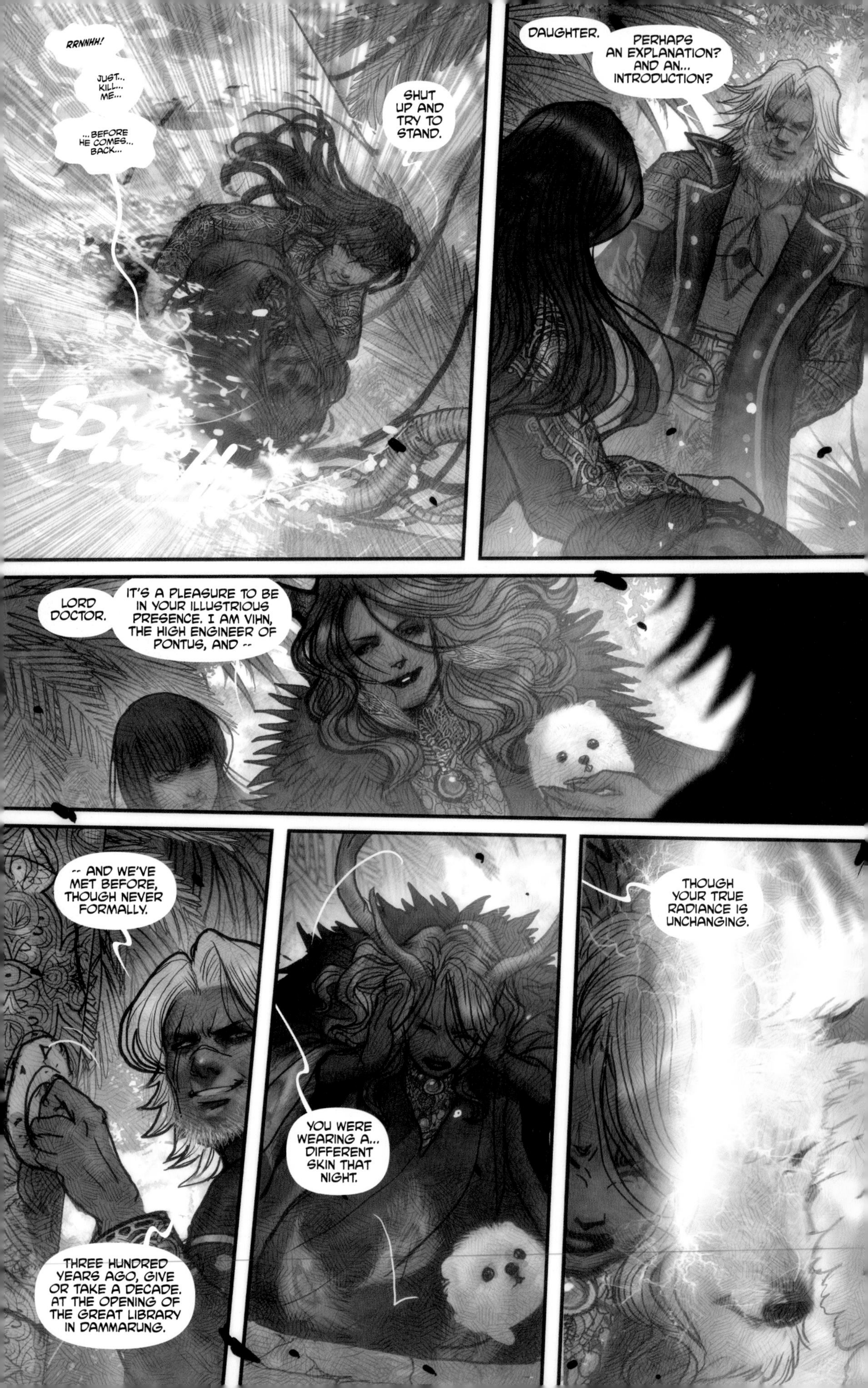
RRNNHH!
JUST... KILL... ME...
...BEFORE HE COMES... BACK...
SHUT UP AND TRY TO STAND.
DAUGHTER.
PERHAPS AN EXPLANATION? AND AN... INTRODUCTION?
LORD DOCTOR.
IT'S A PLEASURE TO BE IN YOUR ILLUSTRIOUS PRESENCE. I AM VIHN, THE HIGH ENGINEER OF PONTUS, AND --
-- AND WE'VE MET BEFORE, THOUGH NEVER FORMALLY.
THREE HUNDRED YEARS AGO, GIVE OR TAKE A DECADE. AT THE OPENING OF THE GREAT LIBRARY IN DAMMARUNG.
YOU WERE WEARING A... DIFFERENT SKIN THAT NIGHT.
THOUGH YOUR TRUE RADIANCE IS UNCHANGING.

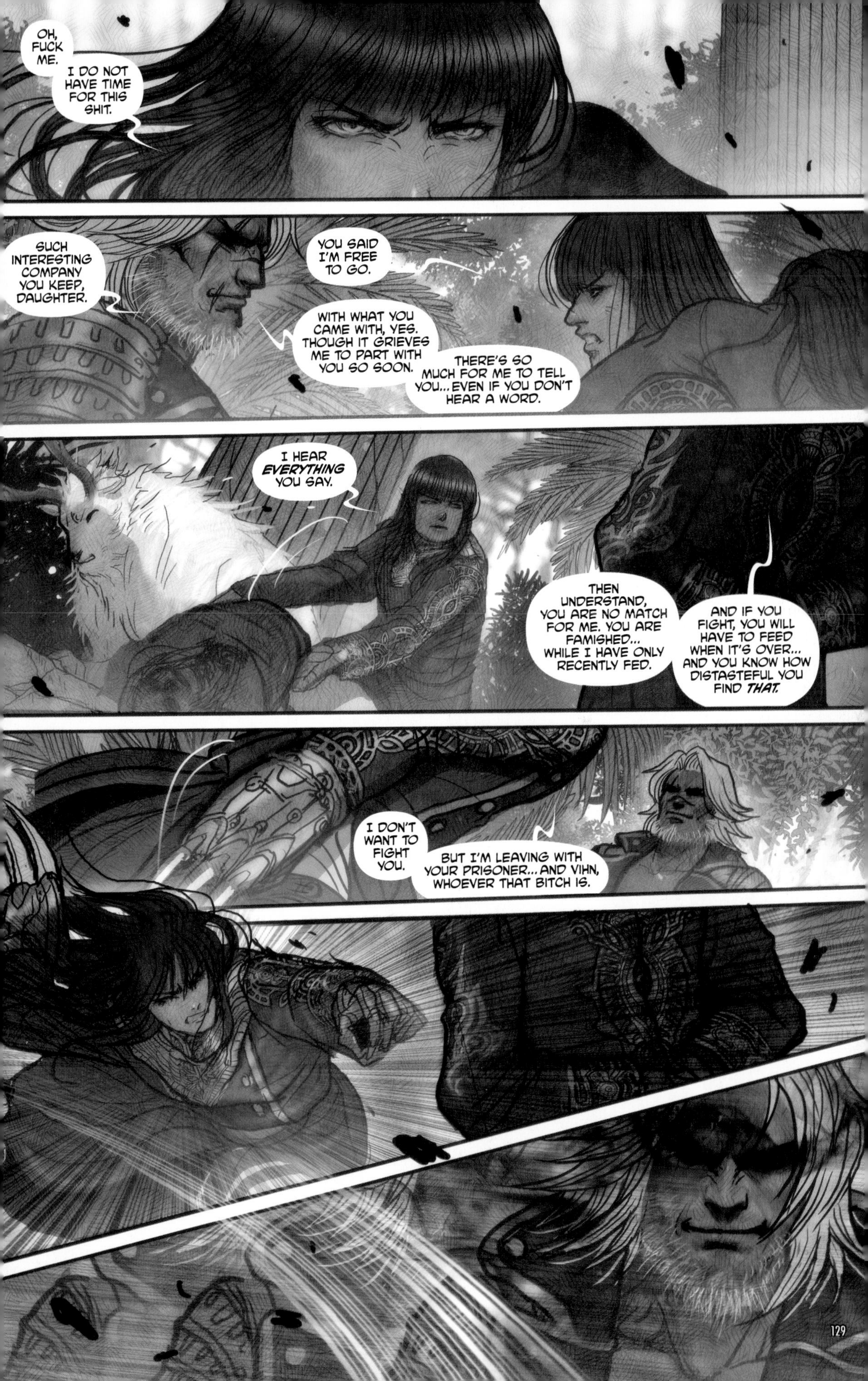
OH, FUCK ME.
I DO NOT HAVE TIME FOR THIS SHIT.
SUCH INTERESTING COMPANY YOU KEEP, DAUGHTER.
YOU SAID I'M FREE TO GO.
WITH WHAT YOU CAME WITH, YES. THOUGH IT GRIEVES ME TO PART WITH YOU SO SOON.
THERE'S SO MUCH FOR ME TO TELL YOU... EVEN IF YOU DON'T HEAR A WORD.
I HEAR *EVERYTHING* YOU SAY.
THEN UNDERSTAND, YOU ARE NO MATCH FOR ME. YOU ARE FAMISHED... WHILE I HAVE ONLY RECENTLY FED.
AND IF YOU FIGHT, YOU WILL HAVE TO FEED WHEN IT'S OVER... AND YOU KNOW HOW DISTASTEFUL YOU FIND *THAT.*
I DON'T WANT TO FIGHT YOU.
BUT I'M LEAVING WITH YOUR PRISONER... AND VIHN, WHOEVER THAT BITCH IS.

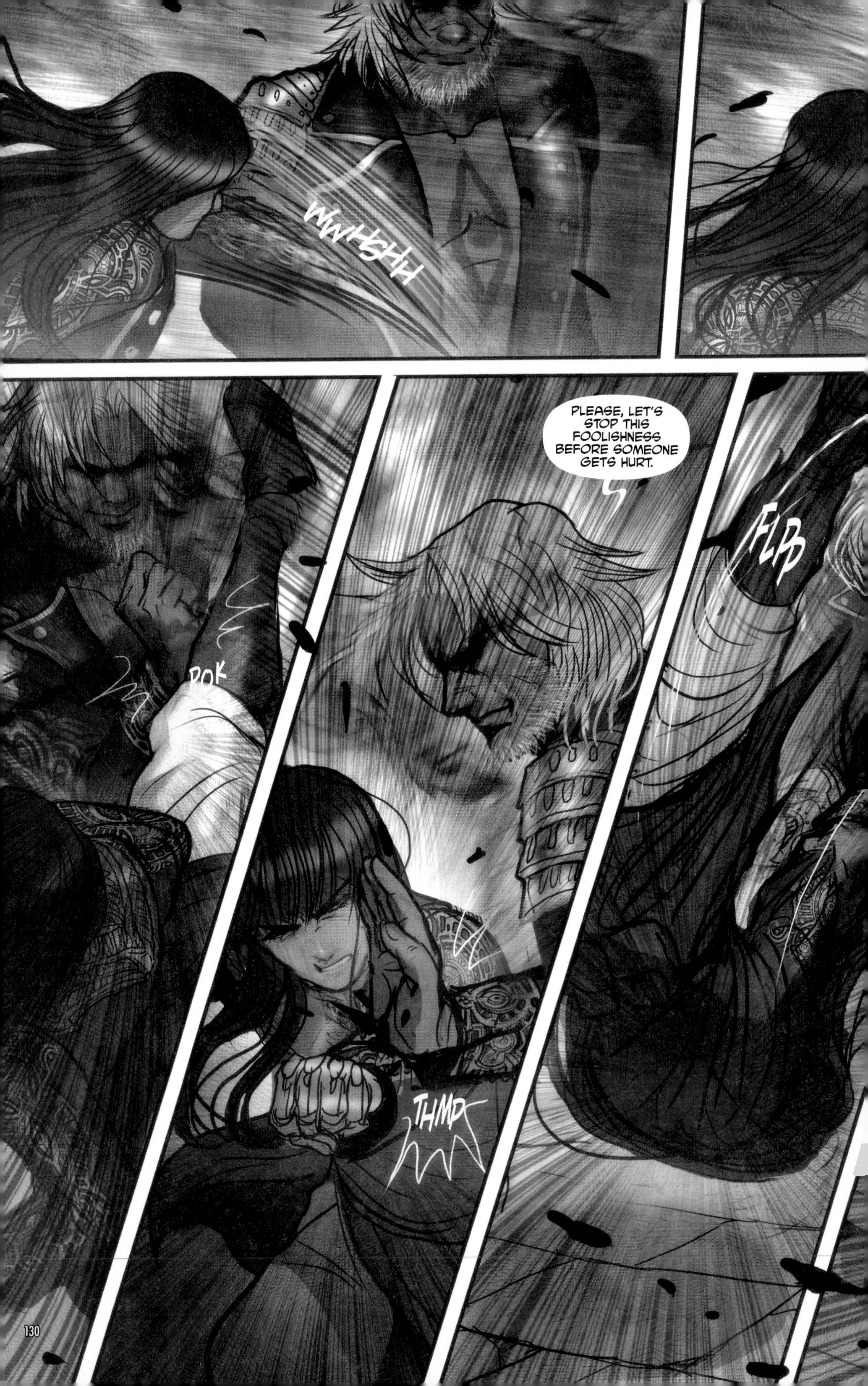
WWHSHH
PLEASE, LET'S STOP THIS FOOLISHNESS BEFORE SOMEONE GETS HURT.
POK
THMP
FLPP

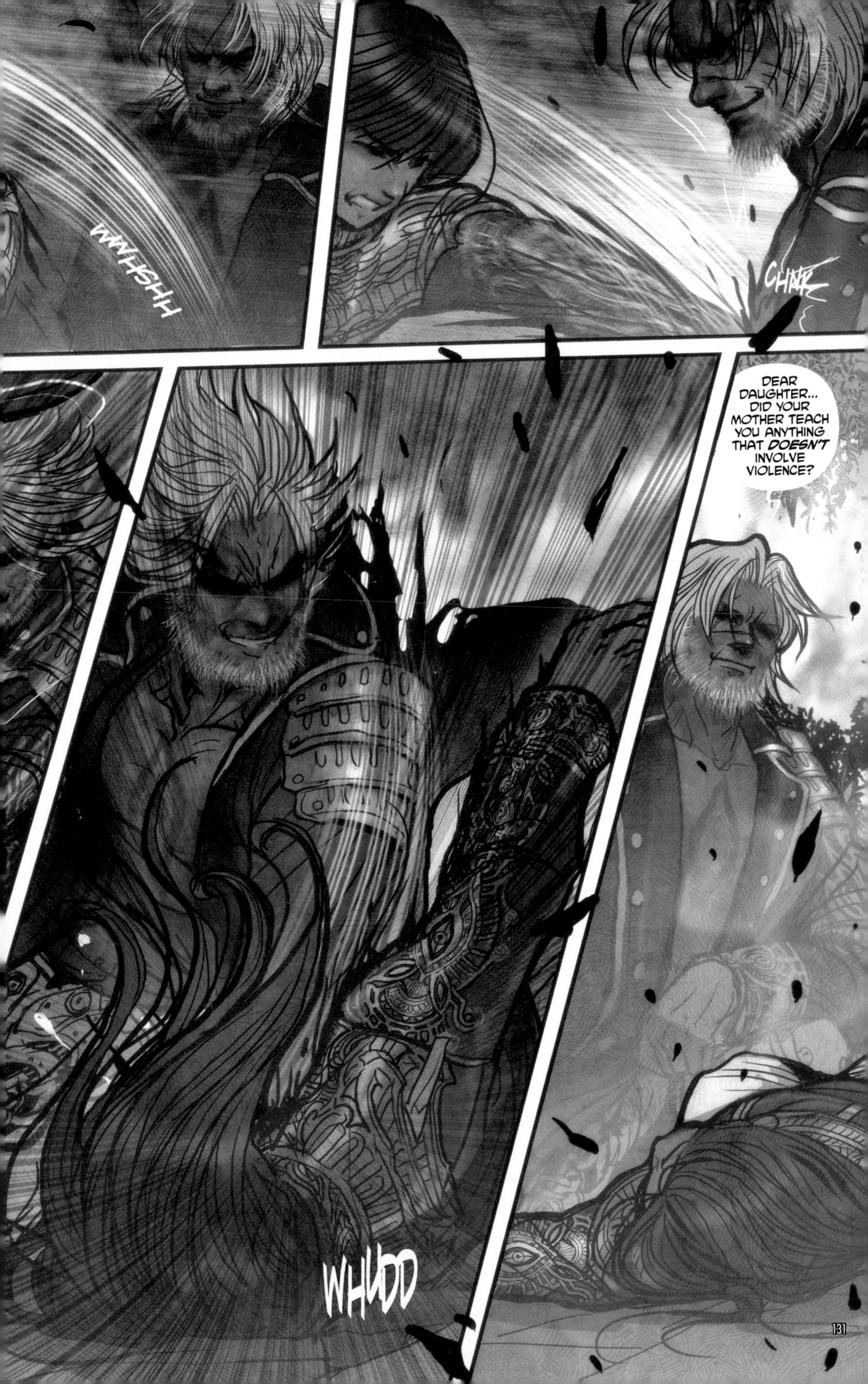
HHSHAAA
CHNK
DEAR DAUGHTER... DID YOUR MOTHER TEACH YOU ANYTHING THAT *DOESN'T* INVOLVE VIOLENCE?
WHUDD

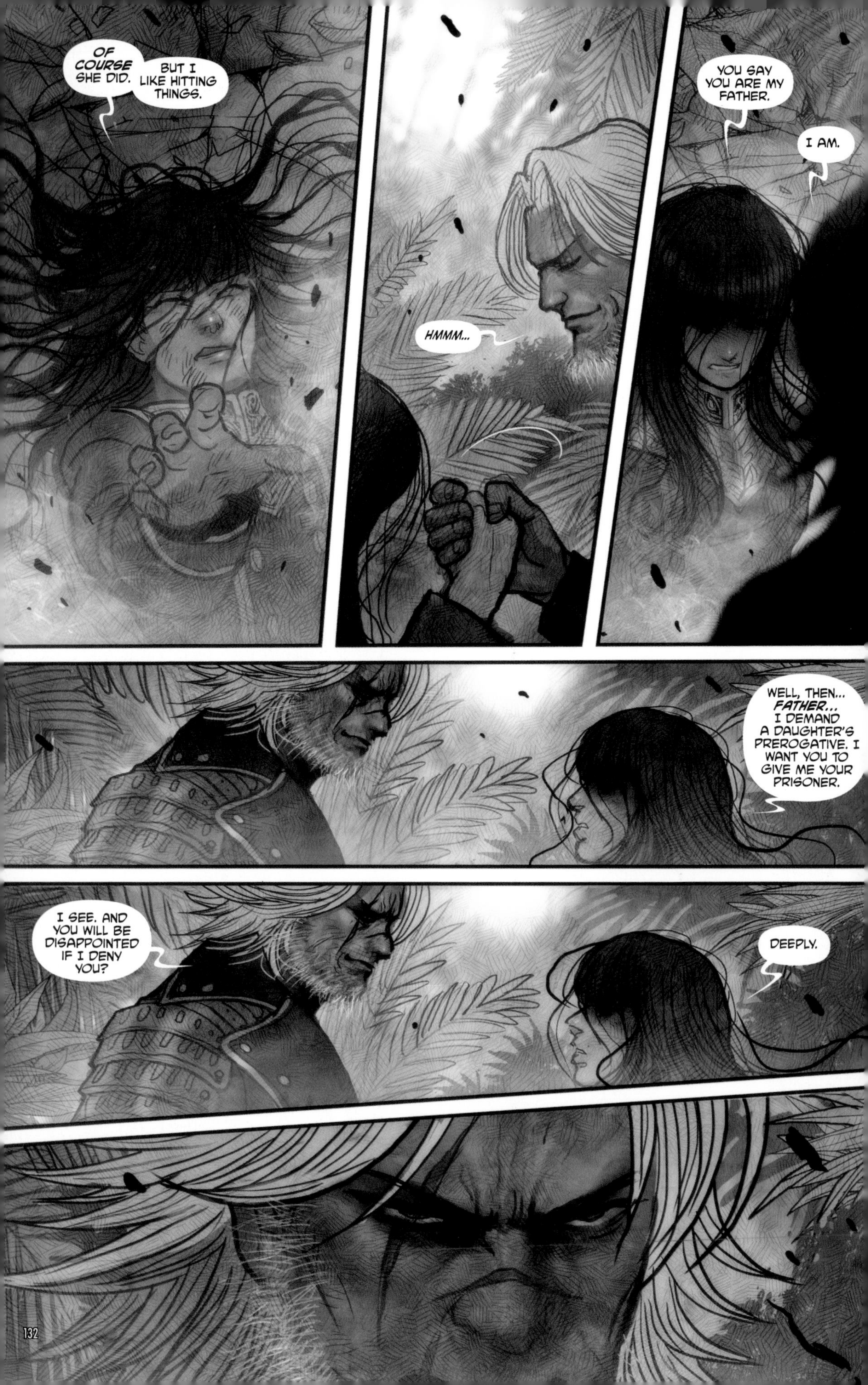
OF COURSE SHE DID.
BUT I LIKE HITTING THINGS.
HMMM...
YOU SAY YOU ARE MY FATHER.
I AM.
WELL, THEN... FATHER... I DEMAND A DAUGHTER'S PREROGATIVE. I WANT YOU TO GIVE ME YOUR PRISONER.
I SEE. AND YOU WILL BE DISAPPOINTED IF I DENY YOU?
DEEPLY.

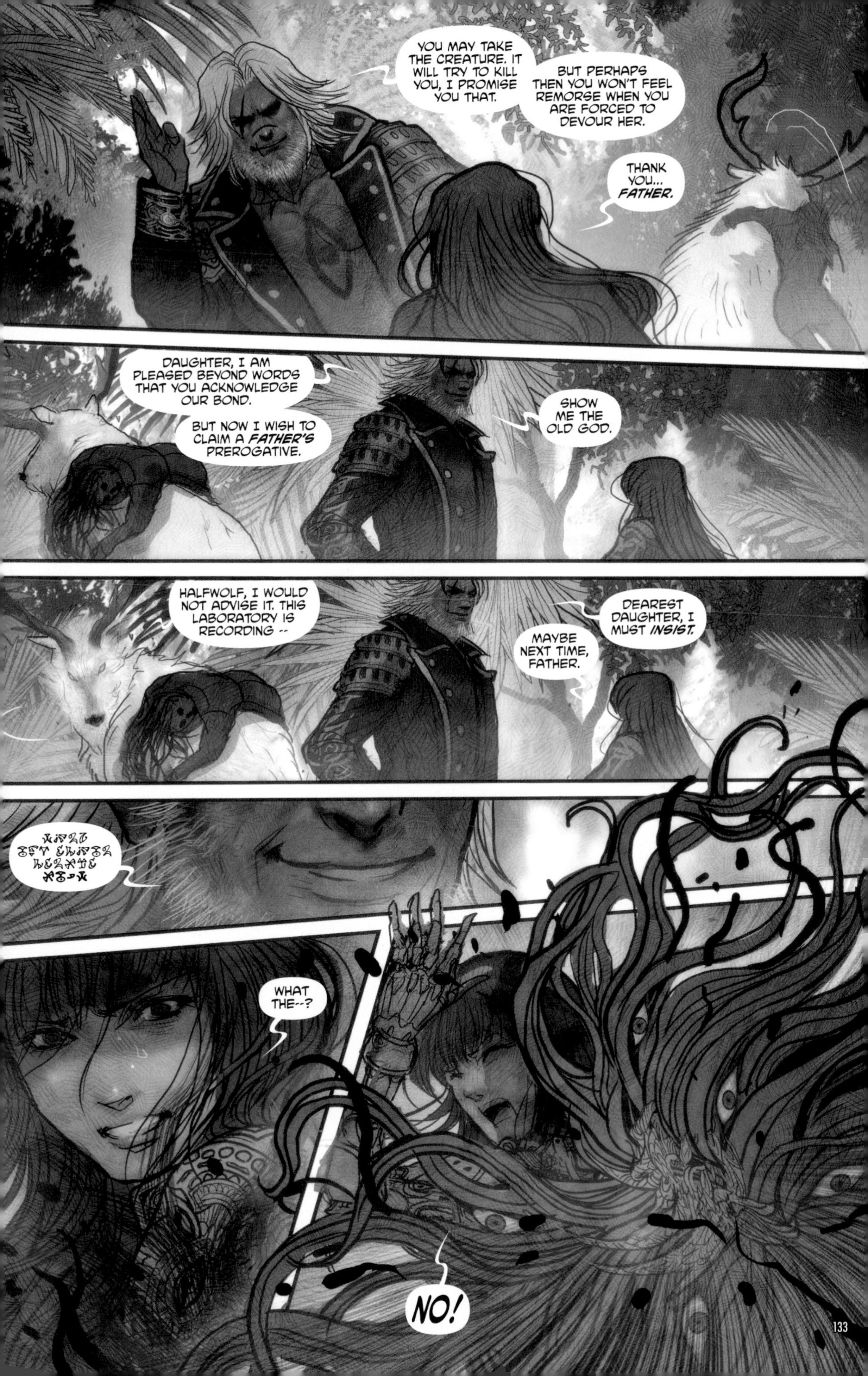
YOU MAY TAKE THE CREATURE. IT WILL TRY TO KILL YOU, I PROMISE YOU THAT.
BUT PERHAPS THEN YOU WON'T FEEL REMORSE WHEN YOU ARE FORCED TO DEVOUR HER.
THANK YOU... *FATHER.*
DAUGHTER, I AM PLEASED BEYOND WORDS THAT YOU ACKNOWLEDGE OUR BOND.
BUT NOW I WISH TO CLAIM A *FATHER'S* PREROGATIVE.
SHOW ME THE OLD GOD.
HALFWOLF, I WOULD NOT ADVISE IT. THIS LABORATORY IS RECORDING --
DEAREST DAUGHTER, I MUST *INSIST.*
MAYBE NEXT TIME, FATHER.
WHAT THE--?
NO!

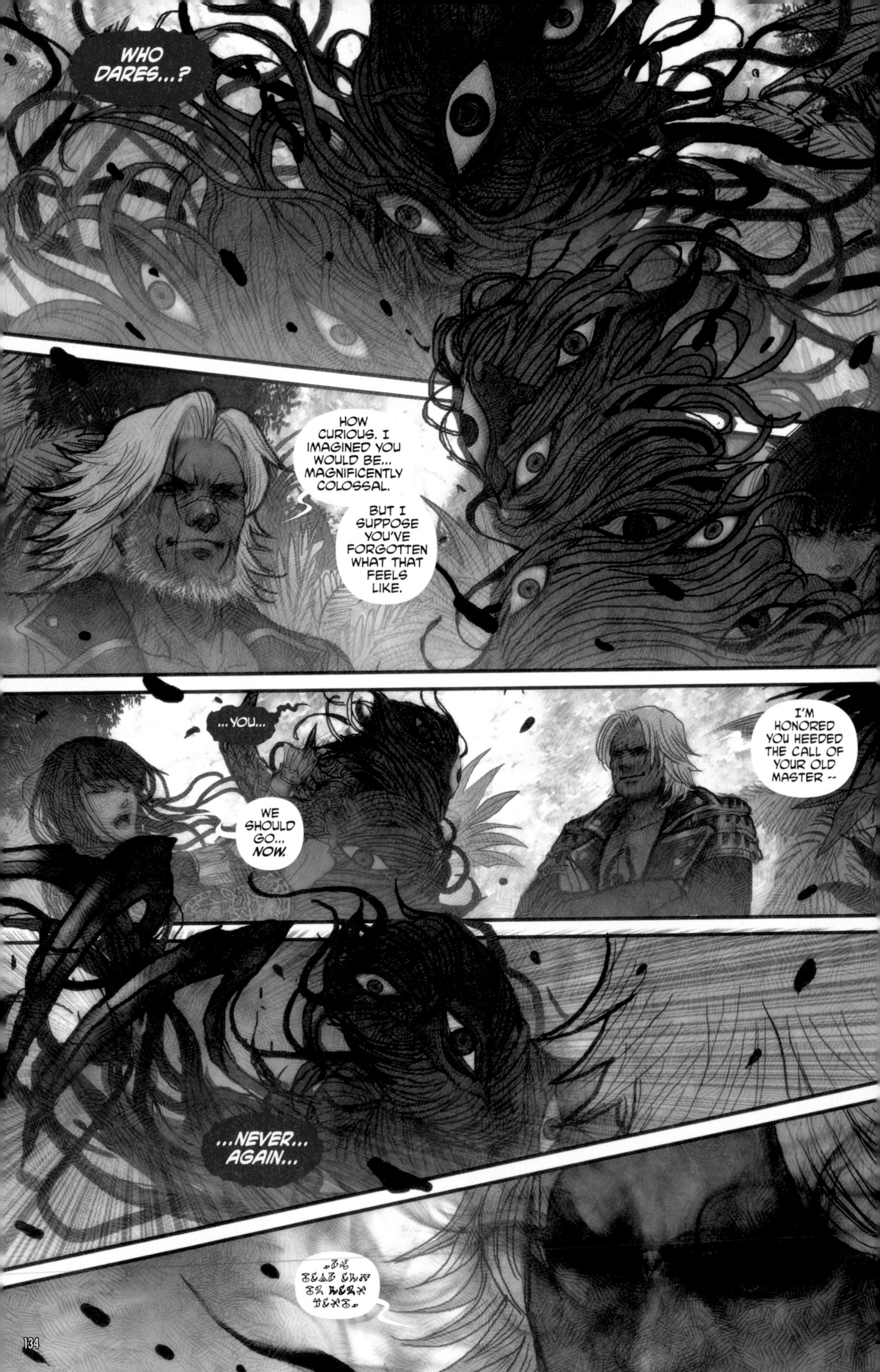
WHO DARES...?
HOW CURIOUS. I IMAGINED YOU WOULD BE... MAGNIFICENTLY COLOSSAL.
BUT I SUPPOSE YOU'VE FORGOTTEN WHAT THAT FEELS LIKE.
...YOU...
I'M HONORED YOU HEEDED THE CALL OF YOUR OLD MASTER --
WE SHOULD GO... *NOW.*
...NEVER... AGAIN...

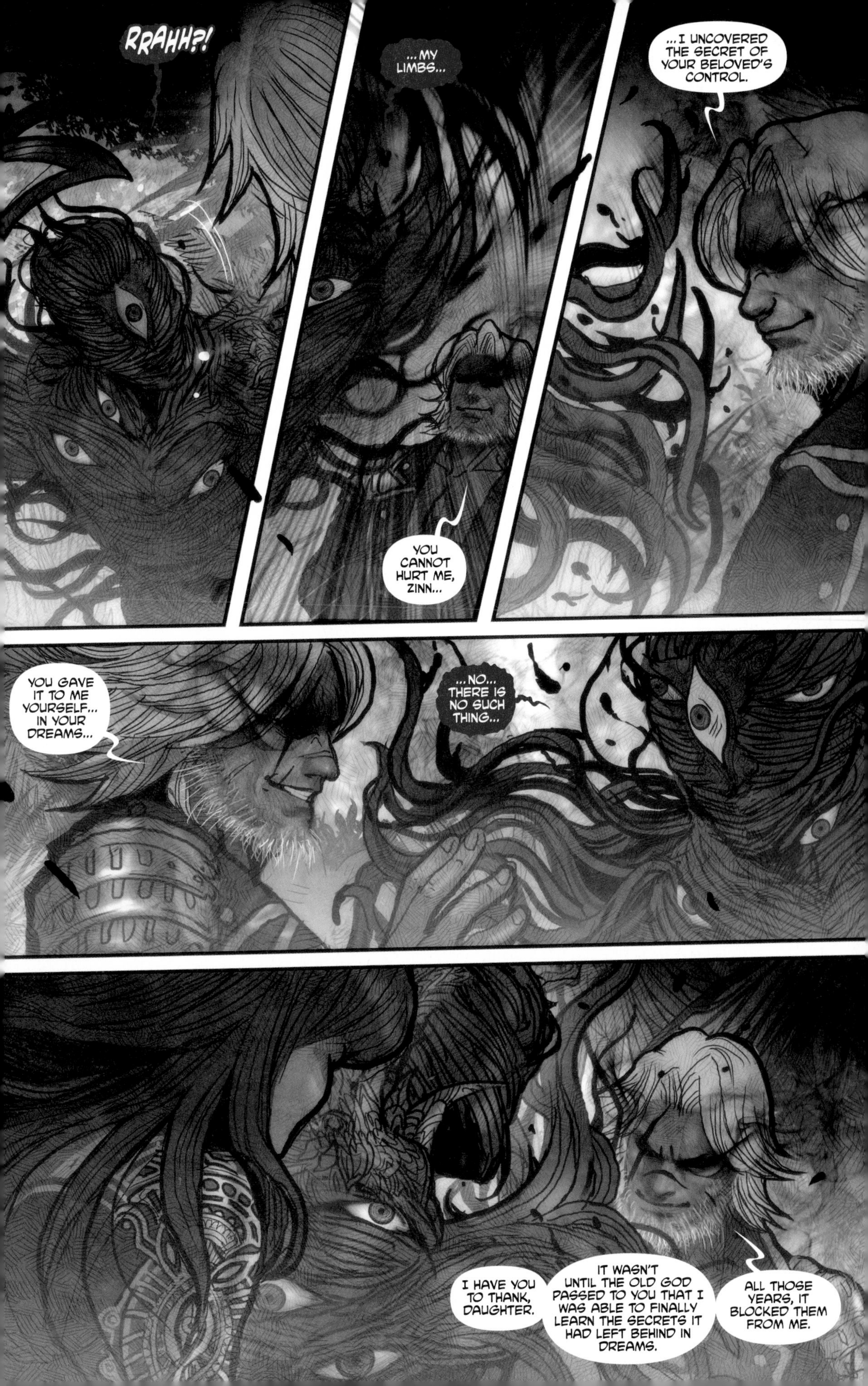
RRAHH?!
...MY LIMBS...
YOU CANNOT HURT ME, ZINN...
...I UNCOVERED THE SECRET OF YOUR BELOVED'S CONTROL.
YOU GAVE IT TO ME YOURSELF... IN YOUR DREAMS...
...NO... THERE IS NO SUCH THING...
ALL THOSE YEARS, IT BLOCKED THEM FROM ME.
IT WASN'T UNTIL THE OLD GOD PASSED TO YOU THAT I WAS ABLE TO FINALLY LEARN THE SECRETS IT HAD LEFT BEHIND IN DREAMS.
I HAVE YOU TO THANK, DAUGHTER.

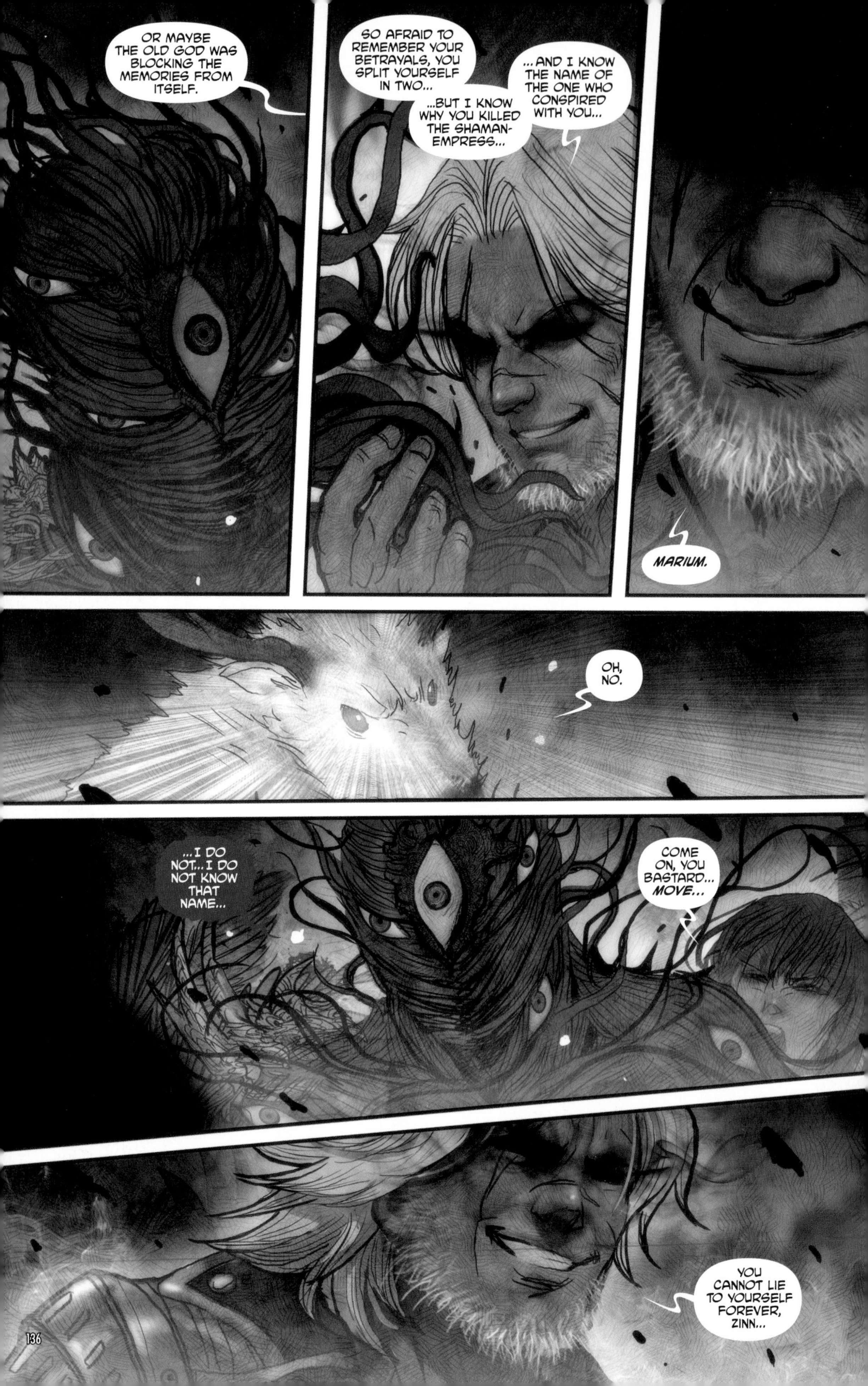

OR MAYBE THE OLD GOD WAS BLOCKING THE MEMORIES FROM ITSELF.
SO AFRAID TO REMEMBER YOUR BETRAYALS, YOU SPLIT YOURSELF IN TWO...
...BUT I KNOW WHY YOU KILLED THE SHAMAN-EMPRESS...
...AND I KNOW THE NAME OF THE ONE WHO CONSPIRED WITH YOU...
MARIUM.
OH, NO.
...I DO NOT...I DO NOT KNOW THAT NAME...
COME ON, YOU BASTARD... MOVE...
YOU CANNOT LIE TO YOURSELF FOREVER, ZINN...

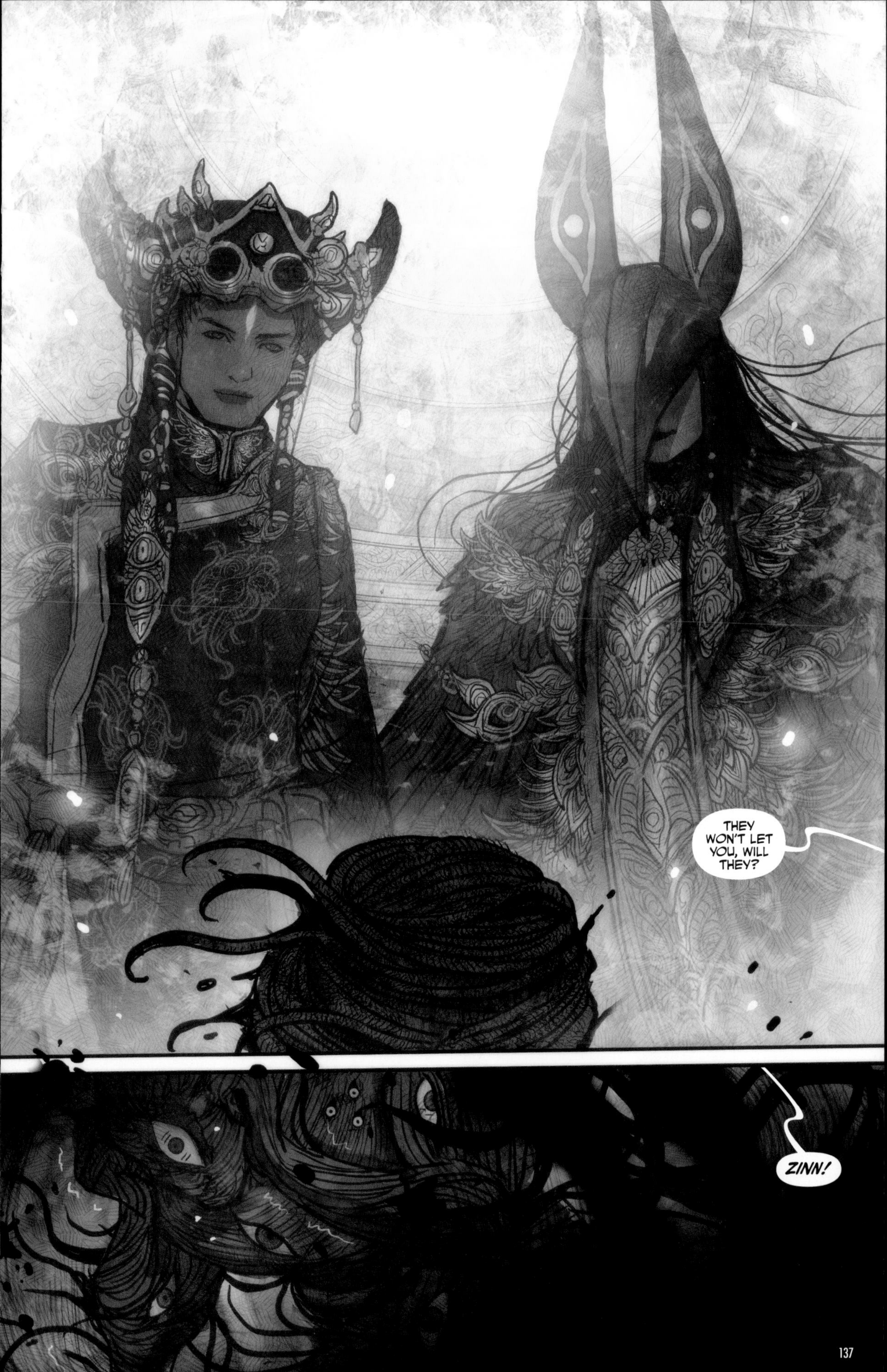
THEY WON'T LET YOU, WILL THEY?
ZINN!

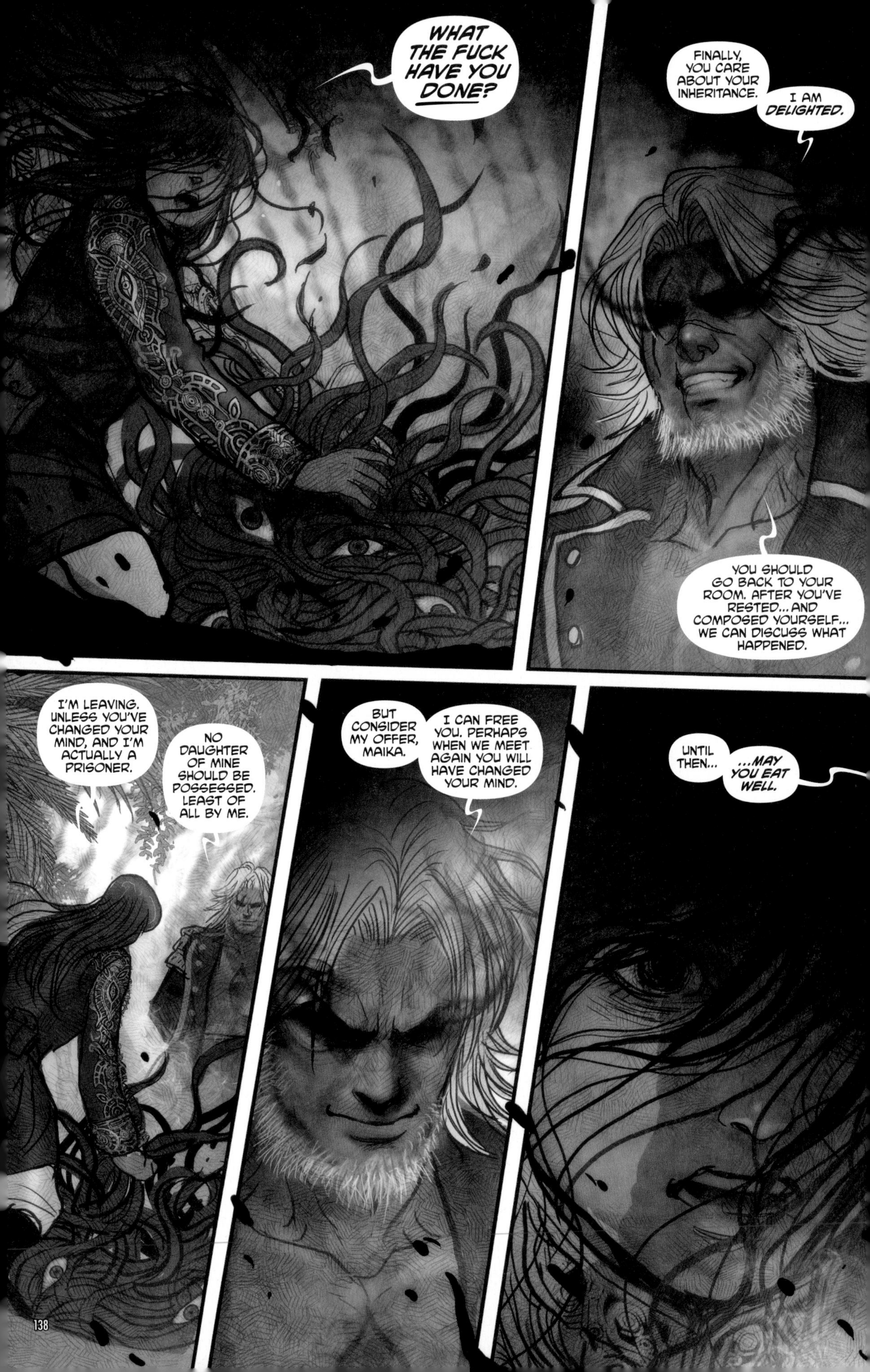
WHAT THE FUCK HAVE YOU DONE?
FINALLY, YOU CARE ABOUT YOUR INHERITANCE.
I AM DELIGHTED.
YOU SHOULD GO BACK TO YOUR ROOM. AFTER YOU'VE RESTED... AND COMPOSED YOURSELF... WE CAN DISCUSS WHAT HAPPENED.
I'M LEAVING. UNLESS YOU'VE CHANGED YOUR MIND, AND I'M ACTUALLY A PRISONER.
NO DAUGHTER OF MINE SHOULD BE POSSESSED. LEAST OF ALL BY ME.
BUT CONSIDER MY OFFER, MAIKA.
I CAN FREE YOU. PERHAPS WHEN WE MEET AGAIN YOU WILL HAVE CHANGED YOUR MIND.
UNTIL THEN...
...MAY YOU EAT WELL.

CHAPTER TWENTY-FOUR

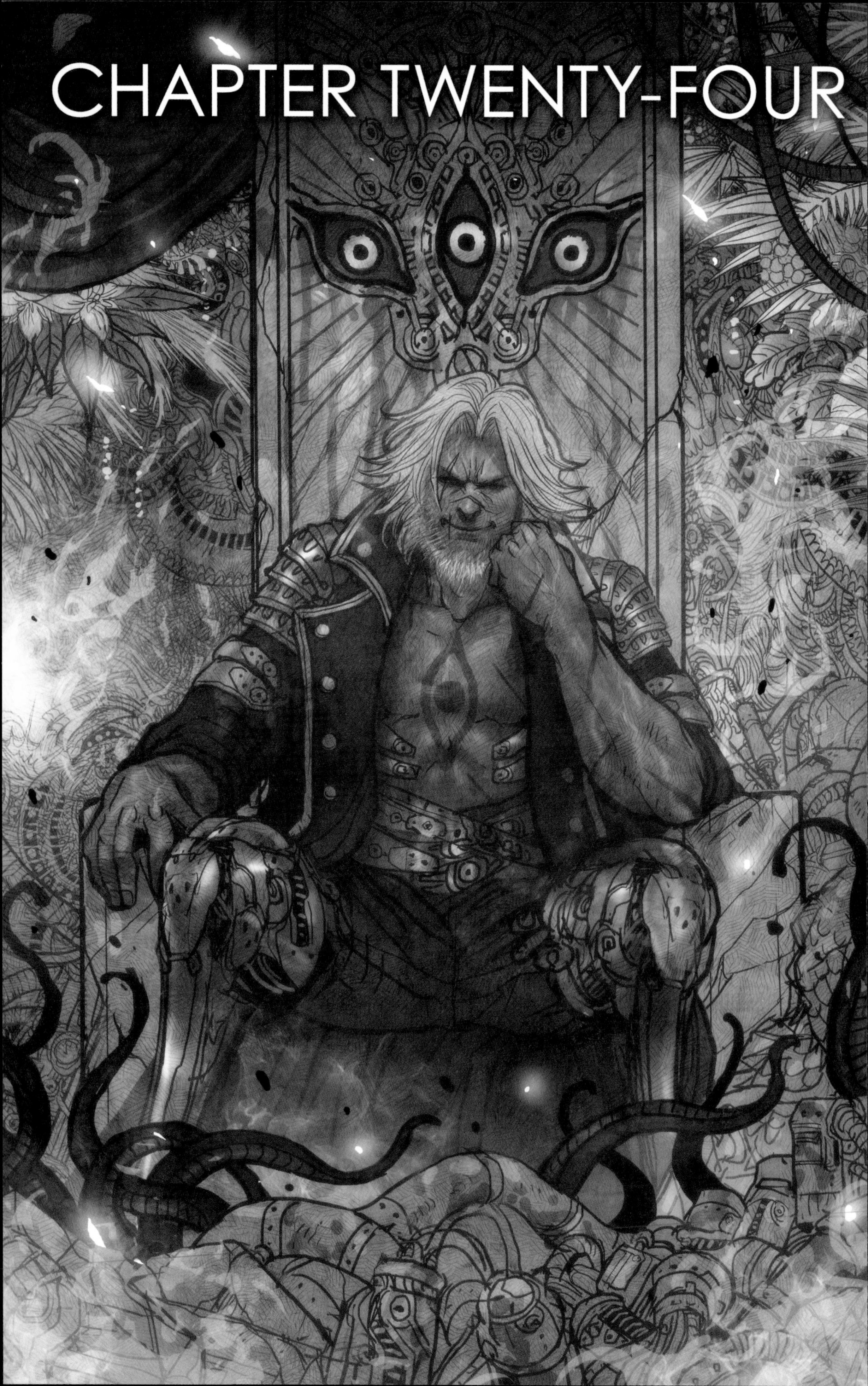

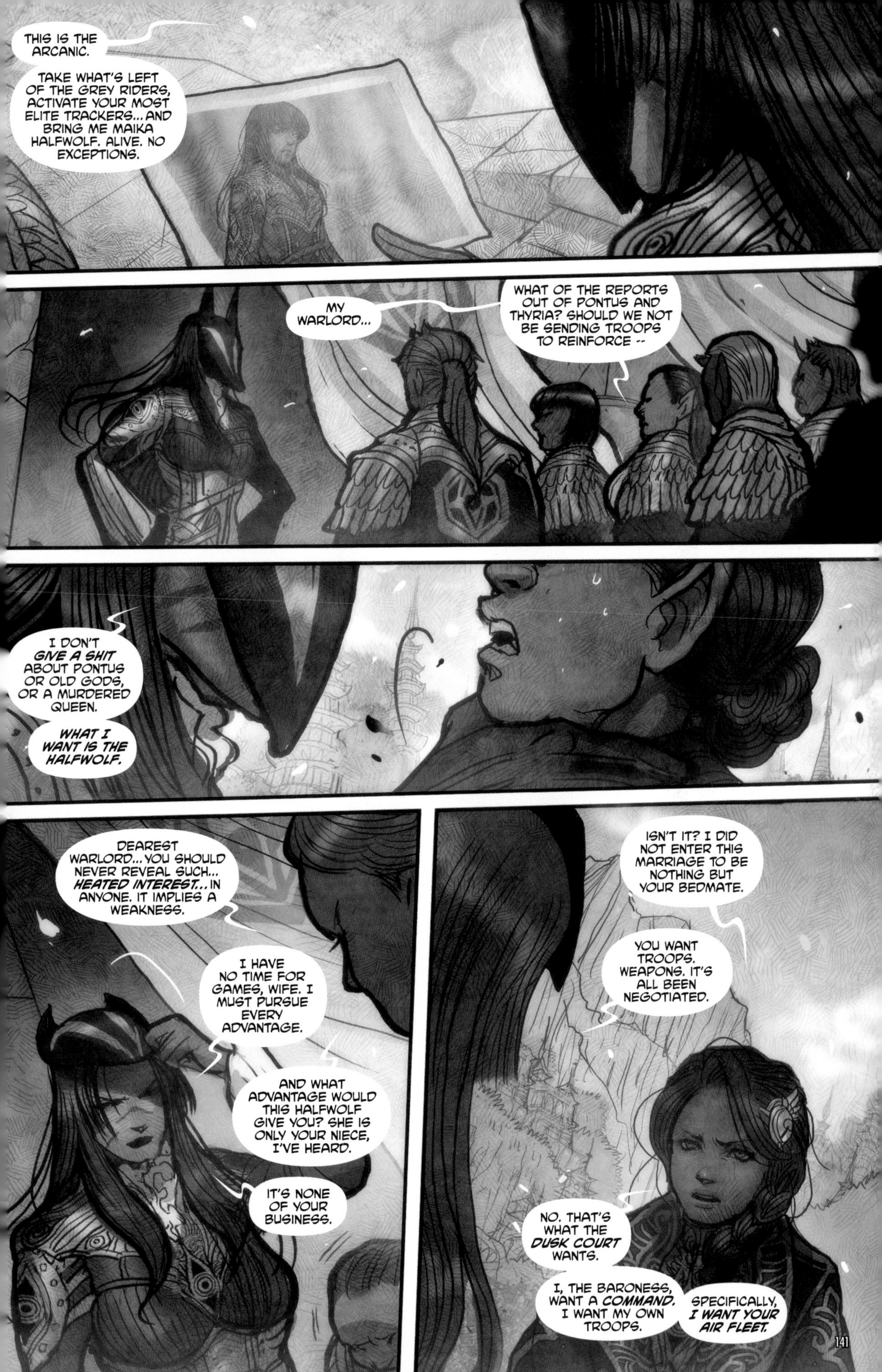
THIS IS THE ARCANIC.
TAKE WHAT'S LEFT OF THE GREY RIDERS, ACTIVATE YOUR MOST ELITE TRACKERS... AND BRING ME MAIKA HALFWOLF. ALIVE. NO EXCEPTIONS.
MY WARLORD...
WHAT OF THE REPORTS OUT OF PONTUS AND THYRIA? SHOULD WE NOT BE SENDING TROOPS TO REINFORCE --
I DON'T *GIVE A SHIT* ABOUT PONTUS OR OLD GODS, OR A MURDERED QUEEN.
WHAT I WANT IS THE HALFWOLF.
DEAREST WARLORD... YOU SHOULD NEVER REVEAL SUCH... *HEATED INTEREST...* IN ANYONE. IT IMPLIES A WEAKNESS.
I HAVE NO TIME FOR GAMES, WIFE. I MUST PURSUE EVERY ADVANTAGE.
AND WHAT ADVANTAGE WOULD THIS HALFWOLF GIVE YOU? SHE IS ONLY YOUR NIECE, I'VE HEARD.
IT'S NONE OF YOUR BUSINESS.
ISN'T IT? I DID NOT ENTER THIS MARRIAGE TO BE NOTHING BUT YOUR BEDMATE.
YOU WANT TROOPS. WEAPONS. IT'S ALL BEEN NEGOTIATED.
NO. THAT'S WHAT THE *DUSK COURT* WANTS.
I, THE BARONESS, WANT A *COMMAND.* I WANT MY OWN TROOPS.
SPECIFICALLY, ***I WANT YOUR AIR FLEET.***

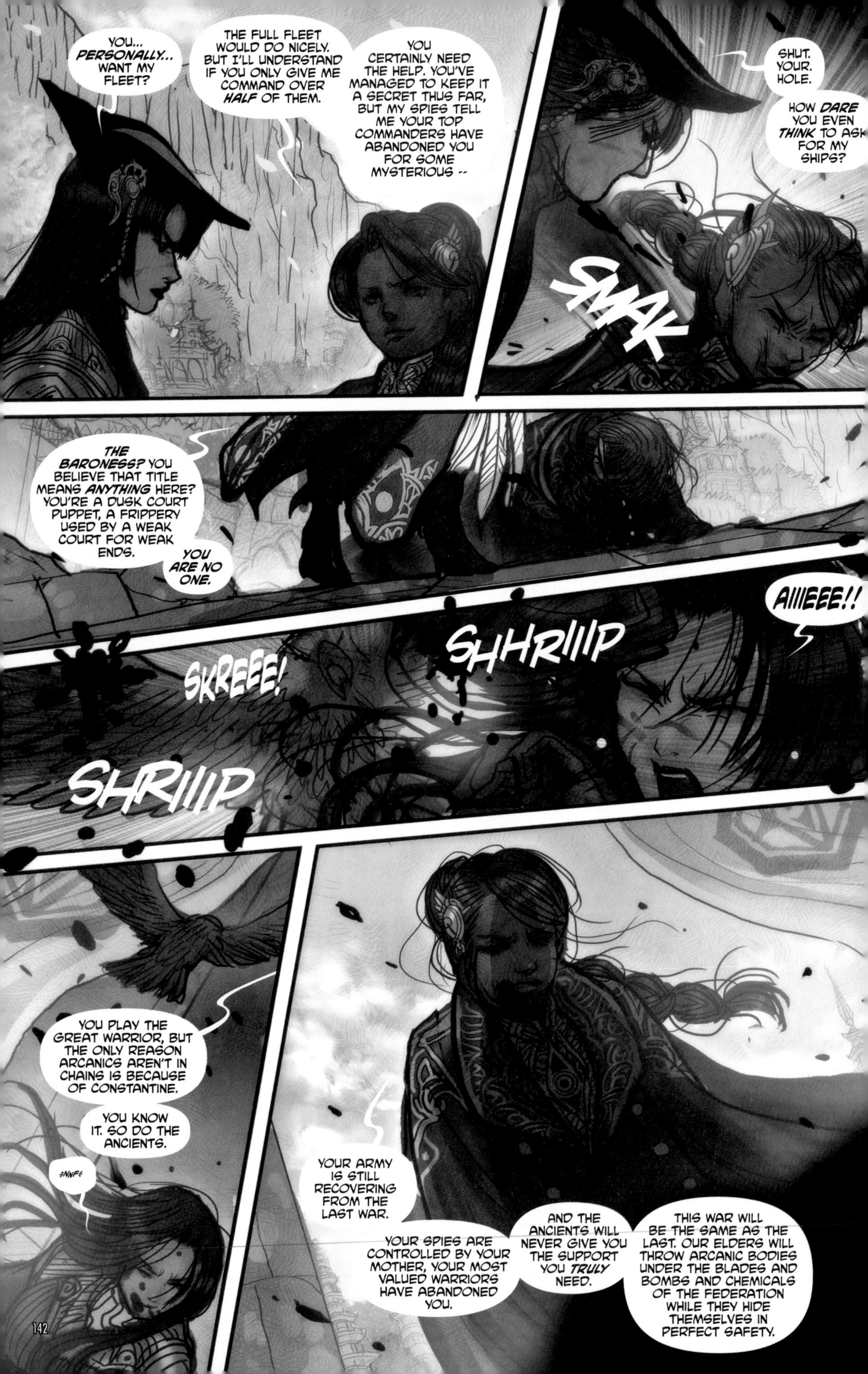
YOU... PERSONALLY... WANT MY FLEET?
THE FULL FLEET WOULD DO NICELY. BUT I'LL UNDERSTAND IF YOU ONLY GIVE ME COMMAND OVER HALF OF THEM.
YOU CERTAINLY NEED THE HELP. YOU'VE MANAGED TO KEEP IT A SECRET THUS FAR, BUT MY SPIES TELL ME YOUR TOP COMMANDERS HAVE ABANDONED YOU FOR SOME MYSTERIOUS --
SHUT. YOUR. HOLE.
HOW DARE YOU EVEN THINK TO ASK FOR MY SHIPS?
SMAK
THE BARONESS? YOU BELIEVE THAT TITLE MEANS ANYTHING HERE? YOU'RE A DUSK COURT PUPPET, A FRIPPERY USED BY A WEAK COURT FOR WEAK ENDS.
YOU ARE NO ONE.
AIIIEEE!!
SKREEE!
SHHRIIIP
SHRIIIP
YOU PLAY THE GREAT WARRIOR, BUT THE ONLY REASON ARCANICS AREN'T IN CHAINS IS BECAUSE OF CONSTANTINE.
YOU KNOW IT. SO DO THE ANCIENTS.
SNNF
YOUR ARMY IS STILL RECOVERING FROM THE LAST WAR.
YOUR SPIES ARE CONTROLLED BY YOUR MOTHER, YOUR MOST VALUED WARRIORS HAVE ABANDONED YOU.
AND THE ANCIENTS WILL NEVER GIVE YOU THE SUPPORT YOU TRULY NEED.
THIS WAR WILL BE THE SAME AS THE LAST. OUR ELDERS WILL THROW ARCANIC BODIES UNDER THE BLADES AND BOMBS AND CHEMICALS OF THE FEDERATION WHILE THEY HIDE THEMSELVES IN PERFECT SAFETY.

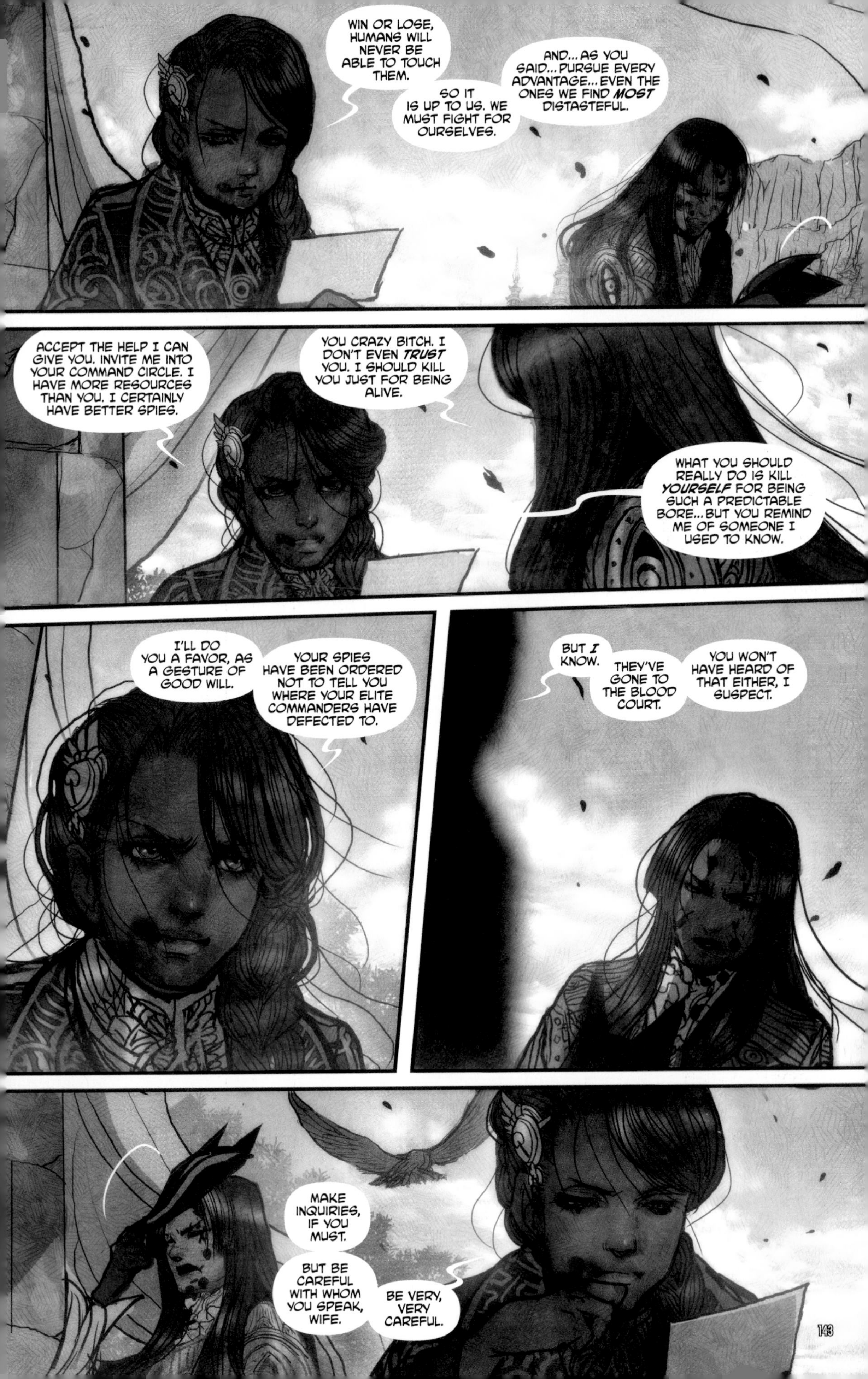
WIN OR LOSE, HUMANS WILL NEVER BE ABLE TO TOUCH THEM.
SO IT IS UP TO US. WE MUST FIGHT FOR OURSELVES.
AND... AS YOU SAID... PURSUE EVERY ADVANTAGE... EVEN THE ONES WE FIND *MOST* DISTASTEFUL.
ACCEPT THE HELP I CAN GIVE YOU. INVITE ME INTO YOUR COMMAND CIRCLE. I HAVE MORE RESOURCES THAN YOU. I CERTAINLY HAVE BETTER SPIES.
YOU CRAZY BITCH. I DON'T EVEN *TRUST* YOU. I SHOULD KILL YOU JUST FOR BEING ALIVE.
WHAT YOU SHOULD REALLY DO IS KILL *YOURSELF* FOR BEING SUCH A PREDICTABLE BORE... BUT YOU REMIND ME OF SOMEONE I USED TO KNOW.
I'LL DO YOU A FAVOR, AS A GESTURE OF GOOD WILL.
YOUR SPIES HAVE BEEN ORDERED NOT TO TELL YOU WHERE YOUR ELITE COMMANDERS HAVE DEFECTED TO.
BUT *I* KNOW.
THEY'VE GONE TO THE BLOOD COURT.
YOU WON'T HAVE HEARD OF THAT EITHER, I SUSPECT.
MAKE INQUIRIES, IF YOU MUST.
BUT BE CAREFUL WITH WHOM YOU SPEAK, WIFE.
BE VERY, VERY CAREFUL.

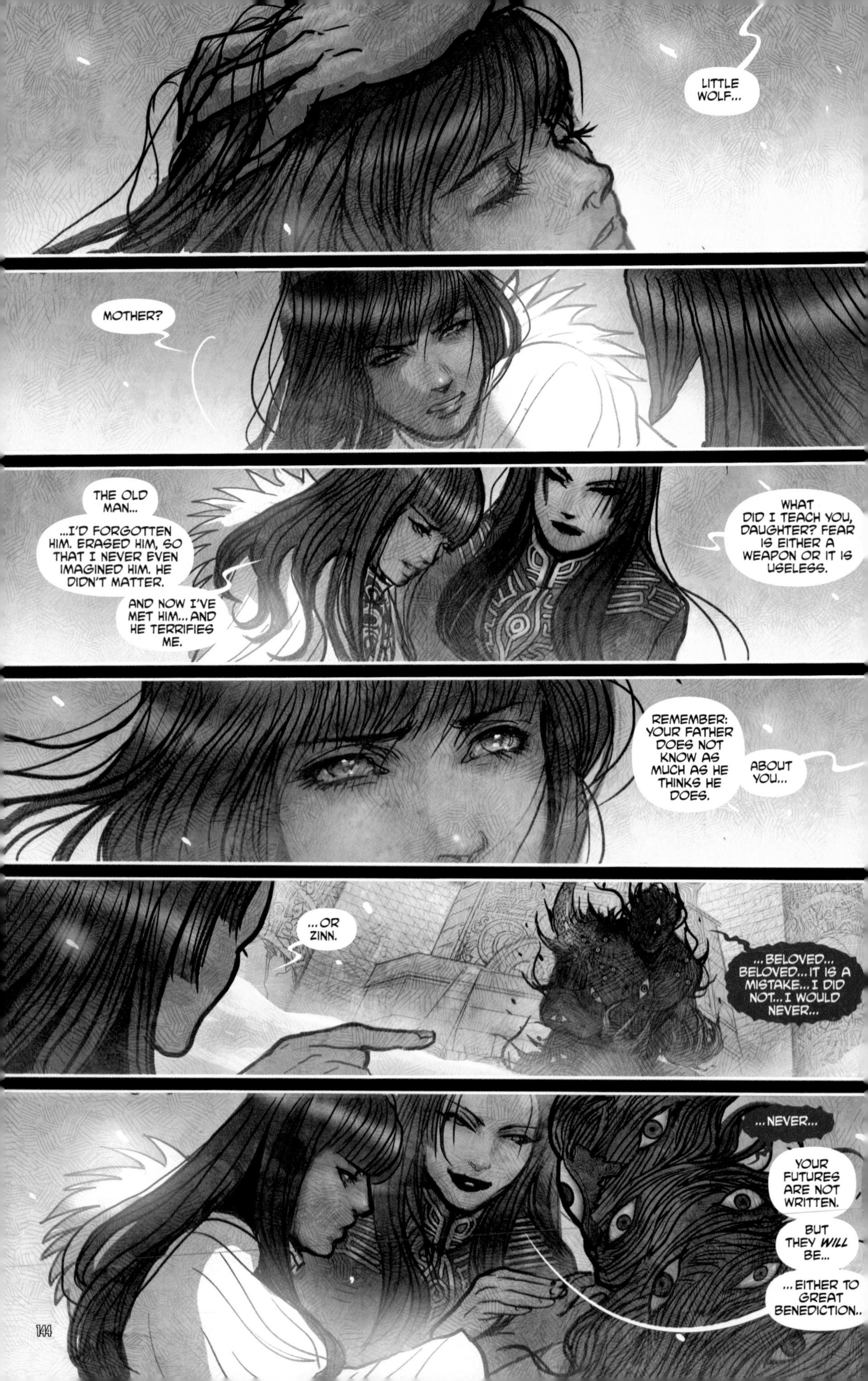
LITTLE WOLF...
MOTHER?
THE OLD MAN...
...I'D FORGOTTEN HIM. ERASED HIM, SO THAT I NEVER EVEN IMAGINED HIM. HE DIDN'T MATTER.
AND NOW I'VE MET HIM... AND HE TERRIFIES ME.
WHAT DID I TEACH YOU, DAUGHTER? FEAR IS EITHER A WEAPON OR IT IS USELESS.
REMEMBER: YOUR FATHER DOES NOT KNOW AS MUCH AS HE THINKS HE DOES.
ABOUT YOU...
...OR ZINN.
...BELOVED... BELOVED... IT IS A MISTAKE... I DID NOT... I WOULD NEVER...
...NEVER...
YOUR FUTURES ARE NOT WRITTEN.
BUT THEY *WILL* BE...
...EITHER TO GREAT BENEDICTION..

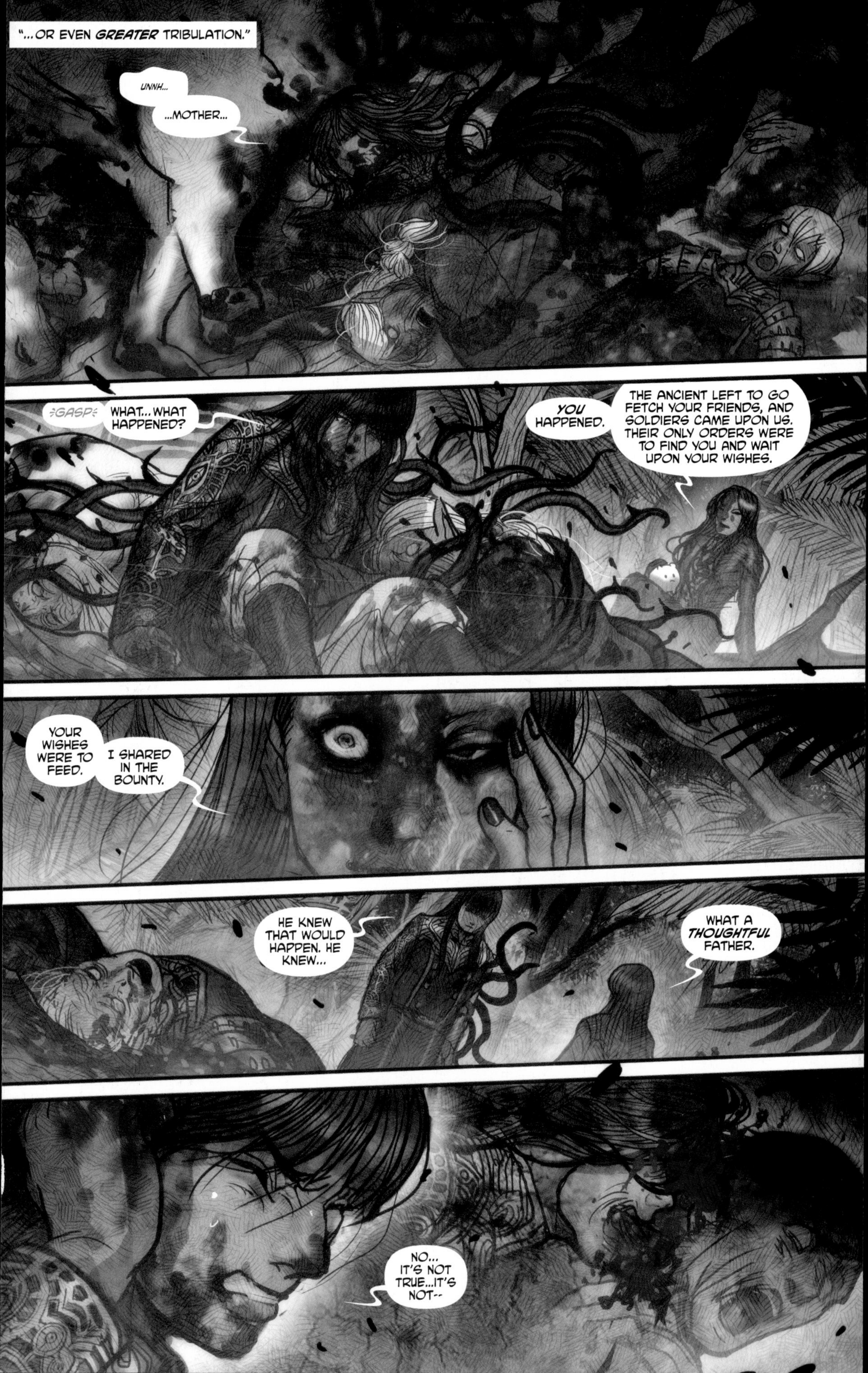
"...OR EVEN *GREATER* TRIBULATION."
UNNH...
...MOTHER...
GASP
WHAT...WHAT HAPPENED?
YOU HAPPENED.
THE ANCIENT LEFT TO GO FETCH YOUR FRIENDS, AND SOLDIERS CAME UPON US. THEIR ONLY ORDERS WERE TO FIND YOU AND WAIT UPON YOUR WISHES.
YOUR WISHES WERE TO FEED.
I SHARED IN THE BOUNTY.
HE KNEW THAT WOULD HAPPEN. HE KNEW...
WHAT A *THOUGHTFUL* FATHER.
NO... IT'S NOT TRUE...IT'S NOT--

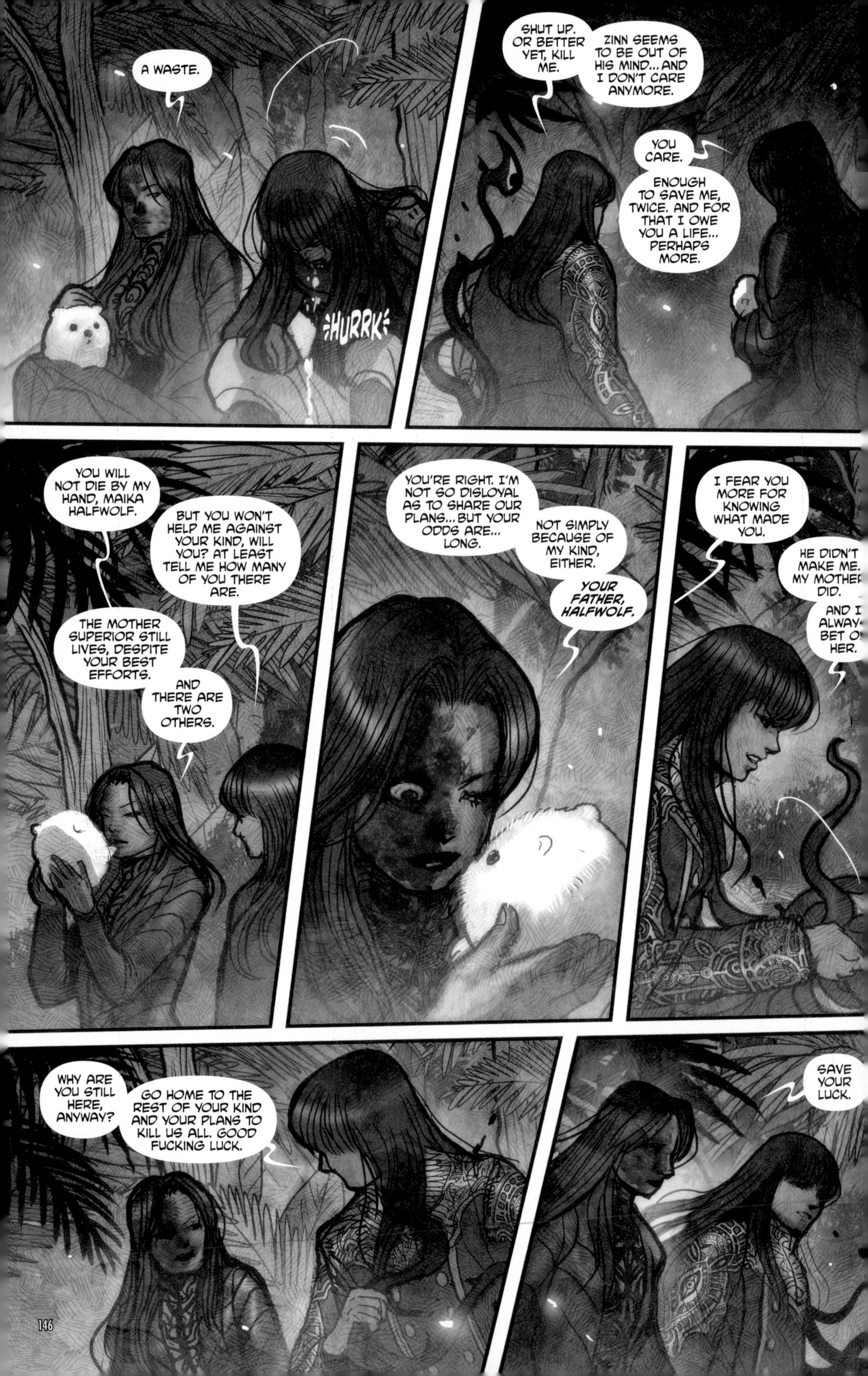

A WASTE.
HURRK
SHUT UP. OR BETTER YET, KILL ME.
ZINN SEEMS TO BE OUT OF HIS MIND... AND I DON'T CARE ANYMORE.
YOU CARE.
ENOUGH TO SAVE ME, TWICE. AND FOR THAT I OWE YOU A LIFE... PERHAPS MORE.
YOU WILL NOT DIE BY MY HAND, MAIKA HALFWOLF.
BUT YOU WON'T HELP ME AGAINST YOUR KIND, WILL YOU? AT LEAST TELL ME HOW MANY OF YOU THERE ARE.
THE MOTHER SUPERIOR STILL LIVES, DESPITE YOUR BEST EFFORTS.
AND THERE ARE TWO OTHERS.
YOU'RE RIGHT. I'M NOT SO DISLOYAL AS TO SHARE OUR PLANS... BUT YOUR ODDS ARE... LONG.
NOT SIMPLY BECAUSE OF MY KIND, EITHER.
YOUR FATHER, HALFWOLF.
I FEAR YOU MORE FOR KNOWING WHAT MADE YOU.
HE DIDN'T MAKE ME. MY MOTHER DID.
WHY ARE YOU STILL HERE, ANYWAY?
GO HOME TO THE REST OF YOUR KIND AND YOUR PLANS TO KILL US ALL. GOOD FUCKING LUCK.
SAVE YOUR LUCK.

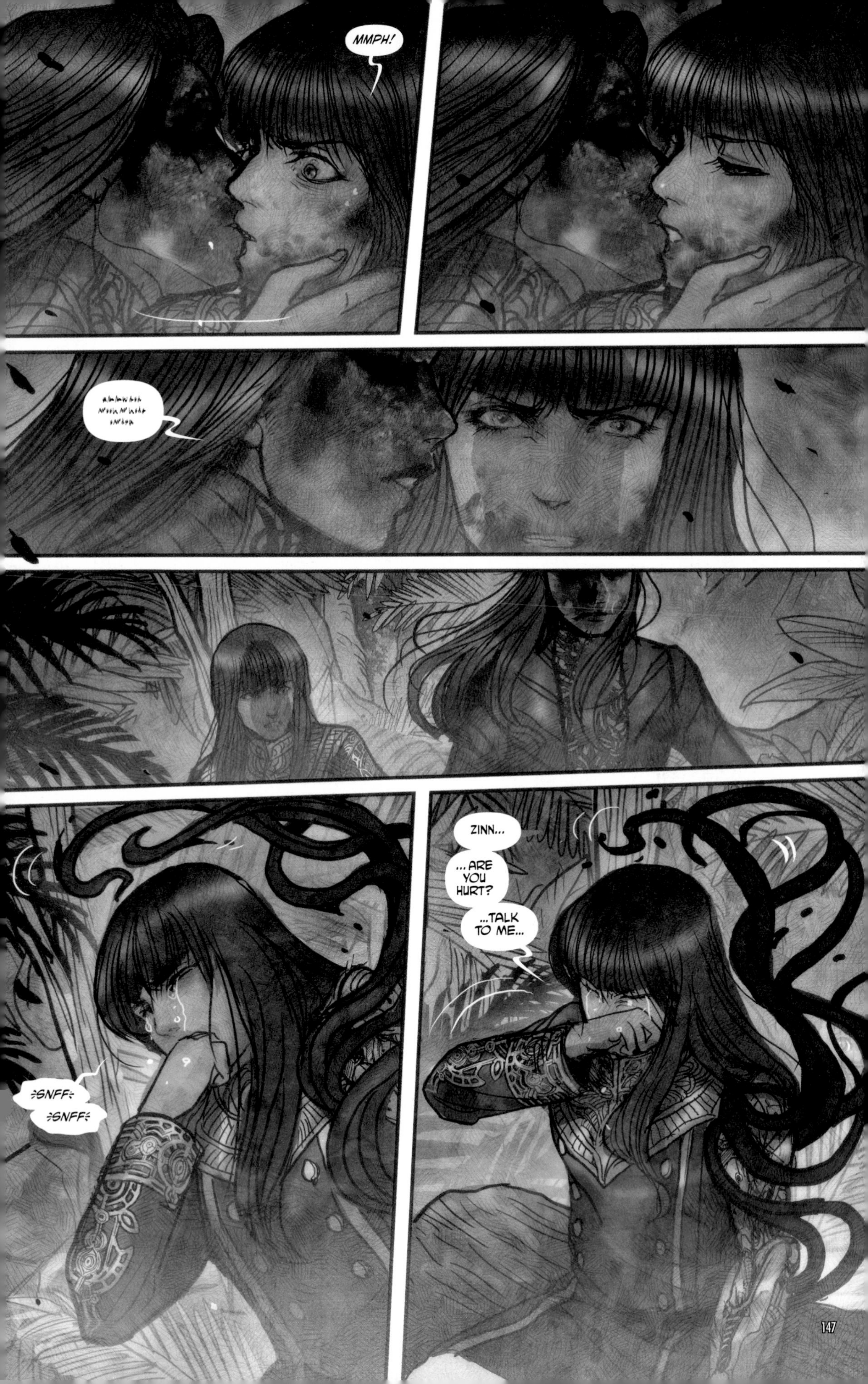
MMPH!
ZINN...
...ARE YOU HURT?
...TALK TO ME...
SNFF
SNFF

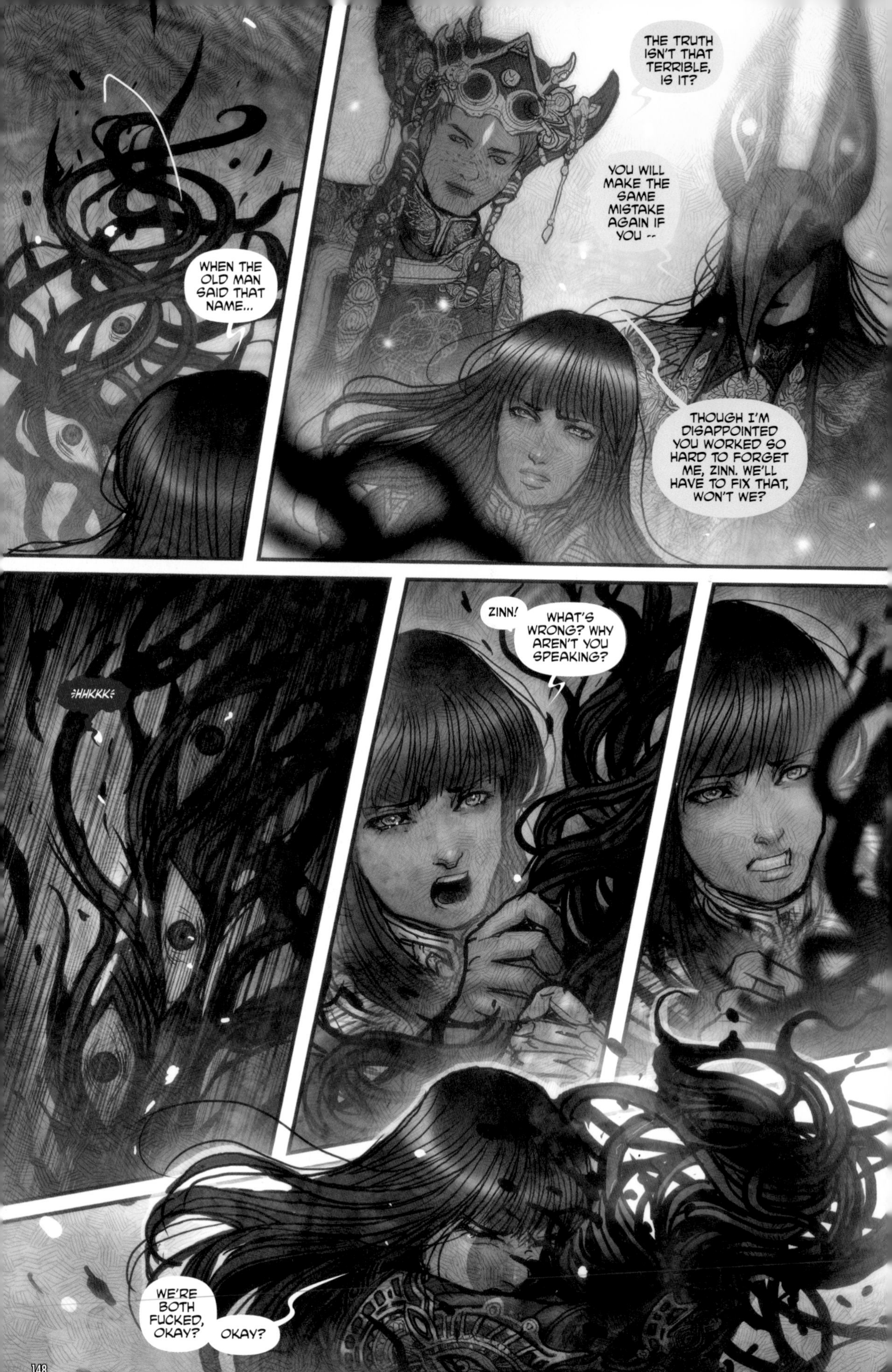
WHEN THE OLD MAN SAID THAT NAME...
THE TRUTH ISN'T THAT TERRIBLE, IS IT?
YOU WILL MAKE THE SAME MISTAKE AGAIN IF YOU --
THOUGH I'M DISAPPOINTED YOU WORKED SO HARD TO FORGET ME, ZINN. WE'LL HAVE TO FIX THAT, WON'T WE?
HHKKK
ZINN!
WHAT'S WRONG? WHY AREN'T YOU SPEAKING?
WE'RE BOTH FUCKED, OKAY?
OKAY?

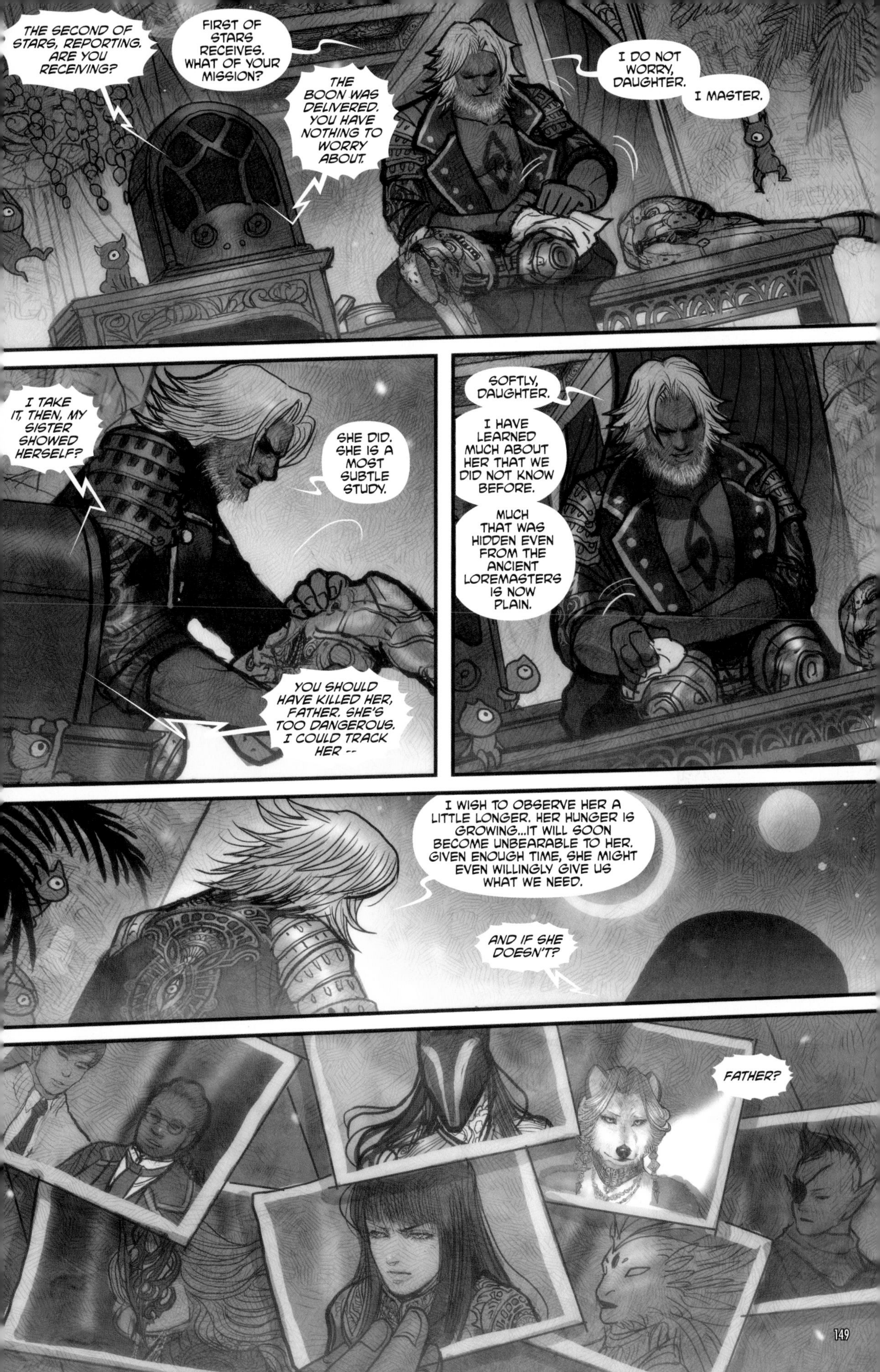
THE SECOND OF STARS, REPORTING. ARE YOU RECEIVING?
FIRST OF STARS RECEIVES. WHAT OF YOUR MISSION?
THE BOON WAS DELIVERED. YOU HAVE NOTHING TO WORRY ABOUT.
I DO NOT WORRY, DAUGHTER.
I MASTER.
I TAKE IT, THEN, MY SISTER SHOWED HERSELF?
SHE DID. SHE IS A MOST SUBTLE STUDY.
YOU SHOULD HAVE KILLED HER, FATHER. SHE'S TOO DANGEROUS. I COULD TRACK HER --
SOFTLY, DAUGHTER.
I HAVE LEARNED MUCH ABOUT HER THAT WE DID NOT KNOW BEFORE.
MUCH THAT WAS HIDDEN EVEN FROM THE ANCIENT LOREMASTERS IS NOW PLAIN.
I WISH TO OBSERVE HER A LITTLE LONGER. HER HUNGER IS GROWING...IT WILL SOON BECOME UNBEARABLE TO HER. GIVEN ENOUGH TIME, SHE MIGHT EVEN WILLINGLY GIVE US WHAT WE NEED.
AND IF SHE DOESN'T?
FATHER?

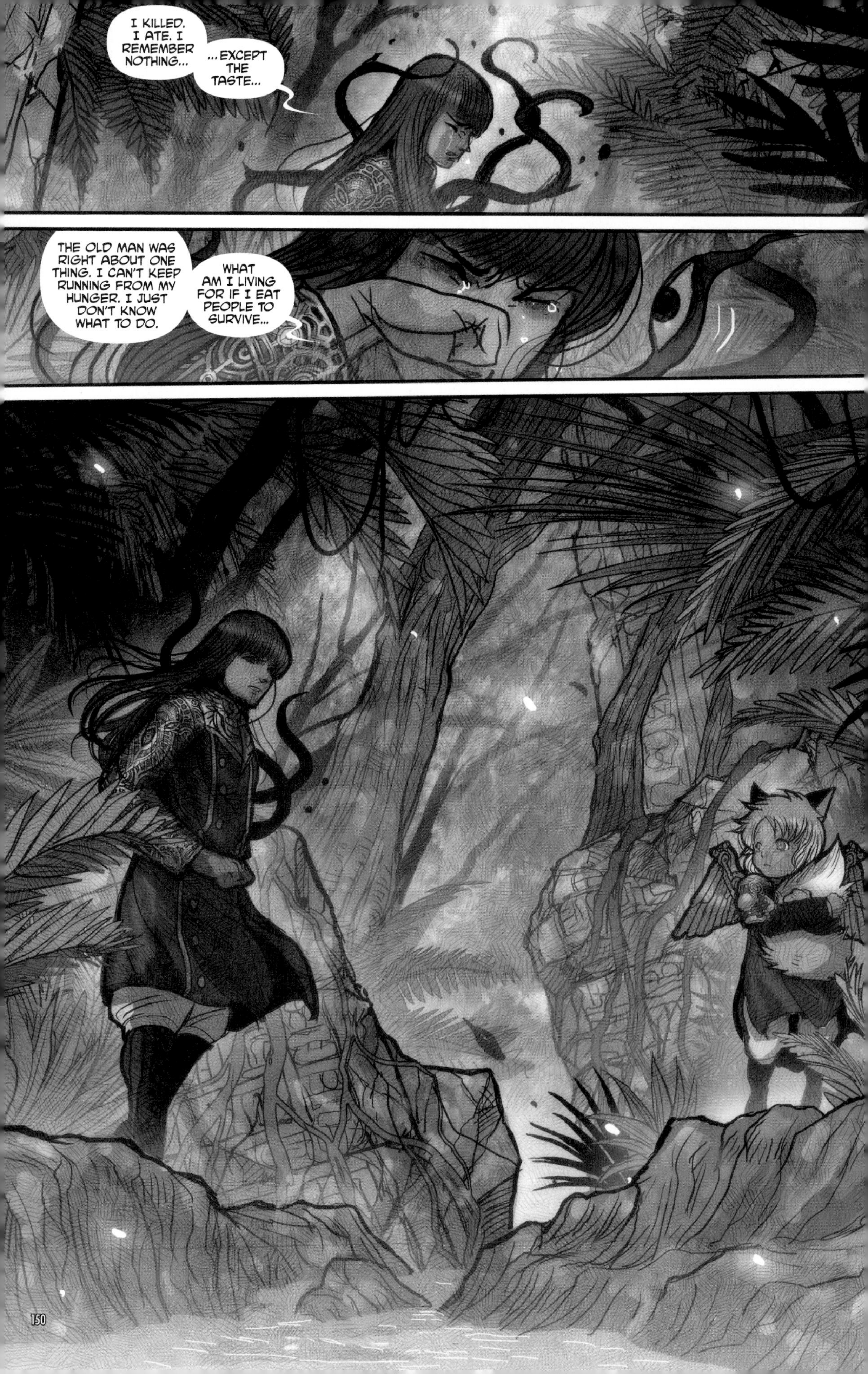
I KILLED. I ATE. I REMEMBER NOTHING...
...EXCEPT THE TASTE...
THE OLD MAN WAS RIGHT ABOUT ONE THING. I CAN'T KEEP RUNNING FROM MY HUNGER. I JUST DON'T KNOW WHAT TO DO.
WHAT AM I LIVING FOR IF I EAT PEOPLE TO SURVIVE...

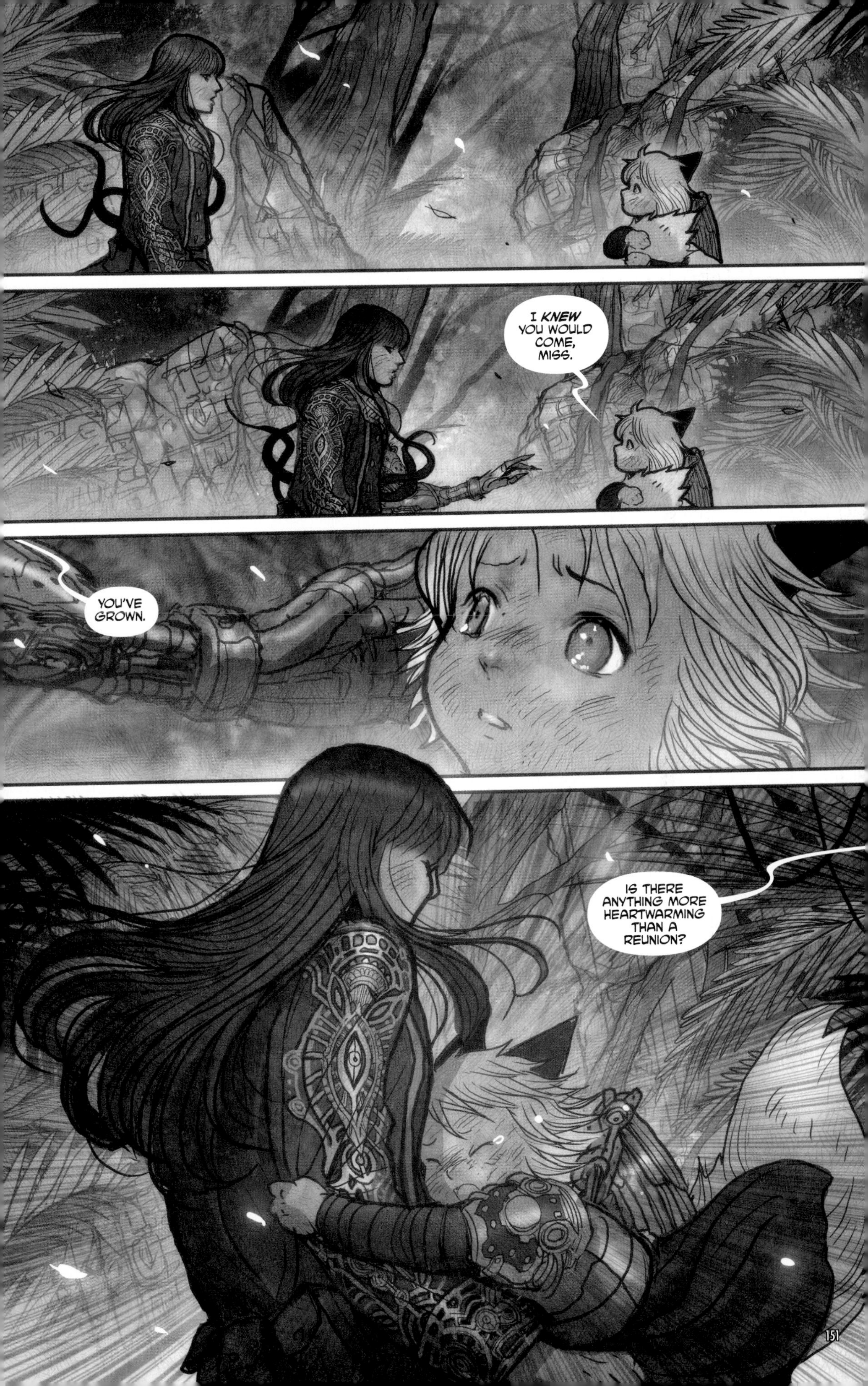
I KNEW YOU WOULD COME, MISS.
YOU'VE GROWN.
IS THERE ANYTHING MORE HEARTWARMING THAN A REUNION?

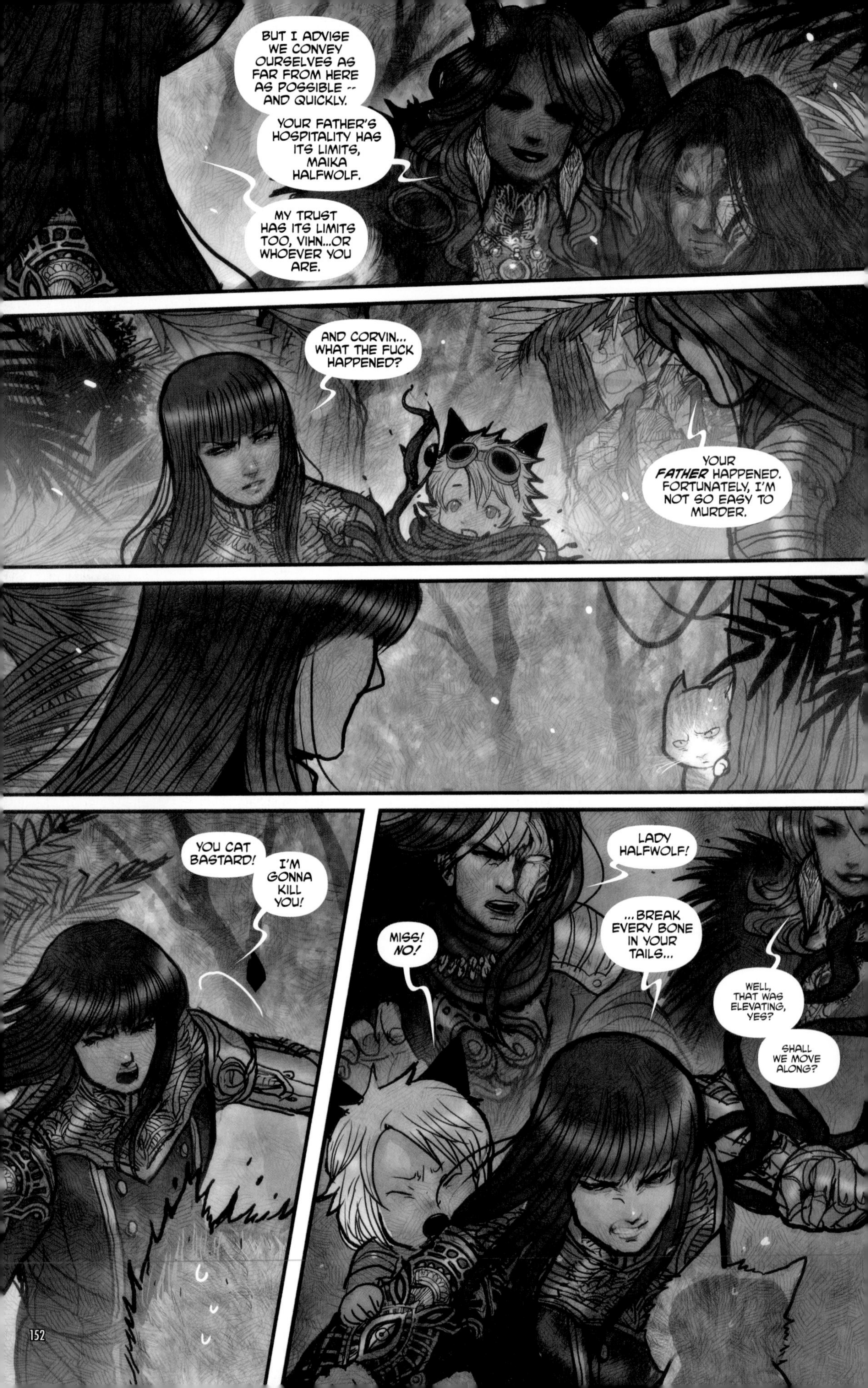

BUT I ADVISE WE CONVEY OURSELVES AS FAR FROM HERE AS POSSIBLE -- AND QUICKLY.
YOUR FATHER'S HOSPITALITY HAS ITS LIMITS, MAIKA HALFWOLF.
MY TRUST HAS ITS LIMITS TOO, VIHN...OR WHOEVER YOU ARE.
AND CORVIN... WHAT THE FUCK HAPPENED?
YOUR *FATHER* HAPPENED. FORTUNATELY, I'M NOT SO EASY TO MURDER.
YOU CAT BASTARD!
I'M GONNA KILL YOU!
LADY HALFWOLF!
...BREAK EVERY BONE IN YOUR TAILS...
MISS! *NO!*
WELL, THAT WAS ELEVATING, YES?
SHALL WE MOVE ALONG?

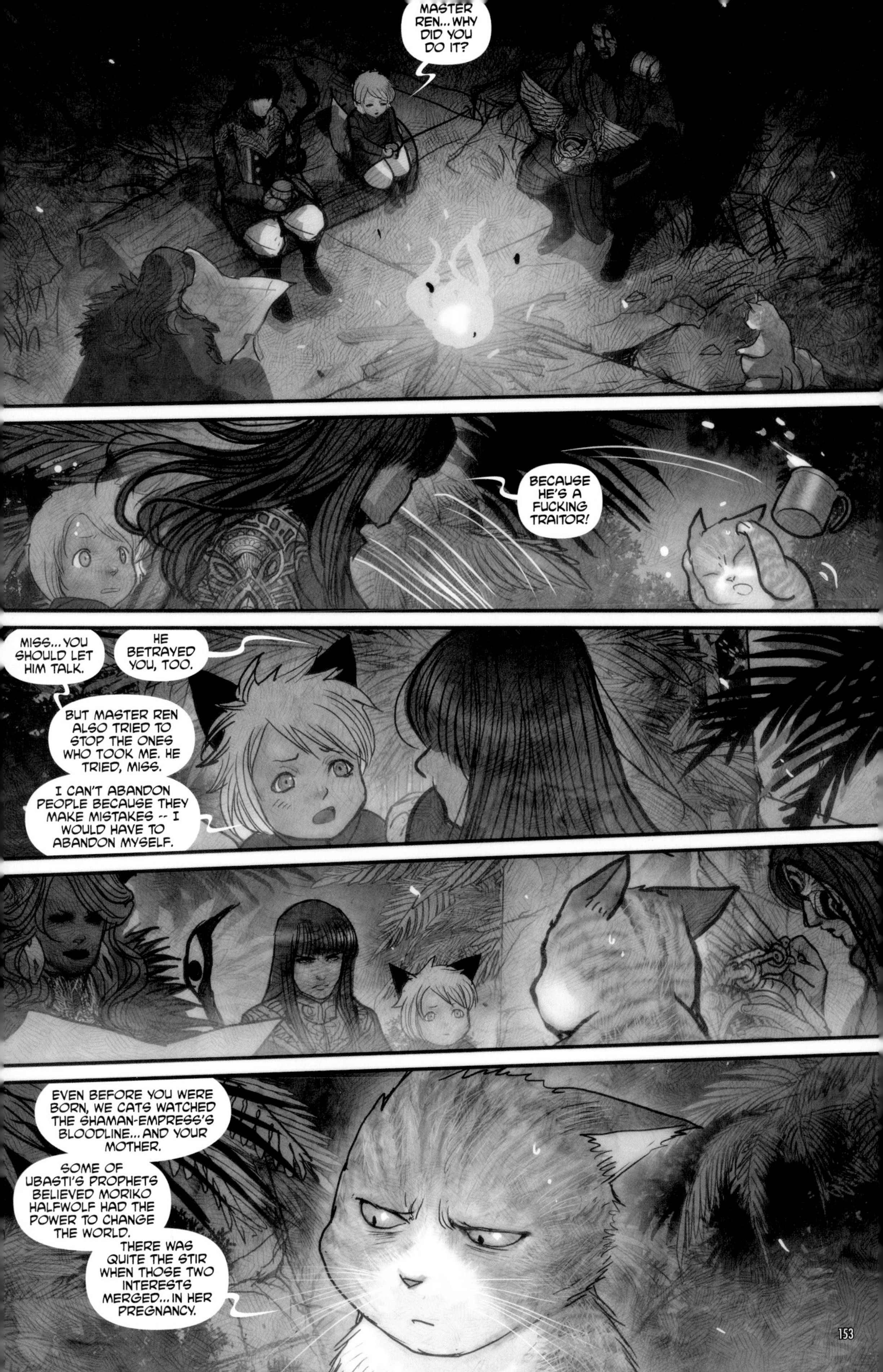
MASTER REN... WHY DID YOU DO IT?
BECAUSE HE'S A FUCKING TRAITOR!
MISS... YOU SHOULD LET HIM TALK.
HE BETRAYED YOU, TOO.
BUT MASTER REN ALSO TRIED TO STOP THE ONES WHO TOOK ME. HE TRIED, MISS.
I CAN'T ABANDON PEOPLE BECAUSE THEY MAKE MISTAKES -- I WOULD HAVE TO ABANDON MYSELF.
EVEN BEFORE YOU WERE BORN, WE CATS WATCHED THE SHAMAN-EMPRESS'S BLOODLINE... AND YOUR MOTHER.
SOME OF UBASTI'S PROPHETS BELIEVED MORIKO HALFWOLF HAD THE POWER TO CHANGE THE WORLD.
THERE WAS QUITE THE STIR WHEN THOSE TWO INTERESTS MERGED... IN HER PREGNANCY.

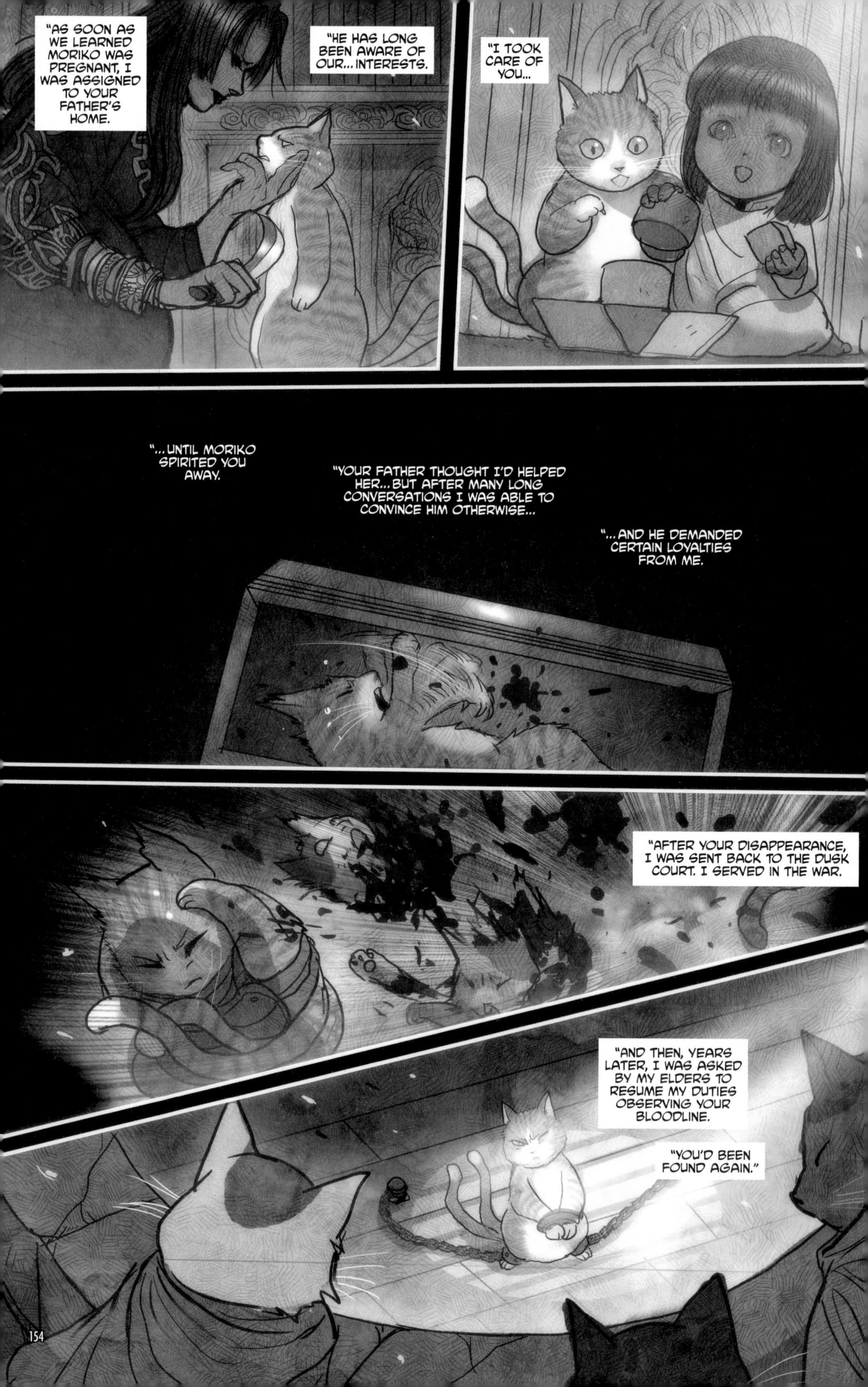
"AS SOON AS WE LEARNED MORIKO WAS PREGNANT, I WAS ASSIGNED TO YOUR FATHER'S HOME.
"HE HAS LONG BEEN AWARE OF OUR... INTERESTS.
"I TOOK CARE OF YOU...
"...UNTIL MORIKO SPIRITED YOU AWAY.
"YOUR FATHER THOUGHT I'D HELPED HER... BUT AFTER MANY LONG CONVERSATIONS I WAS ABLE TO CONVINCE HIM OTHERWISE...
"...AND HE DEMANDED CERTAIN LOYALTIES FROM ME.
"AFTER YOUR DISAPPEARANCE, I WAS SENT BACK TO THE DUSK COURT. I SERVED IN THE WAR.
"AND THEN, YEARS LATER, I WAS ASKED BY MY ELDERS TO RESUME MY DUTIES OBSERVING YOUR BLOODLINE.
"YOU'D BEEN FOUND AGAIN."

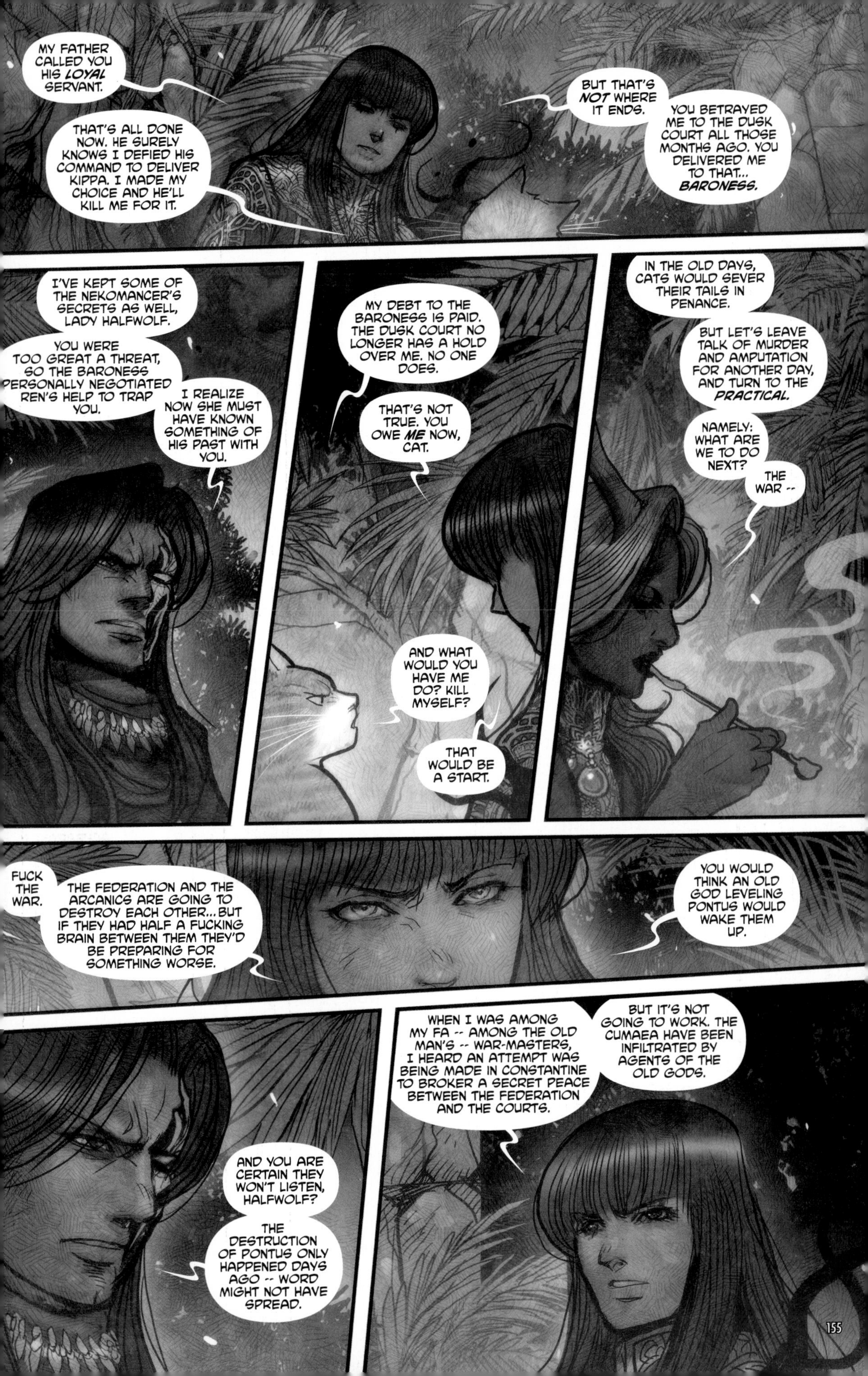
MY FATHER CALLED YOU HIS LOYAL SERVANT.
THAT'S ALL DONE NOW. HE SURELY KNOWS I DEFIED HIS COMMAND TO DELIVER KIPPA. I MADE MY CHOICE AND HE'LL KILL ME FOR IT.
BUT THAT'S NOT WHERE IT ENDS.
YOU BETRAYED ME TO THE DUSK COURT ALL THOSE MONTHS AGO. YOU DELIVERED ME TO THAT... BARONESS.
I'VE KEPT SOME OF THE NEKOMANCER'S SECRETS AS WELL, LADY HALFWOLF.
YOU WERE TOO GREAT A THREAT, SO THE BARONESS PERSONALLY NEGOTIATED REN'S HELP TO TRAP YOU.
I REALIZE NOW SHE MUST HAVE KNOWN SOMETHING OF HIS PAST WITH YOU.
MY DEBT TO THE BARONESS IS PAID. THE DUSK COURT NO LONGER HAS A HOLD OVER ME. NO ONE DOES.
THAT'S NOT TRUE. YOU OWE ME NOW, CAT.
AND WHAT WOULD YOU HAVE ME DO? KILL MYSELF?
THAT WOULD BE A START.
IN THE OLD DAYS, CATS WOULD SEVER THEIR TAILS IN PENANCE.
BUT LET'S LEAVE TALK OF MURDER AND AMPUTATION FOR ANOTHER DAY, AND TURN TO THE PRACTICAL.
NAMELY: WHAT ARE WE TO DO NEXT?
THE WAR --
FUCK THE WAR.
THE FEDERATION AND THE ARCANICS ARE GOING TO DESTROY EACH OTHER... BUT IF THEY HAD HALF A FUCKING BRAIN BETWEEN THEM THEY'D BE PREPARING FOR SOMETHING WORSE.
YOU WOULD THINK AN OLD GOD LEVELING PONTUS WOULD WAKE THEM UP.
WHEN I WAS AMONG MY FA -- AMONG THE OLD MAN'S -- WAR-MASTERS, I HEARD AN ATTEMPT WAS BEING MADE IN CONSTANTINE TO BROKER A SECRET PEACE BETWEEN THE FEDERATION AND THE COURTS.
BUT IT'S NOT GOING TO WORK. THE CUMAEA HAVE BEEN INFILTRATED BY AGENTS OF THE OLD GODS.
AND YOU ARE CERTAIN THEY WON'T LISTEN, HALFWOLF?
THE DESTRUCTION OF PONTUS ONLY HAPPENED DAYS AGO -- WORD MIGHT NOT HAVE SPREAD.

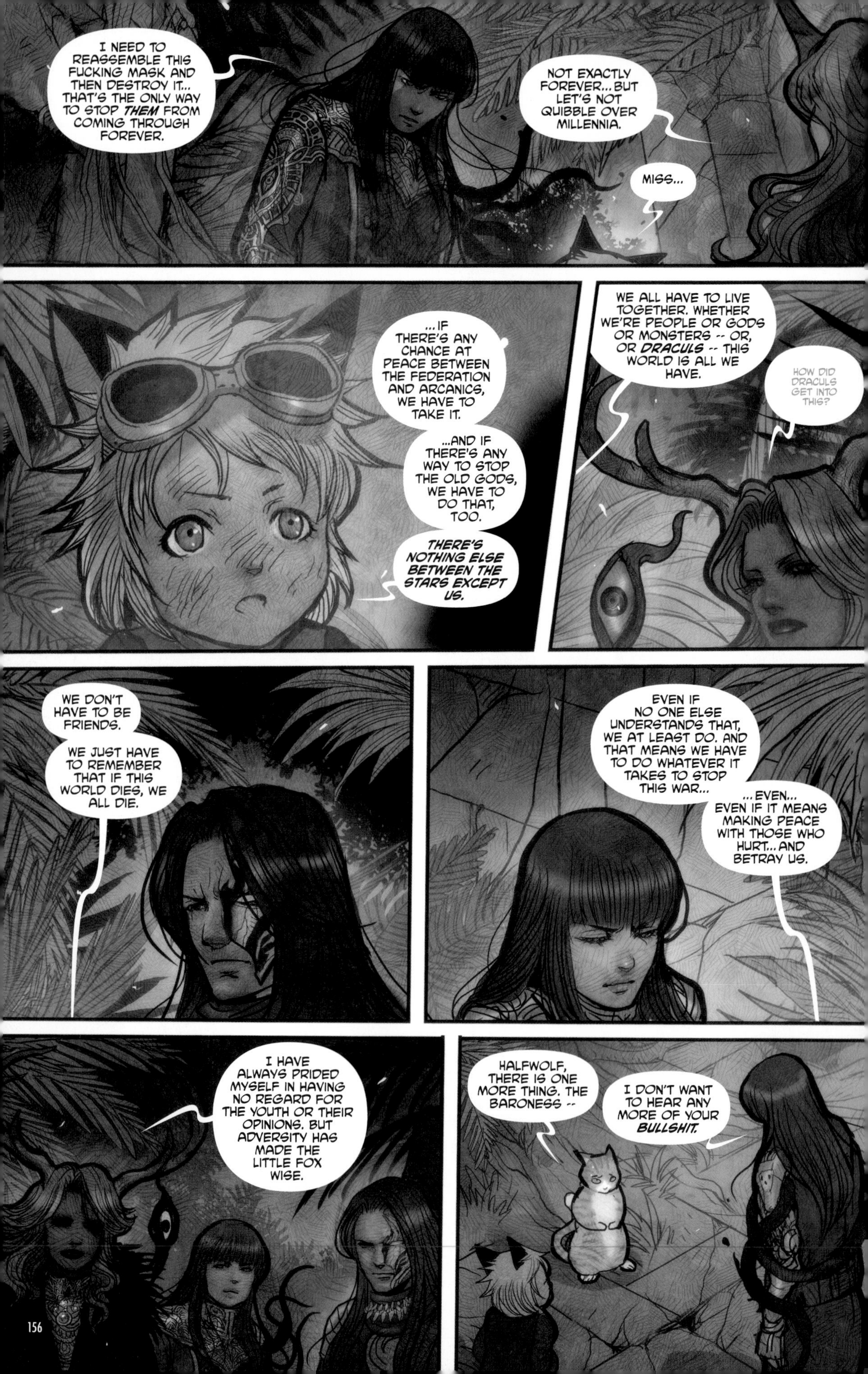
I NEED TO REASSEMBLE THIS FUCKING MASK AND THEN DESTROY IT... THAT'S THE ONLY WAY TO STOP *THEM* FROM COMING THROUGH FOREVER.
NOT EXACTLY FOREVER... BUT LET'S NOT QUIBBLE OVER MILLENNIA.
MISS...
...IF THERE'S ANY CHANCE AT PEACE BETWEEN THE FEDERATION AND ARCANICS, WE HAVE TO TAKE IT.
...AND IF THERE'S ANY WAY TO STOP THE OLD GODS, WE HAVE TO DO THAT, TOO.
THERE'S NOTHING ELSE BETWEEN THE STARS EXCEPT US.
WE ALL HAVE TO LIVE TOGETHER. WHETHER WE'RE PEOPLE OR GODS OR MONSTERS -- OR, OR *DRACULS* -- THIS WORLD IS ALL WE HAVE.
HOW DID DRACULS GET INTO THIS?
WE DON'T HAVE TO BE FRIENDS.
WE JUST HAVE TO REMEMBER THAT IF THIS WORLD DIES, WE ALL DIE.
EVEN IF NO ONE ELSE UNDERSTANDS THAT, WE AT LEAST DO. AND THAT MEANS WE HAVE TO DO WHATEVER IT TAKES TO STOP THIS WAR...
...EVEN... EVEN IF IT MEANS MAKING PEACE WITH THOSE WHO HURT... AND BETRAY US.
I HAVE ALWAYS PRIDED MYSELF IN HAVING NO REGARD FOR THE YOUTH OR THEIR OPINIONS. BUT ADVERSITY HAS MADE THE LITTLE FOX WISE.
HALFWOLF, THERE IS ONE MORE THING. THE BARONESS --
I DON'T WANT TO HEAR ANY MORE OF YOUR *BULLSHIT.*

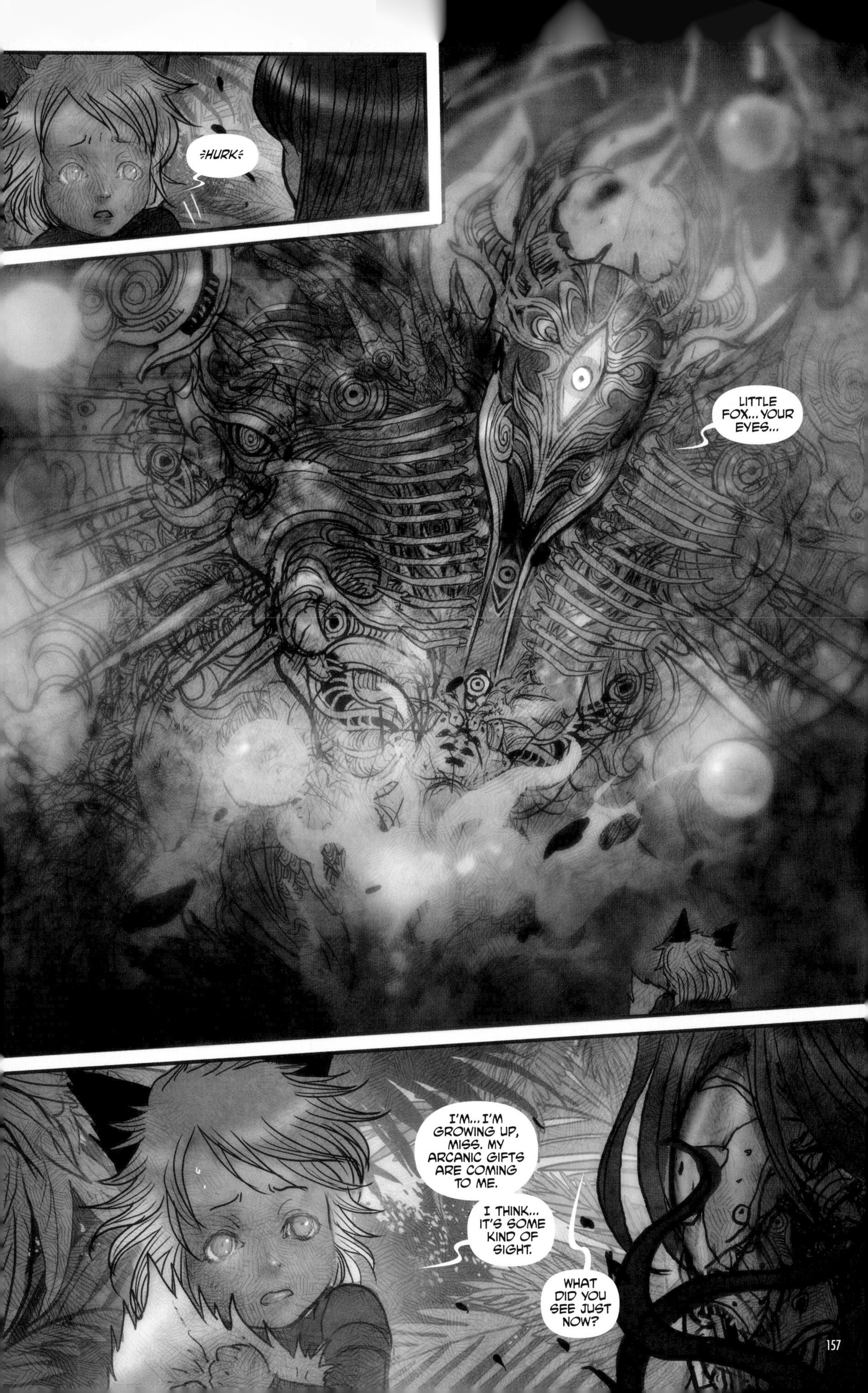
HURK
LITTLE FOX... YOUR EYES...
I'M... I'M GROWING UP, MISS. MY ARCANIC GIFTS ARE COMING TO ME.
I THINK... IT'S SOME KIND OF SIGHT.
WHAT DID YOU SEE JUST NOW?

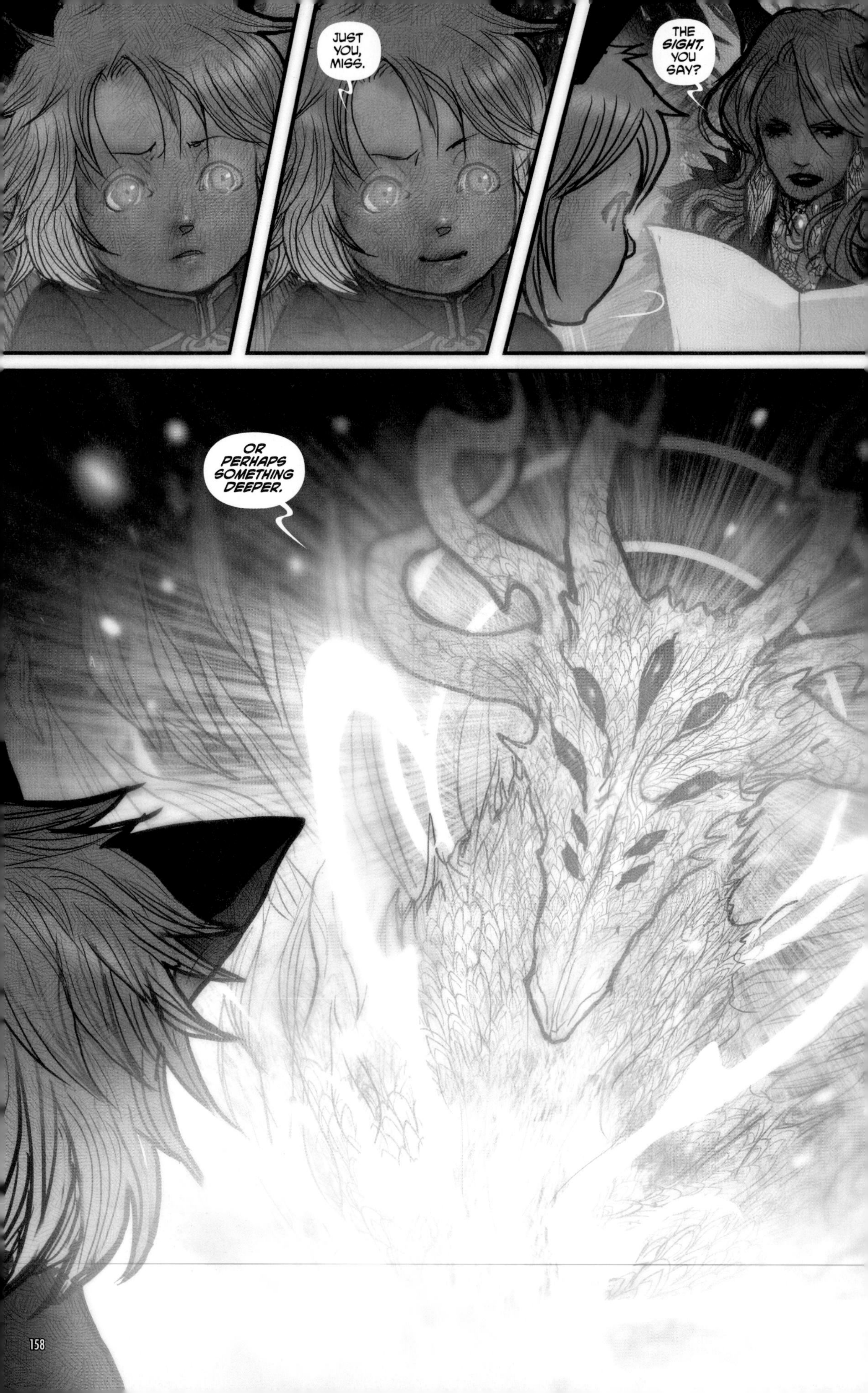
JUST YOU, MISS.
THE SIGHT, YOU SAY?
OR PERHAPS SOMETHING DEEPER.

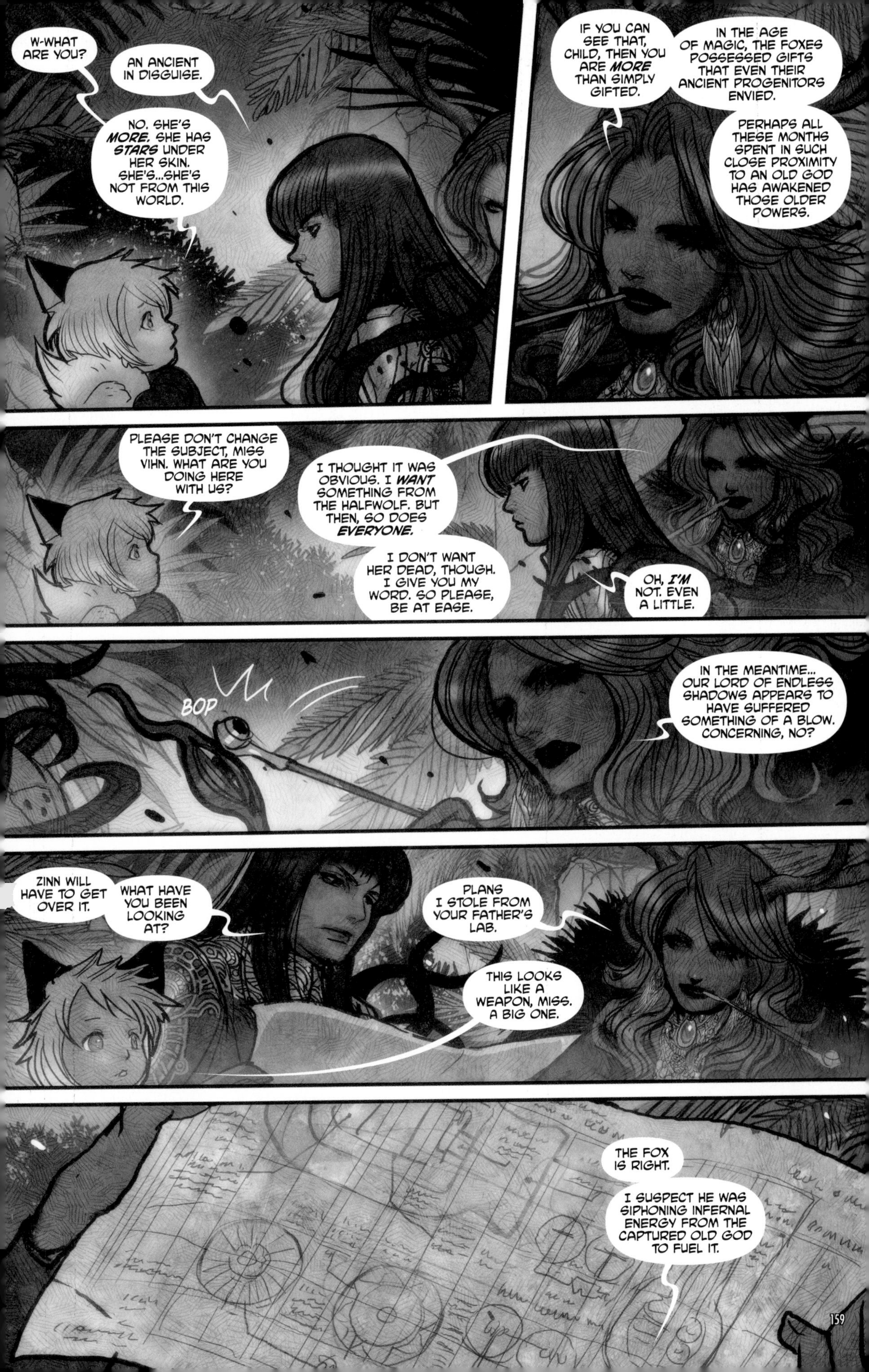
W-WHAT ARE YOU?
AN ANCIENT IN DISGUISE.
NO. SHE'S MORE. SHE HAS STARS UNDER HER SKIN. SHE'S...SHE'S NOT FROM THIS WORLD.
IF YOU CAN SEE THAT, CHILD, THEN YOU ARE MORE THAN SIMPLY GIFTED.
IN THE AGE OF MAGIC, THE FOXES POSSESSED GIFTS THAT EVEN THEIR ANCIENT PROGENITORS ENVIED.
PERHAPS ALL THESE MONTHS SPENT IN SUCH CLOSE PROXIMITY TO AN OLD GOD HAS AWAKENED THOSE OLDER POWERS.
PLEASE DON'T CHANGE THE SUBJECT, MISS VIHN. WHAT ARE YOU DOING HERE WITH US?
I THOUGHT IT WAS OBVIOUS. I WANT SOMETHING FROM THE HALFWOLF. BUT THEN, SO DOES EVERYONE.
I DON'T WANT HER DEAD, THOUGH. I GIVE YOU MY WORD. SO PLEASE, BE AT EASE.
OH, I'M NOT. EVEN A LITTLE.
BOP
IN THE MEANTIME... OUR LORD OF ENDLESS SHADOWS APPEARS TO HAVE SUFFERED SOMETHING OF A BLOW. CONCERNING, NO?
ZINN WILL HAVE TO GET OVER IT.
WHAT HAVE YOU BEEN LOOKING AT?
PLANS I STOLE FROM YOUR FATHER'S LAB.
THIS LOOKS LIKE A WEAPON, MISS. A BIG ONE.
THE FOX IS RIGHT.
I SUSPECT HE WAS SIPHONING INFERNAL ENERGY FROM THE CAPTURED OLD GOD TO FUEL IT.

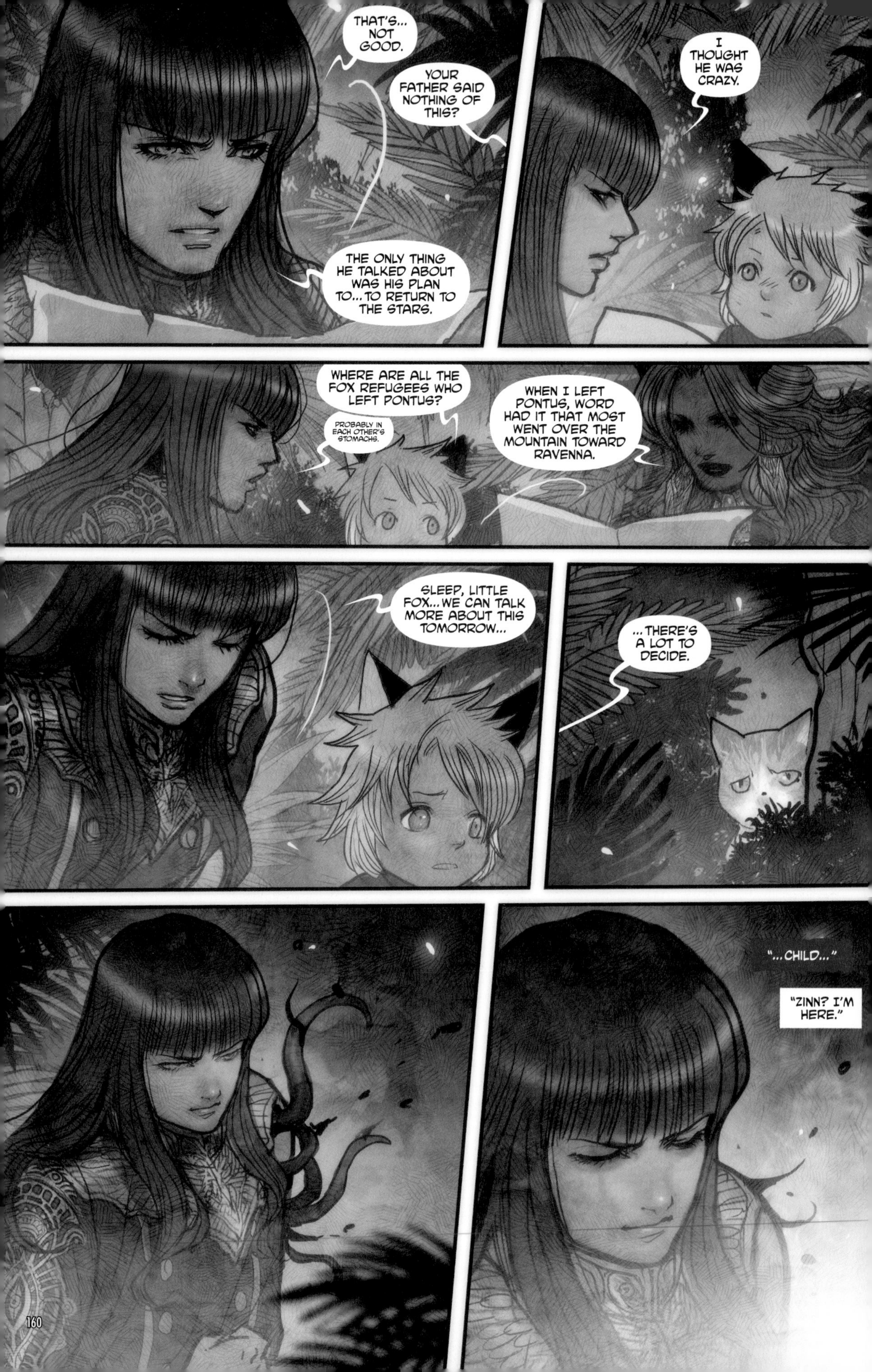
THAT'S... NOT GOOD.
YOUR FATHER SAID NOTHING OF THIS?
THE ONLY THING HE TALKED ABOUT WAS HIS PLAN TO... TO RETURN TO THE STARS.
I THOUGHT HE WAS CRAZY.
WHERE ARE ALL THE FOX REFUGEES WHO LEFT PONTUS?
PROBABLY IN EACH OTHER'S STOMACHS.
WHEN I LEFT PONTUS, WORD HAD IT THAT MOST WENT OVER THE MOUNTAIN TOWARD RAVENNA.
SLEEP, LITTLE FOX... WE CAN TALK MORE ABOUT THIS TOMORROW...
...THERE'S A LOT TO DECIDE.
"...CHILD..."
"ZINN? I'M HERE."

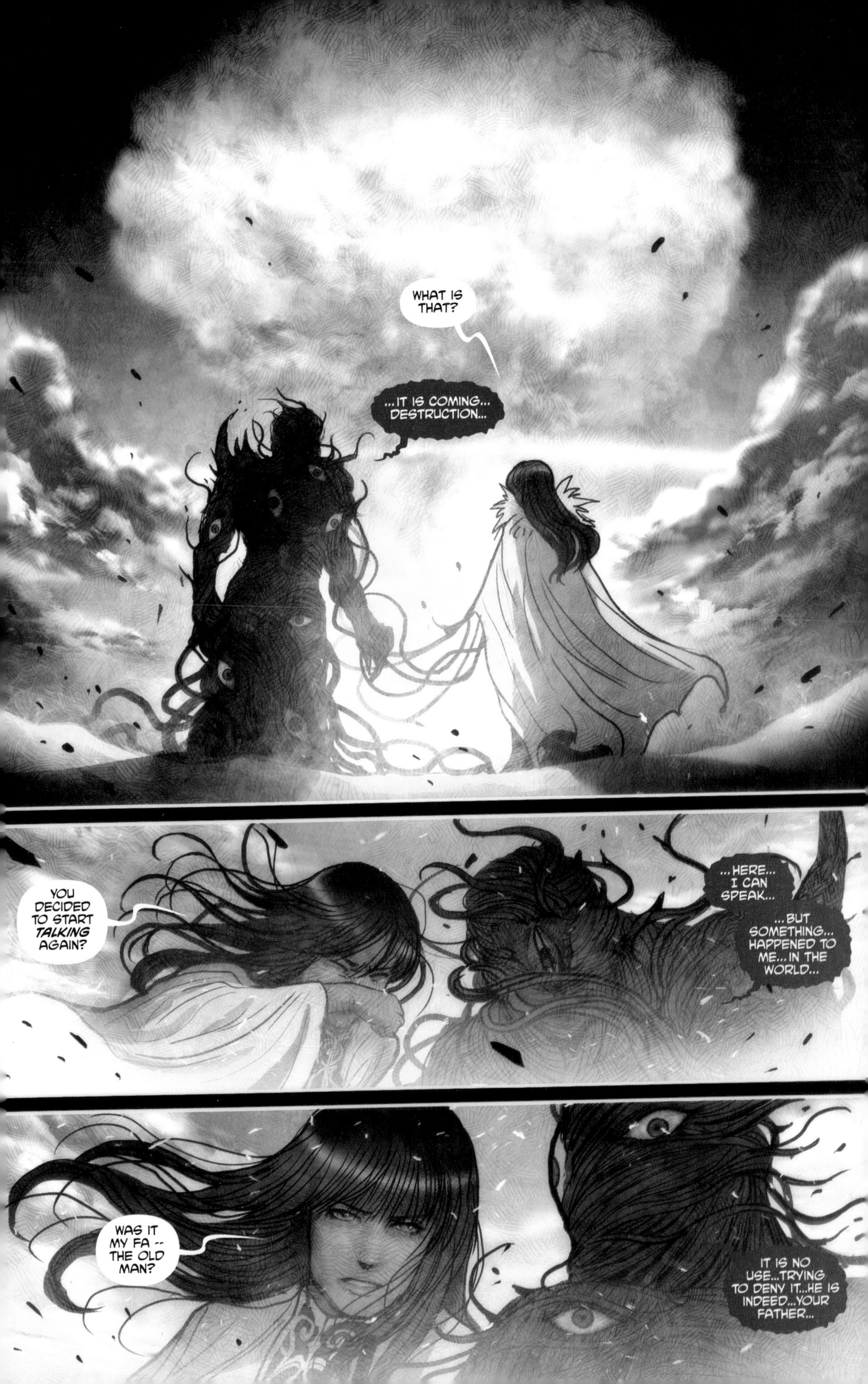

WHAT IS THAT?
...IT IS COMING... DESTRUCTION...
YOU DECIDED TO START *TALKING* AGAIN?
...HERE... I CAN SPEAK...
...BUT SOMETHING... HAPPENED TO ME... IN THE WORLD...
WAS IT MY FA -- THE OLD MAN?
IT IS NO USE...TRYING TO DENY IT...HE IS INDEED...YOUR FATHER...

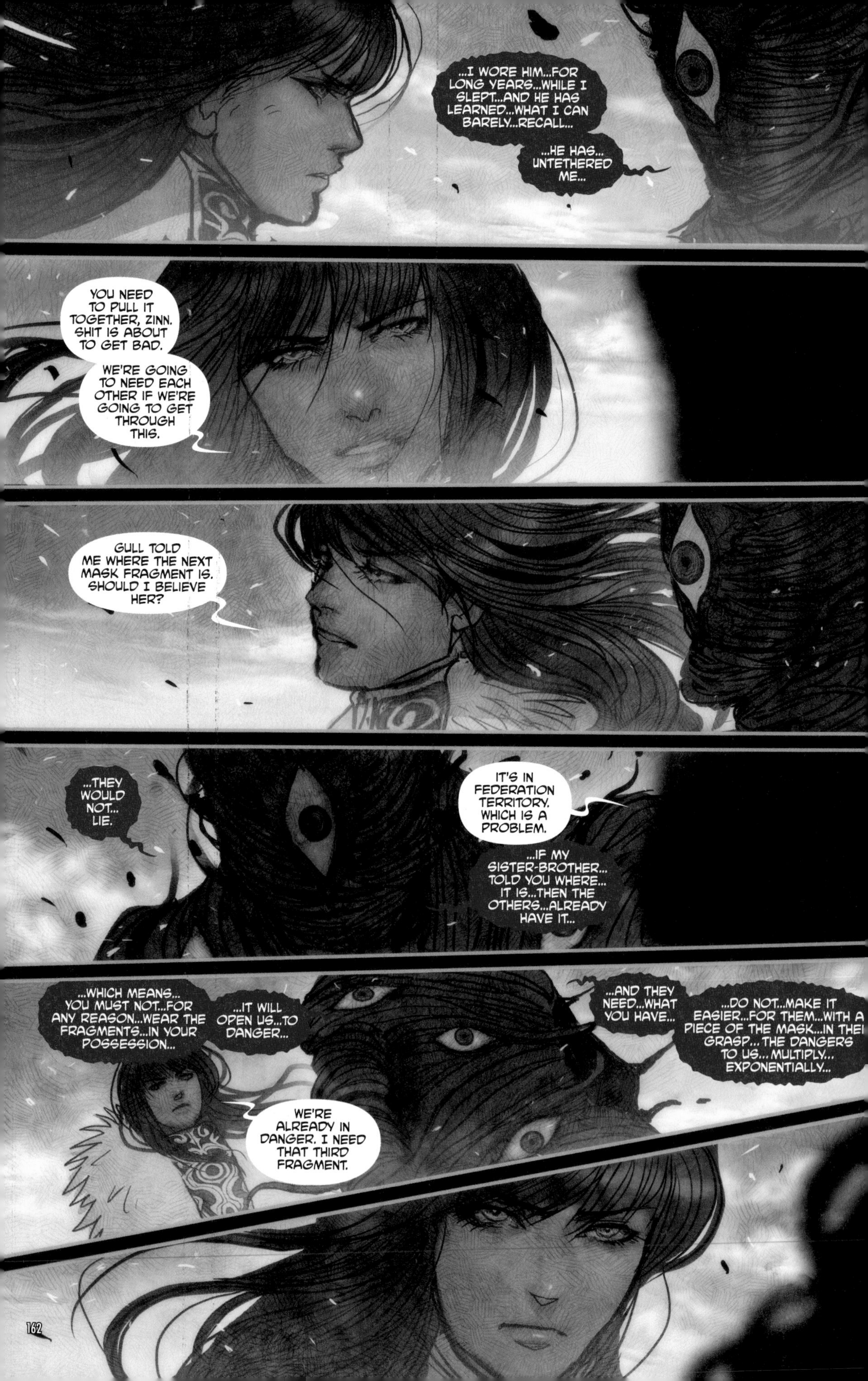
...I WORE HIM...FOR LONG YEARS...WHILE I SLEPT...AND HE HAS LEARNED...WHAT I CAN BARELY...RECALL...
...HE HAS... UNTETHERED ME...
YOU NEED TO PULL IT TOGETHER, ZINN. SHIT IS ABOUT TO GET BAD.
WE'RE GOING TO NEED EACH OTHER IF WE'RE GOING TO GET THROUGH THIS.
GULL TOLD ME WHERE THE NEXT MASK FRAGMENT IS. SHOULD I BELIEVE HER?
...THEY WOULD NOT... LIE.
IT'S IN FEDERATION TERRITORY. WHICH IS A PROBLEM.
...IF MY SISTER-BROTHER... TOLD YOU WHERE... IT IS...THEN THE OTHERS...ALREADY HAVE IT...
...WHICH MEANS... YOU MUST NOT...FOR ANY REASON...WEAR THE FRAGMENTS...IN YOUR POSSESSION...
...IT WILL OPEN US...TO DANGER...
...AND THEY NEED...WHAT YOU HAVE...
...DO NOT...MAKE IT EASIER...FOR THEM...WITH A PIECE OF THE MASK...IN THEI GRASP... THE DANGERS TO US... MULTIPLY... EXPONENTIALLY...
WE'RE ALREADY IN DANGER. I NEED THAT THIRD FRAGMENT.

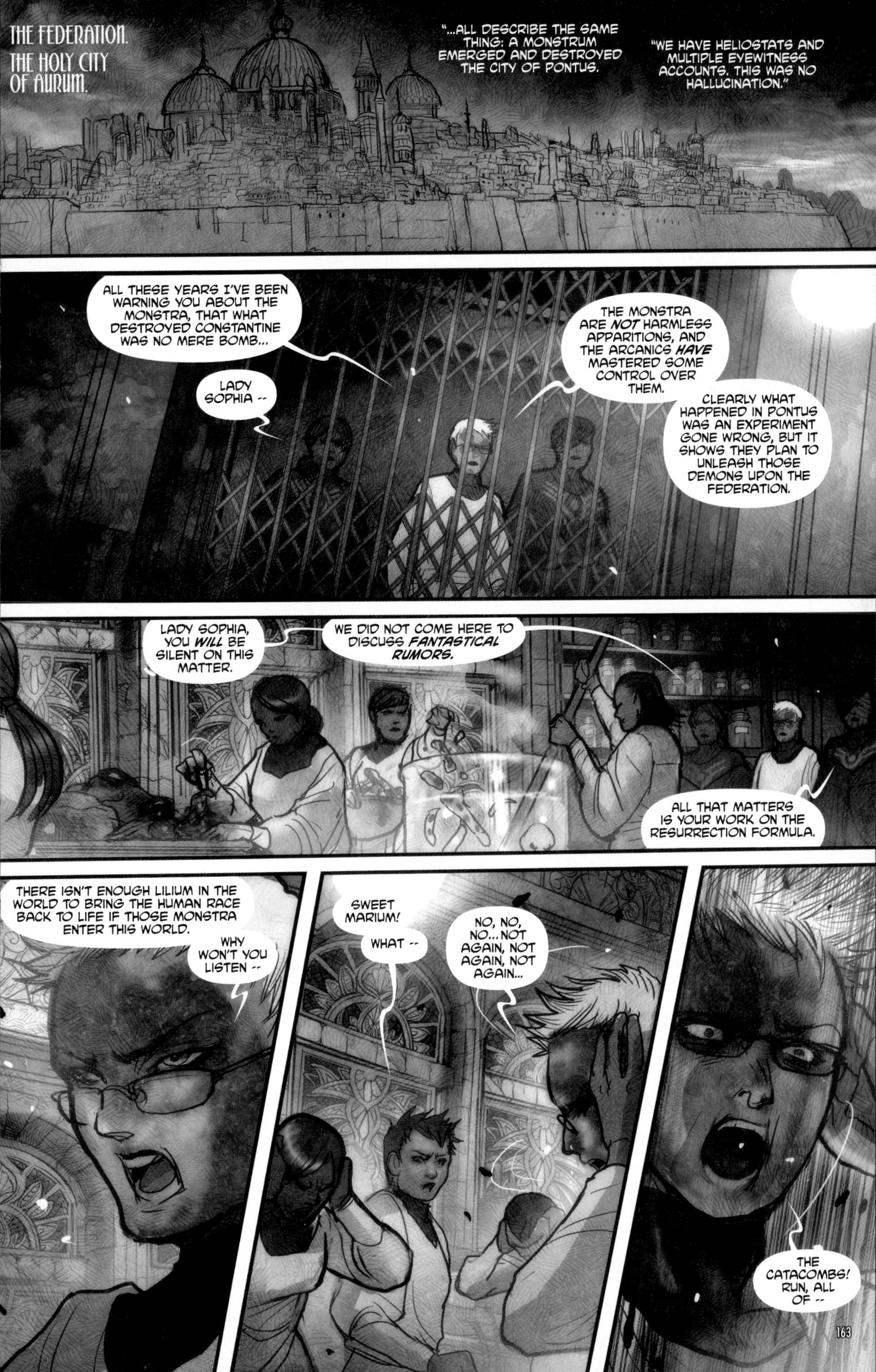
THE FEDERATION.
THE HOLY CITY OF AURUM.
"...ALL DESCRIBE THE SAME THING: A MONSTRUM EMERGED AND DESTROYED THE CITY OF PONTUS.
"WE HAVE HELIOSTATS AND MULTIPLE EYEWITNESS ACCOUNTS. THIS WAS NO HALLUCINATION."
ALL THESE YEARS I'VE BEEN WARNING YOU ABOUT THE MONSTRA, THAT WHAT DESTROYED CONSTANTINE WAS NO MERE BOMB...
LADY SOPHIA --
THE MONSTRA ARE NOT HARMLESS APPARITIONS, AND THE ARCANICS HAVE MASTERED SOME CONTROL OVER THEM.
CLEARLY WHAT HAPPENED IN PONTUS WAS AN EXPERIMENT GONE WRONG, BUT IT SHOWS THEY PLAN TO UNLEASH THOSE DEMONS UPON THE FEDERATION.
LADY SOPHIA, YOU WILL BE SILENT ON THIS MATTER.
WE DID NOT COME HERE TO DISCUSS FANTASTICAL RUMORS.
ALL THAT MATTERS IS YOUR WORK ON THE RESURRECTION FORMULA.
THERE ISN'T ENOUGH LILIUM IN THE WORLD TO BRING THE HUMAN RACE BACK TO LIFE IF THOSE MONSTRA ENTER THIS WORLD.
WHY WON'T YOU LISTEN --
SWEET MARIUM!
WHAT --
NO, NO, NO... NOT AGAIN, NOT AGAIN, NOT AGAIN...
THE CATACOMBS! RUN, ALL OF --

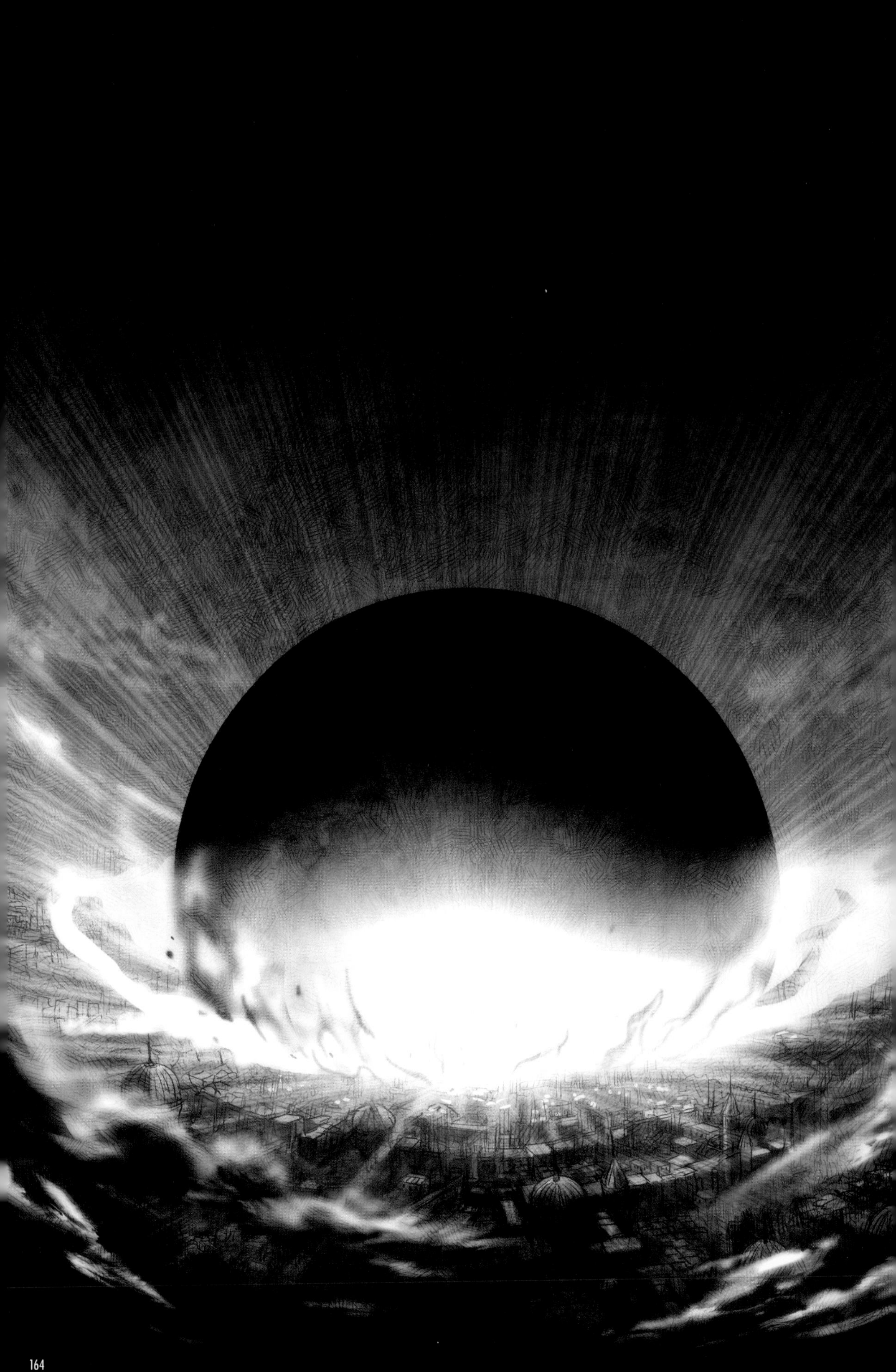

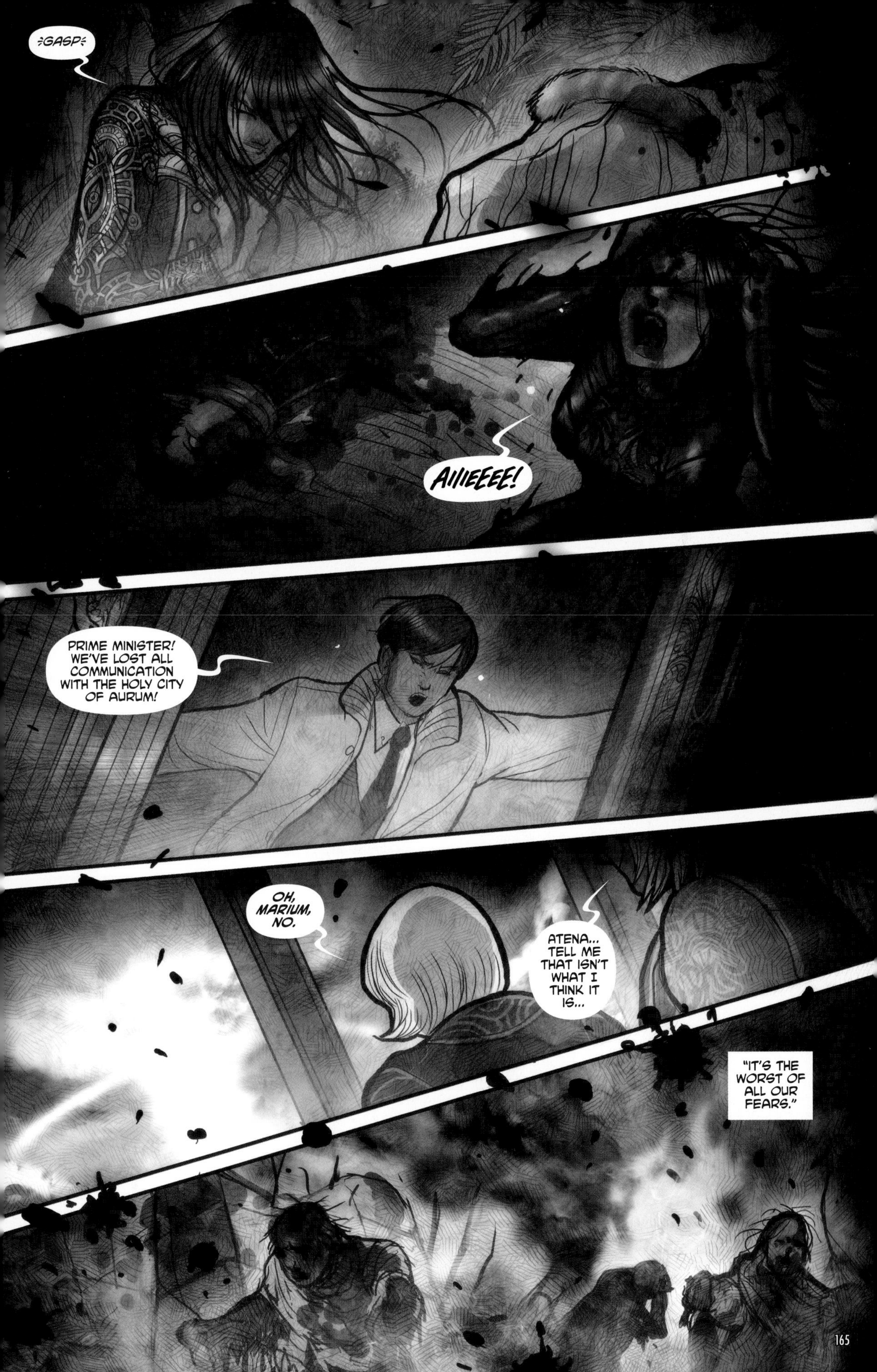

GASP
AIIIEEEE!
PRIME MINISTER! WE'VE LOST ALL COMMUNICATION WITH THE HOLY CITY OF AURUM!
OH, MARIUM, NO.
ATENA... TELL ME THAT ISN'T WHAT I THINK IT IS...
"IT'S THE WORST OF ALL OUR FEARS."

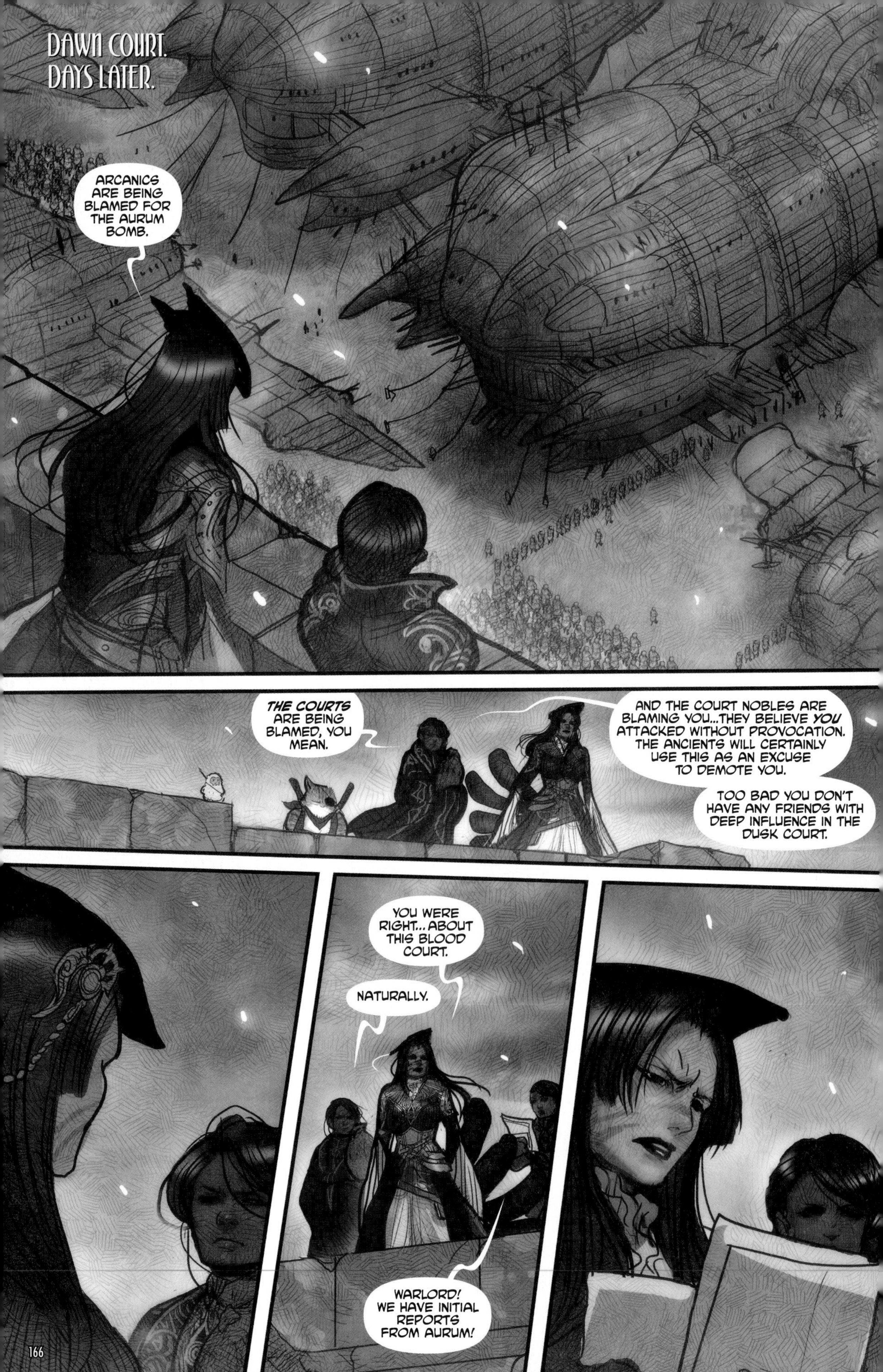
DAWN COURT. DAYS LATER.
ARCANICS ARE BEING BLAMED FOR THE AURUM BOMB.
THE COURTS ARE BEING BLAMED, YOU MEAN.
AND THE COURT NOBLES ARE BLAMING YOU...THEY BELIEVE YOU ATTACKED WITHOUT PROVOCATION. THE ANCIENTS WILL CERTAINLY USE THIS AS AN EXCUSE TO DEMOTE YOU.
TOO BAD YOU DON'T HAVE ANY FRIENDS WITH DEEP INFLUENCE IN THE DUSK COURT.
YOU WERE RIGHT... ABOUT THIS BLOOD COURT.
NATURALLY.
WARLORD! WE HAVE INITIAL REPORTS FROM AURUM!

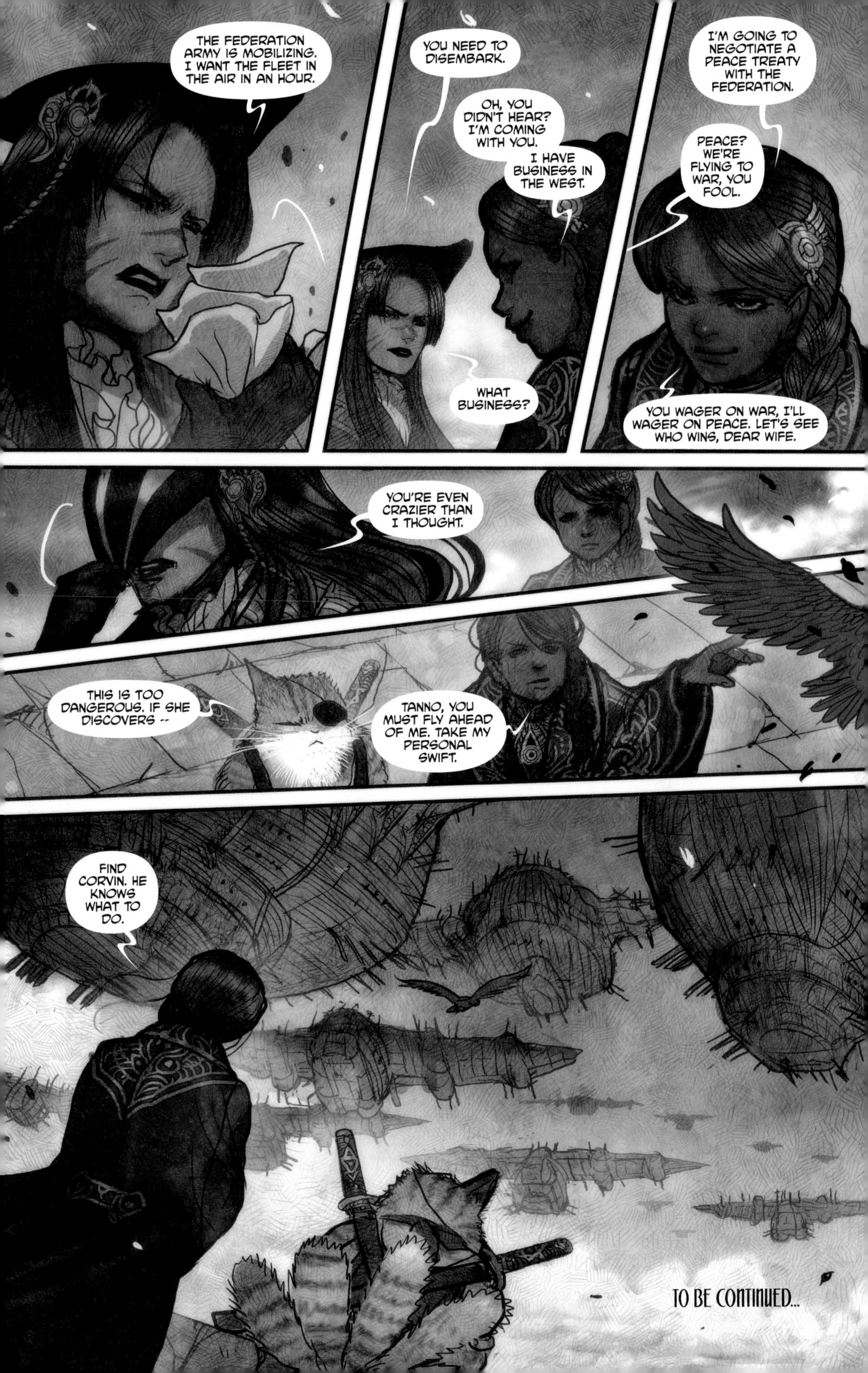
THE FEDERATION ARMY IS MOBILIZING. I WANT THE FLEET IN THE AIR IN AN HOUR.
YOU NEED TO DISEMBARK.
OH, YOU DIDN'T HEAR? I'M COMING WITH YOU.
I HAVE BUSINESS IN THE WEST.
WHAT BUSINESS?
I'M GOING TO NEGOTIATE A PEACE TREATY WITH THE FEDERATION.
PEACE? WE'RE FLYING TO WAR, YOU FOOL.
YOU WAGER ON WAR, I'LL WAGER ON PEACE. LET'S SEE WHO WINS, DEAR WIFE.
YOU'RE EVEN CRAZIER THAN I THOUGHT.
THIS IS TOO DANGEROUS. IF SHE DISCOVERS --
TANNO, YOU MUST FLY AHEAD OF ME. TAKE MY PERSONAL SWIFT.
FIND CORVIN. HE KNOWS WHAT TO DO.
TO BE CONTINUED...

SANA's WAR-MASTERS SKETCHES

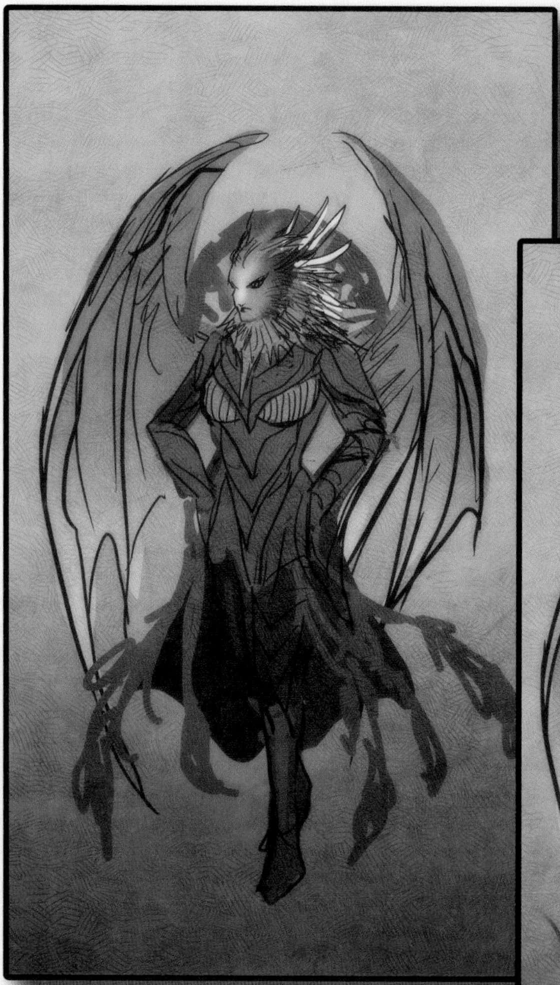

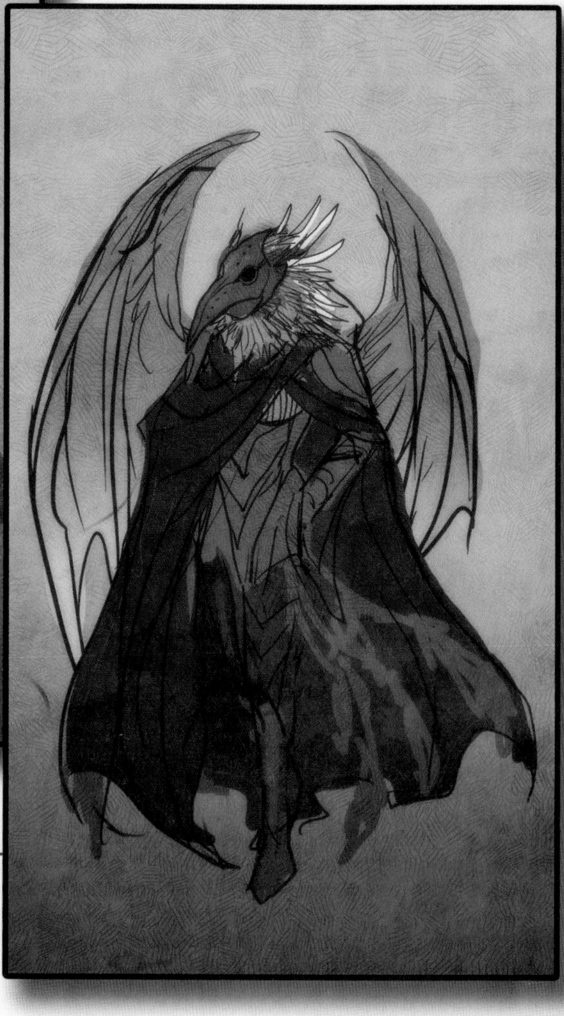

ULIAZA

SENTENUS

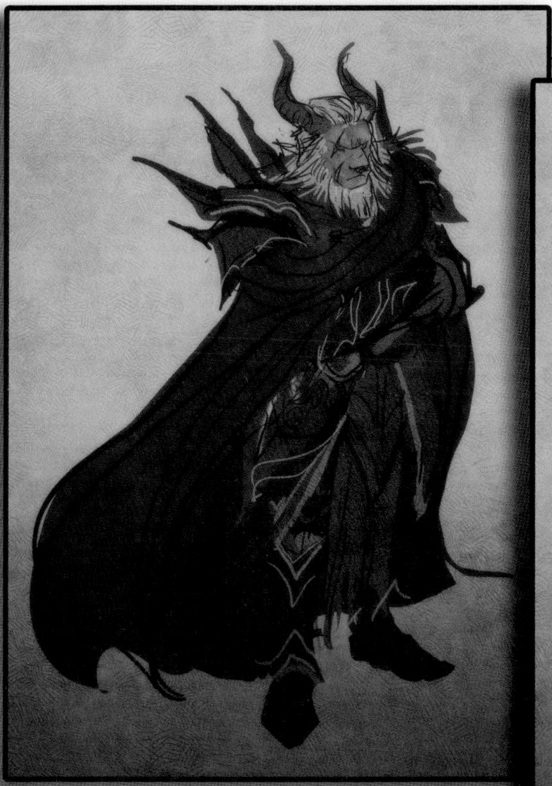

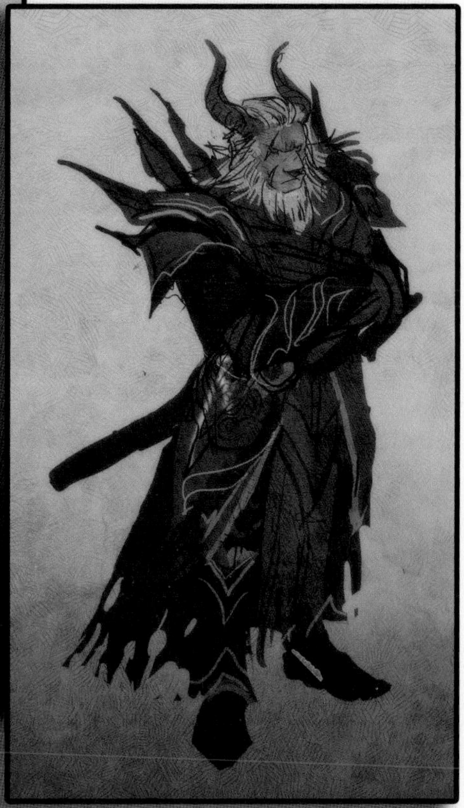

AGATA

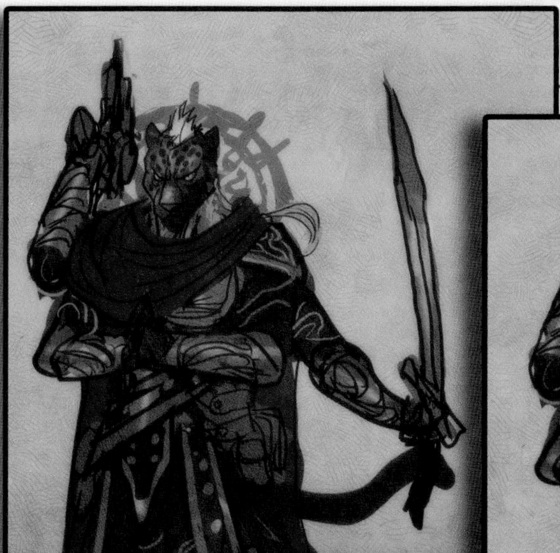

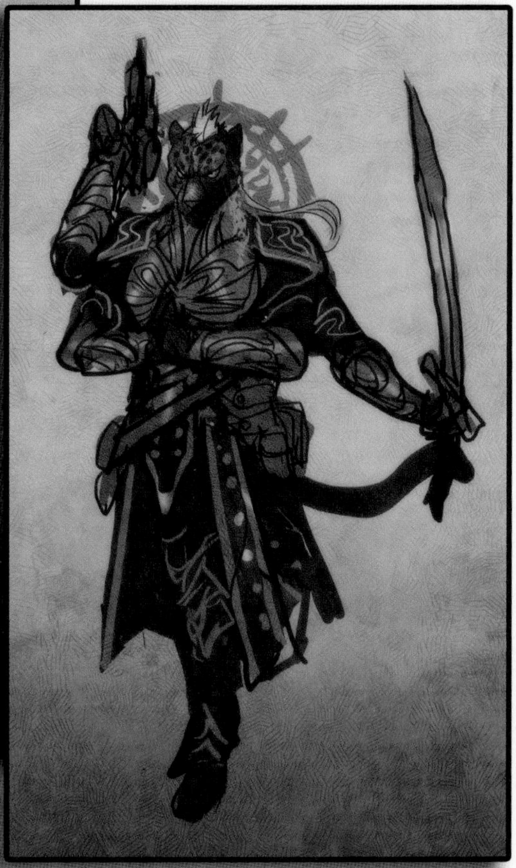

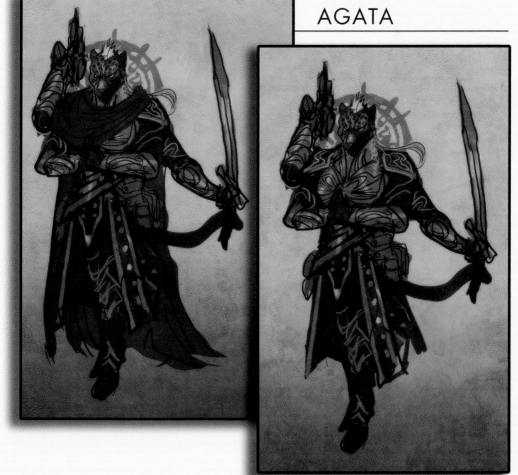

HAPPO KASPIAN NEN-THESTRA

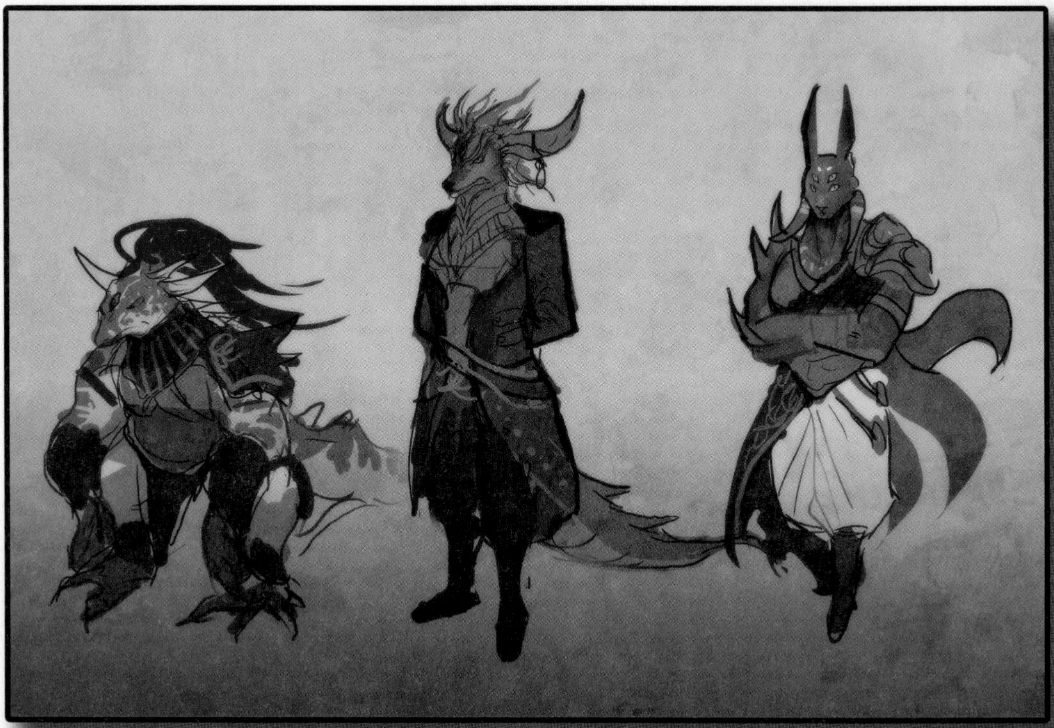

COLDWAY SUPIRA TOH

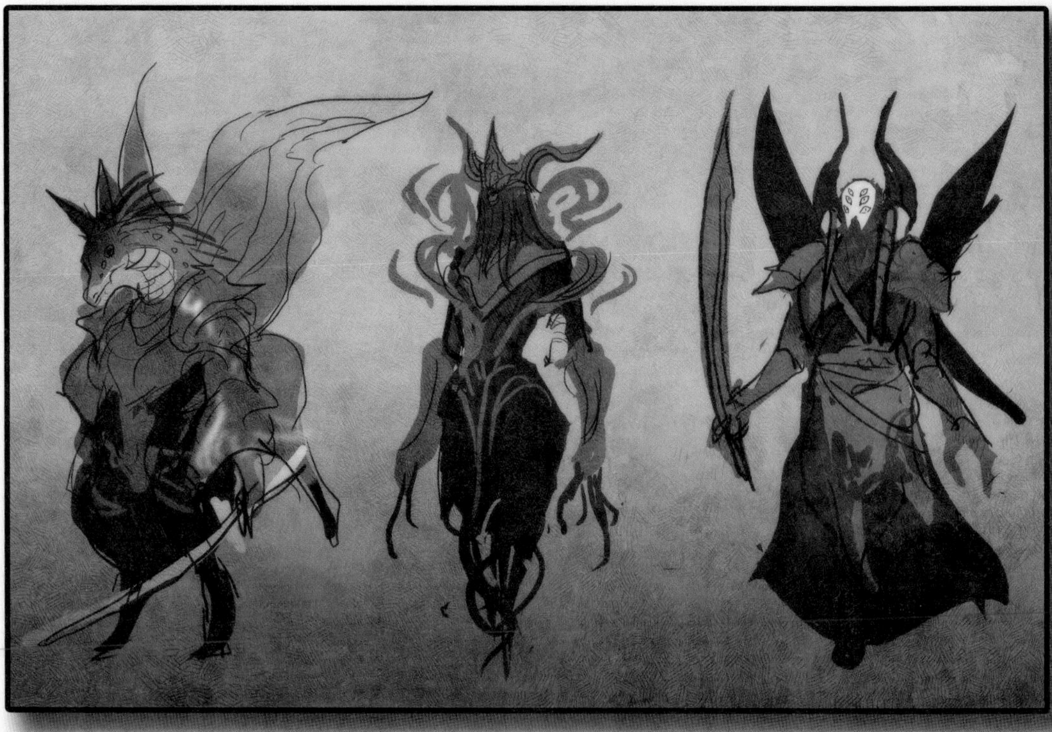

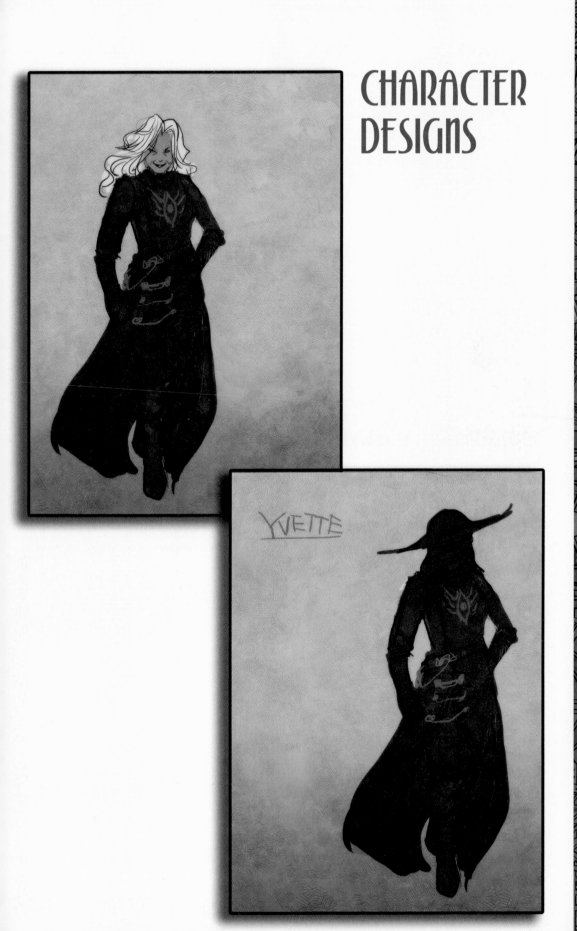

CHARACTER DESIGNS

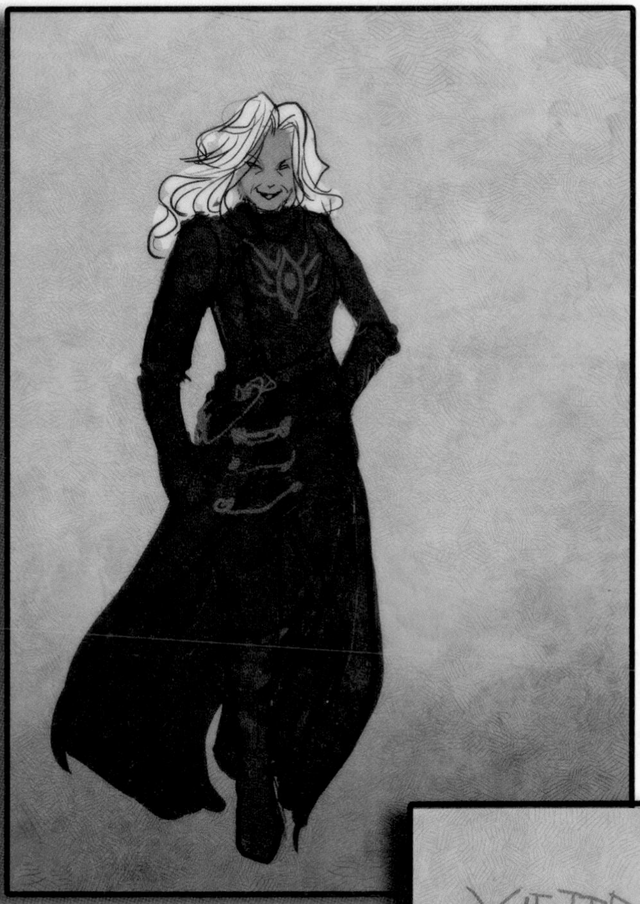

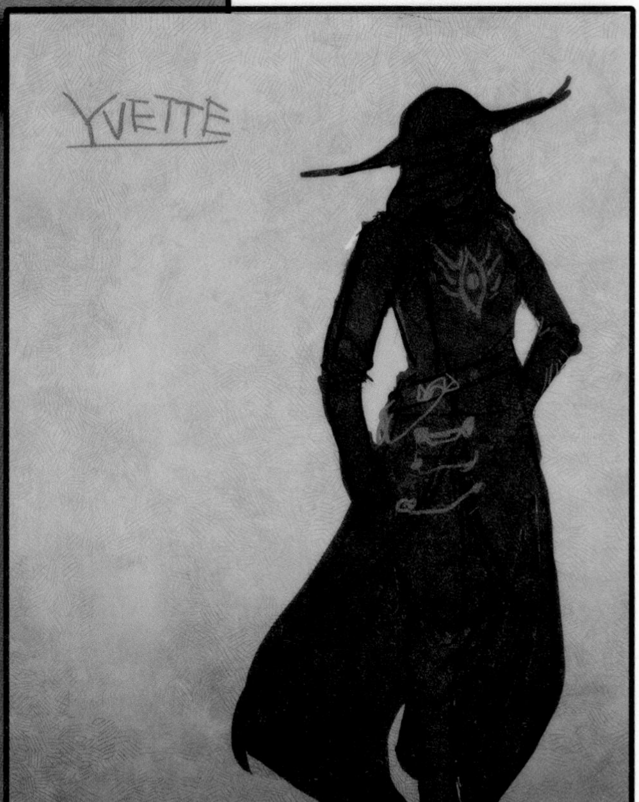
YVETTE

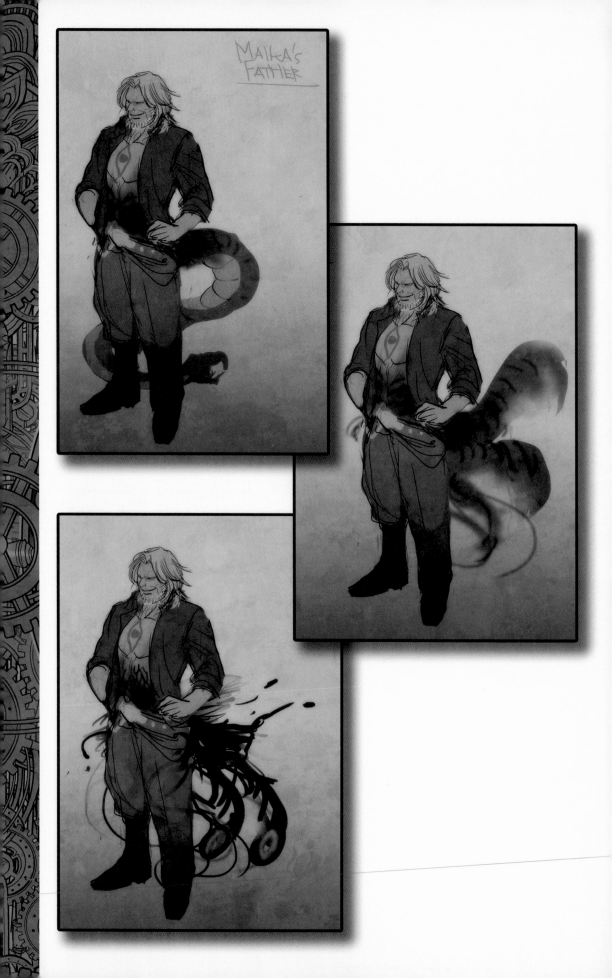

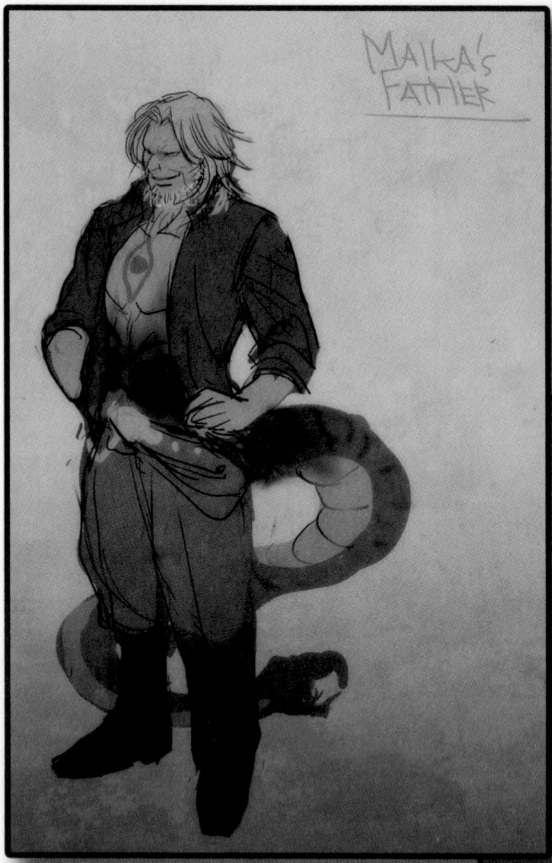
MAIKA's FATHER

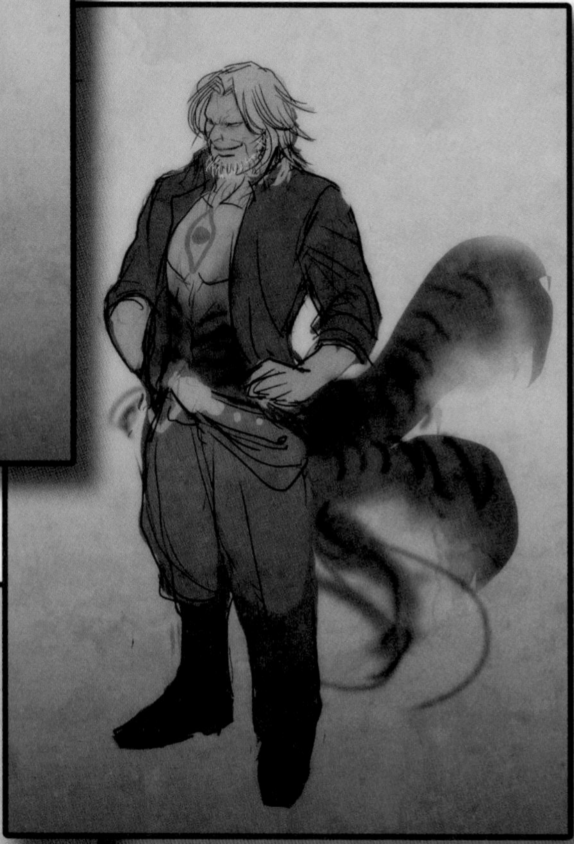

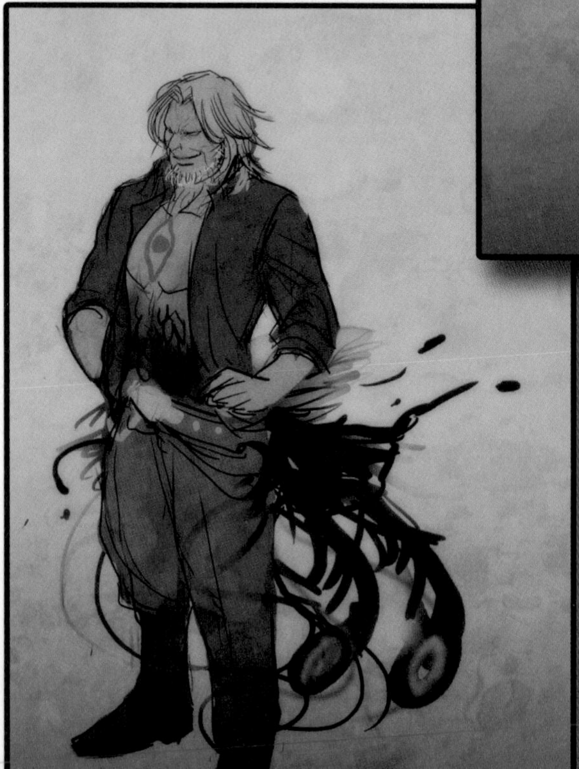

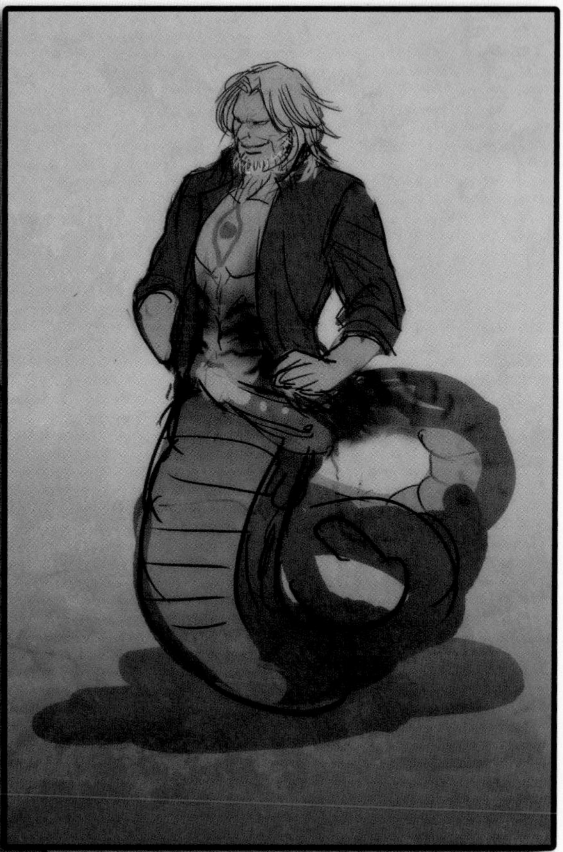

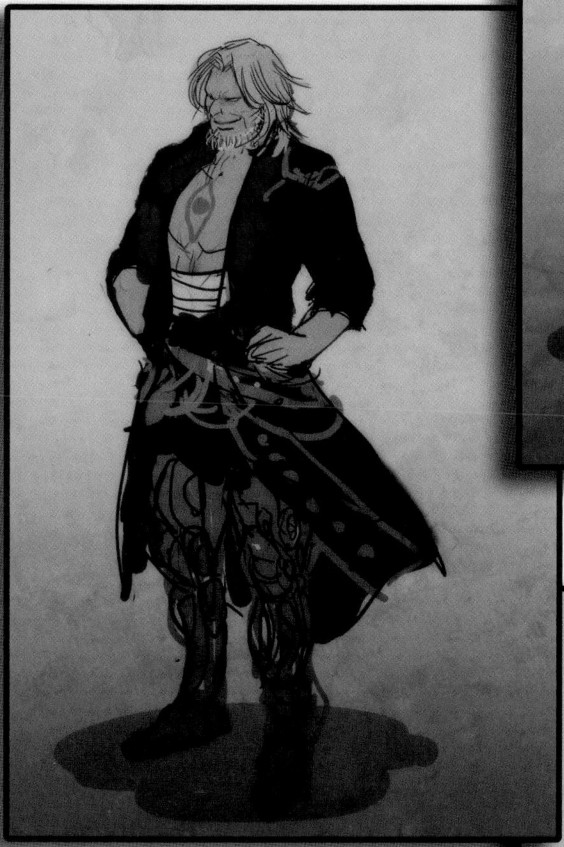

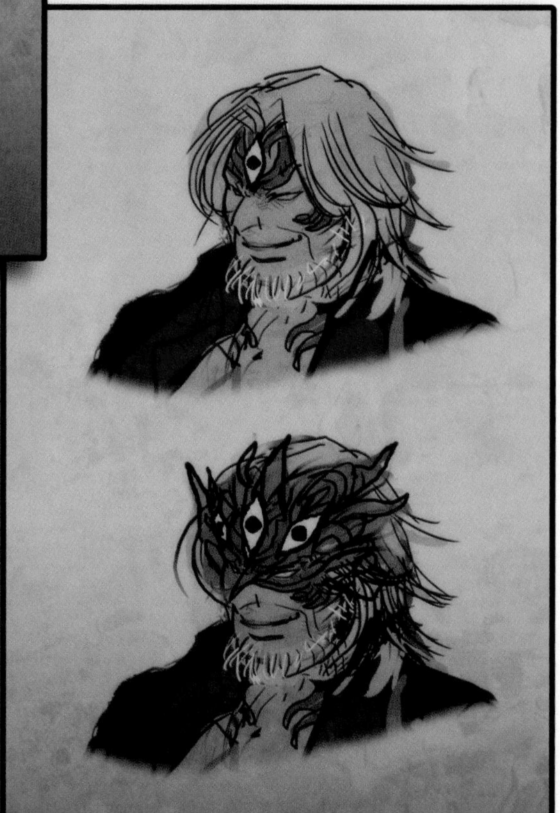

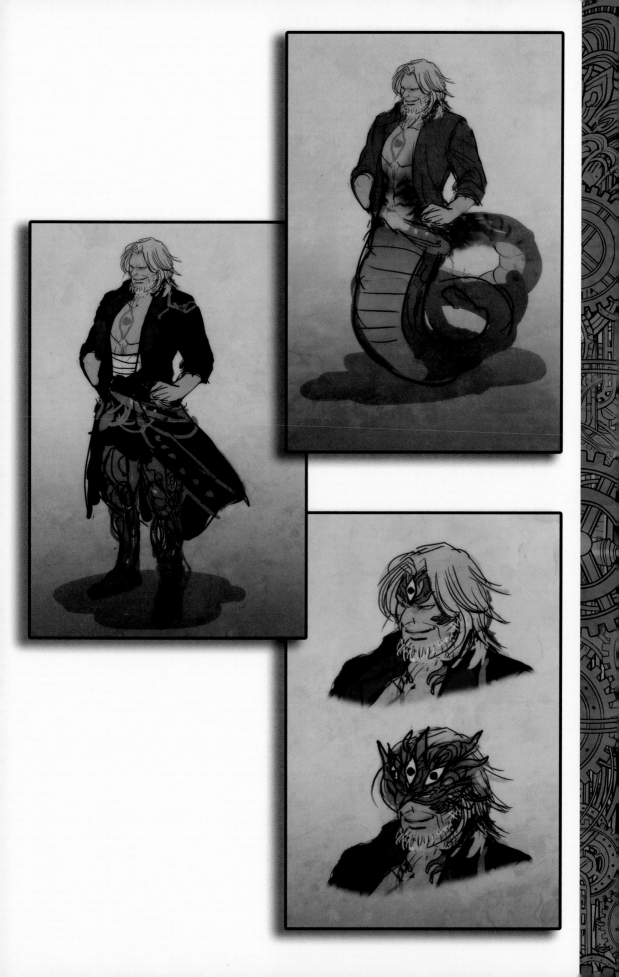

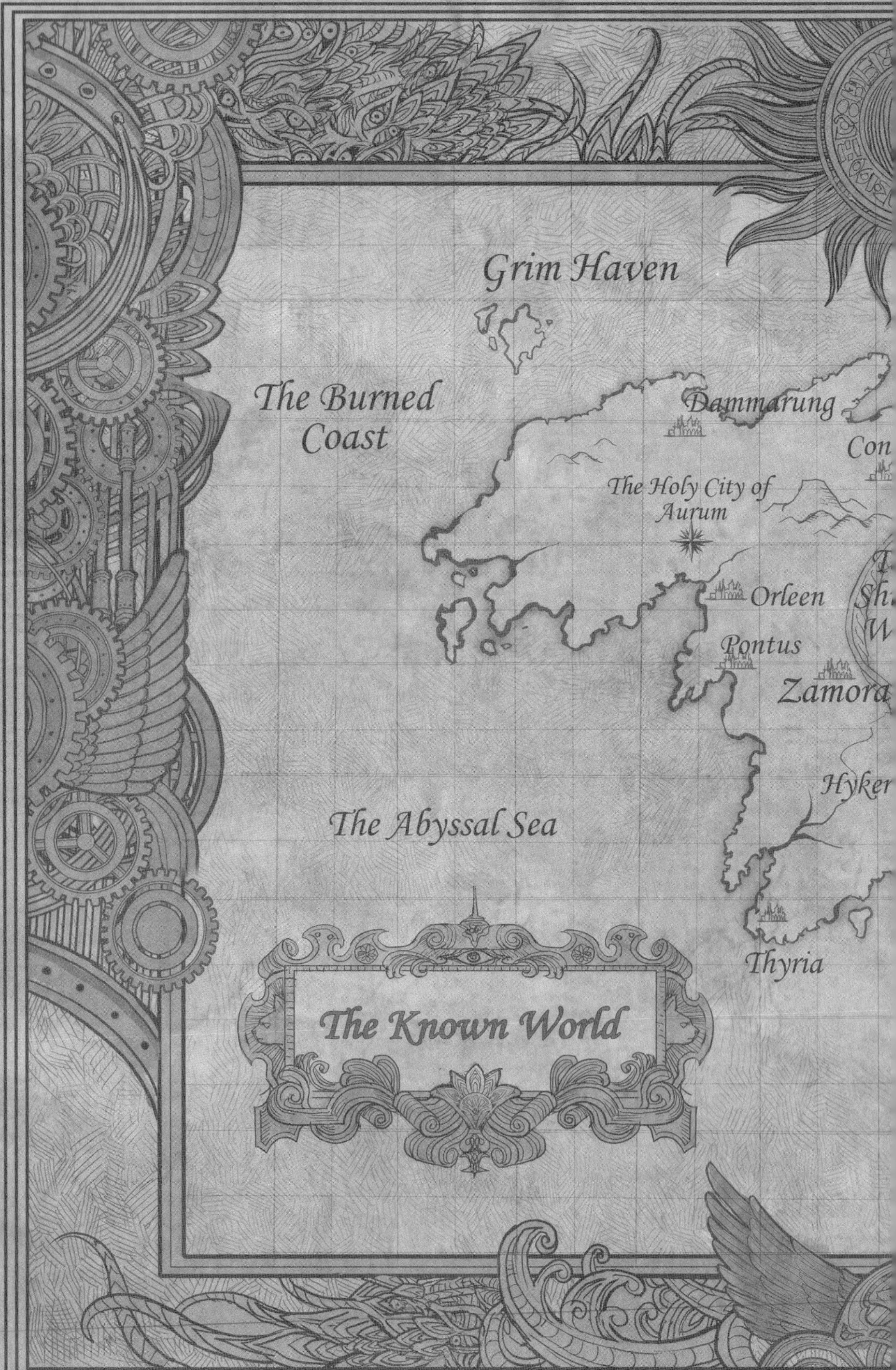
Grim Haven
The Burned Coast
Dammarung
Con
The Holy City of Aurum
Orleen
Pontus
Zamora
Hyker
The Abyssal Sea
Thyria
The Known World

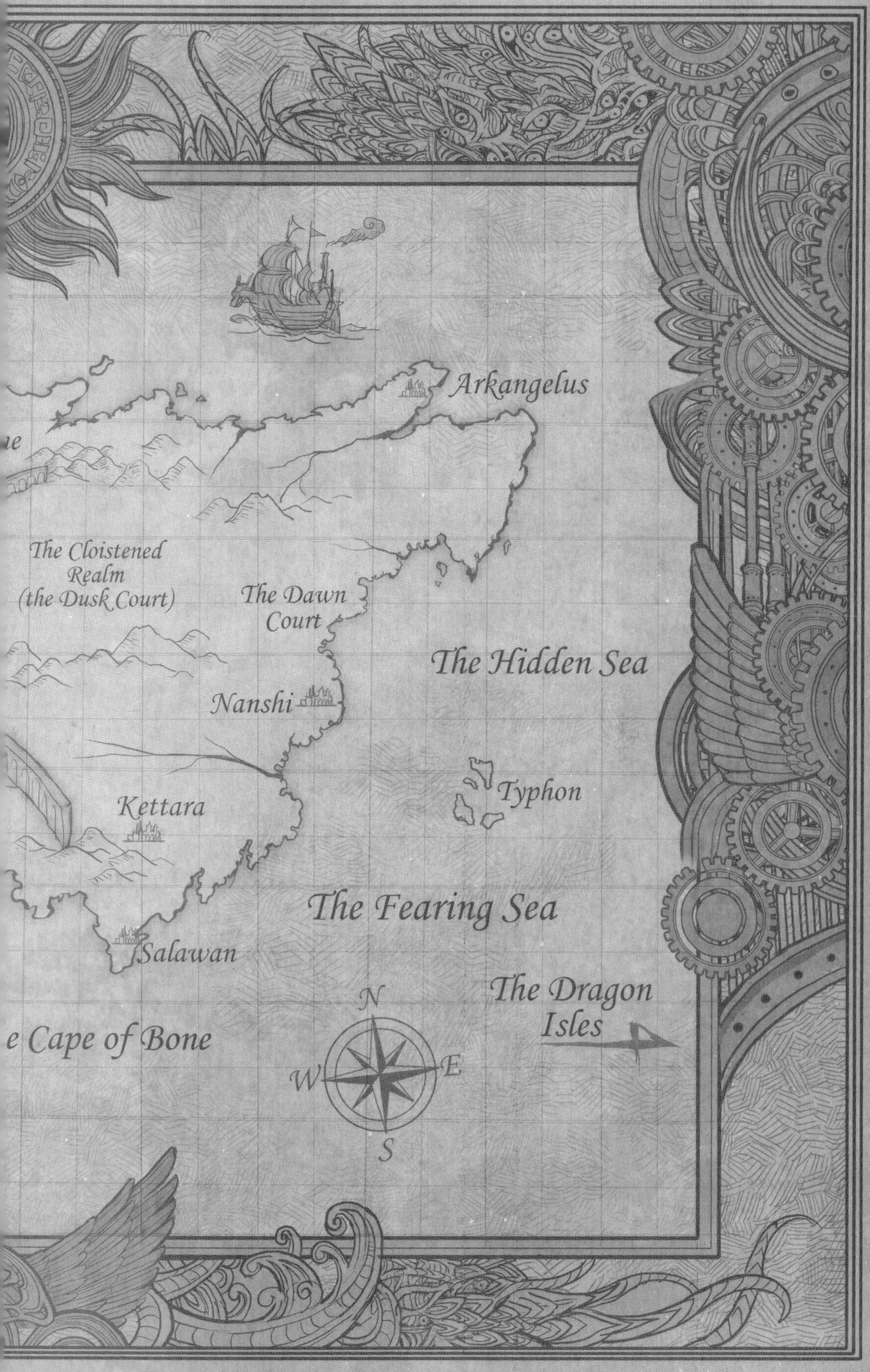

Arkangelus
The Cloistened
Realm
(the Dusk Court)
The Dawn
Court
The Hidden Sea
Nanshi
Typhon
Kettara
The Fearing Sea
Salawan
The Dragon
Isles
e Cape of Bone
N
W
E
S

CREATORS

MARJORIE LIU is the author of over seventeen novels and is the co-creator of the Hugo, Eisner, and British Fantasy Award-winning and *New York Times* bestselling series MONSTRESS, published by Image Comics. Liu's comic book work includes *X-23*, *Black Widow*, *Dark Wolverine*, *Han Solo*, and *Astonishing X-Men*, for which she was nominated for a GLAAD Media award for outstanding media images of the lesbian, gay, bisexual and transgender community.

SANA TAKEDA is an Eisner and Hugo Award-winning illustrator and comic book artist who was born in Niigata, and now resides in Tokyo, Japan. At age 20 she started out as a 3D CGI designer for SEGA, a Japanese video game company, and became a freelance artist when she was 25. She is still an artist, and has worked on titles such as *X-23* and *Ms. Marvel* for Marvel Comics, and is an illustrator for trading card games in Japan.

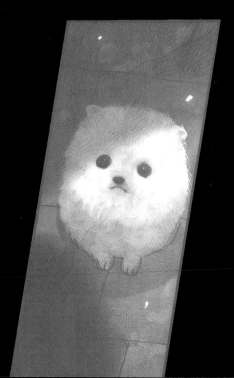